HERO
OF HOLLOWDALE HIGH

HERO

OF HOLLOWDALE HIGH

KATIE LOWRIE

contents

To the City
Farmland
Train Station
Hospital
Supermarket
MARKET
The Divide
Hollowdale Estate
Hollowdale High
To Lakeland

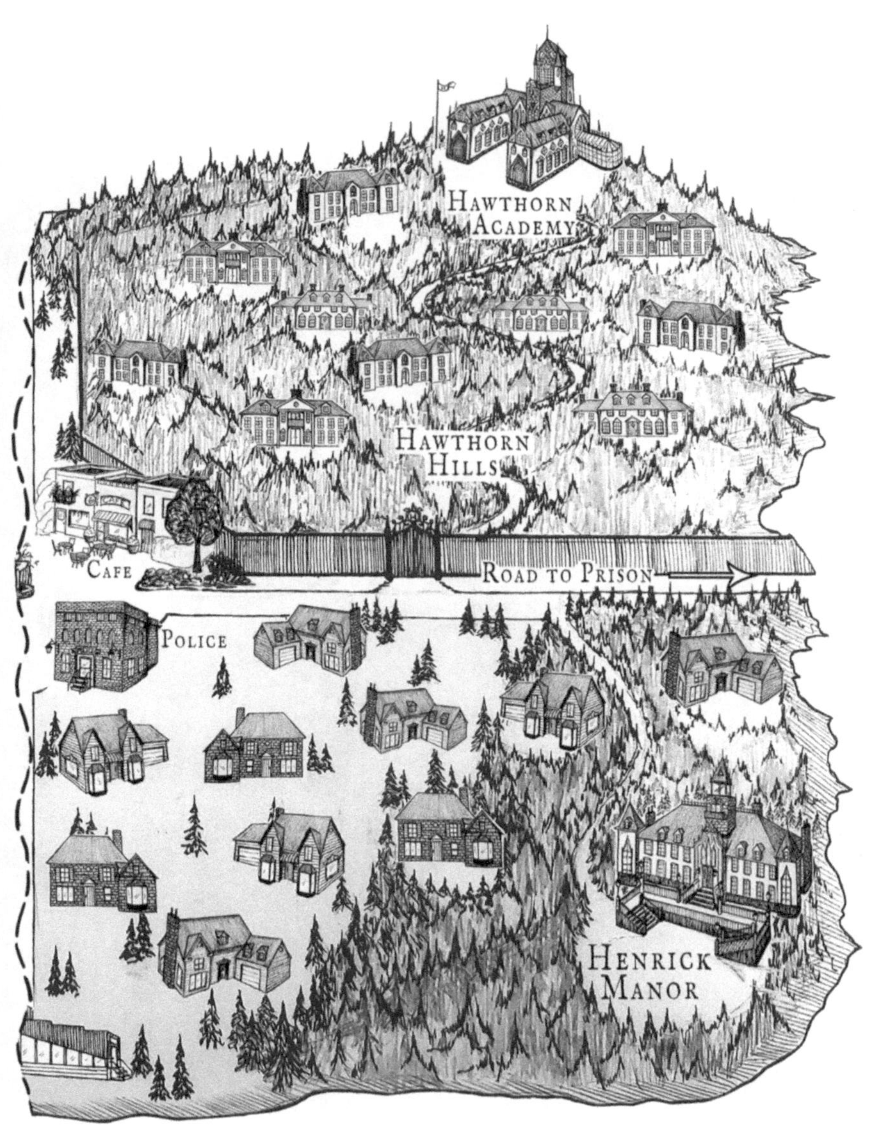

Hawthorn Academy
Hawthorn Hills
Cafe
Road to Prison
Police
Henrick Manor

haven at hollowdale high

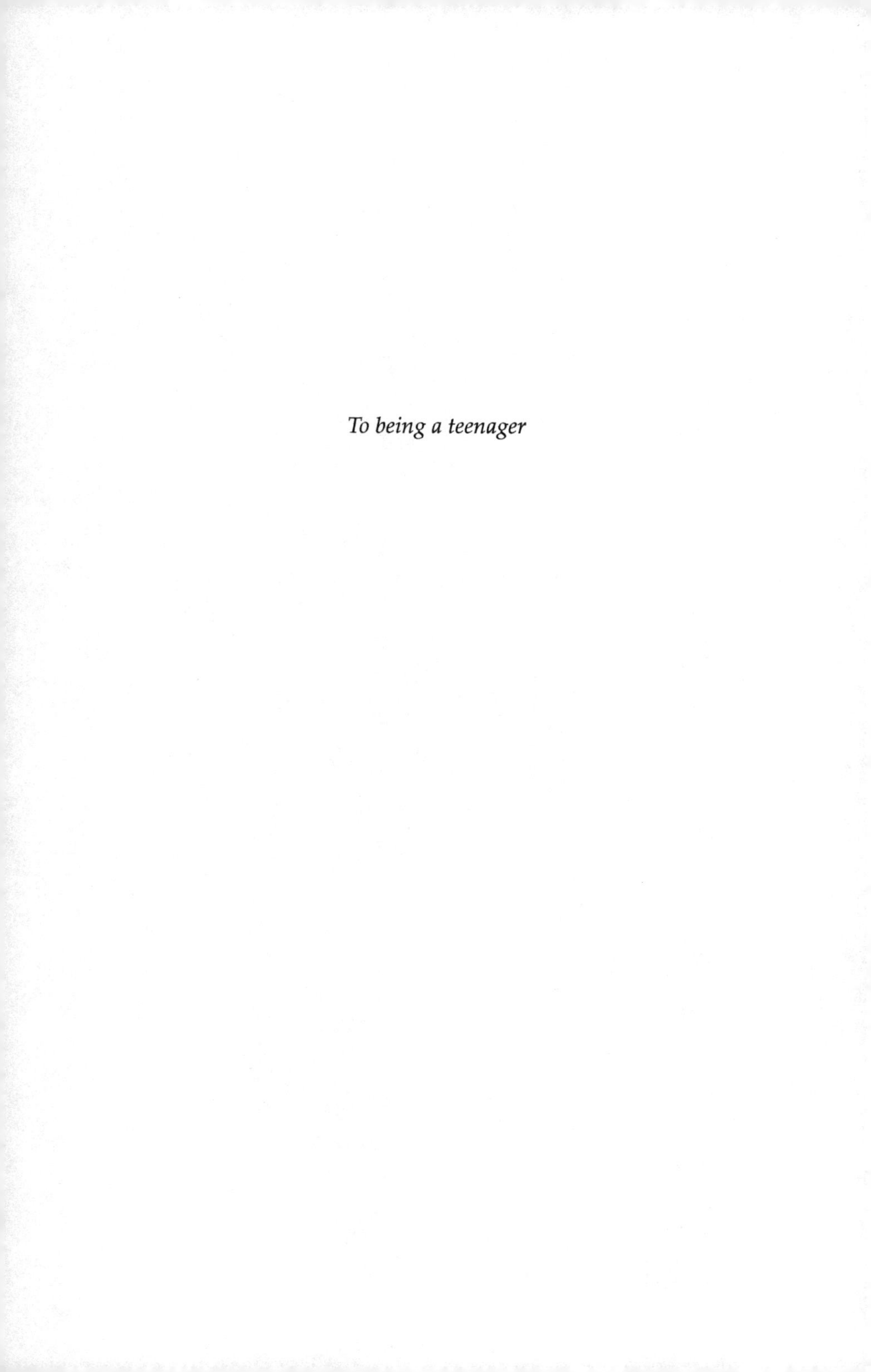

To being a teenager

author's note

This is a short prequel novella to introduce the *Rebels of Hollowdale High* series.

It's a High School series and a bit more real-life than my previous books. As in, less murder, more real-world shit.

You can head to my website for any trigger/content warnings you may need.

Enjoy!

wednesday, 1st september

My name is Layla Williams. I am eighteen years old. I have blonde hair and blue eyes. My mother's name is Darcy and my father's name is Daniel. I have been through hell, but I am safe now.

Those were the words that ran through my head daily, and rather constantly, too. It was a trick my counsellor taught me back at my old school. *"Remind yourself what is real and what isn't,"* she had said and I'd latched on to it ever since.

For the past few months, I had been reminding myself of the facts. I knew most people would wonder why I needed to do it. I mean, surely most people knew their name, age, and who their parents were, right?

Of course I knew. But it was something real. Solid. Factual. Something I could hold on to when the dark memories crept in, fighting at the edges to take over my mind.

Starting at a new school was freaking me out, too. I worried I wouldn't make any friends and if I did, I doubted I'd ever feel like I could open up to them fully.

At the end of the summer, Mum and Dad had moved us to the town of Beurre and I'd barely had time to adjust or meet anyone in the area before term time had come around. If I was being honest with myself, even if I had moved here at the very beginning of summer, I still wouldn't have made any friends. Going to school wasn't something I was looking forward to, but there had been a time when I had loved it. I guess most people my age wouldn't be looking forward to it either, but at least they knew people. At my old school, I was classed as one of the popular girls. But then I'd never wanted to be. The girls I'd known there all seemed so superficial and the majority of them had a serious attitude problem. To survive, you either joined them or were eaten. At Hollowdale, I had the chance to change my behaviour. Make sure that nobody would ever feel threatened by me. I just wasn't a threatening person.

I was staring up at my new school from my old, beat-up Ford. I had mixed feelings about the car. My parents had offered to buy me a new one after everything that happened last year, as if that would make me feel better, but I declined. I was proud of myself for working my butt off to get the car in the first place. One thing I knew was that it had cost me a total of a hundred pounds and it got me where I needed to be. Well. Most of the time.

The entire parking lot was filled with noise and people. Groups of friends milling around on the edges, chatting away and greeting each other like they hadn't spent the entire summer together. The warmth and love emanating off of these groups were creating a buzz of sorts. Nobody else seemed to be apprehensive about returning to school.

Then there was me. The girl standing beside an old banger, both nervous and anxious about being here. My stomach felt as if a thousand butterflies had decided to make it their home and nothing I did made them go away. There *had* been a time when I wasn't a nervous person and I didn't have anxiety flowing through me as natural as blood.

But times have changed. I've changed...

Walking across the busy parking lot, I only realised at the last moment that I was about to bump into an attractive guy who I swore had come out of nowhere.

Like, literally. One second the path in front of me was clear, then the next, this dark-haired Adonis had appeared and wasn't leaving fast enough for us not to become one.

It was like one of those slow motion scenes you see in movies. You know the ones. Where the guy's holding some kind of beverage or has a plate of food, and the girl goes *"Whhhooa,"* as they collide and she's covered in said beverage / food tray.

The guy didn't exactly seem very pleased that I had just walked into his line of vision and when my body collided with his, his face soured further. His top lip curled up into a sneer as he watched his drink cover my head, soaking my blonde hair that I'd spent ages curling this morning. The smell was vile. *What in the name was in that cup?!*

I was counting my blessings that it hadn't been a hot drink, at least. That would have tipped me over the edge. Not that a cold drink was making me feel much better. It was so cold that I could feel it seeping into my pores and travelling throughout my body, right down to my toes.

He scowled in my direction, gave me the once-over, then muttered something about stupid girls who didn't watch where they were walking before he hurried away over to a large group standing by the steps. They were all laughing and joking around, jostling and pushing one another. They looked happy.

I couldn't say I disagreed with him; about the stupid girl comment, I mean. I'd been lost in my train of thought. Lost in my own mind. Something that happened a lot recently.

When I looked over at him and his group again, I overheard one of the boys saying shit about my clothes, and he laughed along with them while staring right at me. I wasn't wearing anything too daring, just a pair of distressed mum jeans and a tour top from one of my favourite bands. I tried not to let my face give away my emotions, and I thought I'd managed it. That was until the group began to laugh even louder while all looking at me.

At my old school, I would have still been forced to wear a school uniform. But apparently, here at Hollowdale High, they did things a bit differently. They allowed all students from years eleven to thirteen to wear their own clothes instead of a uniform. Something to do with independence and freedom of expression or something. I wasn't sure, but it sucked. It had been bad enough waking up and putting on a school blazer and skirt every morning, but now that I had to think of what to wear, my mornings had become even more of a stress.

The morning bell chimed across the lot, and the groups of students dispersed slowly. I was still standing in the same spot, the liquid covering me slowly drying and causing my hair to get stuck in position, and I shook myself to attention.

I had to report to the office straight away as it was my first day here and I needed a schedule. It would be a bad first impression to be late on the first day. Especially as I got here with more than enough time. I hated arriving late for things. It was one of my pet peeves. I always showed *at least* ten to fifteen minutes before I needed to.

After I located the main building—you know, due to the big sign on it that said *Reception*—I hurried inside, away from the group that was *still* staring at me. Obviously, they didn't care about being late on the first day. Their laughter followed before the door closing blocked them out once and for all.

The woman at the desk was smiling at me and looked friendly enough. I assumed she'd seen enough new kids to last a lifetime. Part of the job.

Her white hair was up in a neat bun, her lips covered in a coral lip shade, and her teeth were bright and most likely fake.

'Is there anything I can help you with, dear?' she asked gently. Her friendly eyes lit up her face and instantly put me at ease.

'Well, I'm new here. I just transferred. My name's Layla Williams,' I replied. I attempted to smile back, but interacting with strangers had never been my forte. My face just looked like it was contorting to a very unnatural array of features.

'Ah, yes, I see. Here's your new schedule, dear, and there's a small map attached underneath. I hope you find everything okay and feel free to come back here if you need any help.'

This time, I did manage an actual smile.

'I will do. Thank you.' I looked down at the paper she had just handed to me and it said that my first class was History with Mr Daniels. At least it was a subject I enjoyed. The rest of the schedule for the day looked decent, too.

Maybe I'd grow to love this place.

Stranger things have happened.

I MEANDERED THROUGH THE CORRIDORS, using the map the lady at reception had given me to help find my way, but I kept getting turned around.

This school was nothing like my old one.

Each subject had a different building entirely, and each block was a letter. But the blocks didn't run alphabetically or anything, so I couldn't figure out where on earth 'H' block was for the humanities classrooms.

On my way, I passed a group of lockers and the guy I'd accidentally run into earlier was leaning up against them, talking to his friends in an animated fashion. He scowled again when he caught my eye, then proceeded to tell the crowd surrounding him about this morning's incident.

Instantly, I could tell they were the popular crowd. The girls had cheerleading uniforms on, something I never thought this town would be into, and the guys were clearly the football players of the school. Cheerleading wasn't that popular in England, but I'd heard the town of Beurre did things differently. And seeing as this was a sports college, it made sense that they would have a team.

I lowered my gaze and carried on walking as if I hadn't heard them so openly talking about me. Well, actually, I tried not to look at anything except my feet as they moved one in front of the other. It was easier to focus on my scuffed trainers than to show that group my flushed cheeks.

But clearly, I'd already managed to piss off the people I couldn't really afford to piss off. And wasn't that just swell?

After what felt like an eternity, I found room 1H20 and walked into the classroom. Straight away, I noticed everybody was already seated and quiet. There were only two seats still empty in the room. The teacher had assigned our seats if the name cards on the front of each desk were anything to go by.

My name card was in the back row, the last on the right. I assumed the teacher had assigned them in alphabetical order and that would explain why I was in the back. Only one seat remained empty—the desk to the right of mine. The name card read Dean Walters. I just hoped he was nice, or at least that he'd speak to me at some point during the year. If there was anything I knew about teachers, it was that they enjoyed making those who sat next to each other team up on projects and in class tasks.

The seat next to me was still empty when the teacher moved to the centre of the board at the front and started speaking. He was an older man with dark hair that had gone salt-and-pepper around his ears. At first glance, he seemed nice enough. But you never knew with teachers. No matter what age they were.

'Hello, class, my name is Mr Daniels and I will be teaching you History over the next year. I see Mr Walters has yet to show, so while we wait for his highness, maybe we could start with everybody introducing themselves,' he said in an amused tone.

Clearly, he knew who this *Mr Walters* was and that he was a bit of a rogue.

The girl in the first seat, Amanda Adams, stood up and started talking. I tuned out what she was saying, as I was currently having a little mini panic attack about what I would say. I hated things like this. I'd thought this teacher seemed nice, but he was definitely a sadist.

While I was looking around the classroom, anywhere that wasn't the back of the bubbly girl Amanda Adams' head, the door swung open wide and a guy entered through it, acting all nonchalant.

This must be Dean Walters.

On getting a closer look, I noticed it was the guy I nearly knocked out earlier on my way across the car park. The reason I was sitting here smelling like something gone off and rotten. *Oh, great.*

Everyone turned to look at him and fell into a hushed silence as he sauntered through the room. He sneered down at me as he took his seat and whispered, 'Love what you've done with your hair.'

He sniggered and I swallowed loudly. I was tongue-tied and very conscious of my now dried to my head hair. My curls had looked so cute when I'd left the house.

I wished the ground would swallow me whole; or that I hadn't moved here. Moving to the Hollowdale estate in Beurre had seemed like a good idea to begin with. The schools here were great. My parents could find new jobs easily. Plus, it was far enough away from the town I had escaped from.

Slinking down further in my seat, I covered my face with my hair, hoping to look at him again discreetly. I guess you could say he was handsome, in a rugged way. His dark brown hair was floppy and he seemed skinny yet taut.

He was looking down at his textbook like maybe it held all the secrets of the universe, his eyes never deviating from that spot before him. Or maybe he was just putting on a bullshit acting show, knowing I was watching him.

One thing I could see was the small smirk planted firmly on his face. He looked amused but was also trying to hide it.

I had a feeling in my gut that this year was going to be a lot more interesting than my last, not that I'd ever thought *that* to be possible…

Two

Layla

AFTER THAT FIRST LESSON, the rest of the day had gone exactly how I'd expected it to.

Barely any of the other students talked to me, and Dean Walters had been in none other than four of my five classes. In every single one he was seated beside me, and in every single one he spoke not one word to me. All he did was smile or laugh whenever somebody made a joke about my hair. Or about how my tour shirt had holes in it and my shoes were too old.

All stupid high school shit. But stupid high school shit that hurt nonetheless.

I got back to my new house to find my mother waiting at the door for me. Darcy Williams had a jolly smile, but her eyes said something I knew she didn't want to voice aloud. Ever since last year, whenever she looked at me, her eyes were full of sympathy and caring. At first it was exactly what I'd needed, but now it was starting to grate. For once, I wanted Mum to look at me like she used to. The way she did before last year.

Her energy was brimming over the top, and I could tell she really wanted to find out how my first day had gone. It wouldn't surprise me if blood leaked out from her closed smile because she'd bitten her tongue so hard in anticipation.

She opened the front door wide for me to step through, and once I was inside and putting my coat and bag on the stairway railing, she pounced up behind me and wrapped me into a big bear hug.

'Hey, Mum, how's your day been?' I asked with a big sigh. The hug was nice and all, but she'd never hugged me much before, so I hated that she did now.

Another thing that grated on me was how I always tried to deflect conversations away from myself. It was easier, always easier. But I wished I knew how to just open up without somebody having to draw information from me like blood from a stone.

'Darling, your hair!' she exclaimed, touching my dried hair, flattening it down on my head. Guess she was trying to make it resemble something other than a birds' nest but was failing miserably.

'Mum, I'm fine,' I told her, wanting to placate her and take her hands off my hair. She hadn't answered my question, choosing instead to fixate on my hair, so I repeated, 'How was your day?'

'Oh, it isn't my day I want to talk about, sweetheart!' She grabbed my hand and pulled me over to the living room. Once we were seated on the sofa, she asked, 'How was school? Were people nice? Did you make any friends?'

The smile on her face and the way she leaned towards me told me she was hoping I'd had the best day known to man. She wanted to hear about all the friends I'd made. The classes I'd loved.

To her, they were simple questions with simple answers.

To me, they felt like loaded questions.

'To answer your first question, school was fine. The second question is a little harder to answer,' I said honestly. All I could remember were the glares and stares I'd got from everybody I had passed in the corridors. My mother didn't have to know the full extent of my misery and how alone I'd felt. Eating my lunch in the courtyard underneath a tree, trying to keep to myself. She wanted this new start to work out for all of us.

I couldn't disappoint her again.

'I'm sure it was all fine, dear. You're a nice girl and I'm sure you'll make friends in no time,' she said as if that was the end of that. Why was it that mums always believed the best of their children?

Mum looked at me with her biggest smile.

'This is the beginning of the rest of your life, Layla.'

I just hoped she was right.

THE NEXT MORNING, I was feeling a little more prepared for what would happen at school. It couldn't be any worse than the day before and surely couldn't be worse than where I had been before moving here. All I had to do was think of where we had moved from and the circumstances surrounding the move, and I wanted to try my hardest to be happy here. My shoulders felt as if they were carrying the weight of the world on them. My head was so heavy, I constantly wanted to lie down in a dark room and just sleep my life away.

My name is Layla Williams. My name is Layla Williams.

I repeated this thought in my head like a mantra. I was okay, and today at school would be fine. Slowly, the black mist in my head cleared in time for me to see that if I didn't leave the house now, I'd be late for my second day. I looked at my timetable before heading towards my car and saw I had another History lesson today for the fourth period. *Great,* I thought, *another hour to sit next to him.*

And who even knew if he was also in the classes I'd yet to attend. It wasn't like he'd spoken to me much, or anything like that.

I had tried not to think about Dean and his friends, who had made me feel as big as an ant. But it had been hard not to. The looks they had given me were enough for me to know I wasn't the kind of girl they normally associated themselves with. I was too different for them. And by that I meant I wasn't a cheerleader.

Luckily, that was just the way I liked it.

The entire car ride to school, I worried. I worried the day would be just as bad as the one before it. I worried people would be mean about my clothes or my hair. I'd always been a worrier, but the thought of entering the school halls again filled me with pure dread.

The trip didn't last long enough, and within ten minutes, I was parking my car at the back of the lot, hoping nobody would pay any attention to me or my rather wretched car. A chill covered me from my head to the very tips of my toes as I exited my car.

Looking around, nothing in particular caught my eye at first glance, but on a second perusal, I saw the boy from yesterday.

Dean Walters.

He was standing beside a car a little over to the right. A swish, new-looking Audi that I didn't believe he'd paid for by himself with no help from his parents.

Not that I was judging him for that…

Oh, who the hell was I trying to kid? I was *definitely* judging him for that.

On noticing me, he smiled brightly and I shivered. His reaction to seeing me was so different from the one I'd received yesterday that I instantly was on guard. This one seemed sort of friendly and suspiciously genuine, but the moment a petite brunette girl joined him, his smile instantly became a frown.

'Is that the new girl?' asked the brunette who had joined him, overly loud so that her voice carried across the lot to where I was standing. She wanted me to hear her. 'What's up with her car?'

The high-pitched quality of her voice entered my ears and instantly put my teeth on edge. It was as if everything was too much; a sensory overload.

'Not everybody can be rich like us, Rem,' he said to her at the same volume as hers. 'Even the poor have to get around somehow.'

'She'd be better off walking,' the girl—*Rem?*—said. 'No way you'd catch me dead getting in *that* thing.'

'Well, it's a good thing you don't have to, isn't it?' I called back, my thread finally snapping. I wasn't going to stand here and let them talk smack about my car when it was all I could afford. I'd worked hard to afford this and I wasn't going to let this girl shame me.

'Sorry, but did you just speak to me?' Remi huffed and crossed her arms across her cheerleading uniform, then turned back to face Dean, bored with interacting with me. 'Baby, keep a seat for me at lunch.'

She rose on her tiptoes to kiss Dean on the cheek.

I scoffed and laughed a little. As much as I was enjoying the show Remi wanted to put on for me, I needed to get to class.

'Well, as heart-warming as this all is,' I said, waving my hand, gesturing around us, 'I've got a class to get to, so.'

'I'll walk you,' Dean called, stepping away from Remi and making his way towards me. How wonderful. He wanted to walk me to a class that we no doubt shared.

'You really don't have to.'

'It'll be my pleasure.' His lip curled up and his eyes were alight with mischief. 'English, right?'

'Right,' I said, resigned to the fact that he wasn't about to leave me alone. Easier to just let him walk next to me in silence than to fight him on it. 'Let's go.'

Remi stayed beside Dean's car as we walked past, sniffing the air as we did so like she was above me. She could think that all she wanted; I knew the truth.

She was one of those girls who believed she was the shit all because of the friends she kept, the car she drove, and the popularity she had. The reason I knew this?

That used to be me back at my old school.

I may not have been a cheerleader, but I'd been popular enough. My friends and I had acted like we were above everybody else, treating those below us like ants under our shoes. We were vile looking back on it, but at the time, I couldn't see it. I was sure if I asked Beth, my best friend, she wouldn't be able to see it either.

'So,' Dean said to break the silence. I looked up at him, raising my brow, wondering what would come out of his perfect mouth next. 'What school did you move from?'

'Weren't you listening in history class yesterday? I mentioned it in my introduction.'

He shrugged and smiled, sheepish and endearing. *Wanker.*

'I was preoccupied.'

'Doing what exactly? Thinking of all the fun facts you were going to spout after me, Mr popular football guy.'

'Hey! I'll have you know my introduction was the perfect amount of humour and self-deprecation.'

'If you say so,' I replied, looking around the area, hoping to see a friendly face I could latch on to, but then remembering I didn't have any friendly faces here in the first place. 'Plus, if you think it was self-deprecation, then that says a lot about you, doesn't it?'

With that, I moved ahead of him, wanting to create a bit of space between us. A barrier of sorts. Even if it was just the damp September air.

'Hey, wait up!' he called out as I opened the door to the English building entrance. A large part of me wanted to slam it in his face, but the manners my mum had instilled in me from a young age meant I couldn't bring myself to do it. No matter how much he may deserve it.

In what felt like no time at all, the two of us made our way into the English classroom, both finding our seats allocated for us in the back row. Geesh. Was I expected to sit beside him for the rest of this year and the next?

'Hello, Dean,' the teacher said as we took our seats before she turned to face me. 'And you must be Layla. I hope Mr Walters here has been helping you find your way.'

She had a jovial smile that felt warm and safe. Like an older lady you could go to if you needed help or wanted to talk about something playing on your mind. Her eyes were a light blue and her hair must have been blonde once but was now turning an ashy shade of grey.

I smiled at her, instantly feeling a kinship of sorts with the woman, which struck me as odd, seeing as I had an aversion to most teachers and authority figures these days. Too much happened at my old school for me to take easily to them now, but this lady, she was an exception.

'I totally have, miss,' Dean replied with an equally large smile plastered on his face. 'Would I ever turn away from a fellow pupil in need?'

The teacher laughed and I was pretty sure Dean batted his eyelashes at her a couple of times. I couldn't help but join in the laughter—although I was definitely laughing *at* him and not *with* him.

'Is this true?' she asked me and I tilted my head slightly.

'He's been okay…' I trailed off, not sure what else to say now that the attention had landed firmly on my head. And not just from the teacher either, but from the rest of the students in the classroom, too.

Every single head—and therefore pair of eyes—were now turned towards us, focused on the conversation taking place at the back of the room.

'Oh, you must think me terribly impolite,' she spoke again, pretending she hadn't noticed the eyes on us. 'I'm Mrs Dulton. Welcome to Hollowdale.'

I nodded briefly and after she smiled once more, Mrs Dulton turned away from us and walked to the front of the room and pointed at the whiteboard.

'She's my favourite,' Dean whispered in my ear, leaning closer so that I'd hear him. His cologne hit my nostrils and shamelessly I took in a massive inhale. I couldn't help myself. What could I say? The boy smelled *good*.

'I'm happy for you,' I bit out, not turning my head in his direction so he would get the picture and leave me alone. Mrs Dalton was pointing at her header on the board about an upcoming project. One she'd called The Art of Romantic Literature, it seemed.

'And for the next three months, you and the person sitting at your table with you will partner up and combine your efforts in this endeavour.'

Sorry, what now?

Three

Layla

'You mean you want us to work together, miss? For three months?' Dean sputtered, looking at the teacher with an incredulous expression; his eyes wrinkling at the edges. The moment the words had left the teacher's lips, Dean's head had snapped towards the front of the room, his intention of whispering more words to me forgotten.

It made me feel small, the way he was making such a fuss about working with me. He'd been overly friendly to me since I started here—except for the whole spilling a drink on me and laughing with his friends thing on my first day—yet now, apparently he couldn't fathom the thought of working on a romantic literature assignment together.

Was I really that bad of a partner to get lumped with?

'Yes, Mr Walters, I do.' The teacher said in a stern tone. Even after only half an hour, I could sense Mrs Dulton was not one to be trifled with, no matter how nice she appeared. I got the impression she was a no-nonsense woman through and through.

'Well then,' Dean said, turning to face me. 'Things have just got interesting, haven't they, Layla?'

'How'd you figure that?'

'Three months together on a project is a long time spent in close quarters,' he said, raising his eyebrows, a large smile covering his face. 'Gives us enough time to get to really know one another, doesn't it?'

'Lucky me,' I deadpanned.

'A lot of girls in this school would kill to spend time with me,' he said, not an ounce of a joke in his voice, and when I looked over at him, I realised he was dead serious. He really thought that much of himself. I giggled behind my hand, trying to stop myself from exploding into full-belly laughter.

'Well, I'm sorry that I'm not one of those girls,' I said, still laughing.

'I'm not,' he replied, his face still dead serious. It made me pause, the way he was looking at me. As if he was trying to suss me out; figure out all my secrets and then some. 'So…'

'So, what?'

'So,' he said, a cheeky grin covering his face, 'what night am I coming over to work on the project then?'

'Who said you're coming over?' I asked, sassing him with a raised brow. 'Am I not allowed to see the Walters' abode?'

'You can come over if you like, but I'll have you know, I enjoy all the studying I do to take place in my bedroom.'

'Yeah, with that information, you can come over to mine. Next Friday night.'

He nodded, pleased I'd yielded so quickly. I had a feeling he was joking about studying in his room, but I didn't feel comfortable enough yet to take my chances. The boy disarmed me with a smile, and being in such small quarters with him—with a bed, no less—I wasn't sure I'd be able to sit there and focus on books.

'I'll be looking forward to it all week.' His light brown hair gleamed under the bright fluorescent classroom lighting, and his smile was almost as bright.

Looked like I was going to be spending a bit of time with Dean Walters, in private, discussing The Art of Romantic Literature of all things.

Splendid.

saturday, 4th september

'So, what's Hollowdale High really like?' Beth asked me on Saturday afternoon, while she sat cross-legged on my bed eating a bag of fudge.

She had a sweet tooth and fudge was one of her favourite treats. Up until last year, I'd never joined her, but now that I didn't have to worry about my figure as much, I could eat them with her and not feel guilty about it.

'In what sense?' I asked, knowingly being vague.

'I don't mean the building layout or the teachers, do I?'

'I mean, the building layout is interesting...' I started but stopped when a cushion hit me on the forehead and knocked me back a little. 'Ouch!'

'Of course I mean the boys!' Beth giggled. She'd always been a little boy crazy, ever since we first met back in primary school. Every day when we were ten or something, she would have a new boyfriend attached to her hip on the playground. Children were funny when you thought about it.

'What about them?' I asked. I was looking around my room, trying to decide where to place the new *starting a new school gift* that Beth had got me. I had a vast collection of motivational framed quotes covering my bedroom walls, and Beth had got me a new one for this momentous occasion.

It read:

Dream big.

Plan big.

Live big.

I loved it.

'Oh, stop pretending that you haven't noticed anyone.' Her

stern gaze was on me, her eyes wrinkled at the corners, and I wondered how long she'd let me fob this question off for before she started to get pissed off.

'I haven't.' I shrugged. It was only a little white lie.

The only boy I'd noticed was Dean, and I still wasn't sure that was for any of the right reasons. The boy got under my skin like nobody's business. Every class we sat together, he would find a way to irritate me. Like telling me jokes that weren't funny, or picking on my choice of clothing for the day.

'Layla, you're a wicked liar.' Beth threw another cushion in my direction that I ducked from. 'I can tell by the look in your eye that you're hiding something from me.'

'Am not,' I said but looked away because I could sense the blush on my cheeks and knew it would only grow the more I looked into her eyes. She was right. I'd never been a great liar. Most people could read me like a book.

'Just tell me,' she whined. 'I won't stop asking until you give me *something.*'

'Fine, fine!' I put my hands up. 'I admit defeat.'

We both laughed and settled back down again, as I rearranged the cushions back on my bed in their rightful spots. There was nothing I hated more than an untidy bedroom. Okay, so maybe that wasn't true. But it was definitely in my top ten.

'Go on then! Who is he? How'd you meet him?'

'His name's Dean. On my first day, he bumped into me as I walked across the parking lot. No idea what he'd been drinking, but I know it was cold and it smelt bad. Plus, it totally ruined my freshly washed hair.'

Beth laughed, and I joined in, picturing in my mind the sight of Dean's and my collision. It played out in my head like a meet-cute in a film; just without the light pink haze that usually accompanied them.

No. In my head, it was a dark grey colour. All doom and gloom around here.

'Dean,' she sang, bouncing up and down. When it came to boys, Beth's excitement knew no bounds. We may no longer be ten, but her love of having a boyfriend hadn't abated. 'What's he like?'

'You're gonna love this,' I told her and groaned. 'He's a football player.'

'Football player!' she exclaimed, even more excited now. 'Oh em gee, Layla. That's so cool! Hang on. Wait.' She paused and arched an over plucked eyebrow in my direction. 'Is he a *good* football player?'

'He's the captain, if that means anything?' I mumbled, preparing myself—and my ears—for the screech I knew would leave Beth's mouth next.

She didn't disappoint.

'Ahhh! That is so exciting!'

'It is?'

'Yes!' She punched my shoulder and I jolted back. It was always like this between us. Beth was overenthusiastic and excitable. I was realistic and a little more sombre.

It worked.

We worked.

The fact we'd been best friends for as long as we had was a testament to that fact.

I remembered the day I met Beth. She'd had her dark black hair in two pigtails that bounced with every step she took and a gap in her smile. Her two front teeth had been knocked out during a playground game of *Bulldog* and they still hadn't grown back.

The teacher announced my arrival and pointed me to an empty seat at one of the square tables, next to said black-haired girl with pigtails.

As I sat down, she announced loudly, 'You're going to be my new best friend.'

And from that day onwards, that was exactly what she'd been.

No matter what happened, no matter what other friends may have come and gone, we were always there for each other.

The events of last year proved that to me the most.

'That captain of the football team, La! That's pretty impressive, you know. The Hollowdale Rebels have a bit of a reputation from what I've read.'

'When have you read anything about the Hollowdale Rebels?'

'Right now.' She held up her mobile and showed me the page she was on. It was some kind of fan site for the football teams in the local area, all garish and bright. Some fangirl had made this for free, clearly.

'Does it say anything about Dean?' I asked, then winced when I saw Beth's eyes light up. The fact I'd even put that question out there told her I was interested. More interested than I'd wanted to let her know.

'It does.' She scrolled on her phone, her face looking at it intently. 'There's also a team photo if you wanna see?'

I looked at her, not taking the bait.

'I know what he looks like already. Thanks, though.'

'Suit yourself,' she said, slurring her words because of the large piece of fudge she just shoved inside her mouth. 'Doesn't mean I'm not going to.'

Her eyes bulged, and she looked up at me with wide eyes.

'Okay, so I hate to break it to you, La.'

'Break what to me?'

'Dean's a perfect specimen. An Adonis. A god amongst men. A—'

I cut her off before she could say even more.

'Oh, stop!' I laughed, throwing my head back. 'He's not *that* good-looking.'

'Oh, but, my dear sweet child, he is.' She nodded vigorously, as if the motion alone would be enough to convince me of it. 'He's beautiful. Stunning. Perfection. The hair. The eyes. I'm in love.'

Beth placed the back of her hand on her forehead and lay backwards, pretending to swoon at the very idea of Dean. Man, the girl should have taken up drama instead of science; she had a flair for the dramatic, after all.

'You are not in love,' I scoffed. 'And anyway, once I tell you a bit more about him, you may change your tune.'

'I doubt it,' she said. 'But do tell. I want to know all the juicy gossip. You see, I've decided I'm going to live vicariously through you. Nothing exciting ever happens at Mountview.'

I stared blankly at her.

'Oh shit, Layla. I didn't mean it like that. I'm sorry,' she apologised, reaching out a hand to stroke my shoulder in what I assumed she thought was a loving gesture, but to me just seemed sort of odd. 'Forget I mentioned Mountview.'

She zipped her lips together and threw away the key, which caused a small giggle to leave me. I knew she hadn't meant to say that nothing exciting ever happened at Mountview, but she had. And sometimes, whether a person meant it or not, they'd still said it. Had already put the words out into the universe, where they couldn't be unheard even if you wished them to be.

The moment she mentioned my old school, my mood sank to the floor. And for the rest of the day, no matter how hard Beth tried to bring it back, it stayed in a low place, trapped inside my memory.

<h1 style="text-align:center">Four
Layla</h1>

friday, 10th september

THE NEXT WEEK, my life fell into a pattern of sorts.

I'd arrive at school, Dean would greet me by my car, then the two of us would walk together to our first class of the day—all while Remi would stand nearby and give me evil looks as if I'd asked him for this kind of attention.

I definitely hadn't, and I would've told her that if she'd tried to talk to me. But she wouldn't even acknowledge me if we got too close during the one lesson we shared. It was funny to me that she'd stare and evil-eye me whenever Dean was around, but the moment he wasn't, she pretended I didn't exist.

Clearly, the girl had a few self-esteem issues.

Dean had been an absolute charmer the entire week. It was as if he'd had a personality transplant from the moody guy I'd met on my first day who'd bumped into me and spilled a drink on my head.

The whole thing was disconcerting.

'If you could be a character from romantic literature, who would you be?' Dean asked.

It was Friday night, and the two of us were sitting at my dining table, with textbooks and novels around us, as we tried to figure out how to tackle the project binder Mrs Dalston had given us to work on.

Dean had come over straight from football practise, and damn, did he look good. His face had a couple of flecks of dirt on it still, and his chestnut-coloured hair was ruffled. I hadn't asked him how his practice went, but from his appearance, I'd guessed it had been hard work.

'Me?' I asked, putting my hand to my chest involuntarily. *Like, duh, Layla, of course he meant you.*

'Can't see anybody else sat here at this table.' He shrugged, pulling one of the novels towards him, opening it to take a quick peek inside, then putting it back down like it had burned him. 'People actually read this trash?'

'It isn't trash!' I snapped, pulling the book he'd glanced at so I could see the title. It was a battered copy of *Jane Eyre* and I rolled my eyes at him. I highly doubted Dean Walters could read these and understand the language, let alone understand them enough to enjoy them and truly help me on the project. 'I'll have you know that this book is a classic.'

'Yeah,' he agreed. 'Classically *boring*.'

'Wow, Dean. Didn't realise you could be so childish.'

He laughed, throwing his head back before settling his eyes back on my face. He studied me, and I felt a chill cover my body as he did so. Like an ice cube had been placed on my head and was now trickling down, covering me, until there was no part of me left untouched by the chill.

'I'm not childish!' he said through his laughter.

'Oh, sorry. I forgot. You're not childish at all. You're the guy most girls would like to spend their time with, right?'

Throwing his words back at him like that filled me with a small thrill. He must've known when he said it that I'd never let him live it down. The way he'd been so serious about it made it even worse.

The guffaw that followed from his mouth unleashed a part of me I'd been keeping in check. My mouth opened wide, and the laughter left me in a long stream, until my eyes were watering and my sides were hurting from the pain of laughing too much.

'Not afraid to bust my balls, are ya?' His joy shone in his eyes, his entire face animated, and all I could do was look away because of the overwhelming emotions that rushed through me when our eyes locked.

'Not if you deserve it,' I said, still looking elsewhere. I glanced at the books in front of us and decided to answer his earlier question to distract him. 'If I could be a character in romantic literature, I'd probably be Anastasia.'

'Like that cartoon film?' he asked.

'Nope, like *Fifty Shades*,' I answered, keeping a straight face while raising my gaze to look him dead in the eyes. He gulped before clearing his throat.

'Didn't have you down as a BDSM girl,' he replied, then it was my turn to clear my throat before I choked on my own stupidity. I'd meant to make a quip, something witty and out of the blue, but now we'd moved into uncharted territory for me, and I had no idea how to respond.

'I-I,' I stuttered. 'I…'

'Cat got your tongue?' He poked his tongue out and licked his bottom lip, and I shivered, somehow being both hot and cold at the same time.

'Something like that,' I murmured, my cheeks heating. 'Let's get back to work.'

'Nah,' he said, crossing his arms in front of his pecs, drawing my eyes away from his face. 'This topic seems pretty fun, if you ask me.'

'You would,' I muttered, still looking at his chest until I realised what I was doing, then snapped my head to look to my right instead. Sadly, to the right was the wall. So now I looked even more foolish than I'd already made myself look.

Lucky for me—or unlucky, depending on the way you looked at it—my mum called my name from the kitchen.

'Let me just go see what she's yelling about,' I told him,

standing abruptly from my chair so I could make a quick and clean getaway. 'Why don't you look at the project tasks and see what we can tackle first?'

'You can always tackle me,' he said, pure, unfiltered amusement covering his face.

'Shut it!' I hissed, slightly in a joking manner but also slightly embarrassed by how silly I felt with his banter. I knew he meant no harm, that he was trying to make things less tense between us, but actually, he was making it worse.

I made my way to my mum in the kitchen at a fast clip, happy she'd saved me, but not wanting to know what she wanted to say. Mum still asked me every single day after school whether or not I'd made new friends, and every day I had to disappoint her and say no. When she'd found out I had somebody coming over, even if it was just for a school project, she was so happy about it. She assumed we'd chosen to team up, not that the teacher had set us up.

'Hey,' Mum said tentatively once I was standing in front of her as she stirred the spaghetti Bolognese she was working on for dinner. 'How's it going?'

'It's going,' I replied. 'Did you want me for anything in particular?'

'Well,' she started, her face one of worry. I'd seen this face more than once, and my heart sank as I wondered why she was making it now. Before she could say more, my dad walked into the kitchen and smiled broadly at us both.

'Ah, so you've called her in,' he said towards Mum, still smiling widely. 'Perfect.'

He clapped his hands together, and if I'd thought my heart had sunk before, now it was completely gone, missing from my body entirely. Because *that* gesture meant my dad was about to start a conversation you didn't want to be a part of.

'What's this about?' I asked, leaning against the counter in the centre of our spacious kitchen. One thing that was a perk of moving to Beurre was the size of our home. It wasn't a mansion or anything, but it was a fraction bigger than our old one, and the kitchen was to die for.

'That boy in there,' my dad said, nudging his head in the direction of the dining room, his lips pursed like he'd sucked on a sour lemon. 'What do we know about him?'

'In what sense?' I asked, confused about where he was going with it. Did they want to know whether I knew Dean's parents and his entire life story? Or did they just want me to confirm he wasn't a serial killer? Guess it didn't matter in what way they meant it. I didn't have an answer to either question, anyway.

'Who is he?' Dad asked, like some awful knockoff gangster.

Ground, swallow me whole.

My only saving grace was that Dean was still in the dining room with no knowledge of this conversation.

I shrugged, looking over at my mum to see if I was going to get any support from her. She was curling her blonde hair around her finger, her eyes boring back into mine, but her lips were pressed together in a sorry smile. Like a *sorry, Layla, you know what he's like* kind of smile.

Basically, I wasn't going to get any support from her just yet.

'Dean Walters…' I finally answered, making my tone go up at the end in question, still none the wiser as to what the hell my dad was getting at. Then I remembered something that may sway my dad, so I added, 'He's captain of the football team.'

'Well, that's a good thing, I guess. But I don't like him much, La-La.'

My dad's warm eyes made me smile, as did the fact he'd used my childhood nickname, but I still couldn't understand where he was coming from. He'd never even spoken to Dean. We hadn't sat down for dinner yet, so really, he was being very quick to judge.

I knew my parents were coming from a place of love.

After the events of the previous year, they looked out for me a lot more than they ever had before. It was overprotective and overwhelming, but I knew they meant well.

I may be coming to terms with what happened to me, but they were still struggling through the aftermath of it.

'You don't even know him, Dad.'

'Do you?'

'Well, not really.' I shrugged. I knew Dean liked to watch reruns of *Teenage Mutant Ninja Turtles*, but I highly doubted my dad meant his favourite TV show. 'We sit together in most classes because our surnames both start with a "W". But if you're asking about his family or background, then I've got nothing.'

'We're just concerned, is all.'

'Concerned about what? The fact we're doing our homework together out in the open?'

'Don't get smart with me, Layla,' Dad said, pushing his glasses back up his nose. 'You know what I mean.'

'No, Dad. I really don't.'

My parents both sighed in unison, as if I was disappointing them with my obtuseness. And maybe I should be more worried, or concerned, about Dean, but it wasn't as if he'd done anything wrong. Not really.

'If that's all…' I said, trailing off. I looked between my parents, waiting for one of them to speak. Dad's eyes narrowed on me, and he tapped his foot with frustration. Then Mum looked hurt, or confused, about how the conversation had derailed so quickly.

I went back to the table, irritated at my parents' interruption, but also happy they stopped an awkward conversation between me and Dean.

'Everything okay?' he asked as I sat back down in my seat. I nodded and pulled the textbook closer to me.

'Yeah. You get anywhere with these?'

'A little,' he said, fidgeting with the pen grasped in his fingers. I could sense he was looking at me, just waiting for me to turn and look back, but I kept my head down. Reading the same sentence over and over until he coughed.

'How would you like to go out with me tomorrow night?' he blurted out, and I choked on air.

'Er…' I trailed off, finally moving my gaze to stare at him. My parents definitely wouldn't be happy about it, but surely they wouldn't begrudge me a new friend. Especially the only one I'd made at my new school. 'Sure?'

'Perfect,' he said, a wolfish smile covering his features. 'I'll pick you up at seven sharp.'

I nodded and swallowed. What was even happening to me?

Five
Dean

I wasn't sure what to expect when I asked Layla out, but I definitely hadn't expected my stomach to explode in a burst of nerves.

Even just admitting that made me feel wrong. But from the moment I met her, I knew I needed to get to know her better. The way she'd reacted when I spilled my drink on her amused me. Plus, she was new to town and didn't know anything about anything that had happened in the past.

After leaving Layla's house, I made my way to the field, like I did every single Friday night. The whole school did—or at least those fifteen or older.

The field was owned by the Matthews family, and ever since Maxwell Matthews started at Hollowdale High, it became *the* place for everybody to go on a Friday night. After he died, his younger brother Spencer took over the tradition.

Everybody in town knew about it. Even the cops knew about it and gave the area a wide berth. We were on private land and not harming anyone, so as long as nobody ended up in hospital to have their stomach pumped, it was all gravy.

'How was Layla?' James asked, waggling his eyebrows at me, handing me a can of beer. 'Kissed her yet?'

I nudged him in the rib with my elbow before taking a swig of the beer.

'Don't talk about her like that.'

'Mate,' he said, putting his hands up. 'Didn't ask if you'd fucked her. Just if you'd kissed.' He rolled his eyes and looked at Alex and Peter, who were standing beside us. 'Touchy.'

'Don't know what he's so touchy about,' Alex piped up. 'Not like he's asked her out.'

His smile was smug, and all I wanted to do was wipe it off.

My mouth opened before I could stop myself.

'Actually, I've asked her out tomorrow.'

'You have?' Alex's eyebrows rose high on his forehead, and his smug smile slipped away as fast as it arrived. 'Where you going?'

'Haven't decided yet.' I shrugged. I'd asked her on a whim, with no real plan. Shit. What if I didn't make it clear I meant it as a date? Did I even specify it was a date?

Double shit.

He broke out into a deep chuckle. My face must be giving away the sheer panic that had settled within me. Maybe Layla thought I'd asked her out as a friend? How was I even meant to know for sure?

I could text her, sure.

But that could make everything awkward as fuck.

'You should take her to the bowling alley over in Lakeland,' Alex said, dangling his bottle of beer between his fingers. James and Peter, bored with my fretting, had started talking between themselves about who even knew what. Alex assessed me. 'The owners have sold up, so in a month's time it'll cost a fuck ton to go.'

I mulled it over in my mind. Bowling was fine, right? Everybody loved bowling. And surely Layla wouldn't feel uncomfortable with bowling or as if I was inviting her out to hook up. The way her cheeks flushed when we spoke about *Fifty Shades of Grey* earlier told me more than she probably wanted to.

'Bowling?' James piped up, pausing his conversation with

Peter, his eyes alight. 'I'm game! We should all go tomorrow. What time are you thinking?'

'Well,' I started, needing to make it clear they weren't invited.

'I'll pick you up at seven.'

'I have to pick Layla up at seven,' I told them. All three of them smiled, smug as fuck.

'We'll pick you up at half six, then,' James said. 'Then we can go get Layla.'

'I—' My mind scrambled for a way out of it. A way to make it clear I wanted time with Layla all to myself without them around, but the words wouldn't come. My tongue glued to the bottom of my mouth, unable to speak.

Maybe it wouldn't be the total clusterfuck that my mind was envisioning. Maybe Layla wouldn't mind, or had thought it was a friend thing?

Shit. Only T-minus twenty-one hours until I found out.

Six

Layla

saturday, 11th september

I STILL COULDN'T BELIEVE I'd agreed to go out with Dean.

Ever since he'd asked me on the spot the previous night, I was trying to come up with an excuse to stay home, but nothing sounded satisfactory.

Moving here was supposed to be my fresh start, sure, but I'd also never intended to get involved with anybody at Hollowdale. Graduate and get out; that was the plan.

I didn't even know what to think about it, to be honest. It seemed strange to think back to the first day of school and how we had completely got off on the wrong foot—after that whole spilling the contents of his drink all over me, situation.

My nerves were building with every hour, and all I could do was stare at the time and count down the minutes until he arrived at my front door. I finally understood why people sometimes said they had gymnasts in their stomachs doing umpteenth somersaults. I still hadn't told him about why my family had moved to Hollowdale, but tonight didn't feel like the night to tell him the truth. And actually, when I thought about it, he'd only asked me that one time and then dropped it pretty fast.

By the time the clock turned half past six, I had worked myself up to a full-on state of distress. What if he didn't like what I was wearing? What if my outfit didn't suit the activity he had chosen? What if he had reconsidered the whole evening and was going to blow me off?

Stop thinking so negatively, Layla. I reprimanded myself; a constant battle between my heart and my head waging a war at all times.

I heard the doorbell ring and rushed to open it before my parents got there first. That was one meeting that could be prolonged, although I had a feeling I wasn't going to be quite so lucky.

'I'm going out with some friends. I'll text you later!' I shouted behind me as I ran down the stairs and made it to the door before Mum or Dad could appear and accost me.

Opening the door, my hands shaking, I saw Dean standing with his hand raised, about to ring the bell again. He was wearing dark denim jeans and a white polo T-shirt that fit him tightly, his abs from playing football on display underneath. He looked gorgeous. But then again, Dean looked gorgeous all the time—and he knew it.

'Hey, gorgeous. Ready for an evening of fun-filled excitement?' he asked, running his hand through his slight quiff.

My heart fluttered when the word gorgeous left his lips, but I kept it to myself—or at least I hoped I had. To cover up the flutter, I rolled my eyes at him as if it was the lamest sentence I'd ever heard. And coming from Dean, that wouldn't have been too difficult. He hadn't mentioned what this date involved, and I was unsure what *an evening of fun-filled excitement* entailed. The evening with Dean would be my first ever date, meaning I didn't have much knowledge to go on.

'Hey, yourself,' I replied, biting my bottom lip but stopping when his eyes gravitated towards them. 'I'm ready if you are.'

I was trying to sound confident, but even I heard the waver in my voice.

He led me to the car, and I paused before getting inside. The car wasn't empty. I could make out three others in the car, meaning it was about to become a bit of a tight fit.

I tried not to look too disappointed as Dean opened the back door for me to slide into the centre seat. *Wonderful, I've really pulled the short straw, haven't I?*

'I know you've met them briefly before, but this is James, Alex, and Peter.' Dean didn't sound fazed that he was introducing me to his buddies on what was supposed to be our date night. 'Alex is driving, and these other two bozos decided to come out for the ride.'

I nodded, strapping my seat belt across me, trying not to wince when it cut into my neck. It was one of those awkward ones that came down from the ceiling. I'd often wondered about what was more likely to decapitate you? The seat belt or the car accident it was meant to save you from?

I hoped I wouldn't be finding out. I'd never seen Alex drive before, and a flutter of anxiety sat low in my stomach at the thought of putting my life into his hands.

Would they be joining us all evening? Or were they literally along for the ride? I didn't have time to make sure as Alex had started the car and was moving along the road with alarming speed.

Already, I was starting to regret agreeing to this date; it didn't seem like much of a date if three of his friends were tagging along.

As if sensing my worry, Dean looked at me and gave me a short shrug and an embarrassed smile, buckling himself into the seat beside me. The smile he gave me just made me like him even more, but I played it cool. Didn't want him to think I was totally uncool or something like that.

Maybe there was a very valid and reasonable explanation as to why I was currently sharing the car with three random guys, right? And the last thing I wanted to do was to come across as needy or rude. Nobody wanted a needy girl, especially before you'd even started officially dating. I'd always witnessed Beth acting like a needy girlfriend and I was fully aware it was the reason everybody had broken up with her within a couple of months, tops.

Maybe it was never meant to be a date date. Maybe it was me who'd got the wrong end of the stick?

Either way, I needed to roll with the punches.

My name is Layla Williams. I am eighteen years old. I have blonde hair and blue eyes. My mother's name is Darcy and my father's name is Daniel. I have been through hell, but I am safe now.

I repeated my mantra, needing to calm down the swirling thoughts in my mind. One time I'd mentioned it to Beth, the words I told myself, and she didn't understand.

'But why do you need to remind yourself who your parents are? Seems a little weird to me.'

That was the last time I mentioned my coping mechanisms to her. And Beth didn't even mean it in a horrible way—she was merely asking. But it had got my back up, anyway. As if she thought I was silly. As if she thought I was being overdramatic. And she, of all people, knew what happened to me. She knew the torment I'd lived through.

'... they insisted.' Dean looked at me, his face sheepish, and I cocked an eyebrow back. I'd totally missed the start of his sentence and I wasn't sure whether I should look rude and ask him to repeat it because I wasn't listening or if I should pretend I'd heard it and hope it wasn't something serious I would need to recall later down the line.

'Who insisted?'

Dean nudged his head to the two in the front seats and I nodded.

Ohhh, he meant his friends.

'That's okay,' I said, not sure what the correct response was.

Should I make it clear I would've been happy for it to be just us two? Or did I play it coy and keep it to myself?

Why did I care so much?

'It's not,' he said with a chuckle in my ear, leaning closer to me. Not that he could get much closer. We were squashed together in the back of the car enough as it was. 'I wanted it to be just us two.'

My stomach filled with butterflies. Turned out I did need to know what he wanted, because the moment the butterflies dissipated, a calm settled over my entire body. He wanted the night to be a real date, the same way I did, and that made me feel pretty good.

'So, what's the deal with Remi?'

'Huh?'

'Oh, don't play shy with me. You know exactly what I'm asking. The girl hangs off you like a bad smell and ever since I started here, she's given me evil glares and avoided me.'

'Remi's... she's something else.' He rubbed his chin in deep thought. 'We dated for a while.'

'And how long exactly is a while?'

'Three years? Something like that.'

'That's more than a while,' I said with a laugh, heading back to the ball return for my turn. Three years at our age was a little more than mere 'dating'. It was a full-blown relationship, even if it was more of a puppy love type thing. They knew each other well.

No wonder Remi had taken an instant dislike to me on the first day of school.

I bowled the ball down the lane, making sure to miss the

gutter and give it a slight curl. The ball connected with the pins and every single one fell down one by one.

Instead of cheering and rubbing my hands together with glee, I turned around and sashayed back to the spot I'd left Dean in. His mouth was agape, his eyebrows hidden by his fringe.

'And when did you split up?' I asked, resuming our conversation as if I hadn't just bowled a damn good strike. 'Please don't tell me something stupid like the end of summer.'

'Well, no, actually'—he shuffled on the spot, his eyes downcast—'it was the beginning of summer.'

'Oh, perfect,' I said, nodding. 'Was it serious?'

'As serious as a relationship can be when you're fourteen.'

'No wonder the girl hates me.' I may not get along with Remi, but I could understand her. She felt cheated out of something she wanted back.

'She doesn't *hate* you,' he murmured, walking to the ball return. 'She just strongly dislikes you.'

'That makes it better, does it?'

'I don't know.' He shrugged before picking up the light ball once more and throwing it down the lane. The pins split and he groaned. 'How come you're so good at this?'

I smiled, his sour tone amusing me. I'd known the boy would be competitive. What football player—and captain of the team—wouldn't be? But I hadn't expected him to be so ready to take me down.

We were on to our second game and I beat him on the last one by quite a bit. The boy was yet to get a strike and his irritation at it was clear for everybody to see.

'Practise,' I answered, a bright smile playing on my lips. Then I realised my answer made it sound like I'd spent a lot of time hanging in bowling alleys, so I felt the compulsion to add, 'My dad used to take me a lot when I was younger.'

'You're lucky,' he said, standing in front of me once more. At the same time, we both sat down on the bench, putting our game on pause. 'That you got to spend quality time with your dad like that, I mean.'

My eyes locked on his, and I saw the hurt swimming in them. We'd never spoken about his parents before. Honestly, most of our conversations had either revolved around our English Lit project or something else equally as surface level.

'My dad's pretty great. Sorry if he made you uncomfortable last night. He's super protective of me.'

'I get that. You're his only kid. Of course he's gonna protect you.'

I took a deep breath. I may as well tell him why my dad acted so protective of me. It wasn't like it was a big secret or anything. Not like the other thing I never wanted to talk about again if I could help it.

'Well, that. And the fact that when I was younger, I was super ill for a little bit. I had meningitis and had to be hospitalised for a bit. It's pretty irritating, you know, how overprotective my dad can be. My illness is actually the reason I was held back a year in school.' It was something I didn't talk about often because I didn't remember all too much of it. It affected my parents a lot more than it did me.

The loud background music changed to a slow song and I smiled, happy in that moment for the first time in a while. Even though I'd only known Dean for two weeks, it felt right to open up to him. I could see him being a good friend, even if the whole dating thing didn't work out between us. And I needed friends.

'You were?'

'Yep. I'm eighteen already.'

'Who knew I was on a date with an older woman?' he said, and we both laughed. It always amazed me that when you were older, a year's age difference was nothing, but as a teen it felt like a lifetime.

'My parents have never let me forget about it. That I should be in the year above, I mean.'

'My dad passed away a couple of years ago,' Dean said, his

voice cracking at the end. My heart twinged for him. There was me complaining about my dad being overprotective, all while he was sitting there, knowing he would never see his dad again. I felt like a grade-A dickhead.

'I'm so sorry, Dean.'

'Nah, don't be,' he said, his eyes glazed over and lost to me. 'It's not your fault. It's nobody's fault.'

'I know,' I whispered, leaning closer, placing my hand on his knee for comfort. 'But I'm sorry nonetheless.'

His eyes widened at my touch, and he swallowed. I watched as his Adam's apple bobbed in his throat, and his eyes blinked fast.

His face came closer to mine, and my brain began malfunctioning. I knew what it meant. Knew that his face looming closer to mine, his lips puckered, meant he was going to kiss me. And I had a split-second decision to make.

Did I lean in, too?

Or did I back away and make the situation more awkward? He'd opened up a bit, telling me about his dad, and we'd been having such a good date that I didn't want to be the one to ruin it.

The decision really wasn't a decision after all.

I moved towards him and placed my lips on his. And when our lips touched? It was magic. Pure magic. Like electricity sparked and crackled between us—a connection I couldn't deny.

Dean Walters could kiss, that was for sure. And I wanted to fall deeper into his depths.

I just hoped I'd allow myself to.

wednesday, 15th september

'MAYBE I SHOULD WRITE the report and you present it when the time comes?'

I raised an eyebrow at Dean, confused why he wanted *me* to make the presentation. Standing in front of the class and talking wasn't something I was capable of doing. If I even tried, I felt certain I'd stand and cry. Or worse. Mess everything up. Say everything wrong. Then run out embarrassed and unable to live it down.

And from what I'd seen, he wasn't the right man for the job when it came to the report side of it all. He barely tolerated English Lit. Made all kinds of comments about how unenjoyable it was. Yet here he was, offering to write up a report on it. Something didn't add up.

'Why do you wanna write the report? You're much better at being in front of people.'

He coughed, his cheeks flushing a light shade of pink. His eyes darted around the room, looking at everybody, making sure whatever he said next wouldn't be overheard.

'If I tell you something, will you promise not to repeat it?'

'Oh, I don't know if I can promise that.' I bit my bottom lip, enjoying the tease. 'Depends on just how juicy it is.'

'Layla, I'm serious.'

'And so am I!' I giggled. It was just too easy to rile him up at times. My fingers grazed his and I straightened my features. 'I promise.'

He leaned in, a look of determination crossing his features. My mind was instantly intrigued. What was so serious that he needed me to keep it quiet?

'I actually really love English Literature,' he said, the expression on his face sheepish as a pale pink tinge entered his cheeks. The flush was adorable and I smiled at his embarrassment.

'Okay…' I trailed off, wondering if there was more to his declaration, but he just stayed silent, moving back in his seat again. 'Is that it?'

'Yeah.' He ran his hand through his fringe, looking at me dead serious. 'I can't have that getting out! People will never look at me the same way.'

'I doubt that,' I said with a full belly laugh. 'Who cares what other people think, anyway? You're still one of the coolest guys in school. Plus, you're the captain of the football team. Pretty sure people would overlook your love for Dickens.'

'I'm more of an Austen man, actually.'

'Really?' I asked, trying not to sound too disbelieving. But honestly, I couldn't imagine him sitting down with a cup of tea and *Pride and Prejudice.* Not that he needed a cup of tea at all to enjoy the classics.

'No,' he said, laughing at me. 'No, you had it right the first time.'

'Well, why don't we work on the report together and then we both give the presentation? A happy in between,' I suggested, hoping I'd twist his arm closer to the time to give the presentation without much input from me.

'Sounds like a plan!' he said enthusiastically, grabbing his pen and beginning to write away on the notebook in front of him. 'How about this Friday night? I can come over again after practice?'

'Well…' I looked around, not sure if I should tell him the truth or not. I inhaled slowly through my nose and decided to go with the truth. 'Actually, Friday's my birthday. My mum and dad might have plans for us.'

'It's your birthday on Friday?' He gasped, dropping his pen and holding his hand up to his chest. 'Why am I only now just finding out about it?'

'Because we've not talked about birthdays yet?'

'Pft! I'm taking you out.' He was adamant, his tone sure.

'You really don't have to do that.' It was my turn to flush, my cheeks heating under his intense gaze.

'I know,' he said, 'but I'm going to anyway.'

friday, 17th september

Nothing I said the rest of the week could convince Dean that I didn't need to go out for a birthday date. That I was perfectly fine spending the night at home with my parents and ordering in a Chinese takeaway.

Just the fact he wanted to spend my birthday with me at all was enough to make me smile. Since our date at the bowling alley—if we could even call it that—the two of us were in constant contact. We messaged each other all night or sent random voice notes filled with crap about what we were watching, reading, or even the games we were playing. And then at school, we spent all our time together, both in lessons and during lunch.

Because I'd met his friends the night we all went bowling, I sat with them at lunch and the rest of the footballers. It was a large crowd of people and even though it overwhelmed me, I enjoyed being a part of something bigger. A group of people who had banter and were genuinely happy to spend time with one another. Not like my old group of friends who stuck together out of convenience and to keep up appearances.

'You ready for burgers?' he asked, and I nodded before he'd even finished his sentence.

'I'm starved,' I said, and he laughed. It was a light laugh, and it made the muscles in my stomach clench with nerves and butterflies. Being alone with him made me feel all the things and I wasn't sure how to handle it.

With everything that happened in my past, I never expected to want somebody in a sexual way. To want to have somebody see me naked because I asked them to, I *allowed* them to.

'You ate half of my lunch and at least two of the cupcakes Alex baked for you!' Dean brushed his hair away from his forehead, and the blue of his eyes caught me off guard. They were the brightest of blue.

'But that isn't the same as having burgers, is it? I want cheesy chips too.'

'And whatever the princess wants, the princess shall have,' Dean said, opening the door to Carillo's. It was a burger restaurant in the city and I was surprised when he suggested it. I thought at most he'd take me somewhere in Beurre itself, or maybe at a push in Lakeland. But nope, he'd gone all out.

The waitress showed us to a booth once Dean told her his name, and it was a window booth in the back that was away from most of the restaurant. It was secluded, private, and perfect for a birthday date.

Once we were settled and had ordered our drinks, I looked at Dean and smiled, happy with how my first few weeks in a new town had gone. When I decided to change school so close to finishing and heading off to university, my parents and Beth thought I wasn't thinking clearly. That I would grow to resent my decision. But they were wrong. The decision was the best one I'd made. I wished I'd thought to do it earlier.

'Thank you for bringing me here.'

'No need to thank me,' he said, fiddling with the napkin in front of him. Maybe he was more nervous than I realised. It was the first time we'd been out, just us two, after all. 'D'you know what you're gonna have?'

'I always get the same thing,' I admitted. It was a habit of mine. Why change something that wasn't broken?

If I knew I liked something, I was going to keep having it until it was either removed from the menu or I decided I didn't like it anymore.

'What about you?' I asked. 'You know what you're getting?'

'Well, funny enough, I always get the same thing, too.'

'Great minds think alike.' The two of us gave each other that look you give to somebody when you realise you have something in common. 'You up for a game of twenty-one questions?'

'Sure!' he said, rubbing his hands together. 'Hit me with it.'

'Okay…' I thought about what I could ask that wasn't too heavy. 'How old were you when you got into football?'

'Young. Maybe five? I've grown up my whole life being into it. My dad loved football and it was something we would watch together.'

I wanted to ask him about his dad. I was itching to know more. But I also wasn't going to bring down the tone either.

'I've got one for you,' he continued talking, not giving me any time to ask him to elaborate. 'Why did you move to Hollowdale High?'

'Er…' I didn't know how to respond. I wanted to tell him, wanted to open up, but I also knew it wasn't the time or place to. Even if it wasn't my birthday, I wouldn't have wanted to tell him sitting in a restaurant. 'Pass.'

'You can't just pass!'

'Well, I just did,' I said, chuckling a little to brush it all away. 'Ask me literally anything else.'

'Fine,' he said, his widening smile causing my pulse to thump faster. There was something slightly sinister within it. 'What age were you when you lost your virginity?'

I'd lifted my glass to take a small sip of my water, and I coughed, the water having made its way down the wrong hole.

'Sorry?'

His devilish smirk grew, and he said, 'You heard me. Now answer the question, Williams.'

'I haven't,' I mumbled. My face was so hot I was close to having to fan myself with the menu that was untouched on the table in front of me.

'You haven't what?'

'I haven't lost my virginity,' I admitted, feeling ashamed and then pissed at myself for that. I shouldn't feel bad for sticking to what I believe in. And it shouldn't embarrass me that I hadn't.

'You're a virgin?' Dean asked, his face incredulous. My heart sank to my stomach, and I began wringing my hands in my lap. And even though I'd guessed he wasn't one, it still hurt to hear otherwise. Even if I hadn't *actually* heard otherwise yet.

Remi's bitterness towards me was making a bit more sense. I'd thought it from the start, but clearly she wasn't over him and saw me as the biggest hurdle in her way. The reason she couldn't be happy. Even though that wasn't the case. If Dean wanted to be with her, he would be. Simple as that.

'How?' he sputtered. Then he recovered, catching himself. 'I didn't mean it like that.'

'It's okay,' I said, even though I couldn't settle whether it was or not. The waiter came over and we ordered our food. I was twiddling my thumbs, wondering how I should react. What I should say.

But then Dean spoke and I relaxed a little.

'Layla,' he said, his eyes softening. 'I'm not judging you or anything like that. It's cool. And honestly, fair play to you. I think it's good that you've stuck with what you want. I admire that.'

'Thank you,' I said, smiling shyly.

My heart fluttered. Dean admired me, and it made me feel so good inside.

Katie Lowrie

Happy birthday to me.

monday, 25th october

SCARE MAZES DIDN'T ALWAYS shit me up, but apparently the ones at Pleasure Park were the exception to that rule.

'Fuck!' I shouted as a man ran at me with a chainsaw. His face covered in fake blood, his teeth covered in grime as he sneered at me. The smell of the diesel from the chainsaw entered my nose and I screeched. Instantly, I grabbed onto Layla's waist. She walked in front of me, and although we were supposed to make our way through holding on to the shoulders of the person in front of us, my hands moved of their own volition.

The chainsaw dude signalled the end of the maze, and the two of us burst out the doors at the end, back into the outside world, laughing as we went. Adrenaline filled me, my breathing laboured.

Layla grabbed my hand and dragged me off to the side so we wouldn't get caught up in the crowd that was flooding out of the maze behind us.

'That was a lot scarier than I thought it'd be,' she said with a wide smile, causing two small dimples to appear on her cheeks. Every time those dimples appeared, a sharp stab of emotion travelled through me. Her smile brightened her entire face.

Made her blue eyes sparkle and stand out on her face like the brightest of oceans.

We'd been dating for over a month, and the entire time, I couldn't believe my luck. She was funny, smart, and beautiful. The perfect trifecta.

'I was totally cool, calm, and collected,' I said, forcing myself to keep a straight face. She saw through it in seconds.

'Oh, sure you were! Your screeching in my ear made me jump more than the scare actors did!' She laughed. She was almost a little *too* amused by it all. I needed to distract her. Looking around, I spotted a booth over to the right selling candy floss and popcorn buckets. That would have to do.

'Fancy a snack?' I asked, reaching out my hand to take hers. Layla must have seen in my eyes how much I wanted her to drop her ribbing, because she nodded and placed her hand in mine with no argument and let me lead her to the snack cart.

We joined the queue of other couples waiting and I squeezed her hand, happy to feel her and know she was standing beside me.

Her hand in mine was slightly chilled, but that was to be expected. It was nearly Halloween, and the weather turned icy, especially towards the evening.

You know what else was pretty icy? Layla herself.

She'd told me back on her birthday that she was a virgin, and I respected that. I really admired the fact she'd stuck to her guns and hadn't given it up to somebody she didn't think was worthy. There weren't many girls at school who could say the same. Or at least not the girls I knew and hung around with.

It was a couple of years ago that I lost my virginity. Remi and I had been dating since we were fourteen and we'd grown together. Experimented with foreplay, and having sex seemed the next logical step. We'd believed ourselves to be in love. And if you were to ask Remi, she still believed we were destined to be. That Layla was a blip in our timeline. But even if Layla was exactly that, I knew Remi wasn't where I would end up either. So much had changed since we were thirteen. *Remi* had changed. In her bid for popularity, she'd forgone all her real, genuine friends and sold out to befriend the older, more popular girls on her cheer team.

'I bet you're a salt guy, right?'

'Huh?' Her voice broke me from my thoughts. She'd caught me off guard.

'Popcorn,' she clarified. 'I bet you're a salt popcorn guy.'

'You bet! And of course you have to mix chocolate in with them,' I told her as if it was the most obvious thing in the world. Ever since I was young, I remembered putting chocolate into my salt popcorn. It was something my dad introduced me and my sister to, and after he passed, it became something we did religiously to honour him.

'Any chocolate in particular?' Her pouty lips pulled up into an amused smile.

'I mean, if I had to choose, I'd say M&Ms. But really, any chocolate will do. My dad always said that it didn't matter what chocolate he had, as long as the brand was Cadbury.'

'You don't talk about your dad much,' she pointed out and I gave a stiff nod. She already knew that my dad was dead—something I rarely chose to talk to anybody about—so why she was trying to dig over popcorn at a theme park was beyond me.

'Just the same as you not talking about your past much,' I snapped back. The moment I said it, I wanted to take it back. Take it from the air and put it back into my stupid, big mouth. But I couldn't. So I just shrugged and murmured, 'Sorry.'

'No,' she said, squeezing my hand. 'It was my fault for trying to pry and doing a poor job of it at that.'

'You definitely could've done it better,' I said with a low chuckle in an attempt to ease the tension that was surrounding us like a thick fog. The date was going so well and I didn't want shit to get messed up because I couldn't talk about my dad.

'Forgive me?' she said, batting her eyelashes at me, her ocean-coloured eyes swimming with regret. She looked so cute, her oversized jumper swamping her and her long eyelashes framing her face, and I leaned down on impulse to give her a kiss on the lips.

When I moved back, the smile on her face took my breath away.

'Of course I forgive you,' I told her. 'I'm sorry for snapping back.'

The two of us got to the front of the queue and ordered our popcorn, plus a sharing bag of chocolate to put inside. If I worried that snapping at her would change the tone of the date, then I needn't have. We went straight back to the easy banter and flirting, and when we went to sit on a picnic bench to eat, my mind wandered to a previous date I'd been on in the same place.

My time with Remi was filled with ups and downs. We may have dated for just under four years, but we'd never connected the way I was connecting with Layla. Mostly, it was a teen lust thing. It was the two of us experiencing our firsts together and in a safe way. The first kiss. The first time seeing each other naked. Rounding out all the bases and then losing our virginity to one another. It was a journey of discovery. One I looked back on with fond memories but knew I no longer needed.

I also discovered that Remi wasn't a nice person. That she needed a lot more than I could give her, or wanted to give her at our age, and that she felt a lot more for me than I did for her.

And although I broke things off, I wasn't going to cut her out of my life if she needed me. I'd hoped that after a summer apart she would've moved on a little. Set her sights on somebody else.

But apparently she'd just doubled down on trying to make me "see sense".

One thing Remi didn't understand was that I had seen sense. It was the seeing sense that led to me ending things with her in the first place.

Layla hadn't mentioned anything about how Remi treated her at school, so I hoped it meant Remi was leaving her alone.

And all I could do was hope she *continued* to leave her alone.

Nine

Layla

thursday, 28th october

'You have to tell me,' Beth whined, crossing her legs underneath her as she sat on my mattress, popping a cherry drop into her mouth.

'I don't have to tell you anything,' I said, laughing. 'What do you even wanna know?'

'You hab to tell me erything,' she said, her words jumbled from the cherry drop she still had in her mouth. She swallowed and I moved to sit facing her on my bed as I waited for her to finish. When she was done, she repeated, 'You have to tell me everything.'

'Everything as in…'

'You're dating one of the hottest guys at school, right?' she asked, and I nodded. Automatically. It was only after her sentence settled in the air that I realised what I'd just agreed to. Dean *was* quite popular, and he *was* the captain of the football team. 'There has to be something you can tell me about him.'

'I've told you most of it,' I told her, grabbing a strawberry cable sweet from the stash in front of Beth. 'Hopefully, you'll get to meet him soon.'

'Why couldn't he join us today again?'

'He has football practise on a Saturday morning. Plus, I wanted to talk to you about something without him being here.'

'Okay,' she said, her face settling into one of utter seriousness. Beth may be upbeat most of the time, and boy crazy all the time, but she also knew when I needed her to be real with me. To listen to me and help me with whatever silly notion was running through my mind. 'Shoot.'

'Okay, so…' I started, then paused, not sure how to word it. I knew I could talk to Beth about everything, and I often did, but what I wanted to talk about was something she didn't have much experience with either. 'Things between Dean and me have been getting a little… heavy?'

'Heavy? How?'

'Okay, so at first it was just kissing and stuff, right? And I can handle that. Heck, I enjoy that. But then his hands start to wander or he'll whisper something in my ear that tells me he wants to take our relationship to the next step and I don't think I'm ready for that.'

'Well, then tell him that,' she said with a shrug as if it were the most simple answer. And I supposed that to Beth it was. She didn't have the demons in her past like I did. Plus, she was always pretty vocal in life about what she was and wasn't okay with. 'From what you've told me about him, he'll understand.'

'I know.' I toy with the sweet between my fingertips, too agitated to eat it. 'But I worry he'll ask me why.'

'Okay…' Beth looked at me closely. 'And I'm guessing you don't want to tell him?'

'Not really.' Even just the thought of telling him has my pulse quickening and my palms sweating. 'What if he judges me for it?'

'Layla,' Beth said, her tone filled with sympathy and understanding. 'Why would he judge you for something that wasn't your fault?'

I shrugged my shoulders, my tongue glued to the roof of my mouth, unable to form an answer.

'And,' she continued, 'if he *does* judge you for any of it, then you dump his arse, no questions about it.'

'I know,' I whispered. 'I hate that it still has such a grip on me.'

'Layla, that's understandable. Everything only finished last year properly,' Beth pointed out. 'Plus, it makes total sense that it still has a grip on you. Fuck, Layla, it would have a grip on anybody. I think you're crazy strong for how you've handled everything.'

'Thanks.' My hands stopped wringing together in my lap and I inhaled deeply through my nose. 'I wish I could talk about it more. My parents always want me to tell them how I'm feeling. And I feel so crappy because I just can't. It's like a block in my mind that stops my tongue from moving. Like years of being told to keep it a secret overrides the logical part of my brain that tells me it isn't a secret—that it *never* should've been a secret in the first place.'

Beth's hand reached out and grabbed mine. Her thumb rubbed soothingly over the top of my hand, and her comfort trickled through me into my very being. There were times when Beth and I didn't see eye to eye, but ultimately, she was my best friend. My *only* true friend. One who had stuck by me throughout it all. And I could never repay her for that. Even if I kept her in a lifetime's supply of fudge and cherry drops, it would never be enough.

'You're right,' she agreed in a hushed whisper. 'It should never have been a secret.' The precaution was an actual necessity because my mum liked to listen in at doors to see if she overheard me opening up. Or talking about something that worried her. It was a very big invasion of privacy—one we'd discussed during a family counselling session—but apparently it made her feel as if she was being proactive. The same way my dad's overprotectiveness made him feel as if he was being proactive.

I didn't point out to both of them that listening at doors and knowing who I hung out with back then wouldn't have changed any of what happened.

'But, Layla,' Beth continued, squeezing my hand for a brief moment. 'The fact that it was a secret isn't your fault. You were a kid and you didn't know any better. *They* took advantage of you and your naivety. Simple as that. And I know you hate talking about it, and I'm gonna stop in a moment. I promise. But I do think you should talk about it with Dean. If you really like him, that is.'

I nodded. She had a point. I wanted to talk to Dean openly and honestly. Wanted to tell him I wanted to take the next step with him, but that I just didn't know how to without the demons of the past creeping up and dragging me under.

'No, no. You're right.' I squeezed her hand. 'And I should get better at talking about it with people who aren't paid to listen to me ramble on.'

'Nah,' she said, brushing me away. 'Nothing wrong with trauma dumping on a paid professional. Better that than doing it to your friends.'

'Very true.' I finally bit into the strawberry cable I'd been toying with, savouring the synthetic taste of strawberry and sugar as it trickled down my throat. 'Beth?'

'Yeah?' she said, popping another cherry drop into her mouth.

'What if I tell Dean the truth and he doesn't want me anymore? What if my fear of intimacy scares him off?'

'Then he isn't worth your time,' she said, her gaze boring into mine. 'If he makes you feel anything less than, then you tell me straight away and I'll deal with his stupid boy brain.'

I smiled, a small laugh slipping through the cracks.

'Thanks, girl.'

'No problem! You're my best friend, Layla. I'm not gonna let anybody treat you like shit for something that was completely out of your control, okay?'

'Okay.'

SCHOOL ON MONDAY started the same way as any other.

Dean met me in the car park. We walked into school together, then we headed to our first lesson of the day together—English.

At lunch, Dean had a team meeting that he couldn't get out of, which meant I needed to somehow survive by myself for a couple of hours. The cafeteria seemed daunting and the field was no doubt going to be too cold, so I decided to head to the students' lounge. It was one of the rooms in the school solely for the use of upper year students.

My feet carried me there at a fast clip, and I kept my head down so I wouldn't make eye contact with anybody I didn't know. Or worse, those I did.

'Look at the loser walking alone,' Remi's voice said from somewhere nearby. 'Honestly, what kind of a twat has no friends except a boyfriend they shouldn't even have?'

Do not rise to the bait. Do not rise to the bait, I repeated in my head, ignoring Remi as I continued walking down the brightly lit school corridor. She was being followed by her gaggle of girls, the type who looked up to her as their fearless leader and chose to never question any of her actions or their own while with her. It sickened me.

'Dean could do *so* much better than you,' one of her cronies spat, and they all descended into giggles.

'Yeah! Dean's only with you to make Remi jealous!'

I held in my breath and kept walking, hoping I would get away. But they must have turned to follow me as their voices stayed behind me as I went.

'He and Remi are endgame. You're just trash in the way.'

I scoffed at that. And, unluckily for me, it wasn't just in my head like I hoped it would be. Nope. It came out of my mouth, entered the air, and made its way to their ears.

Wonderful.

'Did you just scoff at us, bitch?' Remi said, her voice like thunder. All of a sudden, she was in front of me, standing there with her friends beside her, and I couldn't make it around them without force. My eyes focused on a scuffed part of the carpet near the wall that was coming up. The frayed deep red edges stuck up in all directions.

'Oi!' one of the girls shouted, shoving my shoulder. 'Remi's talking to you. You can at least show her the respect she deserves and reply to her, skank.'

'It's fine, Monica,' Remi said, soothing the girl who shoved me. 'The skank will learn her lesson soon enough.'

She turned to face me once more.

'I'm in contact with some people from your old school. I'm sure they'll dish the dirt on why you left.'

'And what makes you think I left for a reason? My parents could've got a new job or something.' Seemed odd to me that Remi was adamant I left for some nefarious reason. Even if I did leave for a reason other than my parents getting a new job, why did it matter to her?

And who the heck was she contacting at my old school? Not that I believed her for longer than a mere moment. Although, if she did get to talk to somebody, what would they say?

An icy chill trickled down my spine and I shivered at the implication of just what that could bring. If she really *was* talking to somebody, then they could tell her the truth.

And then I would have to face it.

Would have to tell Dean everything.

And I just wasn't ready for that. No way, no how.

friday, 5th november

SINCE I STARTED DATING DEAN, I'd heard a lot about the Friday night field parties that took place, but every time I suggested we go, Dean made up an excuse as to why we shouldn't.

Apparently, bonfire night was a whole different ball game because here we were.

Fireworks were happening in the next field for the rest of the town, and we had a great position for them. After all, fireworks happened in the sky, so it wasn't hard to get a good view.

'Are you cold?' Dean whispered in my ear, pulling me closer into his chest.

I shook my head, but I was lying. My nose was turning into ice, and I felt certain it was bright red, shining like Rudolph's. Once November hit, the weather took a turn for the worse. Everywhere was frosted over, and when you were outside, you could see everybody's breath any time they exhaled or spoke.

'Are you sure?' he asked again and I laughed. Guess the fact I was shivering wasn't helping my cause. Dean placed a kiss on my forehead, and I tilted my head up to look into his azure blue eyes. They were the colour of what I imagined the lightest sea would look like and I found myself getting lost in their depths frequently. It caught me off guard, honestly. It was rare that I looked into somebody else's eyes and saw safety. Saw something that made me feel whole.

'I'm freezing,' I admitted with a laugh. 'Remind me again why these field parties are fun?'

'Well, it's definitely better in the summer.' His eyes warmed when he laughed, and it instantly warmed me. Figuratively, not literally. Because it was still bloody freezing.

A loud cheering came from the group standing across the field, drawing my attention. In my peripheral vision, I saw Dean roll his eyes, and the tension that bristled through him emanated off him in waves.

The group in question was referred to as the 'Rebels'. I didn't know why, and when I'd asked, Dean had been less than forthcoming. Apparently, he'd been friends with the leader, Grayson, for years, but something happened to change all that. It didn't bother me that he hadn't told me more about it—I was keeping a secret from him, so it wasn't like I could judge.

Over the last month, I'd opened my mouth to tell him so many times, but every time, I stopped myself. We kissed. Man, had we kissed. But anytime D tried to take things further, the brakes went on, no matter how hard I tried. It was as if my brain couldn't associate the touch with anything but fear. Pain. Humiliation.

'Want a drink, babe?' Dean asked and I nodded, rubbing my hands together in front of my chest. I wished I'd remembered to bring gloves, but it had slipped my mind. It was as if my mind turned to mush whenever Dean showed up at my front door to take me out. 'I'll be right back.'

Dean went off in the direction of the drink buckets, and I shuffled from foot to foot, trying to keep warm now that his body heat was gone.

'Well, look here,' a voice said from behind me and I rolled my eyes. Of course it belonged to Remi Riley. She still hadn't forgiven me for "taking her man" even though I'd done no such thing. 'The trash is standing alone. Dean get bored of your frigid arse?'

'He just went to get me a drink, actually.' I pointed over to where Dean was standing, chatting to his football friends, who were also over by the drinks table. 'He's happy with me.'

'I highly doubt that,' she spat, her thin, arched eyebrow rising even higher. Everything about Remi was perfect. Never a hair out of place. Never caught off looking harried or anything like that. Even in a field in the freezing cold, she looked cute wearing a cream knit beanie with a large pom-pom on the top. Her coat matched the beanie and looked a lot warmer than mine was. Go figure.

'Well, if he wasn't happy with me, then why would he have sex with me?'

The words left my mouth before my brain could catch up with them. They were out in the world and they couldn't be taken back.

Remi's mouth dropped open in shock and her eyes started twitching.

'You're a liar,' she spat, looking around at her friends for them to back her up. None of them did, though. They just shrugged, looking unsure of what to do or say. 'Whatever, you skank. I hope you haven't passed along a deadly disease. But don't worry, tomorrow I'll know for sure why you moved here. I've got a source.'

'Course you have,' I said, not taking her seriously. She'd mentioned already that she was in touch with somebody from my old school, but if that was the case, then they clearly hadn't told her much yet. 'Just piss off, Remi. Leave me and Dean alone.'

She screamed and stamped her foot on the ground. She and her minions flounced off and away, and I could finally let out the breath I was holding. Even though I'd lied to her face, I couldn't bring myself to regret it.

monday, 8th november

I arrived at school happy and invigorated. The bonfire party with Dean was really fun, and I loved watching the fireworks burst in the night sky while wrapped up tightly in his arms. It grounded me. Made me feel safe. Secure.

Stepping out of my car, I looked around for Dean but couldn't see him. It was the first inkling of something not being right. Every morning he was standing in front of his car, waiting for me to arrive, and then he'd head over. I swore he kept his eyes peeled on the entrance, watching intently for my car to arrive on the lot.

I grabbed my phone from my pocket and sent him a quick text.

HEY BABE, **I'm waiting by my car. You gonna be long?**

WITHIN A MOMENT, the two ticks underneath his name turned blue, meaning he'd read my message. I watched, waiting for the screen to tell me *Dean is typing*, but it didn't come.

Maybe he was running late and was still driving?

But then he wouldn't have read the message. He wasn't the type to read his messages while driving. Not after what happened to his dad.

Shuffling from foot to foot, I wondered how long I should wait for him to arrive. It was only fifteen minutes until the bell for first period rang, and Dean knew that being late made me anxious.

Five minutes went by.

Then another five.

And that was when Dean's car peeled into the car park, the tyres screeching on the tarmac as he took the corner so fast. I swallowed, nerves building in my gut.

Dean was a careful driver. He didn't make careless mistakes or silly decisions, yet the way his car turned the corner could've been considered both of those things.

Then I saw the passenger sitting next to him.

It was *her*.

Remi.

What was he doing giving her a lift to school? Was that why he was so late to meet me? I could understand if she needed a lift last minute because her car broke, or her other ride to school had bailed or wasn't coming in because they were sick.

But any other explanation didn't make sense.

I waited for him to park, then headed over to the vehicle with tentative footsteps.

'Hey,' I said as he stepped out of the car. If him arriving with Remi hadn't told me something was up, the way he proceeded to the school entrance without acknowledging me told me all I needed to know.

Then I heard the whispers from the students standing at the car next to Dean's.

She had sex with her teacher.

They were in a relationship for five years!

He dumped her and only then did she tell the police.

My heart stopped beating in my chest. My skin prickled and a slight sheen of sweat rested there. Remi had finally done it. Had found the information that could destroy me. And destroy me she had.

And the worst part of it all?

Dean believed her lies, without once having tried to talk to me first.

tuesday, 9th november

I was avoiding Layla.

And I knew avoiding her was shitty, but I wasn't sure how to *not* avoid her.

Okay, that was also a lie. What I really meant was I wasn't sure how to look her in the eye and not feel betrayed by her actions. Not feel as if she'd been lying to me for the last two months.

So many times I'd given her the chance to talk to me about her past. To tell me the truth.

And I had to find it out from *Remi* of all people.

It was Sunday night when Remi appeared at my door, wanting to come in and tell me about what she learned. At first, I brushed her off. Didn't want to hear what she had to say. I knew it wasn't going to be kind, especially as Remi had been doing everything she could since the first day of school to undermine Layla by using her own social standing at Hollowdale.

But then she showed me the messages from somebody who'd gone to Layla's old school, and I knew I needed to at least hear what Remi came to tell me.

Even though I knew Remi might be lying, or at least twisting the truth to fit her agenda, it still didn't change the fact that

Layla didn't open up to me. Didn't think I was worth being honest with. And that cut me deeper than I would admit out loud.

I'd given her so many chances to tell me what held her back. To tell me why she couldn't let me in. And I thought we'd got somewhere at the bonfire.

We'd only been dating for a couple of months, but I really liked her. I could see myself with her for longer than the school year. I was waiting it out, but I planned to talk to her about her future plans, like where she wanted to attend university and things like that. Get a sense of what she wanted in life, and whether it was worth me dropping the 'L' bomb.

Not that I loved her yet. But I was well on the way to it.

Our relationship was nothing like the teenage puppy love I'd experienced with Remi either. With Remi, I always walked on eggshells, constantly embarrassed by her when she acted like a bitch to everybody in her vicinity. But with Layla, I always had a smile on my face. A spring in my step.

And I fucked it up by brushing her away and ignoring her.

'Dean!' her voice called from somewhere behind me and I winced, not wanting to turn around and face her, but knowing I should. 'Dean!'

I had a split second to decide what to do. Whether to keep walking ahead and continue to ignore her, or to turn around and face the fucking music.

I turned.

'Dean, wait up.' Layla hurried towards me, a look of determination fixed on her features, her curly blonde hair swishing around her. Once close enough, her eyes pleaded with me. 'Please, can we go talk?'

'Fine.' The one word came out as a grunt, and I followed her into the nearest classroom. Being alone with her was messing with my head, and it had only been a mere minute. The scent of her shampoo and perfume entered my senses, messing with my brain. 'But you've got five minutes.'

'Why are you being such a dick?' she asked, her bottom lip wavering. 'You can hear me out and it'll take as long as it takes.'

'Class starts in five minutes,' I reminded her, which was why I said five minutes in the first place.

'Oh,' she said, looking a little sheepish. 'Okay then. Five minutes it is.'

I watched her take a deep breath, preparing herself for whatever she wanted to say to me.

'I don't know what Remi has said to you in private to make you want to avoid me in public, but why didn't you just ask me? I thought we were closer than that. We've been exclusively dating for a while now and I thought that meant something to you like it did me. But clearly I was wrong. The way you've treated me the last two days isn't okay, Dean.'

I stayed silent, tapping my toe on the floor. Her words went in my ears, but I was acting so irrationally that they went straight out the other side. The only part I grasped onto was that she thought she meant something to me.

'You did mean something to me,' I said, watching her wince when I used past tense. 'But I hate that you felt like you had to lie to me. That you couldn't open up about what you went through. I hate that you didn't trust me enough.'

'That's not fair, Dean. You've barely talked to me about your dad and I've asked. I've given you enough chances to tell me about him.'

'I've spoken to you about him more than I've ever spoken to anybody!' The words rumbled from my throat, the deep-rooted anger bubbling up to the surface unbidden. It wasn't Layla's fault. She just happened to be the person in front of me at that moment, saying the words that harmed me most. Because I would love to talk about my dad with her. Tell her things from my childhood that were fun and happy. But it was like a mental block. A memory too painful for me to even whisper.

And the rational side of my brain knew that was how Layla

felt. Knew the memory was too painful for her to talk about, especially with somebody she'd known for a brief blip in time.

But it still hurt me to the core, regardless.

'I'm sorry,' she whispered, tears in her eyes, unshed.

The image was wrong. It should be me apologising to her. But my mouth wouldn't move. My tongue was heavy, as if it were made of toffee, and it didn't budge an inch.

'I know,' I croaked out.

And then I fled. I couldn't look at her any longer without horrible thoughts swirling through my head aimed at her. I had to get away before I said something I would come to regret.

Twelve

Layla

wednesday, 10th november

It was lonely eating lunch at a table by myself.

Guess I hadn't noticed how well I'd integrated myself into Dean's life before we broke up. But sitting at the lunch table alone definitely highlighted the problem to me. In every lesson we shared, we sat together. During any free periods or lunch breaks, we stayed together with his football friends. Not having any female friends here meant I didn't have another group I could be with.

'Is this seat taken?' A girl's cheery voice entered my ears, and I looked up from my sad-looking plate of food. Even my sandwich was wilted and in pain.

'No?' I said, but it came out as if I was asking her. I shook my head a little, trying to clear the cobwebs that were gathering there. I hated spending too much time alone with my thoughts. Maybe I should try again? I coughed, clearing my throat. 'I mean, no. The seat's free if you want it.'

The girl didn't need more than that as she pulled the chair out, the metal legs scraping across the linoleum floor in an awful screeching sound, and plonked herself down in it.

'Thanks!' she said, her smile wide. 'My name's Amber.'

'Layla,' I replied, glancing at her outstretched hand. Did she expect me to shake it, or?

'My hand isn't poisonous,' she said with a laugh, but pulled it back anyway, pushing a strand of her hair behind her ear. Her red hair was tied up in a high ponytail, and except for the loose strand she'd just placed behind her ear, there wasn't a hair out of place. Then I looked at her clothing for the first time.

Wonderful. A cheerleader.

'If you've come here to bully me,' I started, unsure how I was going to end the sentence, but knowing I needed to stand up for myself somehow.

'No,' she said, touching my wrist. I flinched away, pulling my hand out of her reach, but gave her a small smile. Hopefully, she wouldn't take my action to heart. I just didn't like being touched by strangers. Heck, surely nobody did? 'I'm sorry. I forget that not everybody seeks comfort through touch.'

'Do a lot of people?' I asked, caught off guard by her manner. She was putting me at ease without even really trying. It was the first time I'd smiled since everything went down between me and Dean.

'Depends on their love language.' Her face was deadly serious as if love languages were something everybody should know by heart. Maybe Beth had made me take that test one time for fun, but I couldn't remember the result. No doubt Beth's love language would be anything to do with kind words.

'What are the love languages?'

'Well, there are five of them,' Amber said, sitting back in her chair and getting comfortable. The rest of the cafeteria faded away as I focused on her melodic voice. 'There are words of affirmation, acts of service, receiving gifts, quality time, and physical touch. Mine's physical touch. It's how I show love.'

She shrugged and I nodded. I wondered what mine would be. Beth's was for sure words of affirmation. I didn't care much for gifts, so it wasn't that one.

'I think mine's acts of service,' I said, blinking at her, speaking the words before my mind caught up.

'Yeah.' Her ponytail bounced as she nodded. 'I can believe that.'

'Is that a good thing?'

'Course it is! No love language is bad, silly. Everybody's different, so of course everybody has a different way of understanding and showing love. You're good.'

'Well, now that you've confirmed it, I must be.'

We both laughed, and I felt at ease around her. She was stunning, and her rich chestnut-brown eyes were wide and welcoming. I didn't want to get my hopes up or anything, but maybe she could be a friend to me. I would need one to survive. It was only November, which meant another six months until I graduated and could leave Hollowdale High—and what had happened—behind me.

The two of us started to eat our food, a comfortable silence falling upon us. It was harder to tune out the noises and whispers of the other students in the room, but I needed to get used to it. The rumour Remi spread wouldn't be disappearing overnight.

'Remi's a bitch.' As if she could read my mind, Amber said what I was thinking. 'She's just jealous of you and knew that the only way she'd be in for a chance with Dean was if he split up with you.'

'Isn't there some sort of cheerleader code you're meant to stick to?' I asked, a wry smile on my face.

'Screw that!' Amber said, her face screwing up as she bit into her sandwich. I waited for her to swallow before she continued. 'The girl's been a grade-A arsehole since we were in primary school. She isn't used to not getting her way. Dean breaking up with her really threw her back.'

'He said they split because he wasn't as interested in her as he should've been, but that they'd remained close friends.'

Maybe that was why he believed the lies she'd spouted over what I had to say.

'They have.' She looked over her shoulder and surveyed the room before leaning in closer to me. 'And the entire time Dean's made it super clear he isn't interested in becoming anything more again.'

'Doesn't matter,' I grumbled. 'He's still not talking to me regardless.'

'Well then. Either we need to get him to talk to you, or we ignore it and do something even better.'

'And what's even better?' I raised my eyebrows as she sipped her drink through her straw. The epitome of cool and calm.

Amber put her drink down on the table and smiled.

'There's a spot on the squad,' she said casually. *Too casually.* She'd been building up to it. I could tell. Maybe it was the reason for her sitting with me in the first place. 'And I've heard it through the grapevine that you used to dance at your old school.'

'Dance, sure. But that's a little different to cheer.'

'Maybe in America.' She laughed, waving away my concern. 'You know that here it's basically the same thing. There's a football game, we stand on the sidelines and ra-ra some pom-poms, and dance at half time. We're not even allowed to try a pyramid or stunts anymore. Not after what happened a couple of years ago.'

'What happened?' I asked, not remembering much about it, but then again, a couple of years ago I was focused on something completely different.

Her face soured and her eyebrows knitted. Amber opened her mouth, then closed it again. When she finally spoke, it was more of a non-answer than I expected.

'A stunt went wrong,' she said, her voice sombre. Then, as if she remembered her whole point was to convince me to join, her face brightened once more. 'But that was an anomaly! And like I said, we're not allowed to do it anymore. Much to Remi's chagrin.'

'I can imagine being robbed of the chance to climb the pyramid weighs on her.'

'You don't even know the half of it,' Amber stated and took a sip of her water. 'But that's a story for another day. Right now, I need to convince you to help me out.'

'And what do you gain from it?' I asked, suspicious of her true intentions. 'Because we've never spoken before today, so sorry if I'm sounding like a bitch.'

'You're not,' she said with a laugh. 'And if I were you, I would be reacting in the same way. I know you've got no reason to believe me, but I really do just want to help you. While also helping myself.'

I nodded. She sounded genuine enough. And really, what did I have to lose? Everybody at the school was already giving me a wide berth and ignoring me. They all believed Remi's lies. Hadn't even asked me for the truth. Including the person who should've known better.

'I'm in,' I told her, making a snap decision. I enjoyed dance and maybe dancing would bring me out of the funk I'd slipped into.

'Great!' She smiled, showing every single one of her straight teeth, and bounced her head with enthusiasm. 'Want to come over to mine tonight? I can teach you some combos and we can go grab pizza for dinner?'

'I do love pizza, and it would be good to not go home. Ever since people started talking about what happened at my last school, Mum's been even more freaked out than before.'

'Your mum's pretty protective then?'

'Yeah.' I nodded, thinking back on the many times Mum had been protective of me—some would even argue that she was *over*protective of me. 'I was ill as a kid, and ever since then, she's never been able to forget that. And, I mean, I understand it. Of course I do. But it doesn't help me in the long run, you know?'

Amber's chestnut-coloured eyes filled with warmth and her head tilted forward in a slight nod.

'Sorry, I shouldn't be offloading on you.' My laugh came out awkward and stilted. I was airing my frustration with my mum to a girl I'd only known for a half hour, and my cheeks flushed. Amber seemed friendly for the time being, but what if she was a minion of Remi's and I just didn't know it? She could be over here gaining info to take back to the others to help them in their vendetta to bully me.

'It's okay,' she said. The red strand of hair she'd tucked behind her ear broke loose once more and my eyes fixated on that spot. It was the only way I could think to stop myself from crying—or worse—running out of the cafeteria while everybody watched on with amusement. 'Do you wanna talk about any of it?'

Her eyes were soft, and maybe there was a shade of pity there, too.

'No,' I bit out, the word grating out. It was harsh, and she didn't deserve it, so I added, 'Not now. Maybe one day, if you can put up with me?'

'You bet! Don't feel like you have to tell me shit if you don't want to. I know that Remi's version of events is just that—a version.'

'Thanks.'

'No problem. What are friends for?'

thursday, 25th november

'I can't believe I've let you drag me into this.'

'You're gonna do amazing!' Amber said, her ponytail swishing from side to side as she fidgeted with excitement. 'And you look HOT! They *have* to put you on the team.'

'Isn't Remi in charge, though?' I asked, tightening the laces on my shoes as I rested my foot on the bench for the umpteenth time. Apparently, I'd developed a new nervous habit within the space of ten minutes. 'She'll just block me from joining.'

'She's the captain, yeah. But it's also a vote from all the girls on the panel. And lucky for you, they aren't all Remi fans.'

'That's good to know, I guess. I didn't expect that.'

'Well, there was an incident a couple of years ago…' Amber trailed off and looked into the distance, her eyes lost in the past. It wasn't the first time she'd hinted at an incident on the team, but it always seemed pretty serious and I didn't want to pry. She'd really been a great friend so far, so I didn't want to piss her off. Or make her talk about something she wasn't ready to open up about. 'It doesn't matter. Either way, the captain of the squad can no longer decide things without at least two others agreeing.'

I nodded as if I understood any of the team politics. If I was being honest, I didn't even really want to try out. Amber was so excited, teaching me all the moves and helping me with everything, and because of that, I couldn't let her down by bailing at the last second.

'Right, I'm gonna go take my seat and watch everybody, okay? You're gonna smash this shit. I promise!'

Before I could stop it, her outstretched arms pulled me into a tight hug. It shocked me. Amber knew that touch wasn't my jam, and so far she'd respected that.

'Oh my God. I'm so sorry, Layla,' she said, stepping back from me, her face showing how annoyed she was at herself. 'I forgot myself for a moment. Forgot you hate being touched.'

I shook my head and murmured, 'That's okay. It was a nice hug.'

She smiled, and her top lip lifted enough to display her perfect teeth underneath.

'Nice?' she barked. 'Well, next time I'll get permission and aim for a *great* one.'

My laughter burst from me, all high-pitched and awkward, and I realised what she'd done. She'd managed to distract me from my overthinking—my anxious thoughts that had been playing through my mind ever since I woke up that day—and I appreciated her and her friendship even more.

I had to go out there and give it my all. Amber deserved that much.

Her ponytail swished as she walked away from me, and I watched her back until she exited the changing room door. With one last glance in the mirror, I took a deep breath, trying to centre my swirling thoughts.

My name is Layla Williams. I am nineteen years old. I have blonde hair and blue eyes. My mother's name is Darcy and my father's name is Daniel. I have been through hell, but I am safe now.

A rustling noise came from the other side of the room. My head snapped in the direction of the noise, but I couldn't see anything. I relaxed once more, knowing I was the only person in the room. Everybody else had already left, too excited to get to the tryouts to wait around.

I wished my mind worked that way.

'Those leggings really make your arse look good. Did you know that?'

The voice rumbled through the room, and I froze, my brain scrambling to place the voice with a face. It didn't instantly register, and I wasn't sure I even knew who the voice belonged to.

I stayed still, too worried to turn around, but also knowing that I should.

'Sorry,' the voice said with a chuckle. 'I should probably introduce myself. People call me Wilson, but you can call me Daddy.'

Wilson? I didn't recognise the nickname, so that didn't help. And there was no way in fucking hell I'd be calling anybody *Daddy*. Who on earth was he?

Remi's rumour had died down, but clearly not enough. The whispered calls of *slut* and *teacher's whore* followed me through the corridors every day and although I ignored them, they still settled heavily on my consciousness.

'I definitely won't be doing that,' I said, turning around to face the intruder. The fact he'd snuck into the girls' changing room told me more than enough. He wasn't here with good intentions.

He was medium build and probably around five-foot-nine. So not much taller than me, but his strength more than made up for it. The guy in front of me was an athlete, maybe even a member of the football team alongside Dean, and the sneer on his face curdled my stomach. Amusement marred his features, thrilled that I turned around to face him, and if I could get out of the room without having to push past him, I would.

But he was blocking my exit.

'So it's okay to fuck a teacher but not a footballer?' he said with a sneer. 'We all know you've fucked Dean, too. So maybe only the captain of the football team is good enough for you?'

I swallowed, biting my retort down. The flush in my cheeks was growing, and my thoughts were racing.

Must get out. Must get away. Must find somebody and tell them.

'You scared of me, little girl?' His lips turned up into an amused smirk. A smile that told me he relished in the power he had. Enjoyed the fear of his prey.

'No, not at all.' My words said one thing, but my tone said another. No matter how hard I tried to stay calm, to ignore the fear trickling through my veins, I couldn't do it.

'It can be our little secret,' he continued, his smile wide. 'Nobody would have to know.'

He took a step closer. Then another.

The scent of his aftershave reached me and made me gag. It was too strong. Too overwhelming. It smelled oily, like his actions.

'There's nothing for anybody to know.'

'Doesn't have to be that way,' he said. Another small step. 'I can show you things that even your teacher wouldn't have.'

Inching backwards, I tried to move away, but my legs hit the bench and I couldn't go back any further. He loomed over me. I may not be short, but I wasn't as tall as him either. He easily had a couple of inches on me, and that was before you took into consideration his build.

The reminders of what Mr Long did to me were still there, like a snake slithering through my skull. A poison that could never disappear. The fact that Wilson was using those against me and spurting shit he knew nothing about pissed me off more than anything else.

How dare he try to use my trauma against me?

'I think you should leave.'

'You do, do you?' He laughed. Maniacal. The glee on his face only grew the longer we stood there. 'Are you going to make me?'

My eyes narrowed on him. We both knew I couldn't make him do shit.

He took another step, bringing his torso flush up against mine. Should I knee him in the balls? Jut out my elbow and catch him in the gut?

As I ran through my options, analysing every single one, he made his move. Strong, large palms pushed my shoulders down, rooting me to the spot.

And then multiple things happened at once.

My knee thrust upwards, into his crotch, the strength of it surprising even me. And as he crumpled, bending in half in front of me, Dean burst through the door.

Fourteen
Dean

'WHAT THE FUCK is happening in here?' I roared, barging my way further into the changing rooms and grabbing Wilson by the shoulders and pulling him away from Layla.

'Captain,' he said, bent in half. 'Did you see what she just did to me? That's assault!'

'There was only one person attempting assault here, and it was *not* me,' Layla growled, her face red with anger.

'The bitch hit me!' Wilson whined, glaring at Layla. 'She deserves everything coming to her.'

'Get away from her,' I bit out through gritted teeth, losing my patience with him.

'Didn't realise she was your property.' Wilson raised an eyebrow with a smirk on his face. One I wanted to get rid of.

'She's not,' I growled, pushing him back a little. 'But she's not yours either. Get away from her.'

'No need to be so touchy,' Wilson said, as if I was over-reacting.

And I wasn't.

He'd been about to touch Layla. To try and force her into something she didn't want to do. No matter what rumours were going around about her, it didn't give him—or anybody for that matter—the right to touch her against her will.

'You should learn to take a joke,' Wilson said, his words

aimed at Layla. I hadn't looked at her yet, and the moment I did, my gut squirmed. Her eyes were holding in tears, and her bottom lip was wobbling. Other than that, she wasn't moving at all. She was frozen on the spot, her body statue-still, and I was worried she was too shocked from the events of the last few minutes. Because that was all it could've been. I'd hovered outside the changing room, waiting for her to come out. When Amber left, I knew it was only a matter of time until Layla came out, too. But then I got distracted by Remi, who came to tell me something unimportant. Next thing I knew, I could hear Layla's muffled cries and my gut told me that something was wrong. And it had been right.

'A joke?' I scoffed, moving to stand in front of Wilson and using myself as a shield between him and Layla. 'Think it was a bit more than a joke, *mate*.'

'Remi thought it'd be funny.'

'Remi put you up to this?' I asked, my anger climbing in my veins. What the fuck was Remi thinking? I knew she disliked Layla, but after I broke things off with her, I thought she'd left her alone. After all, Remi had got her way.

'No.' He shook his head, his smile growing wider with every second. 'But when I told her somebody should put the bitch in her place, she didn't try to stop me.'

'Of course she didn't.' I was resigned to Remi's behaviour, and I would be talking to her about her shitty actions. Whatever way you looked at it, it wasn't the way to win me back.

'Ever since this bitch started here, she's believed she's above us all. She needed knocking down a peg and I was more than willing to be the one to do it. Just a shame you interrupted us.'

My clenched fist connected with the prick's face.

And as Layla moved out of the way of his body crashing to the ground, all I could think was *fuck, there goes my football future.*

But I couldn't bring myself to care. The wanker deserved it and some.

'Do you know why I've invited you in here, Mr Walters?' the headteacher asked, walking around her desk to sit down in the large chair across from me.

'Probably because I punched Wilson,' I said, not beating around the bush. If they wanted to strip me of my title, then so be it. Wilson entered the changing room with the intent to hurt Layla. I couldn't just let that slide because hitting him wasn't the *proper* thing to do.

'And why did you punch Mr Wilson?' she said, putting her hands together in front of her, seemingly poised while waiting for my answer.

'Because he was attempting to harm Miss Williams,' I said, the boredom in my tone evident. I'd already explained what happened to the coach, who'd stormed into the changing room the moment Wilson went down.

I couldn't help but think that it was Remi's doing somehow. Maybe she saw me enter the changing room and knew shit was about to hit the fan, so she alerted the coach right away.

'And you didn't think to alert a member of staff?'

'What, and let him touch her against her consent?' I scoffed, my temper rising. 'I'm sorry, miss, but that seems a little messed up if you ask me.'

The headteacher's office was relatively small, the large desk in the centre taking up most of the room. Framed certificates graced the wall behind her, but I wasn't sure what accolades she was celebrating. Before that moment, I'd never even seen the inside of her office. I never got in trouble. Had never had reason to be there.

'That's a very serious accusation to make, Mr Walters,' she said, resting her chin on her hands, her face stern. 'I want you to think carefully about what you're saying.'

'I don't need to. I know what I'm saying and I stand by it.'

'Very well then.' She moved back in her chair, resting her hands on her table, looking at me square on. 'We will speak to Mr Wilson and Miss Williams to get their versions of events. However, you're suspended until Monday. When you return, we'll discuss your position as captain of the football team.'

I took in a deep breath and exhaled slowly. Fucking hell.

Apparently, in my last year at Hollowdale High, there was a first time for everything.

friday, 26th november

EVERYTHING after I kneed Wilson in the crotch happened so fast that I didn't process any of it.

Dean was whisked away by Coach Matson, as was Wilson, and Amber flew into the changing room once my name was called and I didn't enter the sports hall. After that, I had to tell my version of events to the headteacher and then I got sent home early.

The next day, I arrived at school, ready to talk to Dean and sort things out between us. Enough time had passed since everything blew up surely for him to hear me out. To let me open up the way I should've from the start.

'Hey!' Amber said, bouncing on her tiptoes as she made her way over to me, her ponytail with a life of its own as always. 'What are you doing here?'

'Huh?' I asked, not really focusing on her as I looked around the lot for Dean's car. I couldn't see it anywhere. Remi was standing over with her friends, and there was no Dean anywhere.

'Surprised you weren't suspended like the boys,' she said, her head bobbing up and down.

'The boys were suspended? For how long?' How did I miss

that? I'd even messaged Dean when I got home the day before, thanking him for sticking up for me, but he didn't mention he got suspended.

'Think Dean's allowed back Monday, but even then his captainship might be taken away. Wilson's been suspended for a couple of weeks and has lost his spot on the team.'

'Dean might stop being captain?' My heart sank. If there was one thing Dean loved more than anything, it was football and leading the team. I couldn't believe his position on the team was in jeopardy all because of me. 'Would they really do that?'

'Oh, I doubt it,' Amber said, her tone easy-breezy. 'They never took it away from the cheer captain before Remi after what happened, so doubt they'll take it from Dean. It's just a threat, isn't it?'

I nodded, unsure.

'Have you not spoken to him?' she asked, looking me in the eye.

'I texted him but nothing too in depth.' I opened my car door, making my decision within a split second. 'I'm going round there.'

'To Dean's? Now?'

'Yep. I need to talk to him. Maybe now he'll listen to me.'

'Here's hoping! I'll see you later, alligator.'

'In a while, crocodile!'

I MARCHED up to the front door, having parked my car on the road, and knocked.

Karen opened the door, her apron covered in flour and her dark black hair in disarray.

'Oh, Layla,' she said, her face lighting up at the sight of me.

'How nice to see you! I was gutted when Dean told me we wouldn't be seeing you anymore.'

I swallowed, my gut dropping to the ground. Wonder what Dean told her to explain my absence.

'Hey, Karen. Is Dean home?'

She narrowed her kind eyes, a smile playing on her lips.

'I think we both know the answer to that. Shouldn't you be in school?'

'It can wait,' I said, brushing off her concern. 'Talking to Dean can't.'

'He's in his room,' she said, opening the door wider for me to enter. When Dean and I were dating, we spent most nights either at my place or his. From the first time I came over, his mum was friendly to me. She cooked my favourite meals, asked me how I was. All of the things. And I truly appreciated her.

Dean's little sister, Tillie, was a little harder to win around. Remi was her idol, and she looked up to her. Plus, she'd known Remi for years and, of course, I didn't measure up in her eyes.

At least she was at school and not here to witness my grovelling.

I made my way up the stairs and knocked on Dean's bedroom door.

'Come in,' he called out, and I wondered if he knew it was me. Surely he would've heard my car or the front door. My hand paused on the handle, daring myself to enter.

I pushed it open to find Dean lying on his bed, a controller in his hands, focused on the large television screen in front of him.

'Shit!' he cursed, scrambling to sit up when he realised it was me. 'Layla, it's you. I thought you were Mum about to come and pester me about something boring.'

'Nope,' I said with a chuckle. 'I skipped school to see you.'

'That's pretty badass for you,' he said, a smirk gracing his lips, and I smiled back. Even though there was still tension between us, it didn't feel as bad as it had before. 'Living on the wild side of life, aren't you, Layla Williams?'

I hovered by his door, unsure where I should sit. Dean was sitting up, his back against the headboard of his double bed, looking at me with amusement.

'I won't bite,' he drawled, the look on his face at odds with his words. 'What are you doing here?'

I sat down on the opposite end of his bed, crossing my legs underneath me, getting comfortable. I shook off my nerves. It was *Dean*. There was no reason to be nervous around him.

'I came to say thank you,' I said, picking at the fluff on my tights to distract myself. 'For yesterday.'

'No need to thank me.' My senses told me he was looking at me, but I couldn't bring myself to raise my head. 'Looked like you had it sorted when I walked in.'

I winced, imagining what it must have looked like to him when he came into the changing room.

'He's lucky I didn't do worse,' I said, my voice cracking and faltering at the true implication of my words. Because even if I had wanted to, I probably still wouldn't have done worse. 'It just reminded me of the past, and I snapped. I knew I had to do something.'

'Shit, I'm sorry. I didn't even think about that,' he said, and I looked up at his face. His round eyes softened and I could see sympathy shining within them. I hated that. Hated that he was looking at me differently.

'That's okay. I can tell you a little about what happened.' I wasn't sure how much I could tell. Or how in depth I could be without cracking. But for him, I would try.

'Only if you want to.' He grabbed my hand away from my tights and gripped it in his. 'Babe, I was a dick. I should've never got angry at you for not opening up to me. And then after I'd made such a big deal about all of it, I felt like I couldn't just apologise for acting like a prick.'

'I don't think I'm ready to tell you everything. I've not spoken about it with anybody besides my therapist. My parents wish I would, though.'

'Do what's best for you. I don't want to pressure you into *anything*.' The double meaning of his sentence was clear to me and I relaxed.

Dean cared about me, and I shouldn't be scared.

'When I was about thirteen, one of the coaches at my old school took an interest in me. At first, I thought it was because they thought I was talented. Looking back, he groomed me from the very start.' I blinked, focusing on Dean, doing all I could to stay present. 'Up until last year, I didn't say anything to anyone. Too scared to tell the truth. But then another girl came out and accused him of rape, yet nobody believed her. And I knew I couldn't stay silent. That I had to speak up and tell the truth. And the guilt ate at me. If I had told somebody earlier, then the other girl wouldn't have suffered.'

'That's not your fault. That man abused his power.'

'I know,' I agreed. 'But it doesn't stop the pain. Or the guilt.'

'What happened?'

'The other girl ended her life. And I knew I would do everything in my power to make sure Mr Long lived the rest of his days behind bars.'

'You're brave. You know that, right?'

I shrugged. Most days, I didn't feel brave at all.

'I'm sorry I didn't tell you earlier. But that's why I have intimacy issues.'

'He touched you?' Dean asked, pissed off. All I could do was nod. I didn't want to go into any more details. 'Hey'—Dean lifted my chin so we were looking into one another's eyes—'we don't have to talk about it. Not until you're ready.'

'Thanks. Do you forgive me?'

'Layla, there's nothing to forgive. Do you forgive me?'

I pretended to think about it for a split second before I said, 'Of course I do. Just don't act like a knob again and we'll be all good.'

He laughed. 'So does that mean I'm forgiven enough to become your boyfriend?'

'Hmm…' I rubbed my chin with my pointer finger. 'Maybe. But let's just spend the day together first, yeah?'

'Sounds like a plan to me.'

Dean shuffled across the bed so our faces were directly across from each other. He leaned in, and I did the same.

Our lips touched, and electricity sparked between them. It felt like safety, and that was something I hadn't experienced in quite some time.

saturday, 18th december

'YOU'VE GOT THIS, DEAN!' my dad shouted, standing up from his seat, his fist pumping the air.

I laughed along with my mum, who was sitting beside Karen, rolling my eyes at Dad's antics. Ever since Dean and I had sorted everything out, and I sat down and talked with my rents about everything that had happened at school, my parents were on board with us dating. Well, maybe they would've preferred it if I wasn't dating at all, but because I *was* dating, they were happy it was with Dean and not some other "hooligan". Dad's word, of course.

'Thanks again for coming,' Karen said to me and Mum, her kind eyes crinkled at the edges. 'He doesn't say it, but I know Dean really appreciates the support.'

'Honestly,' Mum said through a laugh, 'I think Daniel is just as excited as Dean is. He was always hoping Layla would get into sports, but she never did. At least now he has somebody to discuss the weekend games with.'

'Yeah, and he can stop pestering me.' I was thankful that my dad had stopped begging me to watch football with him. Although it was still a little difficult for me now that Dean and my dad wanted to hang out at the weekend. The pizza they ordered in was always a plus, though.

Scouts were at the game and I knew Dean was nervous about it, but from the way he flew across the pitch, you wouldn't have known it.

The rest of the match flew by and I couldn't take my eyes off Dean the entire time. There was something about a guy in a football kit, sweating on a pitch, that just made my insides melt. He was just sexy; it was as simple as that. And although we still hadn't had sex, I was okay with that. But I hoped it would happen sometime soon. The more time I spent with him, and the more he made me feel normal for not being ready yet, the more I *wanted* to.

As if the pressure being off made me feel the opposite way.

When the game finished, and Dean's team won by a long shot, we made our way down the steps alongside the rest of the crowd. Because of everything that happened the day I was supposed to try out for the cheer team, I never got to audition, but there was one coming up at the start of January that I would give my best shot.

'We're heading home,' Dad said once we were at the bottom of the stairs. 'Tell Dean we said hi!'

'Will do,' I replied, hugging my mum and placing a kiss on her cheek and then doing the same with my dad. 'Not sure what time I'll be home.'

'As long as it's before curfew,' Mum said, furrowing her forehead in my direction.

'Yeah, yeah,' I said, waving her away.

Once they retreated, Karen came up to me with Tillie in tow. She'd watched the game with her friends but was probably trying to talk Karen into letting her go hang out at the diner. We still weren't super close, and Tillie still looked up to Remi, but once she heard I was trying out for the squad, she started to view me a little differently. I was a lot cooler in her eyes than I was as the new girl, that was for sure.

'Let Dean know we've headed home too, please,' Karen said, pulling me into a tight hug. 'You're coming over tomorrow for Sunday lunch, right?'

She let me go and I took a small step back, nodding. Her roast dinners were amazing—and a lot better than my mum's. Not that I would tell her that.

'Can we perfect that routine tomorrow, La?' Tillie asked, clapping her hands together. 'I want to make sure you're ready for the new year.'

'Sounds good to me! I'll see you both tomorrow,' I said, giving them a little wave before I turned around to head towards the clubhouse.

To get to where Dean was changing, I needed to pass the area where the cheer team was located. To be fair to them all, they'd done a great job. They kept spirits high and the routine they performed at halftime was pretty decent. It made me excited to join them—even if I wouldn't admit that out loud.

As I passed the girls cleaning away their stuff, I smiled, catching Amber's eye, and she beamed back at me.

'Did you see how hot your man looked out there?' She fanned her face with her hand, and I laughed at her joking around. Amber wasn't into guys, and I knew she meant no harm. We were genuine friends, especially as she was the only person who believed me and talked to me after Remi's crap.

'He did look mighty fine, didn't he?' I could feel the evil glare Remi was giving me from her spot a few metres away, but I chose to ignore it. The two of us would never be friends, but I hoped that when I made the team, she wouldn't make my life miserable. She'd never apologised for the rumour she spread, and I never expected her to. It wasn't in her to apologise. 'Are you meeting us at the diner later? Beth's hoping she'll be able to come.'

Since Amber and I became close, I'd introduced her to Beth and luckily, the two of them got along okay. I wouldn't say the two of them would ever be the best of friends, but I didn't need that. The worst-case scenario would've been if the two of them hated each other on sight, but thankfully that wasn't the case.

'You bet!' The way she bounced on the balls of her feet amused me. The girl was always moving, no matter what was happening. 'I need to get some fries in this body pronto.'

'I'm off to meet Dean. I'll see you later, alligator.'

'In a while, crocodile!'

With a spring in my step, a smile wide on my face, I walked over to the clubhouse where Dean and the rest of the team were showering and getting changed. It was our routine that after the game, I would wait for him. Beth had tagged along to a couple of them, but she couldn't make this one. Said something about her sister wanting to tell her some big news. Beth's sister Cara was basically her guardian these days after her mum, Tara, fell off the face of the earth. But that was a whole other story for a whole other day.

'Hello, beautiful,' Dean said, coming into view. Fresh from his shower, his dark brown hair wet, his fringe swept away, out of his eyes. 'The rents gone home?'

'Yeah, my mum and dad told me to tell you that you played great. And your mum locked us in for Sunday lunch tomorrow.'

His lips touched mine in a brief kiss and I relished in the fresh, clean scent he was exuding.

'Oh, and your sister's adamant we're perfecting the routine tomorrow.'

'Have I mentioned that I love that you're getting on with my family?'

'You may have,' I said, biting my bottom lip. 'But you can always remind me.'

'Can't keep telling you the things I love about you. Otherwise, you'll go getting a big head.'

'Oh, there are multiple things you love about me, ay?' I teased, looking into his eyes and getting a slight thrill from the discomfort that flickered through them.

'You know how I feel about you,' he said, vague. A little

laugh escaped me, and I reached out to place my hands on his waist.

'No, actually, I don't.' And I wasn't lying. I knew he obviously enjoyed spending time with me, and I knew he was considering attending a university close to the one I wanted to go to.

'Layla,' he whined, dragging my name out. 'Are you going to make me say it?'

'Say what?' I said, acting coy. Like I didn't know what I was doing. It wasn't like I wanted to force words out of him if he wasn't feeling them, but I did genuinely want to know where we stood.

Three months had flown by so fast and it was probably a little naive of me to be so into him so quickly, but I couldn't help it. Couldn't help myself. Couldn't help the way my head and heart were feeling.

'Not here,' he said, grabbing my hand with one of his and pulling me away from the crowds of people that were still milling around. Once we were secluded underneath the stands, Dean took a deep breath, his eyes swimming with emotion. 'Layla, I'm falling in love with you.'

'You are?' I asked, trying to keep my happiness from being too obvious in my voice.

'Of course I am.' His voice cracked and every word, every breath, every action was genuine. He meant it—maybe even more than he ever meant anything else he said to me before. 'And I feel like a dick that you even had to ask me. I should've told you without nudging, but to be truthful with you, I was scared. Scared that you wouldn't feel the same. Scared that you would run away when you learned how deeply I feel towards you.'

'I wouldn't run away because of that.'

'Pfft,' he said, brushing his fingers along my forehead and down my cheek. 'You would've run a mile and only when you stopped would you have even considered whether you felt the same way.'

'Oh, shut up,' I said through a laugh. In the shortest time, he knew me. Had picked up on my flaws and the things that caused me to flee certain situations. 'But I guess you're all right yourself.'

'All right?' he asked, pinching my waist, making me laugh even harder.

'Okay, okay.' I moved my hand to cover his and squeezed. 'I'm falling in love with you, too.'

'You are?' His eyes were filled with hope, slowly turning the colour of a deep hazelnut as the emotions swirled within them.

I nodded, smiling wide. The fact he even had to ask to make sure gutted me. He should just believe me no matter what.

'I must be a dick, too, then if you need to make sure I'm telling you the truth.'

'How about we make a deal to always tell the truth, even if it isn't the right thing to say?' His fingers trailed underneath my jacket and moved slowly up and down on the bare skin at my waist, the touch soothing.

'And how do you propose we know whether or not it's the truth?'

'Other than just trusting each other?' he asked, a slight laugh escaping him, but I was deadly serious. Of course we could trust one another, and we would both assume the other was always telling the truth, but I wanted a way to know for sure. An under-standing. Something we could say that solidified the seriousness of the vow.

'I just want us to be sure.'

'Okay…' he trailed off, looking at a point over my shoulder, deep in thought. 'How about when we want to know for defi-nite, we say pinky promise?'

'Pinky promise?'

'Yeah!' he said, slowly getting more enthusiastic about the idea. 'The pinky promise is sacred and must be upheld.'

'Okay,' I agreed, enjoying his amused grin and the slight wrinkling at the corners of his eyes. 'Pinky promise it is.'

'Are you ready for our first one?'

'Lay it on me.'

'Pinky promise me that you're falling in love with me.'

'I pinky promise. Do you pinky promise that you're also falling in love with me?'

'Pinky promise,' he said, his smile filling my insides with a warmth I only ever experienced when he was looking at me that way.

And honestly? Nothing had ever felt so right in my life.

Epilogue
Beth

christmas eve, 24th december

'MERRY CHRISTMAS!' I raised my glass of snowball and clinked it with the glasses of those around me.

'Merry Christmas,' Layla replied, laughing at the yellow froth that had settled on Dean's top lip. I looked around and smiled wide. I couldn't wait to share my news with them. I was beyond excited.

I just hoped they would all feel the same.

'Guys,' I started, glancing at them in turn. 'I've got some pretty cool news.'

'Let me guess,' Amber said, interrupting me. 'There's a new boy at school that you've set your eyes on?'

Dean and Layla laughed, and I rolled my eyes.

Don't get me wrong, I was glad that Layla had found a friend in Amber during a hard time—especially as I was unable to be there for her—but I wasn't sure if I gelled with her. Layla was my best friend, always had been, and I hated that it felt as if there was a large distance between us these days. But that was all about to change. And they'd know that, if they'd just let me speak.

I tried again.

'I mean, there could be a new boy at school to set my eyes

on…' They all looked at me expectantly. 'Anybody at Hollowdale worth my time?'

'Huh?' Layla asked. 'What are you chatting about now?'

'I'm transferring to Hollowdale,' I told them, my smile wide. 'Cara's got a new job and they've asked her to relocate.'

Cara was my older sister and guardian. My mum, Tara, was a mess of a human and really wasn't worth the time of day.

'Seriously?' Layla squealed, her snowball sloshing over the side of her glass as she jumped. 'We're gonna have so much fun!'

'Right!' Amber agreed, nodding, her smile tense. 'I'm excited for us.'

'It's gonna be so good. Plus, I'll be starting with friends.' I was beyond happy that I wasn't starting completely fresh like Layla did at the start of the school year. And joining the first day of January term shouldn't be *too* bad. 'You *will* show me around and that, won't you?'

'Of course!' Amber said, locking her arm with mine, her previous tense smile gone. I couldn't get a handle on her at all. Maybe I never would. 'I've got your back.'

'Thanks!'

I looked at Layla again, wondering why she hadn't been the one to lock arms with me. But then I saw her arm locked with Dean's and I remembered again, not for the first time, that she had a boyfriend now.

And I had to admit that I was a little envious of it. Of her.

I shook my head. Cleared away the cobwebs and the dark thoughts.

'Hollowdale High, here I come.'

We all cheered, raising our glasses high in the air for another toast.

The clinking of glasses, the laughter and smiles, all made it one of the best nights.

Little did I know that things were going to rapidly change— and go downhill—from that moment forward.

hero of hollowdale high

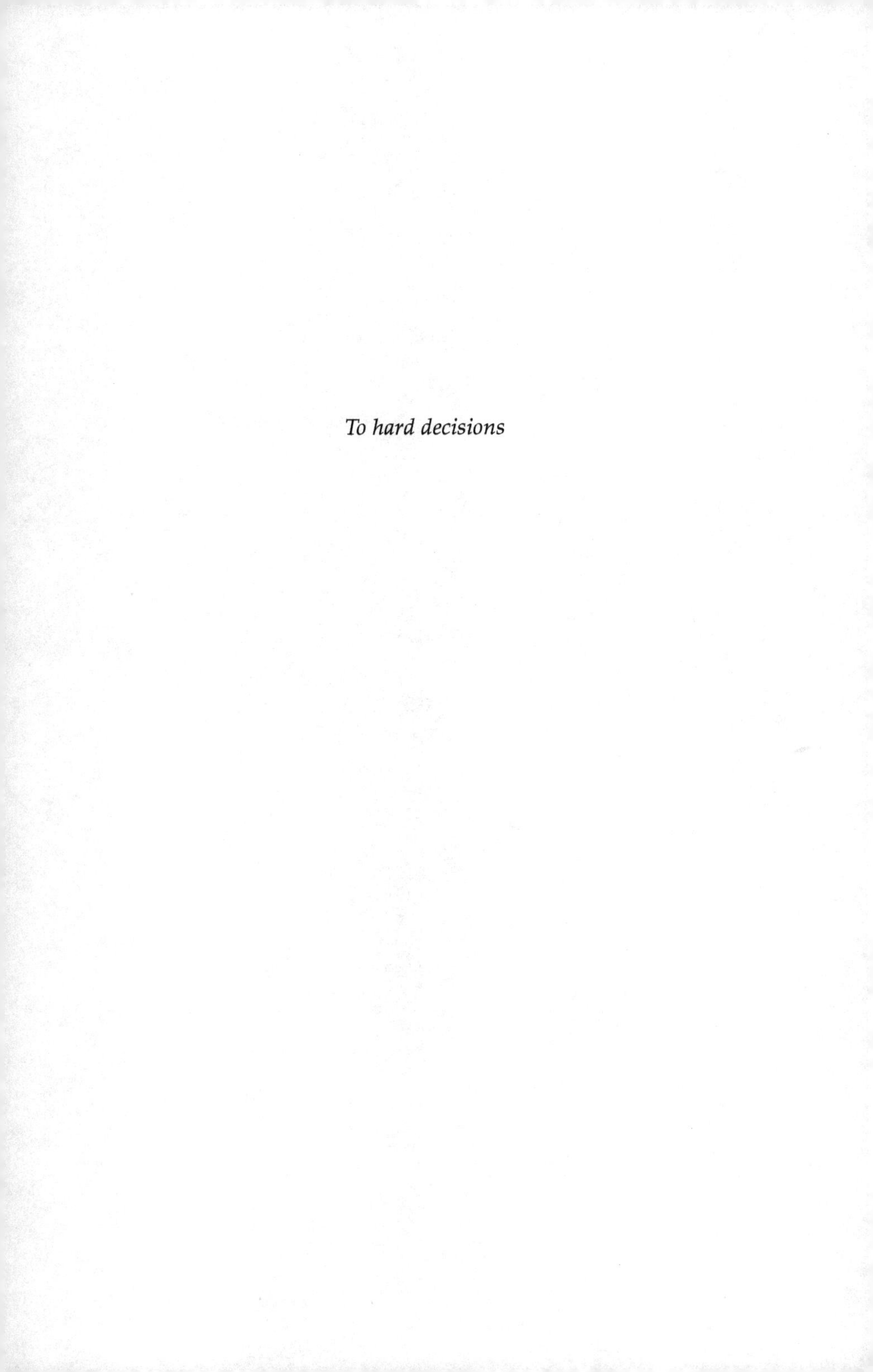

To hard decisions

author's note

Thank you so much for picking up a copy of *Hero of Hollowdale High*.

Beth and Grayson have wormed their way into my heart, and I hope they bury themselves deep in yours too... not in a creepy way or anything.

This story deals with some real life themes and issues that could be potential triggers.
You can head to my website for any trigger/content warnings you may need.

Enjoy!

One

Beth

I'D BEEN in Hollowdale High for all of two minutes when I first saw *them*.

They were walking towards me in the hallway and I found myself, just like everybody else, staring in their direction and not being able to tear my gaze away. I'd recently transferred from my old school and had moved to Hollowdale High in order to spend more time with one of my only friends in the world. Layla and I had been close when I was younger, but after her traumatic year, we were even closer. I could see she was finally happy and that only made me happier.

Walking towards me in the school corridor was a group of six teenagers that I assumed to be in the year above me. Each of them was beautiful, and they stood out amongst the typical students I'd witnessed in the car park. There was a girl with long dyed red hair. Her face was scowling at everybody who dared to glance in her direction; she was beautiful. She stood next to five guys, all of equal hotness. They were all extremely gorgeous.

'They're something to look at, aren't they?' I heard Layla's voice before I saw her. She was standing behind me with Dean, leaning up against a block of lockers.

Layla was my best friend and had been since primary school. The two of us were super tight, and it had gutted me when she left our old school to join Hollowdale. So when my sister told me we were moving to the town of Beurre—and therefore would join Hollowdale myself—I was thrilled. Dean was her boyfriend, and after a brief spell last year, they were back together and completely in love.

The two of them looked so happy together, and it pleased me that Layla had found somebody to open up to and be herself with, especially after everything.

'Oh, hey, you two.' I slammed my locker and looked at the hall. 'Who are *they*?'

I hoped I didn't sound *too* interested. But I think I failed.

'They're the *"Rebels"*,' Layla said, making bunny ears with her fingers to mock them and the stupid name. I could hear in Layla's tone it didn't impress her that they had a collective group name. 'Most people will tell you they're one of the most popular groups in school, aside from the football team at least, but they don't seem to give a shit about that. Dean used to be good friends with them, didn't you?'

Dean's lips pursed, and he shrugged. 'Only when we were young. Haven't really spoken to any of them since we started high school.'

'There's a rumour around here that the girl got into a real load of trouble because she got caught with a teacher.' Layla's face gave nothing away, but her bright blue eyes did. I knew the secret she hid behind them and I knew Dean did, too.

'What's the girl's name?' I asked, choosing a straightforward question. I didn't want to dwell on the teacher thing. We all knew that maybe that rumour wasn't the way it seemed. That gossip changed even the simplest of statements.

'That's Arianna. The guy with the muscles is Rock. Pretty sure that isn't his real name, but that's what everybody calls him. Then there's Tyler, Ace, and Spencer. The best-looking one there by far is Grayson.' I looked at who she was referring to and my God, he was definitely the best-looking of the six. He was perfect. All chiselled jaw, sinewy muscle, and just plain fucking hot. His hair was a light brown, the colour of caramel, and it looked good enough to eat.

'Oh, so Grayson's good-looking, is he?' Dean turned to Layla, and I could see the teasing glint in his eye as he raised the question to her. She had the bravery not to blush and just shrugged whilst smiling at him with complete adoration. How sickening.

'You don't want to get involved with them, Beth.' Layla's voice reprimanded me as if she'd known exactly what I'd been thinking about.

'Oh, Layla, ye have little faith in me, it would seem. I wouldn't even know how to get involved with them.' It wasn't a lie. Approaching them seemed daunting.

'Good,' Layla said like that settled the matter. 'What class have you got first, anyway?'

'English Literature and I can't say I'm looking forward to it.' I knew my tone bordered on stroppy, but I couldn't help it. There was something about reading novels by dead people that got my back up. It was Layla's thing to enjoy humanities like English lit. I much preferred maths and science, the type of subjects that always had a definite answer. Sometimes I wished life were as simple as maths; and that there was only one answer and only one way of reaching it. That no matter what the sum, the equation, everybody would end up with the same answer. The same interpretation.

It was solid. Reliable.

And that was what I liked life to be like.

'Oh, hush,' Layla said with a smile, but before she could say more, Amber disrupted her by hurtling towards us. Amber was a cheerleader like Layla, and the two of them became firm friends back when Layla joined the school and Dean was ignoring her. But that was a whole other story for another day. 'You're gonna love it here.'

Amber bobbed her head, her red hair swinging in the high ponytail she favoured. The two of us weren't exactly the closest of friends, *but* we were friendly, for Layla's sake. Plus, I was really trying not to be that childhood friend who acted possessively. Wouldn't be a good look for a seventeen-year-old, would it?

'Well… maybe I wouldn't use the word love,' Amber said, joining the conversation. 'But it's definitely not dull around here.'

'Sounds good to me.' I laughed, looking back to where the *Rebels* were standing together in front of the lockers. Each one of them gave off an air of superiority, and I could just tell they thought they were the shit. Believed their own hype. 'Who knows, right? Maybe I'll find myself a Prince Charming and have him sweep me off my feet.'

'Girl, I'm not gonna lie to you, but when you say shit like that, you really make me die.' Amber's tone was light, and I could hear the laughter within it, but I also knew that she judged me for it, too.

I'd always been a dreamer. Always been the girl who watched movies and dreamed of a situation unfolding like that for me. Be the girl who the popular guys dared the hot guy to date, and once he saw her true beauty, would defy said popular guys and do his own thing.

Or be the new girl in school who intrigued everybody and then, when in the cafeteria, was spotted by a guy who wasn't quite human, who couldn't hear her thoughts and therefore was interested in her.

Those movies were my bread and butter. The cheese to my macaroni. The peanut butter to my jelly.

No matter how I felt about myself, or my life, or my mum, those movies got me through.

'I just love, love. Is that an issue?' I asked, bringing myself back to the conversation, looking into Amber's large chestnut brown eyes and seeing her amusement lingering in them.

'No! You totally do you. Just guess I've never met somebody who wears their heart on their sleeve.'

I nodded, biting my lip—and my tongue. Not that she meant

any harm by her words, and to an extent, I understood what she was getting at. I wore my heart on my sleeve. I believed that love could be around any corner and that we should always be open to it, and I would never be ashamed of that, either.

'Well, get used to it,' I said, locking my arm through hers. 'It's just who I am.'

Science club.

The one club at school that excited me the most. It was a no-brainer when I transferred to Hollowdale High that I would sign up. Even tutoring those who needed it didn't bother me. I took it in my stride that I could help anybody learn about the wonders of science. If you had a life skill, why wouldn't you use it to help others?

'Let's all welcome our newest member, Elizabeth Jacobs.' The teacher gestured in my direction and I smiled widely.

'Beth, please,' I said, correcting him the way I'd corrected all of my teachers that day.

'Beth it is.' He nodded and pointed at the whiteboard behind him. 'These are the topics and experiments we plan to cover this term. For those of you who plan to study one of the sciences at university, I suggest you show up for all of them. However, you may pick and choose the subjects that interest you the most. I will post the tutoring schedule next week.'

In my school planner, I scribbled down the dates and experiments, excited to get started.

I looked up at the board again, and that was when *he* walked through the door, a pissed off expression covering his face. It was the guy from the hallway earlier.

One of those *rebels* that Layla pointed out.

The leader. The hottest guy by far.

Grayson.

'Yo, teach,' he called out, waving a sheet of paper in his hand. His gaze focused on Mr Taylor, who was sitting behind his desk, arranging something on his laptop. 'What the fuck is this about?'

'No swearing in my classroom, Mr Smith, or I'll have to send you to the office.'

'Fine,' he barked out with a laugh. 'What the *heck* is this about?'

'Better.' Mr Taylor grasped his hands together in front of him, his elbows on the desk, and my attention was now solely on the conversation taking place at the front. Writing down experiments be damned. 'That, Grayson, is your grade as it currently stands.'

'Bullshit!' he roared, slamming the paper down on the desk, the thud echoing. 'I deserve better than this.'

'Language!' Mr Taylor said, his tone still calm, but with an edge of warning underneath. 'I won't tell you again. If you wish to improve your grade, then I'm sure one of the science club members can fit you into their schedule.'

I bent my head down, not wanting to look too interested in their conversation, but I couldn't help myself from taking another glance at them.

Grayson's eyes locked with mine. The anger on his face was apparent, as his eyes narrowed, a glint of some emotion or other I couldn't place.

'Fine,' he snapped, turning back to face the teacher. 'I choose that one.'

He nudged his head in my direction, and a blush covered my cheeks. *That one?* As if I were so far beneath him.

Mr Taylor looked at me, too. He tilted his head, his eyes assessing the situation.

'*That*, Grayson Smith, is our newest member of the science club. Beth, could you come up here for a moment, please?'

I nodded, making quick work of getting out of my stool and making my way to the two of them. Part of me was excited, and yet a larger part of me was apprehensive about what Mr Taylor wanted.

'Yes, Mr Taylor,' I said the moment I stood before his desk. I tried to ignore the fact I could smell Grayson's cologne—a cedar scent I loved—and that our arms were about an inch away from touching.

'I know you've already committed to tutoring the younger years, but your grades are amazing and you seem like the kind of student who likes a challenge.'

I nodded, even though there was no possible way for him to know I liked challenges. Heck, I wasn't even sure I did. But there was no way I was gonna voice that.

'Grayson here needs a tutor, and I think you're the perfect person for the job.' He looked at us both. 'You could learn a lot from Miss Jacobs, Grayson. Just make sure you're actually listening to her, and your grades will improve tenfold.'

'You seem to have a lot of faith in me, sir,' I said with a little laugh. 'Of course I'll be happy to help.'

'Then it's sorted,' Mr Taylor said, sitting back in his chair, giving us both a contemplative look. 'You have until the mock exam in March to show an improvement, then we can discuss the next steps.'

'Sounds wonderful,' Grayson said, his tone saying the opposite. 'I can't wait to *study* with you, Jacobs.'

My stomach dipped and my nerves tingled.

Funny enough. His emphasis on the word study made me think he wanted to do anything but that.

Two
GRAYSON

'*I can't wait to* study *with you, Jacobs.*'

My words played through my mind for days after the fact, and every time they did, they amused me. When I'd suggested to the dickhead science teacher that he should let me choose her as my tutor, I didn't think he'd actually agree to it. Not like I'd asked politely or anything.

No, if anything, I acted like a wanker so the teacher *wouldn't* let me choose her. I thought the way I spoke to her would piss him off so much that he'd team me up with the biggest science geek to grace the halls—or should I say science labs.

But nope.

Apparently, the new girl was either a much bigger geek than I'd realised, or he saw through my shit and wanted to match me at my own game.

Either way, it had happened, and I couldn't stop thinking about it.

'Did you see the new girl?' Tyler asked, resting his back up against the back of his truck, swigging from his bottle of beer. 'Bit too short for me, but her tits looked good in her shirt.'

I stayed silent, wondering what the responses would be from the others.

The entire gang was at Spencer's family field, as we were every Friday night, and even though I was drinking and joking

118

around with them all, I couldn't take my mind off of everything going wrong in my life.

God. Even that sentence sounded pathetic as fuck.

I drained my beer, listening to the guys talk about Jacobs, knowing they wouldn't be saying half the things they were if Arianna were there with us.

The people at school called us the Rebels, and honestly, it was silly that they still called us that. It was a remnant of a different time—a much more innocent time.

The name itself was ironic back then. We were as far from rebels as was possible for any eight-year-old to be. It was the summer before starting at Hollowdale High that others adopted it not long after. All because of the events of a summer's evening the last week of school break before we joined Hollowdale.

TYLER, *Spencer, Ace, Rock, and I were all hanging out on the Matthews' family farm, when Maxwell Matthews, Spencer's older brother, came up to us. A swagger in his walk that we all looked upon in awe. Maxwell was three years older than us, and that made him the coolest guy around. Even if he looked down on us.*

'Hey, pipsqueaks,' he said as he approached. 'What are you doing out here?'

'We're playing,' Arianna said, crossing her arms across her chest and staring Maxwell down with a look filled with venom. She'd never acted like the other girls at school. She was one of us—always had been —and always made it clear she could run with the boys and keep up. If we ever doubted that, she made us remember why. Usually through some kind of physical fight.

I'd had more beatdowns from Arianna than I had from my dad, and that was saying something.

'Looked to me like you were all standing around doing nothing.'

'Believe what you want,' she said, stomping her foot down on the grass hard. 'What do you want, Maxwell?'

'Haven't I told you to call me Max?' He smiled at her, showing all

his teeth. Ever since he became a teenager, Max had changed. Only a little, but enough for us not to want to spend as much time with him anymore. 'Anyway, I've decided this is the last Friday night you're spending on this field. Unless you become worthy of it.'

'What are you talking about, Max?' Spencer asked his brother, his walnut-coloured hair long in the front, flopping into his face. 'Cut to the chase.'

'The popular kids need a place to hang on Friday nights, and this field is the perfect place. Mum and Dad are okay with it, too, so it's decided. If you dorks want to be popular enough for an invitation, then you need to give yourselves a reputation. Half of you are about to turn eleven, and you're gonna be the new kids in school. The youngest. You've called yourselves the Rebels since you were five. Now it's time to live up to that name.'

'And how do you propose we do that?' I asked, scuffing my trainer against the pile of mud in front of my foot.

'I don't give a shit how, Grayson,' he said with derision. 'Just that you do. Don't mess this up for me or you'll regret it.'

Maxwell smiled and turned around. We all stayed quiet as we watched his retreating back.

After he'd disappeared from sight, Arianna spoke up.

'So... we become true Rebels. How?'

'What does being a rebel even mean?' Tyler whined, his eyes wide as saucers. 'Not that it matters to me yet. Or Spencer and Ace. We're not joining you at Hollowdale for another year.'

'True,' I said. 'But you'll still be here on Friday nights with us. Especially as Spencer is the little Matthews. We need to establish our presence. If the whole town learns of these parties, Maxwell will become a legend. And one day, Spencer will inherit that.'

They all nodded, musing on my words.

'Rebel,' Ace said, rubbing his hands together. 'A person who rises in opposition or armed resistance against an established government or leader.'

Of course he knew the dictionary definition of the word.

Ace was the smart one. The one with book smarts and not just street smarts. He retained information, and none of us could figure out where he stored it all.

'Well, we're not gonna arm ourselves,' I said.

'And we don't care about the government,' Tyler stated.

'So guess that means we go against an established leader... The headteacher?' Arianna asked, and my mind started whirring at her words. It was the most sensible option.

'Or just the teaching staff in general.' I raised my head from staring down at the mud pile and smiled at them all. 'From the moment we join Hollowdale, we do all we can to become the coolest crowd in school.'

'You mean popular?' Tyler sneered, the word sounding sour.

'The opposite,' I replied. 'I said cool.'

'Means you might want to distance yourself from Dean Walters,' Rock said, his tone low. Rock spoke little, but when he did, it always made an impact. He didn't waste words on nonsense. 'The boy's a part of the popular crowd and you know he's gonna do all he can to get into the football team.'

I nodded, knowing Rock was right, but hating it anyway. It seemed stupid to stop being friends with somebody to be seen as cool, but I supposed that was the sacrifice needed.

'From this day forth,' Spencer shouted, 'we shall become the Rebels. Truly.'

'Hear, hear!' we all chorused back.

'WHERE IS ARIANNA, ANYWAY?' Rock asked, and my ears tuned back into the conversation and out of the past. 'I asked Mum before I went out, but she wouldn't tell me shit.'

Once again, I stayed silent. I knew exactly where Arianna was and there was no way I'd betray her trust in me by telling these dipshits. Arianna and I were close. She was the one in the group I could speak to about anything. The one I knew didn't judge me.

I couldn't put my finger on the turning point in our friendship, either.

Maybe it was when her dad married Rock's mum a few years back. That was the summer we didn't speak about. Ever.

'No idea. Said she'd meet us here.' Spencer took another sip of his drink and surveyed the crowd. 'Thought the new girl might be here.'

'Why would she show up?' Rock spat, anger filling his features. 'She's best friends with Layla Williams, which means she's also in with Dean Walters. That douche isn't gonna let her come here.'

'Why not?' Spencer replied. 'He comes to these parties enough.'

'Not anymore,' I said, my tone low, moving to the bucket of beers in ice and pulling myself out another. 'Ever since he shackled himself down with Layla, he's barely been here.'

Nobody questioned how I knew that. How I'd noticed such a thing. But I was certain they were all thinking about it.

Even now, five years later, the way I dismissed Dean from my life was a sore spot.

'Maybe I'll invite her next week,' I said, wanting to stop them from looking at me with pity in their eyes. 'She's my new science tutor, after all.'

'Oh yeah?' Rock elbowed me in the side. His voice was completely changed from how it sounded when he asked about Arianna. 'Let me guess. You plan to seduce her.'

I laughed, as did the rest.

Of course they'd think that of me.

I was the one with the less than stellar reputation. The playboy. The lothario who bedded everyone and anyone.

Little did they know I didn't like that about myself.

But when I was drinking—or already drunk beyond measure —I couldn't help myself. Slipping my dick into a warm body was better than returning to the hovel I called home and the man who I called father but had never acted loving or caring towards me once.

And, with the sentence I couldn't get out of my mind, was I any better than their opinions of me?

'I can't wait to study *with you, Jacobs.'*

From the flare in her eyes as I said it, she knew the double meaning behind my words, too. And it didn't put her off.

'FUCK,' I murmured, my eyes rolling back in my head. 'Fuck.'

I glanced back at the girl whose mouth was wrapped around my cock as she sucked me like a lollipop and my heart roared with lust.

There was nothing quite like watching my dick disappear into a girl's mouth, her lipstick leaving a mark, her teeth softly grazing the underside of my shaft.

'Fuck, yes, like that.'

She moaned, taking me further into her throat, and my balls tightened. That tingle at the bottom of my spine.

Then I locked eyes with Arianna, who was standing a metre away, her arms crossed over her chest, her left foot tapping away with irritation. Her bright red hair was gathered on top of her head in a bun, and she looked severe.

Well. That was one view that'd stop you from shooting cum down a girl's throat.

'Get over here,' Arianna growled, and I rolled my eyes, fighting to decide whether I was gonna listen to her or defy her and finish first. I hadn't seen her arrive at the party or heard her car arrive, but then again, I was pretty preoccupied.

'Can I—'

'Grayson,' she growled. 'I'll come and remove your dick from her mouth myself if you don't wrap it up.'

'Okay, okay,' I said, raising my hands before placing them on the shoulders of the girl on her knees. 'Show's over.'

She popped my dick out of her mouth and looked up at me with wide, innocent eyes.

'Are you sure you're gonna let little Miss Ari ruin our fun?' she asked, batting her eyelashes in a way I assumed she believed was attractive, but if anything, it just made my dick go limper.

'We're done here,' I repeated, taking a step back and putting my dick away, adjusting myself before I walked over to Ree, who was still tapping her foot, pissed as all get-out.

My feet carried me over to my best friend and once I got to her, I gave her a questioning look.

'What did you do that for?'

'What did I do what for?' she asked, a disgusted look on her face. 'Why did I stop you from making *yet another* stupid decision? Oh, I don't know, Grayson. Maybe because you need to sort your fucking shit out and stop getting your dick wet with literally any girl who throws herself at you. '

'Maybe if you took one of the dicks who throw themselves at you up on their offer, you wouldn't be so uptight?'

'Are you shitting me?' she spat. 'Are you seriously telling me I need to get laid? Come on, Gray. You're better than that.'

'Am I?' I asked, the buzz from the head and the alcohol slowly wearing off. 'Just tell me what you want.'

'We're going,' she announced, grabbing my arm and pulling me towards her car.

'Like fuck we are.'

'Grayson Smith, do not push me. We're going back to mine now and that is final.'

'Why?' I asked, standing on my tiptoes to look over at the crowd still occupying the field. At first, nothing of note came to me, but then I spotted Rock with his girlfriend, Savannah, and I knew why she wanted to leave. 'Oh. You can't stand to watch your stepbrother get it on, huh?'

'Shut up,' she said, jostling me, so I lost my balance and nearly fell. 'Are you coming with me or not?'

I blew out a breath, weighing up my options, or at least pretending to. We both knew I was going to leave with her.

'I'll come,' I said, looking her in the eyes. 'But you need to tell me what's going on with you and Rock.'

'Nothing's going on.'

'You may fool everybody else, but you'll never fool me, *pipsqueak*.'

She bristled at the nickname. That was what Maxwell had called us, and something we then adopted when talking to Arianna, but after Max died, it didn't feel right to use it anymore.

I was baiting her on purpose. Being a total prick.

Maybe I'd blame it on the booze.

'The same goes for you, arsehole. I see you, Grayson Smith, whether you want me to or not, and I know you're just covering up your many issues with alcohol and stupid girls who think they mean something to you.'

'The girls know the drill.'

'Do they?' she asked as we reached her car. 'Because that one sucking your dick just now was telling her friends earlier about how she was going to be the one to hook you.'

'Hook me? Like a duck in one of those carnival games?'

'This isn't a joke!' She stomped her foot, her temper rising. 'She had a game plan, and you played right into it.'

'I'm not gonna ask her to be my girlfriend because she can swallow my dick, Ree.'

'*I* know that, arsehole. But those girls are hopeful.'

'Okay, okay,' I said, placating her. 'I hear you loud and clear. I'll be a good boy from now on.'

'I'll believe that when I see it,' she said and opened her car door, getting into the driver's seat, waiting for me.

I got into the passenger seat and faced her.

'Thanks, Ree. I appreciate you.'

'I know,' she said, still in a huff. 'Let's blow this joint.'

'Let's.'

Three

Beth

'YOU HAVE TO TUTOR GRAYSON?'

I looked over at Dean, who was giving me a pitying look, tying up the laces on his bowling shoes.

'Yep,' I replied. Popping a cherry drop into my mouth, I relished in the burst of flavour that hit my tongue. 'He's flunking, apparently, and the teacher asked me to help.'

I shrugged, then bent down to put on the pair of bowling shoes the worker handed me. There was something about wearing shoes other people had worn that I couldn't get behind —except when it came to bowling. For bowling, it was a whole other story. And ever since a new family bought the local alley, things had improved majorly. The shoes were newer than they'd ever been.

'Why does it matter if he flunks? Not like he's gonna go to uni to study science, is it?'

'No idea… Maybe they'll hold him back a year if he fails?' I mused, wondering why it was so important for Grayson to pass, but ultimately not really caring too much about it. Maybe he'd tell me during our first session, whenever that would be.

After Mr Taylor asked me to tutor him, and Grayson made his comment about looking forward to it, he left the room with a smirk. Then avoided my gaze for the next two days.

And trust me, I ended up looking in his direction a lot.

I couldn't help myself.

The way his light brown hair shone in the light, a slight golden tint to it, made my insides melt. His bright blue eyes, the colour of a robin's egg, caused butterflies to swarm around in my stomach.

Layla often told me I was boy mad, and I guess to an extent I was, but really I just wanted somebody to care about me. To share in my shit. Or maybe not quite that. But somebody to share my shit *with*.

Ever since she found Dean, and they sorted out their drama, Layla was a much happier person. Always smiling. Always lending a hand to others. Not that she didn't before Dean, or BD as I often referred to it, but she'd gone through such a change in the five months she'd attended Hollowdale High. I was proud of her. And so, so happy for her.

If anybody deserved happiness, it was my best friend. She didn't talk about her past often, and I would never bring it up without her starting the conversation, but I would always be by her side, no matter what happened.

'You ready for me to wipe the floor with you all?' Amber asked, bouncing on her bowling shoe-clad feet, her ever-present ponytail swishing from side to side. 'I feel like I should warn you all that I'm a fierce competitor when I wanna be.'

'You're fierce at all times,' I muttered, holding myself back from rolling my eyes. Lucky for me, she didn't hear me. Layla, however, did and gave me a stern look of warning. It was the look that told me I needed to change the subject and pronto. 'How come we didn't go to the field party tonight?'

We were walking over to the lane, and I noticed everybody bristled a little at my question. Of course I'd seen through their distraction. They invited me to go bowling so we wouldn't go to the field. The real question was why.

Even from the three short days I'd been a student at Hollowdale, I knew the Friday night field parties were a big deal. I knew of them from Layla, Dean, and Amber, but hearing the buzz in the hallways only solidified how much of a big deal they were.

'The first party back after the new year is always rowdy,' Dean said. 'Plus, you don't know anyone yet, so we didn't want to rush you.'

'Rush me into what?' I scoffed, selecting my bowling ball, waiting for Amber to finish her frame. 'And I know you three. Not like you'd ditch me, is it?'

'Of course not!' Layla grabbed my forearm and pulled me to her side. 'Maybe we'll go to the one next week. How about that?'

'Fine,' I replied, squeezing myself further into her side. It was rare that Layla showed physical affection, and when she did, you had to take full advantage of that. 'Next Friday it is.'

Football bored me.

I'd never had much interest in it, but because Layla was dating the captain of the football team, and Amber cheered for the team, we found ourselves in the stands most weekends. Not like I had anything better to do.

'Doesn't he look so good?' Layla hushed in my ear, her eyes fixated on the pitch where Dean was running. 'I swear I'm the luckiest bitch alive.'

'You're definitely one of them,' I agreed, nodding. 'You've snatched a good one there.'

'He's good, isn't he? He just makes me forget all the crap, you know?'

'That's good,' I said, squeezing her hand briefly. 'I'm happy you're happy. Nobody deserves it more than you, Lay.'

'I worry, though,' she said, still looking at the pitch, her tone low enough I needed to lean a little closer to her. 'What's gonna happen when we go off to uni?'

'Have you spoken to Dean about it?'

'Yeah, we've talked about it. He doesn't seem fazed by it at all. Says we'll weather any storm.' A small smile played on her lips, and I could imagine just how much she swooned when he told her that. 'He wants to go to the same uni, but I'm apprehensive.'

'Why? You just said you're worried about what will happen, so I thought you meant you'd be apart.'

'I've not decided either way.' She tore her eyes from the game and looked at me, her beautiful blue eyes wide. 'Because half of me wants to stick together and go to the same place, but the other half of me wants to do our own thing. If it's meant to work out, it will.'

Layla had a valid point. A strong couple would survive three years apart at university, no doubt about it. And even though she was having her doubts, I didn't doubt for a moment that the two of them would figure it out and make it work in a way that suited them. They may have only been a couple for a few months, but there was something about them that made me feel positive about their future. Call me old-fashioned and a romantic, but that was how I felt, deep down in my bones.

'The two of you will figure it out. And then I'll say I told you so!'

We both laughed and focused back on the game. A quick glance at my phone told me there were still another twenty minutes of the half left and I knew I needed an excuse to get away for a bit. The Hollowdale team could score a hundred goals, and I still wouldn't muster much enthusiasm.

'I'm gonna go grab a drink,' I told her, and before she could reply, I bounced up out of my seat and made my way down the stairs.

The school didn't have seating at the football pitch, so most of the games played were at the local football club's stands, so there was enough seating for supporters and parents. Meaning there were some food places open on game days, too.

All I wanted was a bottle of water. It may be cold out, but I wasn't the kind of person who enjoyed warm drinks on a chilly day.

Nope. I always wanted a cold drink, no matter the weather.

The food window didn't have a queue—suppose most people cared about the game a heck of a lot more than I did—and I got two bottles of water for myself and a hot chocolate for Layla. She didn't have the same cold drink belief as I did.

When I turned around, I spotted Grayson outside in the car park, and my heart fluttered a little.

Down, Beth.

Maybe it was the perfect chance to talk to him about our studying session. We'd never nailed down a time or place to meet, after all…

Without second-guessing my decision, I headed to the car park instead of the stands and made my way to where Grayson was standing alone.

'Hey!' I said as I approached, not wanting to surprise him. 'What are you doing out here all alone?'

He checked behind him as if I was talking to somebody else in the deserted lot. 'You talking to me?'

'Does it look like I'm talking to anybody else?' I laughed, looking around the empty lot to make my point. 'Of course I'm talking to you. I literally asked what you were doing out here all *alone.*'

He smirked and gave a little snigger. I'd take it.

'I'm just out here waiting for you,' he said, biting his bottom lip.

'Sure you are.' I couldn't help but smile, though, and giggled. The boy was smooth, that was for sure. 'But seriously, what're you doing?'

'Ah, if I told you that, I'd have to kill you. And that'd be a big shame.' He smiled again. 'Do you mind if I take one of those waters?'

I shook my head and handed one to him, remembering that

the hot chocolate in my hand for Layla was probably gonna be cold by the time I got it to her. Oh well. Not like she knew it existed.

'Thanks.' My eyes were transfixed as he removed the cap and took a big swig of the water, then licked his lip afterwards. 'I am here waiting for someone.'

His tone told me not to ask who he was waiting for, but I'd never been the type of girl to listen to warnings.

'Who you waiting for?'

'Are you always this pushy?'

'Are you always this evasive?'

'Yeah, actually, I am,' he replied. 'It's my only flaw.'

'Why do I find that so hard to believe?' I laughed, raising my brow at him, seeing through his bullshit. 'I get the feeling that you've got nothing but flaws.'

'Ouch! You wound me!' He placed his palm on his heart, staggering backwards, pretending my words were a literal dagger to the heart. 'You always have such a sharp tongue?'

'Hmmm…' I pondered the question, pausing before I answered. 'It's for sure my only flaw.'

He laughed, a proper laugh that time, and my stomach flipped like I'd won a war I didn't even know I was fighting.

'I think I might grow to like you, Jacobs.'

'Thanks… I think?' I shuffled my weight onto my other foot, the cold air making itself known as a shiver ran through me.

'I didn't see you at the field last night,' he said. My breath caught a little at that, and my heart picked up its rhythm. The fact he knew he didn't see me meant he'd been looking.

'Nice to know you've got good observational skills. That'll come in handy when we're studying experiments.' I raised the hot chocolate cup in the space between us. 'I best be getting back to the game. We need to sort a study session out for this week. Shall I give you my number and you can text a time that suits you?'

'You just want my number,' he teased, and a flush warmed

my face in seconds. Maybe I could blame it on the chill in the air…

'So what if I do?' I replied, keeping up the flirting tone we'd established between us. 'It's a pretty genius way to get it, if I do say so myself.'

'Ah, it would've been if you didn't admit to it.'

'Or is it even more genius because I *did* admit to it?'

'Nice to know I'm always gonna be on my toes with you, Jacobs,' he said, a smile covering his face. He pulled his phone from his pocket and held it out to me. 'Put your number in there and message yourself so you'll have mine.'

I handed him the bottle I was still holding and took his phone, quickly inputting my number into it and messaging myself. I even went as far as saving myself under *Jacobs* and adding a quick selfie to the profile.

'Here you go,' I said, handing it back. 'Now don't be getting any ideas that I want an unsolicited dick pic.'

'Ah, but what if it were un-unsolicited?'

'Well, that changes everything, doesn't it?' I said with a laugh and took my drinks back. 'I'll see you later, Gray.'

'See you later, Jacobs,' he called out, and even without looking at him, I could hear the amusement in his voice. 'I'll message you tonight.'

'I'll keep my phone on vibrate,' I called back, not turning around. His laughter followed me back inside, and I smiled to myself.

Goal to Beth Jacobs.

EVER SINCE I'D spoken to Beth on Saturday at the game, I couldn't take my mind off our interaction. Every flirty word and banter-filled phrase repeating in a loop.

If my brain wasn't already occupied with thoughts of her, then the moment she told me not to send her dick pics definitely took away all other thoughts.

That night, once I was over at Tyler's place, I messaged her and told her to meet me after school on Monday at the student study room.

Her response was basically instantaneous.

JACOBS - I LOOK FORWARD to it. I hope you're ready for me, Gray.

Grayson - Surely Jacobs, the question should be, are you ready for me?

Jacobs - I have no idea what you're implying... Are you about ready to combust?

Grayson - My thoughts of a certain girl are definitely getting me closer

Jacobs - What did you think I was talking about? Obviously I meant combustion theory for chemistry.

Jacobs - Why? Was there another type of chemistry on your mind?

Grayson - Is lust a type of chemistry?

Jacobs - Maybe you'll learn the answer to that when we study

Grayson - What are you doing? We could get a head start…

Jacobs - Ah, but then I'll just be dreading Monday with nothing to look forward to.

Jacobs - Night, Gray. Hope you don't dream too hard about me. I'm sure you know what kind of reaction that can lead to.

I'd gone to sleep with a massive smile on my face after her last text. The girl was witty, and there was something about her spirit that just felt good to be around. It was rare I had that strong a reaction to anybody—especially somebody new.

I hadn't heard from her at all on Sunday, and by lunch on Monday, I still hadn't seen her at school, but I knew she was around somewhere.

It was a reaction I couldn't explain, but it was as if my body *knew* she was near. That we were sharing the same space, a GPS pin dropped in town in the exact same spot. Pretty sure she wasn't a witch, though, or something equally supernatural.

Fucking hell, Gray. Jump to witchcraft, why don't you?

'You coming to the field with me after school?' Arianna asked from where she was walking down the corridor beside me. I looked over at her, taking in her outfit of choice for the day, and smiled. No matter how many times she denied it, that girl was dressing to impress a certain person—and not that piece of shit teacher that people spread lies about her being with. As if Arianna would touch a teacher that way.

But people always thought the worst of her. Of us.

'Nope,' I replied. 'Got a study session with Jacobs.'

'Since when?'

'Since I sorted it with her Saturday night.'

'You were with us Saturday night,' she said, her tone sceptical.

'It's called texting. A form of communication where you don't have to be in the same place as the person you're conversing with.'

'Conversing? You're such a knobhead, Gray,' she said, a small chuckle leaking from her lips. 'You don't seem anywhere near as miserable as I thought you'd be to have a forced study buddy. What gives?'

'Not like my partner's hideous, is it?' I asked, mulling over the rest of my response.

Once again, Beth popped into my mind. The way her long black hair curled around her slim face, framing her, as an innocent but devilish smile played on her pouty lips. Even wrapped up in a coat, holding two bottles of water and a hot chocolate, she looked adorable as she bounced over to torment me at the game on Saturday. I was there because I was waiting to meet Arianna. The two of us were planning my eighteenth birthday party. Arianna was throwing it at her house because she had the space. Plus, her dad wasn't a total prick like mine.

'She's not hideous,' Arianna agreed. 'But we know nothing about her. Not really.'

'So? Doesn't mean shit about whether she's a good science teacher or not. I *need* to pass, Ree. I can't stay at this shithole for another year and I definitely can't stay with my old man any longer than necessary.'

'I know,' she said, pausing when we reached the cafeteria. 'Sorry for acting funny. I've just never seen you interested in a girl for more than a quick blowjob behind the trucks at the field.'

'Who said I'm interested?' I asked, turning to face her, holding her forearm so she couldn't escape me and disappear with the crowd into the cafeteria.

'Come off it, Gray. I *know* you, remember? We've been friends since before your mum...' she trailed off, but I knew what she was gonna say. We'd known each other well before my mum left. Left me alone with an abusive arsehole who didn't think twice about hitting his only child in a drunken rage. 'Anyway, I know I haven't seen you smile like this in a while.'

'What about the way you smile when Rock's around, huh?' I teased, taking her hand in mine to walk into the cafeteria and join the long lunch line. 'We just gonna pretend like that doesn't happen?'

'Shut up. There's nothing going on between me and Rock, and you know it. We both know that even if I *did* wanna go there, I couldn't. He's my stepbrother. My dad would lose his shit.'

'Whatever,' I replied, flippant. 'Let's go get some grub before I literally starve to death.'

'The day you starve to death is the day there's no food left on the planet,' she said with a laugh. 'You always have at least three snacks in your bag.'

'Who doesn't?' I shrugged. 'Snacks make the world go round.'

'If you say so.'

'So, what experiment are we starting with?'

'Who said we're starting with an experiment?' Jacobs asked, tilting her head at me and opening the large textbook on the table in front of us. 'You need to learn the basics first, mister. No Bunsen burner allowed for you until you prove yourself.'

'Prove myself, huh?' I ran my tongue along my top teeth and gave her the look that had worked on many girls before her, but she just scoffed and continued looking for the page she wanted.

Once she found it, she turned it so I could read it, too, and began to drone on about bonding. I nodded throughout, half taking in her words and half wondering what her lips would taste like.

Even from where I was sitting, I could smell the scent of cherry on her lips, and I knew it wasn't from her Chapstick. Those damn cherry drops she devoured all day, every day, lingered all around her.

For the next hour, I feigned interest as she talked about whatever it was on the page she'd opened the textbook to.

'I think that's enough for today. Wouldn't want your little pea-sized brain to explode with the overload.'

'It's the only thing pea-sized about me,' I joked. I wanted to see her smile again. It was like a need deep within me to make her laugh, to have her turn her smile in my direction because of something I did or said.

It was pathetic.

But it was true.

'You wouldn't tell me otherwise, even if it was,' she said with a small chuckle. Pride shot through me, puffing up my chest, as her smile stayed in place. 'Do you want a ride home?'

I couldn't drive. Everybody knew I hadn't bothered with lessons when I turned seventeen because who the fuck wanted to spend that kinda money on learning to do something other people could do for them?

Both Ree and Rock learned to drive the moment they turned seventeen, with their parents buying each of them a fucking expensive car, so they were my go-to rides.

Spencer and Ace were still sixteen, so I had no clue what their plans were, and Tyler was taking his test in a month or so.

Clearly, Beth had both the funds for lessons and to run a car. Good for her.

A ride would save me from having to walk home... but it would also let her know where I lived.

Fuck it. If she judged my house and the area it was in, then she wasn't worth my time. That was what I told myself, anyway.

'I'd love a ride, Jacobs. You offering?' I waggled my eyebrows, and she giggled, the sound of it sending a message straight to my dick that it wanted her—bad.

'I mean, my car's a little small for that sort of ride, but I'm sure we can get creative.'

My jaw dropped, and she laughed, wrinkles forming at the corner of her eyes. I gulped. *How on earth was she so perfect?* It pissed me off.

'Yeah, yeah.' I waved her off, closing up the books in front of us and placing them in my backpack. 'I live on the Hollowdale estate.'

'That's cool. It's no big deal.'

'Lead the way, your highness.'

The two of us packed up the rest of our stuff in silence and went to her car in the lot.

She wasn't joking when she said it was too small for a *ride*.

'A Smart car?' I asked, incredulity in my tone that I couldn't mask.

'What?' she asked, a tad defensive. 'It's smart.'

'And there I was, thinking *you* were smart.'

'Hey!' she said, unlocking the door and getting inside. I did the same and had to fold myself to fit into the small passenger seat. The handle on the seat creaked as I pushed the seat back as far as it would go, so my legs weren't tucked together in such a tight space, but even that didn't give me much more room. She smiled, watching me attempt to get comfy. 'I'll have you know that Sally is a great asset. She gets me from A to B and really, that's all that matters.'

'*Sally?*'

'Yes. Sally. That's her name.'

'But *why* is that her name? Why does she even have a name?'

'Everybody names their cars, Gray.'

'No, Jacobs. No, they don't.'

She shrugged, my disbelief at it not fazing her in the slightest. 'Well, I do.'

Okay then…

'Tell me something you love,' she blurted out after putting

the car into drive and the air became stifling. Probably because the contraption on wheels was the size of a tin can.

'Something I love?'

'Yeah! Like how you know I love cherry drops. Don't think too hard about it. Doesn't need to be deep.'

'All right then.' I rubbed my hands together, racking my brain for something I loved that was still surface-level stuff. But also something that didn't make me sound like a super big dork. 'I love old-school video games.'

'Oh, yeah? Like what?'

'Crash Bandicoot, Spyro, Abe's Odyssey, those sorts of things. My mum got me a PlayStation the last Christmas we spent together as a family and I loved it. Played it every single day, no matter what. Even though those games are bare old now and the graphics are shoddy at best, I'd still choose to play them over something new.'

She continued driving, indicating right to enter the estate. The closer we got to my house, the more I wanted to stay in the Smart car bubble with her.

'Tell me something you love.'

'You already know my love of sweets.'

'There has to be more. Sweets can't be your only love.'

'I love Science, too,' she pointed out and I gritted my teeth at how difficult she was being. I gave a small growl from the bottom of my throat and she chuckled, finally relenting. 'Okay, okay. I love old Hollywood movies to the point where you have to force me to watch something new.'

'By something new, you mean?'

'Something made after 1980.'

'Right,' I said, taking in her side profile as she focused on the road. 'Turn right here and it's the last house on the left.'

'That's the name of a film, you know.'

'Thought you said you watched nothing made after 1980?'

'Right...' she trailed off, her brows furrowed. 'And they made that film in 1972.'

I laughed, loving the little wrinkles forming in the corners of her eyes as she scrunched them with confusion.

'There was a remake.'

'Bet it was shit compared to the original.'

'Seeing as I've never seen the original, I can't exactly comment.'

'Fair.' She pulled up at the kerb outside my house and my heart dropped at how short of a ride it was. 'Maybe one day we could watch the remake together?'

It was a potentially insignificant gesture, but one that made my heart soar.

'Not worth it,' I told her. 'It wasn't the best. If I'm gonna force you to watch something "new", it'll be something worth your while.'

She tilted her head, a broad smile causing dimples to form in her cheeks.

'Are you coming to the field party on Friday night?' I asked, the urge to know whether she'd show up overwhelming me.

'Not sure.' She twisted in her seat to face me full-on. 'Why? That an invitation?'

'Yeah,' I said, watching her put a lock of dark black hair behind her ear, a slight shake in her hand. 'I want you there. And then I'll think about letting you pick the first movie we watch another day. Deal?'

'Deal.'

Five

Beth

THE BUCKET of drinks was our first stop on arrival at the field.

The crowd of people looked exactly the way I expected them to. The bonfire raged in the centre of the party, warming the area, and the sheer sight of it made me smile. There was always something so pretty about watching the flames as they snapped and crackled into the sky.

'Be careful tonight, Beth,' Dean warned, handing me a bottle of cider from the ice bucket. 'I don't want to haul you out of here so plastered you can't walk.'

'Nice to know you have high hopes for me, Dean.' I laughed, but inside I found his mother hen act a little insulting. At no point had I given him any sign that I'd be a reckless drunk. Unless we spoke about that one time—New Year's Eve—which we didn't talk about *ever*, so it was all good.

'I just know what these people are like.'

'Well, why don't you two go and huddle together on the edges and enjoy your night and I'll enjoy mine?' Layla's eyes narrowed on me in warning, but I shook off her concern.

'And where are you going to be?' Layla asked, looking around the field at the groups of people hovering around.

'I'm gonna go talk to Grayson. He invited me, so I may as well let him know I'm here.'

'I doubt he's gonna give a shit honestly, Beth,' Dean said with a wince as Layla elbowed him in the ribs. 'There's a girl hanging off him already.'

I turned to the spot Dean nudged his head in and was greeted by the image he'd painted.

There *was* a girl hanging off him, trying to wrap her hands around the back of his neck and pull his head down to hers, but from where I was standing, he didn't look interested in the slightest. I tried to place her, and that was when I realised it was Remi, Dean's ex-girlfriend. Bit odd he hadn't mentioned her by name, but then again, he and Layla pretended the girl didn't exist after what she tried to do to them at the start of the school year.

Her bleached-blonde hair was tied up in a high ponytail and her smile was brittle. A twinge of pity travelled through me, but when I remembered how she'd treated Layla, it disappeared into the wind.

'I'm heading over there,' I announced, beaming at my friends to cover my nerves. A body hurtled towards us and grabbed Layla out of Dean's arms to hug her. 'Hey, Amber.'

'So glad you losers are here finally. It's been a time of it. There was already a fight that got broken up.'

'A fight?'

'Yeah, between Tyler and Rock. Something to do with Arianna, I think? I couldn't really hear it all from where I was.'

'Yet you're spreading the gossip nonetheless,' I said with a smile. Amber smiled back and gave a little shrug as if to say, *you know what I'm like.*

'Somebody's gotta.'

'I'm outta here,' I said again, meaning it the second time. With a small wave at the three of them, I turned and made my way over to where the Rebels were standing on the other side of the bonfire.

They were stationed near their trucks and cars, but I knew none of the vehicles belonged to Gray. He didn't have his licence yet, but he told me he was working on it. According to him, why learn to drive and be saddled with the responsibilities when all you wanted to do at a party was to have a drink and a good time? The boy had a point.

'Hey,' I said when I was close enough, completely ignoring Remi, who was still trying to attach herself to him. 'Fancy seeing you here.'

'Fancy seeing me at a party I invited you to,' he said, a smirk playing on his lips. 'Nice of you to show.'

'You doubted me?' I asked as he extricated himself from Remi's hold. 'I'm not the kinda girl to be a no-show.'

'I'd love to know what kinda girl you are as a whole, Jacobs.'

'I'm sure you would. And maybe one day you'll find out.' I smiled and completely ignored the little stomps of Remi's feet coming from the right of us. Her pissed off face made me smile on the inside, but on the outside, I didn't give her a reaction because really, that was all she wanted.

'Wanna get away from these knobs?' he asked, hitching his thumb towards his friends, who were standing silently watching our exchange.

'How far away can we get on the same field?' I asked with a laugh, looking around at the vast area with nowhere to hide.

Grayson stepped closer to me, completely ignoring the jeers coming from his friends, so I followed suit and disregarded them, too. Taking my hand in his, he walked us away from the crowd to a spot behind the trucks. It wasn't exactly private, but it was away from the others. It was probably the most secluded spot at the party.

'Do you take girls behind the trucks often?' I asked, having no delusions that I was the first. Of course I wasn't. From what I'd heard whispered in the halls, Gray had a different girl on his arm at every party. One group of girls were even arguing amongst themselves in the study hall about which one would approach him next.

'Depends what you mean by the word *take*, Jacobs,' he said, making me giggle. The boy was a walking innuendo and his humour caught me off guard when he displayed it. I got the impression that few people knew the real Grayson. I wasn't saying that I did by any stretch, but I believed maybe I was seeing brief glimpses of him. Little snippets of the guy who lived underneath the guy everybody else saw when they looked at him.

'I take that answer as a yes.' He hadn't let go of my hand, and his cold, calloused fingers were rough in mine, but I didn't mind. 'Don't worry, I won't think of myself as special.'

'You should,' he said, his voice like gravel, and from the slight widening of his eyes, it took him by surprise. He coughed and rubbed his chin with his free hand. 'It's rare I seek a girl out. That I invite them here.'

'Oh yeah?' I raised my eyebrows, my head tilted up, so we were looking at each other's faces. 'You sought me out, huh? Because I'm pretty sure I walked over to you.'

'I invited you here, though,' he pointed out. 'I never do that.'

'So why ask me to come?'

'You make me laugh, Jacobs,' he replied, honesty laced in every syllable. 'I enjoy spending time with you. That cool with you?'

'I'll allow it.' We both smiled, and the hand that wasn't on me came to rest on my hip, warming my skin there that was exposed to the elements from where my jumper had ridden up. Grayson stumbled slightly, and it was then that I noticed his bloodshot eyes. 'How many drinks have you had? Because I'm definitely not drunk enough.'

'I've only had a few,' he said, a glint in his eyes. 'But I'm more than happy for you to drink up.'

I stepped away from his searing touch and took a swig of my cider. And then another. Until I'd drained half the bottle.

It was one of those fruity ciders, strawberry and kiwi, and I loved it. Sometimes having a mum who didn't give a shit had its perks. My sister always treated me like a mature adult, and she let me drink as long as I was sensible about it. We were open and honest with each other—for the most part—and it felt good to have her trust.

'How about something a little stronger?' Grayson asked, removing his hands from my body to walk over to the nearest truck, coming back with a bottle of vodka in his hands.

'You want to drink that neat?' I asked, wondering about his taste buds. A vodka and Coke was all good with me, but drinking vodka neat? Yeah. No, thanks.

'Come on, Jacobs. Live a little.' He twisted the cap off and took a long swig before handing the bottle out to me. I rolled my eyes but took the bottle anyway, taking a tentative sip. *Fuck.* It was definitely the cheap stuff. The liquid burned as it trickled down my throat, and I coughed at the strength of it.

'This is like drinking paint stripper, Gray.'

'Drink a lot of paint stripper growing up, did ya?'

'You know it. Mixed in with cherry drops, it's the perfect pick-me-up.'

'Bet it kept the colds away, too.'

I nodded, my face solemn. 'They did always wonder why I didn't get sick as a kid.'

'Clearly, you've discovered the secret to healthy living,' he teased. 'Why don't we make this a little more fun?'

'But what on earth could be more fun than standing behind a truck in the frigid January air with a cheap bottle of vodka to share?'

'*That* is a brilliant question, Jacobs, and I believe I have just the answer you're looking for.'

'Do enlighten me.'

'We can tell each other some truths, and for every one you skip, you can drink.'

'Sounds delightful…'

'Oh, come off it, Jacobs! You know you wanna learn all my deep and dark secrets.'

'Well, now that you mention it, I have been wondering how you ended up taking chemistry at A-Level.'

'Of all the things you could learn about me, that's the first one you go for? Seriously?' He laughed, shaking his head at me. 'It's one of the subjects I'm best at, believe it or not. Plus, it looks good on uni apps.'

'If you get a grade, it looks good on uni apps,' I pointed out, and he winced at my bluntness. 'But I plan to help you, so I guess it's all a moot point.'

'You're the hottest teacher I've ever had.'

My cheeks flushed at him calling me hot. For some reason, it felt like something special coming from Grayson—even though it was a line he'd used plenty of times; I was sure.

'It's your turn to ask me something,' I said, pushing him away from the embarrassment covering me. 'Make it a good one.'

'Same level good as yours?' he asked, and I scoffed in response. 'Okay… Let me have a think.'

He took a swig of the vodka before pointing the bottle at me.

'I've got one. How many hearts did you crush at your old school?'

The question caught me off guard. Surely the boy was bull-shitting. There was no way he thought I was a heartbreaker in any capacity. Instead of saying a word, I snatched the bottle from his hand and took a deep swig, wanting to drown myself in shame rather than answer.

'That bad an answer, ay?'

I shrugged, not deigning to give him an answer.

'How many hearts have *you* broken?' I asked, not missing a beat. 'Because I would bet money on the number being higher than mine.'

'You would, would you?'

'Thousand percent,' I said with confidence. 'I want a ballpark figure. No need to give me an exact one. I'm sure you don't know it, anyway.'

'You seem so sure of yourself.'

'Oh, I am.' I nodded. 'So what we talking? Ten? Twenty? *Fifty?*'

'You're not gonna leave this alone, are you?'

'The only way to shut me up is to answer the question, Gray, or take a swig and put yourself out of this misery.'

'I've got a better way to shut you up,' he said, throwing the bottle to the ground and stepping closer to me.

His face leaned down until it was level with mine.

'You've sure made things interesting around here,' he whispered, his lips on my ear before they trailed small kisses along my cheek.

His lips grazed mine, and my lips opened up involuntarily, my tongue wanting to dance with his.

He smelled of cheap vodka and something citrus. Then his tongue entered my mouth, and all bets were off. My eyes were closed, but I couldn't help myself from opening them a fraction to see if his were closed, too.

They were.

It was over not long after it began, but the butterflies in my stomach wouldn't stop fluttering around, their wings going insane.

I believed everything happened for a reason and clearly me attending the field party was important, because if I hadn't, the kiss with Grayson would've never happened.

'That was sweet,' he said, his voice a low rumble against my lips. I opened my eyes again and looked into his. They were bloodshot and glassy—definitely drunk—but mine probably looked the same. I wasn't drunk by any means, but I was tipsy. My thoughts fuzzy around the edges.

'Sweet?' I chuckled, awkward, not knowing how to take it. Did he mean sweet in a good way? Did *anybody* ever mean sweet in a good way?

'Yeah. Sweet,' he said, his hand reaching out to brush my cheek. 'You taste like cherry drops.'

I smiled. I always had a packet on hand. I pulled the tube out of my pocket and held it out to Grayson, taking a step back from him.

'You want one?' I asked, and his brows furrowed in confusion. Then he looked down and saw the tube in my outstretched hand and took one.

'They're sticky as fuck.'

'Not the only thing,' I joked. His deep guffaw was genuine, and it caught him off guard.

'You're funny, Jacobs. I think I like you.'

'You think you like me? Even after your lips were just suctioned to mine?'

'Suctioned?' He shook his head. 'Puh-lease. I didn't suction them. If anything, they were...'

'They were?'

'Oh, I don't fucking know.' He laughed. 'I was trying to be clever and smooth and shit.'

'Cute.' We both popped a cherry drop into our mouths and sucked in silence. It wasn't awkward, but it was a little strange. Grayson and I hadn't spent loads of time together, yet there we were, away from the crowd and hidden by Tyler's truck. Any conversation away from others, however, and the banter came thick and fast between us.

'Are you camping out tonight?' he asked. I looked at his dark brown hair and swooned, my stomach swirling up a storm.

'Camping out?'

'Yeah,' he said, placing his hands on my waist and pulling me closer. His crotch was up against mine and the butterflies hit their peak. Everything about our position had me wanting to freak out. To call a timeout to discuss everything with Layla. But I knew I couldn't. Plus, Dean would judge no doubt. 'A bunch of us are setting up some tents and sleeping out. You should join us.'

'Join *us*? Or join *you*?'

He laughed, his fingers playing with the waistband of my jeans.

'I definitely want you to join *me*. Those other fuckers can fend for themselves.'

'I can stay out,' I said, my tone a lot more certain than my mind, which was trying to figure out a way I could convince my sister that I was staying over at Layla's or some crap like that. Maybe I could even be honest. Cara was my sister, not my mum, so it wasn't like she could get too parental on my arse. Not that my mum would care if she knew. She was never around, after all. She didn't give a shit what I got up to—or *who* I got up to. Even if I never had got up to anything with anyone.

'Perfect,' he whispered, leaning down so our lips were on the same level once more. 'You can share my tent.'

'Well, I didn't think you'd invited me to leave me out in the cold.' A warm laugh came from my lips, and he joined in, a spark of lust flashing in his eyes as his pupils dilated a fraction. 'Who else am I gonna share a tent with?'

'True,' he agreed, his intense gaze locked on mine, keeping me in place. 'Not like you're gonna go shack up with Tyler or Ace, is it?'

'Which ones are Tyler and Ace?' I asked, standing on my tiptoes to look over his shoulder at the group over by the fire. 'They the really good-looking ones by any chance?'

'You think they're good-looking?'

'You don't?' I replied, cocking an eyebrow at him.

'I think they're my best friends, and that you shouldn't be looking at them that way.'

'Oh shh.' I batted him away. 'Jealous, Gray?'

'Something like that.'

'Don't worry, pretty boy,' I said, grabbing his hand. 'I've only got eyes for you.'

'Yeah?'

'Yep. Now let me go tell Layla I'm not leaving with her. Wish me luck!' I turned around, heading back to the crowds and to the spot I'd left Layla, Dean, and Amber, assuming they hadn't moved far.

'Good luck!' he called to my back, and I smiled.

The night was going even better than I'd imagined it would.

Yay me!

Six

Beth

'YOU'RE GONNA STAY HERE?' Layla asked, her forehead stretching so high, her eyebrows were about to disappear into her hairline. 'With *Grayson?*'

'Yeah,' I said with a shrug. 'Got a problem with that?'

'No…' she trailed off, looking at Dean for backup. 'Just concerned.'

'Concerned about what exactly?'

'He doesn't exactly have the best reputation,' she said tentatively. 'You've heard the rumours, same as I have.'

'What's your point? Everybody's had rumours said about them. Doesn't mean they're all true.' I gave her a pointed look. 'Shit, I'm pretty sure there was a rumour about me once that said I only ate fudge and nothing else.'

'Not exactly the same as a rumour about having slept with twenty-plus girls, is it?' Dean said with a smile, his head tilted in my direction. 'We just don't want to see you get hurt.'

'Thanks for the concern, but I'm good. I know what I'm doing.'

'Sure you do,' Amber said, nodding, her signature ponytail bobbing with the motion. 'You're about to get chewed up and spat out, and because you fancy him so much, you're willing to go along with it.'

'That's not it—' I started to defend Gray but thought better of it. Fuck them all for being so judgemental about something they knew nothing about. I hadn't told them much about our science study dates, and I definitely hadn't told them anything from our messages, either.

In their eyes, Gray and I barely knew one another.

Barely spoke.

But I knew that wasn't the truth, and I wouldn't waste any time I could be with him explaining that to them.

'Well, if you've got nothing else to say, I guess I'll see you later?'

I waited for more objections, but they didn't come.

'See you later,' they all mumbled, with varying levels of care.

'Just don't fuck him,' Layla whispered. 'You don't wanna be known as *that girl*.'

'Nice to know you have such faith in me,' I said, hiding my disappointment at her words. I didn't want her to know how much it hurt hearing those words leave her lips. 'I'll text you tomorrow.'

With that, I walked away from the three of them and made my way back to where Grayson was waiting a few steps away.

'Everything okay?' he asked in concern, looking back at where my friends were. 'They seem friendly.'

'They are,' I said, feeling the need to defend them even if they were being massive arseholes. 'Just not when it comes to you, apparently.'

'Makes sense. Dean and I go way back.'

'So I've heard. Wanna talk about it?'

'Fuck no,' he blurted out. 'I want to have a good time, not a sad one.'

I nodded and took his hand in mine, rubbing my thumb along his.

'Let's go get another drink'—I walked us over to the bucket and we took out another bottle of vodka—'and enjoy the rest of the evening.'

'I hope you can pop a tent, Jacobs.'

'In your pants?' I asked, biting my bottom lip, loving the reaction on his face when he registered my words. I loved surprising him.

'You've already done that,' he said with a smirk, flipping the script. It was me who went red, and I shook my head. He was just trying to throw me off, and it was working. 'You told me to dream of you, remember?'

'Happy to know I'm a pleasant dream.'

'You're the most pleasant of dreams. Especially when you're naked in them.'

I spat out the sip of vodka I'd taken and sputtered, coughing.

'You okay?' he asked, his smile taking over his face. 'You seem a little flushed.'

'I'm fine,' I replied, still coughing. 'You made me choke.'

'It won't be the last time.' His eyes darkened with an evil glint, and it was at that moment that I knew I was out of my depth.

Maybe drowning with him wasn't such a bad way to go.

ONE WORD for the tent was cosy.

Two words for the tent were *fucking small.*

Three: *very fucking small.*

'Are you okay?' Gray asked, entering the tent and zipping the door behind him, closing us from the outside world. 'My friends weren't knobs to you, right?'

For the last hour, we'd been hanging around with his friends as the rest of the crowd dwindled to maybe twenty or so people. The more intimate the group got, the better the atmosphere. Like they didn't need to put on a show or pretend it was all beneath them once the majority left.

'They all seemed nice enough,' I said with a shrug, sitting

cross-legged at the back end of the tent. 'Arianna doesn't seem to like me much, though.'

'What makes you think that?'

'Well, for starters, the girl barely looked at me. And when she did, it was the evil eye.'

'The evil eye?' he asked with a laugh. 'Arianna was born with resting bitch face. It's her thing. I wouldn't take it personally. She's got no reason to dislike you.'

'She's your best friend, right?' I asked, remembering him telling me about the group dynamics back in our first study session. 'The one in the group you're closest to?'

'Yeah,' he agreed, manoeuvring his tall body in the small space to sit cross-legged opposite me. 'We've known each other the longest. Back when my mum was still around, she worked at their house as a housekeeper and during the school breaks, she'd take me with her. I can't remember a summer without Arianna there.'

'Bit like me and Layla,' I said. 'We became friends back in primary school. I declared on the first day we met that we were gonna be best friends, but that wasn't what really solidified our friendship. The real kicker happened a month or so later. It was World Book Day. You know that day where every kid dresses up as whatever their obsession is at the time, even if it isn't a character from a book?' He nodded, and I continued. 'Well, we were both dressed as Belle and from that day forward, we both knew we were besties. No ifs, ands, or buts.'

'From what I overheard, Layla's not my biggest fan, either. So maybe it's a best friend thing?'

'I thought you just said Arianna has a resting bitch face and not to take it personally?'

'She does,' he said, brushing his hair away from his face, 'but it also takes her a while to warm up to outsiders. The six of us have all been tight for so long and it's rare that we have new people join us.'

'Doesn't Rock have a girlfriend? Savannah or something? How did Arianna react to her joining the group?'

In the dim light, I saw Gray's eyes light up with amusement, a secret sitting on the tip of his tongue.

'Oh, trust me,' he said, leaning forward an inch. 'She didn't take that well at all. Threw a fit about it, actually. It divided the group for at least a week, which may not sound like a long time, but for us, it was an eternity. We've never had anything happen that split us so effectively.' He paused. 'Except for the summer of 2018, but we don't discuss that.'

His tone told me I wasn't to ask about the summer of 2018, either.

'Must be hard for her, being the only girl in your group. Not having other girls to talk about boys with and stuff.'

'Arianna's never needed that,' he said. 'She's got me, ain't she?'

'You her agony aunt, Gray?'

'You bet!' He nodded, his hands coming to rest on my knees, and a shiver ran through me. It was an innocent touch, but my body set aflame. 'Isn't that what best friends are for?'

'True.' I nodded. 'Arianna's lucky to have you. Few guys our age would do it.'

'A lot of guys our age are wankers,' he said, and I laughed. He wasn't wrong. 'My old man's a wanker, and I've never wanted to be anything like him.'

'That's valid. My mum's a wanker, too, and I will do everything in my power to never end up like her.'

'Let's toast to shitty parentals,' he said, grabbing the plastic bottles of pre-mixed vodka and Cokes he'd stashed in the tent the moment we put it up so the others couldn't get their *grubby mitts* on them.

'Let's!' I took the bottle and opened it, touching his before taking a generous swig. It tasted a lot better mixed with the Coke, but it was still cheap as shit and burned my throat as it went down. 'Want to talk about your dad?'

'Fuck no,' he said with vehemence. 'You wanna talk about your mum?'

'Not one bit.'

'You sure?' He nudged, waggling his eyebrows at me. 'I've been told I'm a great listener.'

'Maybe one day I'll take you up on your listening skills, but believe it or not, they weren't the skills I was hoping to experience tonight.'

His eyes widened. Or at least I thought they did. The camping lantern between us wasn't doing the best job of lighting the entire tent.

'You were hoping for my *skills*, huh?' he said. Shivers ran down my spine at his carnal tone. 'And what skills have you heard I possess?'

'Can't say I've heard anything,' I said, which was the truth—sort of. 'Just got the impression from the way you talk to me. Oh. And from that kiss earlier.'

'Maybe we should repeat that kiss. You know, to make sure it was as *skilled* as you remember.'

His face came closer, his eyes a question, wanting to know if I wanted it before he closed the distance completely. I gave a small nod, hoping it looked casual and not as eager as it really was.

That nod was all he needed to swoop in and kiss me again with more pressure and a flick of his tongue. I melted. Fully melted under him, as he lowered me backwards until I was lying down beneath him.

The ground was uncomfortable, and I was pretty sure there was a rock under the tent right where the small of my back was, but I didn't care. Because what was happening in that moment had to be the hottest thing to have ever happened to me. Period.

'I've wanted you under me since the day we met,' he whispered, and a shiver trailed down my spine. I winced, the shiver causing the rock to pierce my back, and Gray moved away the moment he saw my face scrunch up. 'Are you okay?'

'There's a rock.' I shuffled to the left, getting comfortable once more, and gave a little laugh to ease the tension of the moment. 'That's better.'

'Don't want anything poking you,' he said, then added a shade darker, 'well, except maybe me.'

I laughed again, and the noises from outside the tent floated in. People were cackling about something, and there were hushed whispers and people going through the motions of pitching tents and getting comfortable. It was all so normal. A ritual performed every Friday night, rain or shine. Sweating it up in the sunshine or chilly as fuck from the cold.

Grayson reached over to the camping lantern that was lighting the small area and flicked it off, shrouding us in darkness. I blinked, willing my eyes to adjust fast, not wanting to miss a moment. Not wanting to miss even one expression on his face.

'Where was I?' His whispered words covered my arms in goosebumps as his body once more came down to cover mine— his lips following suit, devouring mine.

I felt hot by the time his lips broke from mine, pulling back just enough to let us both breathe. Gray kissed my neck, my exposed collarbone, my shoulder before making his way back to my lips. The kiss behind the trucks paled in comparison. Every gesture, every graze of his fingertips, every brush of his hair on my face, sent my nerve endings into overdrive.

Before I could truly recover, he pressed me deeper into the ground with his hand as the other roamed down my side. His gaze locked with mine, the only thing I could see, and a whimper left my lips.

The pressure of his chest on mine, his hardness pressing through his jeans, were all too much for me. My breathing came out in little pants, the humidity in the tent rising with each moment, with every kiss.

A moment later, he bit my neck, sending another rush of heat through me. He nipped at my neck, gentle enough he would leave no marks. His hand moved to my nipple, pinching it through my thin T-shirt. I was at war with myself, trying to keep my moans as low as possible, not wanting those outside to hear.

Gray's body moved, pressing his hardness into the spot I wanted him most, and my eyes rolled back in my head at the sheer bliss of the friction. There was something fucking hot about it. And even though we were both fully clothed, the heat from his body seared mine.

'The first time I get you naked won't be in a tent with all my friends outside,' he whispered in my ear. 'But there is something we can do right now that'll have you seeing stars.'

I gulped at the delicious picture he painted.

His hips moved above mine, and I was so lost in the sensations that I moved my hips to match his, thrust for thrust.

I wanted that high he'd hinted at. Wanted to feel myself topple over and come down again filled with ecstasy because of his actions.

'Shit, Jacobs.'

His words spurred me on. My release was on the horizon, getting closer and closer with every rub of his hard dick through my thin underwear. The button of his jeans was hitting me in the right place with each buck of his hips, and I knew I was close.

'Gray,' I whispered, shyness shrouding me. 'I think I'm going to come.'

'Good,' he said, the wicked delight there audible. 'I can't wait to see your face when you come undone, Jacobs.'

Those words. His actions. All of it built to a crescendo. One I couldn't stop even if I wanted to. And I sure as fuck didn't want to.

'Fuck.' Before a moan of release could leave my lips, Gray crushed his on mine, stifling the sound before it entered the universe. We rode out my wave together as one.

'Fuck,' he whispered, his movements slowing. 'Fuck, that was...'

'Good?' It came out breathless. His eyes locked on mine, flaring with heat, and he gave a small chuckle.

'Good? It was better than *good*. You made me come in my pants like a love-sick teenager.'

'We are teenagers,' I pointed out, but he just chuckled some more.

'You know what I mean.' He brushed it off, and I didn't think it was wise to let him know I didn't actually know what he meant at all. It was the first time I'd had an orgasm from something other than my own hand—not that I'd tell him that.

'Jacobs,' he whispered, rolling off to lie beside me. He grabbed my hand with his so we were still touching, and my quick worry that we'd lose contact dissipated with his touch. I smiled at the gesture. 'I think this is the start of a beautiful friendship.'

'Friendship, Gray?' I asked, my tone teasing. 'And there was me wondering when you'd get down on one knee and propose.'

He barked out a laugh, squeezing my fingers gently with his, his eyes remaining on the roof of the tent.

'Let's start with friends.' He turned his head to face me and I did the same, our eyes locking in the dim tent.

'Friends?'

'Yeah… you know the type? The ones who get to see each other naked now and then, but still hang out and watch movies while stuffing their faces with popcorn.'

'We'll see,' I said, talking with a nonchalance I didn't feel. The boy had knocked back a lot of alcohol and I wasn't about to trust a word he said. 'Movies sound good, though.'

Once we'd cooled down—literally. Gray had to go outside and get some fresh air before he returned in a much calmer state —the two of us settled down to sleep.

It was already past four in the morning and I would need to leave in a couple of hours to get home before my sister noticed I was gone. But even just a couple of hours asleep in his arms would be worth it.

Our whispered conversation replayed in my mind as he lay

behind me, pulling me close to his chest, one arm underneath my neck. The little spoon to his big spoon.

If he meant friends-with-benefits, then I wasn't game. Or maybe I was? A feeling sitting in my gut told me I would will-ingly make a bunch of stupid decisions when it came to Grayson Smith.

Gray's breathing was as charged as mine, and no matter how much I wanted to turn around and kiss him and continue what we'd started, I knew I wouldn't.

I wasn't going to lose my virginity in a tent in the middle of a field with loads of other kids around us.

Not that I was one of those people who believed there was a right time and place to lose your V-card. Just a right person.

'Night, Jacobs,' he whispered in my ear. 'Sweet dreams.'

'Dream of me,' I said back, my voice carrying in the tent's silence. 'Thanks for asking me to the party.'

'You should come every Friday,' he said. I wanted his words to have a double meaning. I wanted him to mean that he'd give me an orgasm like he had earlier every Friday night, but I didn't want to get too ahead of myself. Maybe he'd do to me what he'd done to the others. 'I like spending time with you.'

'Well, not like I had any other plans,' I replied, my heart rate no doubt giving me away as he'd placed his hand over my heart. Or maybe it was on purpose so he could touch my tit. 'I like spending time with you, too.'

'Night, Jacobs.'

'Night,' I hushed out, waiting for his breathing to slow down before I let myself fall asleep, too.

If my heart wasn't already on the Grayson train, then that evening had solidified it as a lifelong ticket holder.

Seven

Beth

I WAS ON A HIGH.

The events of the night kept playing over in my mind. Every delicious moment with Grayson had burned onto my retinas and branded itself into my membrane. No matter what, it wasn't going anywhere.

When the sun set on the horizon, I woke Gray up and whispered that I had to get back before my sister noticed I hadn't come home. He grumbled, pulling me closer to his body, and placed kisses up and down my neck to convince me to stay, but I couldn't.

I promised myself it wouldn't be the last time I fell asleep in his arms.

Even though a large percentage of me knew it was most likely a one-night thing. A one-time chance to spend time with him—both intimately and literally—that I wouldn't get a repeat of unless I was lucky. I wouldn't let it faze me, though. Not yet.

After all, we still had a lot of studying to do together. The chemistry was there, and if the night before was anything to go by, he knew that.

I slipped into our new house and crept up the stairs, hoping I wouldn't bump into my sister en route. Not that she'd mind too much. Even so, I didn't want her to be disappointed in me.

My relationship with my sister was different from what I saw between my friends and their siblings. Maybe it was because Cara had always acted like a second mother to me, especially when our own mum was letting us down. Letting *me* down.

Often, I wondered why my mum didn't love me the way mothers were meant to love their children. Had I done something wrong? Was I unlovable?

From the age of five, my mum didn't bother with me. Didn't even attempt to parent me or show me she loved me. My earliest memories weren't like that, though. No. My early memories of my mum were happiness and light. The two of us getting along and enjoying spending time together.

But it was as if a switch occurred on my fifth birthday and things were never the same from that day forward.

It was then that my sister picked up the slack. It was Cara who bought me my first bra. Cara who taught me about the birds and the bees and everything in between. About periods and boys.

Everything.

And she never complained about it. Never acted like I was a burden to her.

I just wished she dated more. I kept telling her that the right guy was out there for her, that she just needed to actively go looking for him. He wasn't going to show up at the front door while she stayed in, was he? It had been at least three years since her last proper boyfriend, and of course she could've had dates without me knowing, but we told each other everything.

The seventeen-year age gap between us didn't matter.

Making it to my bedroom unscathed—and unnoticed—I closed my door, pressing my back up against it and slumping down to the ground. All the emotions and feelings hit me in the gut simultaneously.

I made out with Grayson Smith.

No. More than making out with him. He gave me an orgasm and he didn't even touch me underneath my clothes. *Shit.* I couldn't wait to talk to Layla about it all! No longer was I living vicariously through her (albeit limited) experience. I had my own story to tell. My own guy to crush on.

Ten minutes later, I got into my bed, hoping I'd be able to get at least another few hours of sleep. It was only seven in the morning, and on a Saturday the earliest I wanted to see the world was ten. And that was a bare minimum.

My eyes closed, and within moments, I was out for the count.

'I JUST NEED A FEW HUNDRED POUNDS!'

The loud voice woke me, and I bolted upright in my bed, grabbing my phone to see the time.

Nine-thirty.

Fucking wonderful.

'I don't have a couple hundred pounds to give you, Mum!' my sister shouted back.

'You must! Look at you, living in your brand-new fancy fucking home. Think you're above me now, do ya?'

There was no way I could sleep through the shouting match going on downstairs, so the next best thing was to accept that my day had started and save Cara from having to deal with Tara alone.

On eager tiptoes, I went downstairs to join the fray.

'You know why we moved here!' my sister cried, her scrunched-up face coming into view as I turned the corner into the living room. She spotted me and closed her mouth, the words about to leave her lips dying at the sight of me. 'Mum, please leave.'

That was when Mum saw me standing in the doorway.

'Ah, Elizabeth,' she said, turning her venomous gaze to mine. 'How are you doing this fine morning?'

'Hello, Mother,' I said, stepping further into the room.

'What've we done to have the pleasure of your presence so early in the day?'

'As usual, *Beth*, I've come to see my gorgeous daughters. That's the only reason I ever show up here.' Her black hair was manic. It was curly and resembled a triangle atop her head.

'Course it is,' I scoffed, a little laugh coming out of my mouth at the way my mum could lie with such a straight face. 'So the time you showed up last month begging for money was all because what? You wanted to spend quality time with us?'

'Stay out of this, Beth,' my sister said, giving me a stern look. 'Why don't you go up to bed seeing as you stayed out until God knows when?'

My cheeks flushed at having been caught out. Maybe I wasn't as discreet as I thought I was when I arrived in the early hours.

My sister had always told me that for somebody so small, I still made the noises of a fairy elephant.

'Like mother, like daughter,' Mum said, her eyes taking me in from head to toe before turning to my sister and raising an eyebrow at her. 'Allow her to stay out all hours, do you?'

'Not like you give a shit,' I snapped. 'My sister looks out for me a lot better than you do!'

'Does she, ay?' Mum tilted her head back, her laughter sinister. 'Oh, if only I told you—'

'That's enough, Mum!' Cara shouted, her eyes almost bulging out of her head, the need in her to cut off whatever horrid thing Mum was about to spout strong. 'I'll send you the money in the morning.'

'I need five hundred.'

'It was two hundred a moment ago!'

'Well, now it's five. Unless...' Mum trailed off, leaving her sentence hanging in the air. And even though what she was alluding to made no sense to me, it made sense to my sister just fine.

'Five's fine,' my sister bit out through gritted teeth. 'Now leave.'

'I'm going!' The smug tilt of her lips pissed me off. She knew my sister always caved in to her ridiculous demands for money. It was one of the few reasons she showed up. She didn't even live with us. When Cara got the chance to move for her new job, with a swish new house to boot, she offered Mum the chance to move with us, but she declined. Something about her own independence or some crap. And that's what it all was. Crap. 'But I'll be back if that money doesn't drop into my account tomorrow.'

'Whatever. Just go now.' My sister's voice was resigned and so very tired. Were weekend mornings not sacred anymore?

With one final cackle, my mum left the room, showing herself to the front door. The moment it shut with a bang behind her, my sister swung her gaze at me.

'Are you gonna tell me where you were?'

'Just out at the field with a bunch of kids from school,' I told her, deciding to go with the truth rather than some half-cocked lie. 'Everyone goes.'

'Hm,' she replied. 'In the future just tell me, yeah?'

'Yeah,' I said with a nod. 'Right, I'm going back to bed. I'm shattered.'

'Just make sure once you wake up you have a shower,' she said, holding her nose. 'You stink of bonfire and outside.'

EIGHT

GRAYSON

BETH KEPT GLANCING at me when she thought I wasn't looking, and I did the same with her.

It was a game of sorts.

A dance we were both taking part in, knowing the other one was taking part too, but not outright acknowledging it.

'Gray, are you even listening to me?' she asked, waving some kind of apparatus in front of my face.

'Err… Is there a right answer here?'

'The right answer would be, yes, of course, your highness. Not that gormless err that just left your lips.'

'Your highness?'

'What, too much?'

I laughed at her innocent expression and she cracked a smile too, putting whatever it was she was flailing around in her hands down.

'I just want you to pass, Gray. But I need you to work with me here. I can't do the tests for you.'

'Wish you bloody could,' I said, bitterness lacing my tone. If I had a brain like hers, I'd ace the test with no problem. The girl was intelligent—something I'd known even before we partnered up to study. I could tell that first day just by looking at her. Or maybe I could see that I found her attractive, and that was why I

166

picked her, but still, she had the smarts to go far in life. I envied her that. Just a tiny bit.

If I kept going the way I was, I wouldn't amount to shit.

'Well, I can't. So you either need to listen to me and learn, or give up and fail. Simple as that. You get to choose which one you do.'

'Thanks for the arse kicking.'

'That wasn't an arse kicking and you know it. If I ever kick your arse, Gray, you'll know about it.'

'Is that a threat?'

'Maybe,' she said with a shrug. 'You know me. I keep it real.'

'I do know you,' I agreed. 'But I'd like to know you even better.'

'Did you not learn enough in the tent?' she asked, her eyebrows rising on her forehead into her fringe, a teasing smile on her face. 'Maybe we should have a repeat.'

Her face burned as she said it, giving away that no matter how she tried to paint it, she wasn't as casual about what we did as she wanted me to think.

I thought about my response first, not wanting to say something that made me sound like a prick but also something that didn't sound too soppy either.

'I know we should,' I replied. 'I don't think I've mentioned that I like spending time with you, Jacobs.'

'You have, actually,' she said, no longer looking at me. 'In the tent.'

I cast my mind back to that evening, to the words we said, the things we did together, and I couldn't remember telling her that. Everything else was so clear, though. Even though I'd drunk a fuck-ton that night, I could still remember every kiss, every touch. I doubted I could ever kiss her and *not* remember it.

'Well, then you already know,' I said with a laugh. She gave a tentative smile back, but still looked down at the textbook spread out in front of us. 'But I mean it.'

'I'm glad.'

'I'm having a birthday party for my eighteenth this weekend,' I told her. 'I want you there.'

She gave me a sardonic look and started a sentence before abandoning it.

'I—' She twiddled her fingers on the desk, focusing on them. 'Sure. When is it?'

'Saturday night. Arianna and Rock are throwing it at their house in the Hills.'

'Okay,' she said, mulling it over. 'Is Layla invited?'

'The whole school's invited, Jacobs. I just wasn't sure if you knew about it, so thought I'd make it clear just how much I want you there. Just in case you didn't know.'

'Sure. A party sounds like fun. Does that mean the field party's off on Friday?'

'Course not.' I scoffed. 'A double party weekend is peak teenage behaviour, Jacobs. The highlight, if you will.'

'Sure it is.' She laughed but nodded anyway. 'Okay. Field on Friday, Arianna's on Saturday.'

'I look forward to getting to know you better.'

'I hope you mean you look forward to learning my favourite food and my least favourite film.'

'I already know those things,' I said, pointing at my head. 'Everything you say to me is locked away up here.'

'Yet apparently, everything you say to *me* isn't.'

'Harsh,' I said without too much conviction, seeing as she was right. 'I'm forgetful. It's why I can't pass science.'

'Is it?' She leaned forward, entering my bubble. 'Or is it the fact that you don't bother to learn shit in the first place?'

'God, the hits really do keep coming, don't they?'

'Whatever.' She giggled, so close that her hair brushed my hand, and I inhaled deeply. 'We've got chemistry to learn.'

'Will your parents mind you being out two nights?'

'Are you asking me if I have a curfew? Or whether I even have parents?'

'Oh, ha-ha. Answer the question, Jacobs.'

'Seeing as I've never known who the fuck my dad is, I doubt he'll mind me staying out all weekend. Then my mum doesn't live with me and barely knows her own name most days, so I'm sure she'll be cool with it too.'

'Who do you live with?'

'My sister, Cara. She's sixteen years older than me, but she's pretty cool. We're tight.'

'Will she mind?'

'Shouldn't do,' she said with a shrug. 'I'm sure she did the same at our age. What about your rents? Do they give a shit?'

'Nope,' I said, popping the P at the end. Cavalier. 'My mum left when I was younger and my dad's a dick.'

'Oh yeah?'

'Yep. Sounds a bit like your mum, actually. He's drunk most of the time and barely pays attention to whatever I get up to.'

Not exactly true, but she doesn't need to know that.

'Parents suck,' she said with vehemence. 'Family is who you want it to be. Layla's my family, even though we share not one ounce of blood.'

'Like how the Rebels are mine,' I said. 'Every one of them is like a brother to me. Well, sister if we're talking about Ree. She's the one who keeps me sane. Makes sure I don't drown.'

It was more than I meant to admit. But it was the truth.

'Layla's that person for me. She's my anchor.'

'That's a nicer way of looking at it.'

'How do you view Arianna?'

'I've never put a name on it, I guess. But if I was gonna, then I'd use anchor, too. She keeps me afloat.'

Beth nodded and understanding passed between us. We were on the same wavelength; we knew how the other felt. Something I didn't experience with many people.

'I can't wait for this weekend,' I told her, trying to convey with my tone how much I meant it.

'Me neither,' she whispered, brushing her hair back behind

her ear and looking back at the textbook. 'Now we really do need to work.'

'Ay, ay, Captain,' I said with a salute.

She just laughed and shook her head.

'Just admit it,' Ree said, standing beside me by the bonfire. 'You like her.'

The two of us were alone, the crackle of the fire muting our conversation to any outsiders, as we took small sips of our drinks, surveying the area.

Beth was with Layla, Dean, and Amber on the other side of the field. The moment she arrived, she came over to say hello and to let me know she was going to hang with her friends until they left. I nodded and gave her a kiss on the lips before she left, the shock of it clear on her face.

And the faces of everyone else around us.

'I don't need to admit it,' I said, taking a swig of my beer. 'I already know it.'

'Oh,' she said, surprised. 'Saves me a job, I guess.'

'What job's that? The one where you kick me until I'm half-beaten in the grass and admit my feelings for Jacobs?'

'Something like that,' she said, her lips curling into a smirk.

'Maybe I should do the same for you.'

She froze, her cup half-pressed to her lips, her eyes narrowed.

'I don't know what you're talking about.'

'You don't?' I nudged her in the rib with a gentle elbow. 'We both know you have feelings for Rock, yet won't act on them.'

'He has a girlfriend,' she bit out.

'He's only with Savannah because he can't be with you.'

'I'm sure Savannah would be thrilled if she heard you say that.' Arianna paused, her head turning to where Rock and

Savannah were standing, his arm around her waist, as they listened to something Spencer was getting animated about. 'He's my stepbrother. Can you imagine our parents if we started dating? They'd freak and then probably take our money away while they were at it.'

'Probably,' I agreed. 'But when you weigh it up, what matters to you more, money or happiness?'

'Don't get all head shrink on me,' she warned, wagging her finger in my face. 'We're not talking about me.'

'I don't need you to tell me how I feel,' I said. 'I've accepted that I like Jacobs and I wanna see what can happen.'

'Wow. You do like her.'

'I literally just told you that.'

'No, but I mean, you *really* like her if you're willing to see where it goes. You kissed her in front of everyone.'

'I've done more than kiss a girl in front of a crowd before,' I pointed out, and she grimaced at the imagery.

'And every day I wish I could scrub my eyes from the sights they've seen.'

We both broke out into laughter, and I caught Beth's eye across the field. She smiled widely at us both, and I gave her a salute with my beer bottle. She raised her cup back at me and we both took a sip.

'Jesus, Gray, you're smitten.'

'Oh, fuck off.' My words didn't have much bite to them.

'What I meant is you kissed her in front of everyone at the start of the evening. You claimed her in front of all the guys who may have tried hitting on her.' I went to cut in, but she held up her finger. '*Plus*, you made it clear to any girl here that you're taken.'

'Did I?' I asked faintly, even though I knew that was exactly what I'd done. Just watching her walk up to me with such confidence turned me on. At no point had she cowered or waited for me to approach her first.

'You just put a target over that girl's head.'

'Bit dramatic even for you, Ree.'

'Every girl here is gonna wanna know what she did to get your attention. And every girl here is gonna give her hell for it. She's still the new girl.'

'They won't,' I said. 'Otherwise, we'll make it clear she's off-limits. Last time I checked, we still had a reputation.'

'One we didn't do shit to earn,' Ree mumbled but nodded. The power of the Rebels existed, even if we never did much to warrant it. A few fistfights here and a blackmail there meant nobody bothered you much.

'Doesn't matter whether we earned it or if Maxwell handed it to us on a silver platter. People listen to us.'

'Guess I should probably make nice with her,' Ree said, moving her attention once more to where Beth and Layla were dancing together and laughing at something Amber said.

'If you could.'

'I find girls hard to get along with.'

'I know, but this one's different. It isn't like I'm asking you to befriend the girl who sucked my dick that night you interrupted.'

'Grayson!' she shouted, drawing the attention of those around us. 'Do you have to put pictures like that into my head every day? I've seen your dick way too many times for a best friend.'

'Sorry about it,' I said, not sounding apologetic one bit. 'You know you love me.'

'Be easier if I didn't.'

'Hush up, you.' I twirled a red curl of her hair around my finger. 'You gonna stay tonight?'

'And listen to Rock and Savannah in a tent together? No fucking thank you. I'd rather listen to classical music and watch ballet.'

'Wow. Serious stuff.'

Arianna had taken ballet classes when we were younger, and everyone praised her for how talented a dancer she was. But something happened that made her fall out of love with it—and from that moment on she couldn't listen to classical music without it triggering something.

'When you reckon you'll get Beth all to yourself?'

'Few hours' time, I'd say. Her friends won't leave this early and I'm not gonna be the kind of dickhead who takes her away from them if she's having fun.'

'I'm sorry,' she sputtered, 'but who are you and what have you done with Grayson Smith?'

'I'm serious, Ree. I don't wanna fuck this up before we've even got started. She'll come to me when she's ready, and I've got the whole weekend with her pretty much, so I'm good.'

'I'm glad. I'm happy to see you smile, Gray.'

'Now we just need to work on yours,' I told her, but she gritted her teeth and shook her head.

'We may both be waiting a long time.'

Nine

Grayson

The party started at seven.

Well, people were told it started at seven, which basically guaranteed they would show up at eight at the earliest.

Nobody showed at the time stated. It just wasn't the done thing.

People trickled through the front door in small clumps—faces I recognised and ones I'd never seen before. Both rich and poor. Kids from both sides of the 'divide' mingling amongst one another, no doubt hooking up with each other, too.

'Don't you think you should slow down?' Arianna asked me, as I finished my third—or fuck, maybe my fourth—drink of the evening.

'Ree,' I said, jostling her, wrapping my arm around her shoulder. 'It isn't every day a guy turns eighteen. What better way to celebrate it than getting absolutely annihilated?'

'Annihilation is overrated, Gray.'

'You got your stomach pumped one time, Ree. You learned your lesson. We get it.'

She pointed at the empty cup in my hand and muttered, '*Clearly* you don't get it.'

'Lighten up. Enjoy yourself. Your dad's away and you're surrounded by the people you love the most.'

'And those I hate the most.'

'Stop being such a spoilsport. Your best friend's eighteen and would like you to remove the stick from your arse and enjoy the night.'

'Fine,' she grumbled, taking a tentative sip of her drink. I doubted it was a strong one—not after the aforementioned stomach pumping situation. Not that she could remember much of it.

It was rare I got blackout drunk.

I'd only experienced it a few times, and I wasn't in a rush to experience it again. There was nothing worse than not knowing what you got up to. *Who* you got up to. Losing control like that wasn't for the fainthearted.

But my dad's words from that morning had sunk deep into my gut, swirling around in my thoughts, wondering if any of what he said was the truth.

Was I really a waste of space?

Did people tolerate me only because they didn't have the heart to tell me to fuck off?

Without another word to Ree, I headed over to the drinks that were laid out on the dining table. Ree's dad's money had spared no expense.

It wasn't the cheap shit either.

The bottles of vodka called to me and I swiped one off the table, opened the lid, and discarded it in the trash bag by the door, then took a deep, long swig.

Beth's dark hair and hazelnut brown eyes filtered into my mind. Her petite body—those sumptuous curves—would lead me to sin if I wasn't careful. Beth was beautiful, yes, but she was also fucking gorgeous. A real knockout.

My phone vibrated in my pocket and I grabbed it, hoping to see her name on the screen, lighting up my otherwise dark world.

JACOBS - HOPE you've not drunk too much without me

Grayson - Got a bottle of vodka waiting here with your name on it

Jacobs - Hope you mean literally. I love personalised shit.

Jacobs - And I swear to you that if it's the cheap stuff, I don't want it. Name or no.

Grayson - Oh, it's got your name on it all right

Grayson - You'll be drinking it in no time, cheap shit or no. Remember, I'm the birthday boy, and what I say goes.

HOPEFULLY, she arrived soon, and I could show her just what I meant.

THE CLOCK STRUCK EIGHT, and as expected, the clusters of people arriving increased. With every group that showed, my hopes rose that it'd be Beth and her friends walking through the door. And with each disappointment, I drank more.

Some rich dude who went to Hawthorn Academy had offered me pills, *'to have a great night with,'* but I turned him down. I didn't need to add that shit to the high I was already on.

Although when I looked around me, it seemed other people hadn't turned him down.

Hands grabbed my waist, making me jump, and I flew around to see who dared to touch me.

But it was Jacobs standing there, looking smug that she'd startled me. Her smile curved up at the corners.

'Hello, handsome.'

'Hey,' I replied, grabbing her waist and pulling her close for a kiss. 'You look fucking hot, Jacobs.'

A flush crept onto her cheeks and more salacious thoughts flooded in with it. *Down, boy.*

'You look like a treat yourself.'

'A treat?' I asked, cocking an eyebrow at her choice of words before pulling her along with me to the dining table so she could get a drink.

'It was the first thing that came to me!' she said, defending her choice. 'Least it was original. You went with something everyone says.'

'Who else has been telling you that you look fucking hot, Jacobs?' I growled, looking around us as if the offending piece of shit would be standing right there in front of me.

'Oh, hush it up, caveman. I meant in general.' She waved me off and grabbed herself a red cup.

Before she leaned to grab a bottle of vodka, I brandished a bottle in her face and said, 'Here you go, your highness.'

'Huh?' Her expression was one of confusion until she saw what I'd scribbled on the bottle after her text. For *Jacobs only*. 'A bottle with my name on it. You do know how to treat a girl right.'

'Is that sarcasm I hear in your dulcet tones, dear?'

'You bet,' she said with a chuckle, her head tilting backwards, exposing her slim neck. 'Thanks.'

'No problem.'

The two of us moved back into the main room once Beth had mixed herself a drink, hiding her vodka behind a plant so others wouldn't find it.

My eyes surveyed the room, but I couldn't see Layla or Amber anywhere. Or Dean, for that matter.

Spencer and Tyler were standing with Remi over by the fireplace, in what looked to be a very heated conversation. *Not getting involved in that shitshow.*

Rock was dancing in the middle of the room with Savannah hanging off him.

I couldn't see Arianna or Ace, so maybe they were somewhere together, like the kitchen or outside. It hurt Ree to see Rock and Savannah together, even if she continued to deny it whenever asked. She was keeping tight-lipped about it, but we were best friends, and there was nothing she could get past me. Even if she thought she was doing a stellar job of covering up how she felt.

Talking of best friends…

'Where are your friends?' I asked Jacobs, tugging her as I flopped myself down on the sofa so she'd land on my lap. 'I didn't see you arrive, either. How'd you get away with that?'

'We came in the back,' she told me. 'Layla and Dean stayed in the kitchen with Alex and James. Amber went off to find Jaime.'

'You not wanna hang with them tonight?'

'Nah,' she said, a smile covering her face. 'I spent enough time with those losers last night. Anyway, it's the birthday boy I'd much rather spend time with.'

'Oh yeah? And what's the birthday boy like? I hear he's a bit of a wanker.'

'He's okay…' she trailed off, her smile growing wider as she wriggled on my lap, the friction it caused overwhelming my senses. 'He's funny, I suppose.'

'Okay? Funny?' I pinched her waist, leaning in to whisper in her ear, 'Don't remember those being the words you used to describe me last night.'

'Hmm… you may have to jog my memory. I seem to have forgotten.'

'Bullshit,' I swore. 'Just you wait…'

A glass smashing tore my attention away from Jacobs. Screaming and shouting broke out over by the fireplace and I was going to just ignore it, but then I remembered seeing Remi, Spencer, and Tyler standing there hissing words at one another and I knew I needed to go sort it out.

'Wait here,' I said to Beth, placing a soft kiss on her neck before moving her to the free spot on the sofa. 'I'll be right back.'

She nodded, and within moments I was throwing myself on Spencer to pull him away at the same time Rock got there and pulled Tyler back.

'What the fuck do you two think you're doing?' I shouted, shoving Spencer to stand next to me, ready to grab him again if he threw himself at Tyler.

'He started it!' Spencer spat, nodding at Tyler, who was shaking his head with anger.

'That's a fucking lie and you know it,' Ty seethed, narrowing his gaze at Spencer.

Remi was standing next to us, looking down at the ground, as if she'd rather be anywhere else. Something about her downcast eyes told me she was the reason the two were fighting.

Tyler and Spencer were tight. Their friendship was like mine and Ree's, and in all the years we'd known each other, they'd never fought about anything.

Especially something as insignificant as a girl.

Especially when the girl in question was *Remi Riley.*

Not that I disliked Remi. Never really had much to do with her, to be honest. If there was one thing I knew, though, it was that both Tyler and Spencer couldn't stand her. It was one of the things they bonded over, them both hating the same girl.

Tyler hated her because of what she did to his sister.

Spencer hated her because of who was related to her.

'You guys don't fight,' Rock said, looking between the two of them. 'So what's got into you now?'

'Spencer was just telling me what he thought of me, that's all,' Remi said, her voice a low whisper. 'It was nothing.'

'*Remi,*' Tyler growled, and she blinked up at him.

'It was nothing,' she repeated. 'I'll see you later.'

She moved off to another part of the house and left the four of us standing there, two of us confused.

'You gonna tell us the truth?' I said, wondering who'd crack first, but neither of them was playing ball. Tyler scuffed the floor, and Spencer crossed his arms across his broad chest.

'It's like Remi said,' Spencer muttered, glaring at his best friend. 'I told her something she didn't like, and Tyler apparently didn't like it either.'

Tyler didn't reply.

'Go party,' I commanded. 'I don't need my night ruined because of bullshit between you two.'

They both nodded gruffly, and Tyler left in the opposite direction Remi went in.

'Now, if you've stopped needing to be treated like a child, I'm off to spend time with my girl.'

Rock and Spencer nodded at me, and I turned around, my eyes locking with Beth's, who was still sitting where I left her, chatting with Amber and a pink-haired girl about something that amused them all as they broke out into a cacophony of cackles as I approached.

'What's so funny?' I lifted Beth off the sofa and sat down again, placing her back on my lap in the spot we should've been in the whole time.

'Amber was just being a bitch about Remi,' Beth said, leaning back on my chest to get comfortable. 'Usual girl stuff.'

'I won't ask for more details, then.'

'Best not to.' She half-turned so our faces were almost level. 'Wanna dance?'

'Dance?'

'Yes. Dance. Why you making it sound like a dirty word?'

'Just didn't expect you to want to dance, Jacobs.'

'Well, I do. You coming?'

'Nope. I think I'll get a much better view right here.'

'Sit and mope with your vodka, Gray,' Amber said, leaning forward to look at me around the girl next to her. 'We're gonna go party.'

'You don't mind, do you?' Beth's whisper was only for me, but I shook my head, letting her know I didn't mind if she wanted to dance with her friends.

I wasn't lying when I said I'd prefer to watch the show.

'You're the best!' She kissed my cheek and bounced off my lap, going to join Amber and her friend on the makeshift dance floor, which was really just the centre of the stupidly large living room. Layla joined them a moment later, and Dean came to sit next to me.

'Happy birthday, Grayson.' He handed me a beer, and I took it, surprised at the gesture.

'Thanks, man.'

'No problem.'

'You about to do that *if you hurt her* shtick?'

'What makes you think I'd do that?'

I raised an eyebrow, and he laughed, rubbing his jaw with his pointer finger.

'You're right. I was one hundred percent about to do that.'

'Saw right through you, mate.' I drank some of the beer, waiting to see if he'd say anything more, but when he stayed silent, I egged him on. 'Come on. Out with it. Say whatever it was you sat down to say.'

'Beth's special,' he said, and I grunted my agreement. 'And she may talk a big game and act like she's the type of girl who flirts with everyone, but she isn't. She wears her heart on her sleeve and everybody knows it. You can see her feelings on her face in a heartbeat.'

'I know that,' I said with a small shrug. 'Doesn't really bother me.'

'It should,' he said, his tone a shade darker. 'Because no matter what, whether she acts like she's game for a quick hook-up or not, it'd break her heart if you did that to her.'

'What makes you think I'd do that to her?'

'I don't know, Gray. Maybe the way you've acted for the last five years with girls at school and at the field is what's making me doubt your motives.'

'I like the girl. S'not a crime, is it?'

'No,' he agreed. 'Unless you have no intention of keeping her around for more than a few parties.'

'For somebody who believes Beth's special, you don't seem to have much faith in her judgement. Or that somebody like me wants to be with her for more than sex or a hook-up.'

'I—'

'Save it.' My eyes didn't turn to him as they kept focus on Jacobs, who was dancing with Amber and Layla, shaking her hips and shouting along to the lyrics at the top of her lungs. A smile played on my lips, joy finding me in my drunken haze at how happy she looked. Catching my eye, she turned to me and shimmied in my direction, a bark of laughter leaving my lips when she did it again. 'Look, Dean. I'm gonna level with you.'

'Go for it,' he said with a chuckle. 'Let me have it.'

'I'm serious when I say I like her. And when I say like her, I mean more than just a random hook-up or some girl who gives me head at a party or whatever. She's funny, with a wicked sense of humour, and she keeps me on my toes. She listens to me and we talk, ya know?' He nodded, and I continued, 'It means something to me. And I think she feels the same.'

'She does,' he said, taking a swig of his beer. 'That's why I wanted to make sure she wasn't barking up the wrong tree, so to speak.'

'She can bark up my tree anytime.'

We both broke out into laughter at that, and all three of the girls dancing turned their heads to see what the two of us found so funny.

'In the short time I've known her, I've learned that Beth Jacobs is as pure as they come. She's kind, and she has a good heart. Just don't punch it into a pulp, okay?'

'Message received, loud and clear.'

The two of us clinked our bottles together, a silent *cheers* between us, and both took a sip at the same time, a smile playing on our lips. The moment was brief, but it made me remember our friendship as kids, and that maybe I hadn't fucked it up as bad as I thought.

Ten

Beth

I DANCED with the girls for what felt like the entire night but was probably an hour max.

'Gray hasn't taken his eyes off you the whole time,' Layla said as she danced next to me, her smile smug.

'Dean hasn't taken his eyes off you, either,' I said. The two of them still sat next to each other, sipping from their beer bottles and saying the odd sentence when something amused them. 'You've got him wrapped around your little finger.'

'Something like that,' she said, the smile reaching her eyes. Every time I saw her eyes smile like that, my heart soared. Seeing Layla happy made me happy, simple as that. 'He's coming over here.'

'Huh?'

'Gray. He's coming over.'

I swallowed as his hands gripped my hips, his front coming flush to my back, his tongue darting out to graze the outer shell of my ear.

'You look good enough to eat, Jacobs,' he said, his teeth taking a small bite on my neck to drive home his point. 'And I think I'd like to do just that.'

'Are you asking to eat me, Gray?' I turned in his hands, tilting my head so my face was looking at his. My height meant I was always looking up at him. One day, one of us was going to have permanent pain in the neck from trying to look into one another's eyes.

'I'm asking you to come upstairs with me.'

The question in his gaze made my heart flutter, and I gulped, my mouth drier than the Sahara.

'Where to?'

'There's a guest bedroom,' he whispered, his tone alone making me wet. 'Come with me.'

The double meaning wasn't lost on me.

'Lead the way,' I said, turning to give Layla a look that said, *don't you dare ruin this for me.*

She nodded, gave a small little wave, and said, 'Message me later, yeah?'

'Will do.'

'Don't do something I wouldn't do.' *Translation: don't have sex with him.*

'I'll speak to you later, Mum.'

She laughed as Gray took my hand and we walked away from the centre of the room to the entrance hall, then up the sweeping staircase that led to the upper level of the mansion. It was a lot bigger than my new house, let alone the house I used to live in. That shit heap could fit at least five times within the Hollowdales' mansion.

Gray took me down a corridor on the right, a route he knew well. He'd mentioned that he grew up here, so it made sense he knew where to go.

He pushed a couple of people out of the way who were lingering in the hallway, and a couple that were making out further up the corridor slipped into the room they were standing beside before I could make out who it was.

'In here,' Gray said, opening a door and surveying the area first to make sure the coast was clear. 'This is the room I always stay in here.'

'It's… by God, it's hideous.'

He laughed, ignoring me. 'Get on the bed, Jacobs,' he whispered in my ear. 'I've wanted you all night. That dancing you did got me hot and bothered, and I need you to play nice.'

'I always play nice,' I sassed back.

He led me further into the guest bedroom, and I laughed when I saw the interior of the room he'd taken me to.

'Jesus, Gray. This room looks like Valentine's Day vomited all over it.'

'Rock's mum has questionable taste,' he said, placing a fevered kiss on my neck, the scent of vodka lingering on his breath. 'In both room décor and men.'

I didn't ask what he meant by that. I could only assume that Arianna's dad wasn't much of a delight.

The closer we got to the bed, the more my nerves spiked, my blood boiling with need.

Grayson wrapped me up in his arms, and with a gentle touch, he laid me down on the large double bed that occupied the entire left wall.

He remained standing, a slight sway in his actions from the alcohol coursing through his veins, perusing my body from head to toe.

'I can't think about anything else,' he whispered, a quiet admission. 'All I've wanted since that first night together in the tent is you, naked and writhing beneath me. Your body mine for the taking.'

'Then take me,' I said, feeling a boldness in the darkness of the room I'd never felt before. In the tent, the night consumed us —as did the urge to touch each other—and in that guest bedroom, it was even more heightened. 'I'm yours.'

'Are you sure?' Gray asked, his eyebrows furrowing together, his eyes thrilled. 'We don't have to if you're not ready. I know you're a virgin.'

Of course he knew I was a virgin. Who didn't? Most people looking at me, or those learning I was a huge science nerd, guessed it.

'I want to. I've wanted to for a while.'

'Yeah?'

'Fuck yeah,' I hushed out. And just like that, the invisible leash that was holding Gray back from devouring me disappeared. He leaned down, his lips sweeping across mine, and my stomach swooped, a million butterflies dancing around in there.

'I'll be gentle,' Gray said. 'You can trust me on that, Jacobs. I've got you.'

'I do trust you. If I didn't, I wouldn't be here.'

The thumping bass of the party outside the room, the screeching of drunk teenagers, all of it just added to how I was feeling. Even though those other sounds were audible to us, it was as if we were the only people in the house in my head. Our heavy breathing filled the space and my toes curled. All of it was so much *more* than I thought it would be.

Grayson trailed kisses up and down my neck until he was behind my ear. A shiver ran through me, the spot where he kissed sending my brain into overdrive.

'Lie down, Jacobs,' he said, his lips grazing my ear, the smile on his face audible in his voice. Without a word, I obeyed his command. Everything about what was happening was a dream come to life. A dirty dream I'd had most nights since meeting Grayson Smith.

My mouth was so dry that I was gulping down air in a desperate attempt to keep myself from losing control. From losing my cool in front of him.

'I've got you,' he whispered, his fingers trailing a scorching path up and down my ribcage. 'Breathe, Jacobs.'

'I'm trying,' I told him. 'Don't exactly wanna pass out on you, Gray.'

'Good.'

That one word held such promise.

'I need to get you naked,' Gray said before going back to kissing my neck. 'Need to see all of you.'

The kisses were soft, and with each kiss he placed on my neck, a shiver travelled down my spine, causing my thighs to clench together. I was so wet for him that my cheeks flushed at the thought he'd judge me. That I was an embarrassment for being *too* aroused. Was that even a thing?

I didn't know for definite, but my breathing picked up speed, my nerves all-consuming.

Gray's hand grabbed mine, softly pulling me into a sitting position. He took the bottom of my dress and raised it higher until it was off my head, my body bared to him. A matching lace underwear set covered my assets. It was a set I'd got on a recent shopping trip with Layla. I think even when I got the set, I knew when and why I'd be wearing it.

Who I'd be wearing it for.

While placing soft kisses on my lips, my neck, my collarbone, Gray unclasped the hooks of my bra and slowly removed it until my tits were bare to him, my nipples peaked and hard.

Grayson kneeled on the bed beside me and smiled wolfishly in the dim light.

'Lift your hips, Jacobs.'

The demand had me raising my hips in an instant, no doubt or hesitation in my mind. With each minute, my nerves trickled away. Left me and disappeared into the nether.

I sucked in a breath as the cool air hit me when he removed my underwear, and I was completely naked under his touch while he was still fully clothed.

'You are exquisite, Jacobs.'

Lust flashed in his eyes, clear for me to see, and I knew my own were shining back at him with the same emotion.

My flushed skin prickled as his wandering fingertips traced from my collarbone, down my chest, a whooshing feeling in my stomach the lower his hand went until he stopped at the apex of my thighs.

Oh my. I'm letting it happen. I'm going to let him take my V-card.

'You smell divine.'

He moved backwards to stand in order to take off his T-shirt in that hot guy way they do in films. That whole one arm over the head thing I'd never seen in person but could now confirm was as hot as I thought it'd be.

Then he moved to remove his jeans, his devilish gaze locking with mine, and a soft smile played on his lips.

Standing in his black boxers and nothing else, I perused his body in the same way he'd perused mine. Taking him all in.

There were some fading bruises on his arms and his chest, but I didn't ask about them. I could ask another time. Things were heating up, and I didn't want to douse us with cold water by asking about something too real. Too serious.

I could see a faint outline of his dick in his boxers, and I swallowed. I knew what he was packing in there and the thought of it inside me made my mouth water.

Slowly, knowing my eyes were on him, he freed himself from his boxers and a soft moan left me.

'You okay over there, Jacobs?'

'Get your arse here now,' I said, my voice a thin rasp.

He obeyed my demand and came back to the bed. I moved into the centre more, oh so ready for what was to come.

Tingles covered my body, his soft fingers grabbing my hips as he moved his body so he was kneeling between my legs before his body came down to blanket mine.

A wolfish grin. A sinful smile.

His lips dropped to mine in the sweetest kiss. Lingering. Filled with lust, but also somehow pure, too.

Gray's hands dusted up my waist, his thumbs brushing against my ribs, causing butterflies to swarm my stomach as his cock brushed my entrance.

My body recoiled. I braced myself, preparing myself mentally for the precipice I was about to jump off.

The cliff I was teetering on.

Grayson being the person who would take me over. Take me under. Take me with him.

My eyes fluttered closed, the sensations taking me over. The buzz of the party fading away into nothingness. The room was devoid of noise, other than our heavy breathing. Small pants left my lips every time Gray's hands trailed on my hip bones or his lips touched my neck, my collarbone, my nipples.

'Open your eyes, baby,' he whispered, the use of the nickname stopping breath from entering my lungs. 'You have the most beautiful eyes.'

My eyes snapped open, looking into the ones focused on me. Finally, after his teasing fingers had once again returned to my hip bone, they moved lower.

A small gasp left my lips as his thumb teased over my clit. One of his fingers entered me, and I was lost in the sensations.

He added a second finger, pumping in and out in a slow movement, and I thought I would die from the flame engulfing me.

'Are you sure?' he asked again, locking his eyes with mine, his fingers still lazily moving in and out. I nodded, the words I wanted to say stuck in my throat.

He removed his fingers, and then it was the head of his cock breaching my entrance, inch by inch. Taking his time, he slid into me, stopping when he met my inner resistance.

His body came down and fully covered mine, our foreheads touching, as he made one last push into me, snapping that tether to who I once was.

Pain ripped through me, my eyes filling with tears at the sharp sensation, and for the longest time, it didn't ease.

Shit. Shit. Double shit.

At that moment, it felt as if it would never get better. Never soften.

But then, slowly, it did.

'Breathe,' he whispered against my lips, our foreheads still pushed together, neither one of us wanting to break the connection. 'Just breathe, baby.'

I caught his lips with mine, giving him a deep kiss, sweeping my tongue with his. He still hadn't moved, letting me adjust to the feel of him stretching me. The pain had faded into a delicious burn. Still there, but less intense.

After a minute, Grayson rolled his hips, a carnal smile twisting his lips as he sank deeper into me, fully seating himself inside of me.

'You're perfect to me, Jacobs,' Gray whispered, and I glowed from the praise. From the reverence in his tone; the admiration in his eyes.

Tears leaked from mine, both from his words and his actions, no doubt leaving a trail down my cheeks and ruining my mascara.

His hand reached around my waist so he could lift my leg and lock it around his hip. The position had me taking him deeper, and it made my eyes roll back in my head. *Fuck. Fuck. Fuck.*

Gray's moans and my soft whimpers filled the room, both of us completely forgetting about the party that raged on outside. I hoped there was a lock on the door, but at that moment, I didn't even care. We were too far gone for it to matter.

Hurtling off the cliff. Free-falling into oblivion.

His teeth grazed my shoulder, and I clenched around him as he growled, 'You realise, Jacobs, that this makes you mine.'

'I'm yours,' I whispered, the words coming before my brain caught up. 'And I just hope *you* realise you're mine.'

I meant every word. Every part of my being was his, and he was mine.

The two of us had met at the start of term for a reason. He had chosen me as his science tutor because the universe had dictated it to be so.

My words lit a match inside of him. His hips picked up the pace as his thrusts became more demanding. Like he couldn't hold himself back any longer. The pain had mostly subsided, and all I could feel was pleasure zipping through every nerve ending.

His hold on me grew tighter, both of us getting closer to

release. The sound of our bodies coming together was more than I could bear. Everything about it was more than I'd hoped for my first time.

I was glad my first time wasn't going to be a horror story told years down the line with friends over wine.

My toes curled as his cock kept hitting the spot that made me whimper.

'Gray,' I moaned.

My hips bucked, and I tried to control my body as it shook, an orgasm so close I could taste it on my tongue.

Then it hit.

Euphoria seeped into my veins. My blood. Everything became a blur, my eyes struggling to stay open as my body pulsed. In my chest, my heart hammered, and I could've sworn that Gray could hear it, too.

Our eyes locked. An emotion played out on his face I couldn't place. A soft, dazed smile. His eyes were at half-mast.

He growled at my expression, his movements getting jerky as he pumped into me before coming inside of me.

'Fuck, Jacobs.'

Fuck was definitely the right word.

I just had sex with Grayson Smith, and no part of me regretted it at all.

Eleven

Grayson

I woke up the morning after my party with a banging headache.

Fuck. I'd overdone it, that was for sure.

My eyes blinked, trying to block the harsh sunlight filtering in through the window, and I assessed my surroundings. It wasn't my bedroom.

A bright red lamp sat on the bedside table. *Ah.* I was still at Arianna's house, in the guest bedroom that Rock's mum had decorated when they moved in and she was going through a lovestruck phase and everything was a shade of red or pale pink.

Pretty gaudy if you asked me.

Next to the lamp, there was a glass of water and some pills, and I thanked the heavens for Arianna and her ability to know what I needed before I even realised it myself.

The bed was empty aside from me, but the scent of perfume lingered in the air—and a soft underlying hint of cherry filled my senses and made my head swim.

There was only one person who made that happen; whose mere presence was enough to set my thoughts racing with bull-shit that didn't revolve solely around lust.

And she was missing from the bed as if she'd never been in it at all, even though my hazed memories told me she had been at one point.

Maybe her lingering scent in the room explained my dream.

It was a fucking stellar dream. Jacobs was writhing beneath me, naked, and I was having my wicked way with her.

'YOU'RE PERFECT TO ME, JACOBS.' The words tumbled from my lips, and I watched her preen underneath me from my praise. She glowed with it in the dim light, her smile something otherworldly, blinding me.

Tears spilled from them, trailing down her face, a sign of the emotion stirred up inside.

Her leg was in my hand, then locked around my waist, so I could feel her even deeper than before.

Why the fuck was this a dream? The scent of her overwhelmed me and I moaned. Her soft whimpers filled the room.

We were one. Hurtling off the cliff. Free-falling into oblivion.

My teeth bit lightly into her shoulder.

I growled, 'You realise, Jacobs, that this makes you mine.'

'I'm yours,' she said, the words echoing in my brain. 'And you're mine.'

FUCK. Even just thinking about the dream was too much. Precum leaked from the tip of my dick, and I was one moment from heading to the guest room bathroom to *sort the problem* when a knock came on the door and Ree stormed in, her face one of a thunderstorm on a dark, miserable night.

'What do you think you're playing at, Gray?' she spat, lobbing something at my head.

'Huh?'

'Don't play dumb with me, dickhead. I know you, remember?' The words were friendly—the tone, not so much.

'This time, I'm not even playing dumb. I am dumb. I've got no idea what you're chatting about.'

'You had sex with her?'

'No?'

'Gray, I saw you come upstairs with her!'

'And as you can see, Ree, she's not here, so at some point since you saw us come up here and now, she left.'

'But I—' Ree started, but I stopped her from going further. She already thought I'd fucked Jacobs and was pissed about it, and I didn't have the strength to listen to whatever crap she wanted to sling at me.

'But you what?' I goaded her, irritation growing within me. 'Ree, I'm too hungover for this. Can we talk about it later?'

'You bet your arse we're gonna talk about this later,' she mumbled, catching the despair on my face for the first time. 'What's up?'

'I just told you, I'm hungover af.'

'There's something else.' She came closer and cushioned herself at the end of the bed between the wall and me. 'Tell me what's going on.'

'My dad and I got into a fight yesterday.'

'Oh,' she said, uncertain, her voice small. 'What happened?'

'The usual. I did or said something he didn't like. You know how he is.'

She nodded, turning away to glance around the room, wincing at how bad the décor was.

'Gigi really did a number on this room, didn't she? I feel like I'm in some bad tunnel of love at a travelling carnival.'

'It's bad,' I agreed. 'And why is there a cherub figurine creeping at the top of the wardrobe?'

Arianna shivered, mumbling, 'This entire room gives me the creeps.'

Deep down, I knew she was creating a distraction for us both, to get us off the topic of my dad and the argument that took place only an hour before I left to come to my party.

'Where do you think you're going, Son?' my dad grumbled from the edge of the sofa in the same spot he'd landed the night before when he stumbled through the door. Empty beer cans surrounded him, alongside

open bags of nachos and dips, and I knew from his position that he had no intention of moving for the evening.

'Out,' I bit out, not giving an inch. Bet the stupid, useless fuck didn't even know it was my birthday. Why would he? Not like that day meant anything to him.

Other than it being the day his greatest disappointment entered the universe.

'Don't get smart with me, boy,' he growled, his small, beady eyes locking with mine, his anger palpable across the room. At least he was too hammered to stand. But the thing about my dad? He could make you feel smaller than an ant with words—no fists required.

'I thought you told me I'm not smart?'

'You're not. You're a low-life piece of scum who'll never amount to anything.'

'Says the man who smells like he hasn't moved from that spot in twenty-four hours.'

'I've made something of myself, Grayson.' My dad was even more deluded than I thought. The man had nothing to show for his pitiful life. Nothing of merit.

We lived in a small home on the Hollowdale estate. Had done ever since I was born. Dad's job didn't mean shit to me, to the point where I couldn't even tell you what he did. He worked in an office; I knew that much. Something to do with selling insurance.

No matter what it was, nobody would regard it as 'making something of yourself'.

'You keep telling yourself that,' I replied, grabbing my jacket off the hook and making my way to the front door. Not a care in the world.

'You listen here,' my dad shouted, sweeping the bags from his lap and standing to face me. 'Just because my life doesn't look like something you approve of, it doesn't mean I'm not happy with it. But you. You've been a stain on my soul since the day you were conceived. Why else would your mother have left? She left because of you, Grayson. Because you weren't enough for her to stay.'

'That's not true.'

'Got no proof of that, though, do ya?' A flicker of emotion zapped

me, and my dad saw it on my face. His smile became even more sinister, all bared teeth and curved lips. 'You begged her to stay the day she told you she was leavin'. And you know what she said, boy?'

'Enlighten me,' I said, a bravado I didn't feel.

'She told you she couldn't. There you were, standing in front of her, wide eyes and tears pouring down your cheeks, holding your stuffed bear, and she couldn't even stay for you. You asked her if she'd stay for you. Your bitch of a mother said, "No, my darling. Not even for you."'

'You're lying!' I growled, my anger at that day long forgotten, once again bubbling to the surface. A red haze consumed me. 'That's not what happened.'

'Isn't it?' He smirked, oozing cockiness. 'Because that's how I remember it and I was grown enough to see the truth.'

Memories swirled. My mum's face that day, seen through the tears of an innocent, looming at the edges of my mind. Her bright blue eyes. Her dark brown hair reaching her chin, and her wide lipstick covered smile.

My dad was poisoning me. Doing all he could to make me doubt myself. Doubt my memories.

Doubt the truth.

And fuck me, it was working.

Without another word, I opened the door, stepped out into the cool February breeze, and slammed it behind me, wishing I could slam the world out as effectively as the closing of the door.

There was only one thing for me to do.

Time to celebrate my birthday in style and get royally fucked up.

'…LAST NIGHT?'

'Huh?' I zoned back into the room, the bright red of the duvet cover reminding me where I was and why.

'Do you know why Spencer and Tyler were fighting last night?' she asked, and I thanked her internally for the change of subject—and for not asking me where my mind went as I stared gormless at the wall.

'Something to do with Remi, I gathered. Seemed pretty heated.'

'Odd,' Ree said, rubbing her chin with her pointer finger. 'The two of them don't like her in equal measure, so fuck knows why the two of them were fighting over her.'

'Don't think it was *over* her. Think it was something Spencer said to her that Tyler didn't agree with.'

'Fair enough. You and Rock broke it up, I heard?'

'Yeah, where were you? I looked but couldn't see you for most of the night.'

'Oh. I was in the garden with Ace.'

'That all I get?'

'Huh?' She snapped her gaze to mine, lost in her thoughts the way I'd been a moment before.

'Very vague, even for you.'

'It was nothing.' She shrugged, and I took the cue not to prod around anymore about her night. She'd tell me in time if she wanted to. 'So, what're we gonna do today?'

'Let's order in a pizza and play video games. Invite the other pricks over. We'll make a day of it.'

She nodded, raising her hand to salute me, and said, 'Ay, ay, captain!'

The red pillow beside me was in my hand in a moment, and I laughed at the shocked expression on her face when she spotted it coming towards her.

Sometimes, all you needed was a laugh with your best friend to get your head screwed on straight again.

Twelve

Beth

Four Weeks Later

LAYLA and I were chilling in her bedroom, eating sweets and watching some film about a woman who gets pregnant but doesn't know who the father is.

The film was a popular one, the third in a series, Layla had told me when she put it on. I just nodded and let her, not wanting to fight for an old Hollywood film so early on a weekend morning.

'I've never understood how people don't know they're pregnant,' Layla said, musing over the thought before taking a rather vicious bite out of the biscuit in her hand, crumbs trailing from her mouth to her white T-shirt. Her next words were mumbled, swallowing the last of her food, as she brushed the crumbs away. 'You know, like women who give birth on the toilet because they didn't know?'

I nodded—it had always confused me, too. Or like when a character in a film or book didn't notice that their period was late or…

Balls.

My period was late. Or was it? I always struggled with keeping track of it, even with an app on my phone. I always ended up forgetting to mark the start or end day on the app, skewing the data, so it wasn't valid.

Her big brown eyes caught mine, her smile dipping when she registered the look of alarm on my face.

'You okay?' she asked. 'You've gone mighty pale.'

'I was just thinking… About missed periods and pregnancy scares and shit like that.' I swallowed, trying to do the maths in my head but failing. How long ago was the party? Three weeks? Maybe four?

Eurgh. Why was my brain struggling so hard with it? Maths and science were its forte. The thing it knew above all else. Facts and data. No way for it to be wrong.

My knee jiggled, my nerves heightened, all the negative thoughts swirling in my head, fighting for dominance.

'Beth,' Layla said. 'Is there something you're not telling me?'

I bristled. I'd never told Layla what happened between me and Gray at his birthday party. By opening up about it, telling her about it, the memory wouldn't be solely mine anymore. It would live in her mind, too, and I hadn't wanted that. Had wanted me and Gray to be the only two who knew—in cahoots with our own little secret.

Even if he'd never said shit to me about it afterwards and pretended it never escalated as far as it did.

'Maybe?' I blew out a breath. 'So Grayson and I had sex.'

'You did?' she whispered, hurt lacing her voice. 'When?'

'His birthday.'

'You came to mine straight from his and you never told me,' she said, her eyes—like her voice—an accusation. Then her eyes cleared as if she remembered how we got to the conversation in the first place, and her hurt took the back seat. 'Did you use protection?'

I shrugged, knowing we didn't, but too embarrassed to admit that to her. I didn't want her to judge me for my stupid, reckless decision.

'I've got a test in my bathroom,' she said, pointing to the door that led to her en suite. 'If you want to take it?'

'I suppose it can't hurt, right?'

'Right,' she affirmed, nodding with enthusiasm.

PREGNANT?

How could I be pregnant?

Okay, stupid question, Beth. I knew how I could be pregnant, but it didn't change my disbelief at the situation. At *my* situation.

Layla was sitting outside the bathroom door, waiting for me, and I didn't want to disappoint her. When she suggested I take a test, I jumped straight on it, believing that I wasn't, so it wouldn't matter if I did. How wrong I was.

The thought of leaving the bathroom and looking her in the eye, telling her I was pregnant, filled me with dread.

Not that she would judge me in that way, but I knew her opinion of Grayson. It wasn't something she—or Dean—kept secret.

Plus, Layla and I had been through so much together. She was my ride or die. My best friend since the beginning of time, or so it felt like. I didn't want to let her down. Disappoint her.

'Let me see!' she called through the door, her voice so close I knew she was standing with her face up against the door itself. 'Are you okay in there?'

'Yeah,' I said, disguising my feelings in a happy and overly jovial tone. 'I'll be out in a moment. Just overwhelmed.'

'That's understandable. And no matter what the test says, we'll get through this the way we always do. Together.'

Even though I couldn't see her through the door, I knew she was nodding, contemplating everything.

I stayed silent for another minute, wondering how long I could stay in there without Layla becoming too suspicious.

'Are you sure you're okay?' she asked again, the worry creeping in. I needed to get myself together and get out there to her. To physically show her I was okay.

'I promise I'm good. I'll be out in a moment.'

My eyes hadn't left the test. Those two lines got darker by the second, like little lines of doom, making me question my very existence.

There was a human growing inside of me. A little, tiny being yet to fully form that I could feel a pull towards while also not wanting to think that way. I needed to go home. I needed to lock myself in my bedroom, put on an old black-and-white classic movie, and overthink for at least five hours. Minimum.

'So… Is it positive?' her voice asked, tentative, scared to hear the answer.

'No,' I said, knowing the only reason I could lie to her was because there was a slab of wood between us. I shouldn't have lied to her. She didn't deserve that from me. But the word left my mouth before my brain had thought it through.

Quickly, I put the test into the pocket of my hoodie, washed my hands, then stepped out of the bathroom to face Layla.

When I opened the door, Layla had to take a quick step back. I knew she'd had her face flush to the door, and I gave a little laugh at how well I knew her and her predictable behaviour.

'I'm gonna take the test and dispose of it on the way home so your parents don't start asking any funky questions.'

'If you don't mind,' she said, biting her bottom lip, her blue eyes glowing. 'So… I've got something to tell you.'

I blinked, walking back over to sit on Layla's bed, getting myself comfortable.

Already Layla had distracted herself, and I wouldn't bring her attention back to me and my woes. No part of me wanted her to ask to see the test.

She came and sat opposite me, crossing her legs under her body.

Our eyes locked, and I knew instantly what she wanted to tell me.

'You didn't?' I asked with a gasp. 'When?'

'After the field party on Friday. We camped out with a group of people.'

'I thought you didn't like the Rebels?'

'Oh, well, Dean's been talking to them recently.'

I was surprised that I'd missed that. Had I been so caught up in Gray that I ignored what everyone else was doing?

Maybe.

My mind wandered back to the night I lost my virginity, but then I remembered we made a child that night.

Shit. I needed a distraction, and fast.

'Tell me more!' I told her, waiting for her to spill the tea. The excitement was oozing from her in waves and it hit me she'd been waiting all day to tell me before we got distracted by my shit. 'How was it? Worth the wait?'

'One hundred percent,' she said, grinning from ear to ear. 'It was everything I hoped it would be and more. It was really special. And I just knew Dean was the right guy, you know?'

I nodded, although I couldn't exactly relate.

Grayson wasn't 'the one'. He never mentioned that night, and if he did, he acted like the sex part of it never took place. Maybe I shouldn't have bailed before he woke up, but I just couldn't deal with facing him so soon afterwards. And after that, it just never got brought up.

The two of us went back to hanging out at the field on Friday nights and spending time together in the science labs. We messaged each other most nights and had even started watching some classic Hollywood movies on a Saturday night.

We'd even made out and hooked up in the tent since, but we never went past foreplay. Never got close to having sex again.

I wondered if he regretted it or thought he'd pushed me too

fast and was staying quiet in case I regretted it too. It was all a massive clusterfuck, that was for sure.

'Makes me wish I hadn't held out on as long as I did,' she said with a laugh.

'You had your reasons. Valid reasons,' I stressed, not wanting her to second-guess or doubt her decision. It was something I always admired about Layla. She stuck to her gut feeling, never letting anybody sway her, no matter what.

'Oh, for sure,' she agreed. 'And honestly, I'm glad. It meant we knew each other inside and out. There was trust there. Love.'

Even though she wasn't outright saying her words were aimed at me, each one felt like a thin slice of an extra sharp knife.

My experience with Grayson was so far removed from the one she was describing and the judgement sat thick and heavy in the air between us.

I squirmed, and my discomfort must have been plastered plainly across my face because she rushed to correct herself.

'Oh, no, Beth. I don't mean anything like that.' She reached out and squeezed my ankle. 'Let's just be thankful you don't have a reminder due in eight months' time.'

Her laughter trickled through me, settling on my skin like a second layer of slime and filth.

'Super thankful,' I murmured. 'As much as I'd love to hear all the details, I really should head out. Cara will be home from work soon and it's my turn to cook.'

'You sure? I thought you'd want to discuss every detail.' Layla's face fell and my guilt grew. My actions were very unlike me, but it was as if somebody else was in the driver's seat and I was a mere bystander.

'I want to know everything, I promise. How about one night after school this week?'

'Sounds like a plan! Hope you have a good night.'

'You got any plans?'

'Think I'm heading to Dean's later.'

'Fair. Use protection,' I joked, making my way to her bedroom door. Even though no part of me was joking.

'Duh,' she said. 'Your scare earlier is the only scare I need for a very long time.'

'For sure, let me be a lesson to you,' I said, opening the door. 'I'll let myself out.'

'Cool beans. Let me know when you get home.'

I nodded and left the room. Thank fuck, I was finally alone. My feet carried me home as fast as they could muster.

The sanctity of my bedroom called to me.

I needed to be alone with my thoughts.

And try to figure out what the fuck I should do.

I LOOKED DOWN at the grade at the top of the piece of paper in front of me and winced.

Even though I studied as hard as I could, it clearly wasn't hard enough, because the mock test in front of me had a big failing grade at the top.

Jacobs was gonna be pissed.

'Er, sir?' I called out, louder than I needed to, seeing as I was the only student in the classroom. 'This can't be right.'

'I assure you it is, Grayson,' he said at a normal level, tenting his fingertips together underneath his chin. 'It's an improvement on your last score, yes, but it isn't high enough. I hoped having Beth as a tutor would help, but maybe I was wrong.'

'It has nothing to do with her,' I replied, snapping at him. 'She's been great.'

'Nonetheless, you don't seem to have retained much of her teachings.'

'When's my next mock?' I asked, rifling through dates in my head, wondering just how much time I had left to turn shit around. Recently, Beth was acting a lot more sombre than usual, and I didn't know why. Anytime I asked, she brushed me aside, not telling me shit.

Suppose I deserved it.

Ever since my birthday party, things were strained between

us. Not that memories of my birthday were clear to me. They were hazy and blurred. What the fuck even happened that night?

Maybe Arianna would tell me if I asked.

She always looked out for me, especially when alcohol was involved.

'... next one, I won't be so lenient.'

'Can I go now?'

'Remember what I've said, Grayson.'

'Yeah, yeah!' I said over my shoulder, shoving the test into my bag as I headed out the door and slammed chest first into Beth, who was coming into the room.

'Hey!' she squealed, bouncing backwards. 'Just the person I was coming to see.'

'Yeah?' I cocked an eyebrow and leaned against the door-frame of the room, blocking her from entering just in case Mr Taylor wanted to spill the beans about my results before I could tell her.

She nodded, tilting her neck up so she could take in my face fully. Jacobs was so petite that her head was level with my chest, and it was one of the things that made her seem like a little pixie to me. Hope filled her big brown eyes. A hope I would dash when I told her about my grade. Maybe I could keep it to myself a little longer…

'You want to get out of here?' I asked, placing my hand around her waist and turning her around to walk down the corridor with me. She fell into step beside me, not even trying to detach herself from me. A smile broke on my face, but I covered it before she saw. Didn't want her to act funky again.

'Where we going?'

'To the cafe? Can grab some toffee cheesecake or something else sweet?'

'Grayson Smith,' she reprimanded. 'Are you trying to distract me with sweet treats so I don't ask about your science test?'

'What's the correct answer to that?' I coughed and her responding laugh shot straight to my dick.

'Come on,' she said, leaning into my side. 'But you're buying!'

♡

THE LARGE SLICE of cheesecake on her plate had gone mostly untouched for the last hour, and that was one of the biggest red flags.

She twizzled her fork, picking at the food, raising her eyebrow at me.

The conversation was stilted at best. We'd exhausted talk of the weekend, our studies, what we'd eaten for lunch, and the only thing left on the agenda was for me to tell her the truth about my grade for the science test.

'You gonna tell me why you've been acting so funky for the last couple weeks?'

'I haven't been acting "funky" at all. I've just got a lot going on, that's all.'

'Wanna tell me about it?'

'Not really,' she mumbled, still twiddling the fork in the cheesecake. 'What I want is for you to tell me what grade you got on the mock test.'

She looked up from her plate and locked her narrowed eyes with mine.

'So…' I started, realising I couldn't push it off any longer. She was going to find out at some point, so I may as well be the one to tell her. 'I failed.'

'Failed? Define the word failed.'

'So out of the thirty questions on the test, I answered maybe five correctly.'

'Five?' she asked, the first wave of emotion I'd seen in days covering her face. 'How could you have only answered five right?'

'Well, I was a little distracted.'

'Distracted how?'

'You've been avoiding me!' I raised my voice, coughing to cover it when I saw a couple of older ladies at the table next to us turn their heads in alarm. 'And I've no idea why. I've been going over shit in my head for days and I can't figure it out. So yeah. My mind hasn't exactly been on the periodic table.'

'Oh.'

'Yes. Oh.' My lips turned up into a small smile, but hers stayed flat and unimpressed. 'You're all I can think about, Jacobs.'

'I'm flattered,' she said in a tone that told me she felt the complete opposite. 'But thinking about me won't get you into university.'

It was matter-of-fact. No underlying banter or hint of a joke. And it only made me worry about her more. There was something she wasn't telling me. Something that didn't add up.

'The cheesecake no good?' I asked, pointing at her plate. She lifted it and placed it in front of me, fork and all.

'Help yourself,' she said flatly. 'I'm not in the mood for it.'

'You want me to grab you something else?'

'I'm not hungry. Thank you.'

'You? Not hungry for sweet stuff? Maybe I should take your temperature because you're clearly not feeling well.'

'Why?' she bit out, cold as ice. 'Because I'm such a fat bitch that all I ever want to do is eat sweets? That I couldn't possibly turn down a sweet treat because of how gluttonous I am?'

What the fuck? None of her words made sense. I would never say that kind of shit to her—to anybody.

'What's that even mean?' I asked, getting exasperated with her. 'Of course I'm not saying that. I would never say that!'

'I'm sorry,' she whispered, tears creeping into her eyes. Her emotions flipped like a switch. 'I don't know what's come over me recently. Well. Actually—'

She averted her eyes and went back to looking down at the table, fussing with a napkin in her hands. None of her actions were similar to the Beth I was used to. The girl I enjoyed spending time with, laughing with.

Plus kissing and making out with.

'Please talk to me,' I pleaded. 'Or at least if you don't feel like you can talk to me, maybe you can talk to Layla about it?'

'Maybe,' she said noncommittally, and I knew she wouldn't. 'I just can't believe you've failed the test, Gray. We worked so hard on it.'

'I know. I'm sorry. I should've tried harder.' Her change of subject bothered me, but if she wanted to talk about something else for the time being, I couldn't blame her. I'd get whatever it was out of her, eventually.

'It's my fault too. If you hadn't been worried about me, then maybe you would've done better.'

'I guess the only way for us to know that is for you to give me less reason to worry and for me to try harder with my revision.'

'Are you suggesting more study sessions?' she asked, a hint of the flirtatious Jacobs I was used to. 'More time spent together, just us two?'

'I'm not gonna say no, am I? I'd be a fool to turn down alone time with you, Jacobs. Just a Bunsen burner and some gas between us.'

She laughed. A full belly laugh and I felt like a caveman that had finally achieved something right. I was close to beating my chest with my fists and shouting just from hearing that giggle burst from her lips. It had been some time since she'd smiled so freely.

'Is that gas the hot air that comes from your ego?'

'You really do know how to kick a guy when he's down, don't ya?'

'I have been told that it's a gift of mine.' She smiled, her lips pressed firmly together, but curved at the edges nonetheless. 'Along with being able to eat an entire packet of cherry drops in less than an hour.'

'That is an impressive feat, Jacobs. Although not as impressive as my ability to eat an entire jar of peanut butter in less than thirty minutes.'

Through her laughter, she said, 'Why do you even know you can do that?'

'I got dared to once,' I said as if it was the most simple of answers. 'One day, a couple of summers ago, all of us were hanging out at the field and we were bored. Somebody decided we were gonna play dares, and obviously the longer the game went on, the more ridiculous and stupid the dares became.'

'And yours was to eat an entire jar of peanut butter?'

'That, among other things. Pretty sure I ate a lot of shit that day. Although it was Ace who had it the worst. Being the youngest of the group, he always wanted to prove himself, the stupid prick.'

I shook my head, remembering that day. The sun was the hottest it had been all summer, and the six of us were bored with being off school even though it was only the second week of the holidays. We were old enough to know better, yet still young enough to think eating weird concoctions and tagging the fountain in the centre of town in the dead of night were a fun way to pass the time.

'What did Ace end up doing?'

'Oh, so many stupid things. But the worst was that he ran through the animal pens on the farms and ended up falling straight into a large cowpat. Took him at least a week to wash the smell from his body and he still can't look at a beef burger the same way.'

'You're kidding, right?'

'On your life,' I swore. 'Just wait until we throw a barbecue in the summer.'

She laughed, and if I thought I felt good earlier, then that feeling was eclipsed by the one rushing through every bone in my body.

'I'm invited to your summer barbecues, am I?' She tilted her head, her eyes blazing with something I couldn't place. An emotion foreign to me.

'Would you like to be?'

'That's not what I asked.'

'Of course you're invited. I was hoping you'd spend most of the summer with us.'

'And what makes you so certain I'd want to spend my summer with you? I've got friends. Places to go, people to see.'

'I'm sure you do, but I was hoping you'd want to spend time with your boyfriend.'

'My boyfriend? Last time I checked, I didn't have one of those.'

'Pity. I was sort of hoping *I* could be your boyfriend.'

'Grayson,' she said, her smile still in place but a little uncertain. 'Is this your really naff way of asking me to be your girlfriend?'

'I find the word naff insulting, Jacobs.'

'But is it?'

'Yeah.' I coughed, a flush covering my cheeks. 'I never said I was smooth.'

'No, you've definitely proved that multiple times in the short time I've known you.'

'You're really getting all the hits in today, aren't you? I might just take it back.'

'You wouldn't,' she said, confident as all get-out. 'You need me around to keep your head on the ground and not off in the clouds after it floated away because it grew so large.'

'So, what do you say, Jacobs?' Our eyes locked, the noises of the cafe around us having disappeared the moment she began talking to me again. 'Wanna be my girl?'

'I—' She paused, biting her bottom lip. 'I'd love to.'

'No witty remark?'

'Nope. Couldn't think of one. Besides, you're kind of all right.'

'Isn't that a glowing recommendation.'

'Oh, there's a lot more where that came from.' She smiled, showing her teeth, and I beamed back. All the tension from earlier had disappeared. No hint of her personality change or the thoughts that had plagued her mind. 'You'll just have to wait and see what other charming things I can say.'

'I can't wait.'

Fourteen
Beth

BEING Grayson's girlfriend wasn't much different from what we were before. Not really. Although it definitely had its perks.

Did I feel like a totally heinous bitch for not telling him about the baby? Yes.

Was I going to tell him soon? Of course. Or at least I planned to. I just hadn't got around to it.

I wasn't sure what sort of time would be a *good* time to tell him, but I knew one would arise at some point. It had to. Not like I could keep it to myself forever. Once my stomach began to grow, people would learn the truth, anyway.

It was difficult to start such a serious conversation. I'd not told anybody—not even Layla—and I knew it'd come back to bite me on the arse, eventually. Maybe I could confide in Cara? As my sister, she wouldn't judge me too harshly and it wasn't like she'd tell Grayson about it. Or at least I was like ninety-nine percent sure she wouldn't tell Grayson. The two of them got along quite well, and there were even times when they ganged up on me.

Since his birthday, we watched movies together on Saturday nights, and because of my sister's lack of a social life, she usually joined us.

Of course he'd already seen *Wizard of Oz*—who hadn't?—but he was yet to watch *Casablanca* or *Singin' in the Rain*. Although

I'd give it a few more months before I made him sit through the latter. I may love *Singin' in the Rain*, but even I could admit that the dream-ballet sequence lasted a heck of a long time.

Outside of studying science, which was an academic hobby, classic films were my favourite thing to put on in the background and relax to. There was something so soothing about them. Something that transported me to another time. Another country. A different way of living. I loved reading the trivia and learning all about the inner workings of the big studios. The contracts they used to tie in talent for years, and the drugs they plied them with to make them do their bidding. Really, it was all totally criminal—and extremely interesting.

'Is Gray coming over tonight?' my sister asked as she entered the kitchen, and I shook my head.

The toaster popped, and I removed the bread and quickly smothered each slice in butter and chocolate spread. Apparently, according to Layla and my sister, having both butter and chocolate spread on toast was vile, but I disagreed. According to them, the chocolate spread acted as the spread, therefore butter wasn't necessary. I just thought it made them both sound stupid.

'Did you want some bread with that spread?' my sister said as she came closer and saw the mess I'd made. 'Honestly, I know you love the stuff, Beth, but even for you, that's an excessive amount.'

I bit into a corner with a loud crunch and shrugged, the crumbs landing on the countertop.

'I love it.'

'I can see that.' She looked at me disgusted, then smiled, her fondness for me overcoming even her disgust at my eating habits. 'What film did you wanna watch tonight if Gray's not joining us? I don't want to deprive the boy of the pleasure of *Gentlemen Prefer Blondes* or *Some Like It Hot*.'

'I'd never think of doing such a thing. I was gonna let you pick tonight. I'll even let you choose something made after 1980.'

'How generous of you.'

'I aim to please.'

'I'll have a think then if you're not gonna say no to anything.'

'I mean, I said you can pick, not that anything goes.'

'Bet you'd let me choose that.'

'Duh, of course I would. *Anything Goes* is Bing Crosby at his finest.'

'If you say so…' Cara got a mug down from the top shelf and put the kettle on to boil. 'You want a tea or coffee?'

My stomach roiled at the thought and I said, 'Oh, no, thank you.'

'You sure? It's those nice beans you like.'

'I'm good, thanks. I'm off caffeine right now.'

'You are?' she said, raising an eyebrow in disbelief. 'But you love your daily dose of caffeine.'

'Who doesn't?' I shrugged. 'But it's healthier if I don't.'

'What a grown-up decision. Proud of you.' The kettle boiled, and she poured it into her mug and stirred. 'I'll have a think on the film and I'll let you know. We can even get a takeaway if you want? My treat.'

'Like I'd ever turn down food I didn't pay for.' I laughed, as a loud knock came on the front door. I looked at Cara in question and she shook her head. 'You expecting someone?'

'No. Could it be Layla?'

'Layla wouldn't knock like that,' I pointed out, my heart sinking with each second because I had a strong feeling I knew who was lurking on the other side of our front door.

'Very true,' Cara agreed.

The knocking started up again with a vengeance as a voice called through the black fibreglass door.

'Cara! Elizabeth! Open up!'

'How wonderful.' Cara placed her mug down on the countertop and left the kitchen to go let our mother in. I finished my toast, ready to slink away upstairs, but before I could even put my plate in the dishwasher, the two of them appeared, already in a heated discussion.

'It's just one more payment, Cara!' Mum shouted, her makeup from the night before streaked down her face, crusted and cracked. 'Just another couple hundred pounds. Please!'

'Mum, I don't have it. I gave you the last of our money only the other month.'

'Then ask him for some more.'

'I'm not going to ask him for money and that's final!'

'Ask who for money?' I piped up, unsure who the mysterious *him* they were talking about was.

'It's none of your concern, Beth,' my sister said, setting a stern look my way before turning back to our mother. 'I won't ask him, and if I hear that you've asked him, I will lose my shit.'

'Oh, really?' Mum scoffed. 'Lose your shit how, dear daughter? You and I both know that you've got a lot more to lose than I do. I've been keeping my trap shut for some time, but it wouldn't take much for the truth to tumble out, would it?'

I tried to follow the conversation, but I clearly didn't have the context for it. However, Cara did, as her face paled, all colour draining from it.

'You w-wouldn't,' she stammered, thrown off. It was rare to see my sister shrinking in front of Mum. For so long, she'd held her own, letting her know exactly what she thought of her, even while still helping her and keeping her afloat.

'Just watch me,' Mum threatened. 'I wouldn't want to, of course. But if it were to slip out, well, not much we could do about that, is there?'

'I hate you,' my sister said, her tone low and filled with anger. It was the first time she'd said those words. First time she'd lost her cool and said the sentence we'd both thought so many times over the years but never uttered aloud—not even to each other. 'Beth, can you go over to Layla's, please?'

'No, I want to stay and—'

She cut me off before I could finish. 'That wasn't a question, Beth,' she bit out, her anger not aimed at me, but hitting me with the blast, anyway. 'Go.'

I sighed and slowly dragged my feet out of the room, wanting to overhear as much of their conversation as I could before I got kicked out.

It must be serious for my sister to command I leave the house completely.

She'd never done that before.

It just made me want to know what they were talking about even more than if they'd acted less shady. When I got to the front door, I grabbed my coat off the hook and fished my car keys out of the bowl on the side table.

BETH - I'M COMING OVER. Will explain when I arrive. Soz if you have plans with Dean.

Layla - It's eleven in the morning, Dean's not here yet.

Beth - Cool beans. See you in five.

Fifteen

Beth

Within ten minutes, I was sitting on Layla's bed, looking around her room at the many new things that had cropped up in the last few months—relics of her time with Dean.

Things had been awkward between us ever since I took the pregnancy test.

Probably because I still hadn't told her the truth.

And the longer it took for me to open up to her, the harder it was to just open my mouth and spit the words out. Part of me enjoyed having a secret that was mine, and mine alone. And really, Grayson should be the first person I told.

It was only respectful if I did that.

But the thought of telling him made me want to shit myself—something I hadn't done much of recently, what with the pregnancy constipation—and run away and hide in the hills.

I shook my head, clearing the thoughts away, listening to whatever it was Layla had been blabbing about ever since I arrived.

'… and then he asked me if I wanted to move in together.'

'Huh?'

Layla looked at me funny, shuffling in her desk chair, and repeated herself.

'Dean asked me if I wanted to move in together when we move for uni.'

'So you're not gonna live in halls?' I asked, confused. I must've missed more of the conversation than I thought, but it was rude to ask her to repeat it all. Especially as I would have to explain just *where* my mind was instead. 'That's a big step. What did you say to him?'

'I told him I'd have to think about it,' she said, biting her bottom lip. 'You're right. It's a big step and I don't want to make the wrong decision and regret it for the rest of my life, you know?'

Little did she know, I knew exactly what she meant. It was that thought that went through my head daily. The idea that whatever decision I went with would lead to me having regrets.

To me hating my life the way my mum did.

It was clear to me that Mum regretted having me. She had Cara at eighteen and then I didn't come along for another sixteen years, and by then she was already thirty-four and ready to be done with the responsibilities of a young child. She tried her best for the first five years of my life, but then it all went downhill.

'Did you hear me?' Layla asked, and I looked into her eyes, concern shining in them.

'No, sorry,' I said. 'I'm a little distracted today.'

'Want to talk about it?'

'I—' I opened my mouth to tell her about my pregnancy. To tell her the truth, finally. Would she be mad I kept it to myself? I hoped not. And if she was, I hoped it wouldn't last long, and she'd realise why I hadn't told her the moment I found out.

'Assume Tara showed up wanting more money,' she cut me off, and I nodded, half grateful for the topic being handed to me on a platter, and half irritated that I hadn't just spat out the truth.

Secrets were like weights, anchors, dragging you down to the bottom of the ocean with no chance of survival. No chance of breaking free and reaching the surface.

'She did,' I replied, deciding to just go with it. 'But she only came for money last month, and my sister gave her five hundred quid, so fuck knows what she's spending the money on.'

'Maybe on bills and rent?' Layla asked, always seeing the best in people, even my grubby mum. Layla knew as well as I did it was rare Mum spent the money she got from my sister on actual practical things like rent and food. No. Most of the time it went on alcohol, or drugs, or designer clothes, depending on the frame of mind she was in.

'Either way, the money's gone now, and she wants more.'

'What's Cara gonna do?'

'No idea. But Mum kept telling her to ask *him* for more.'

'Who is *him*?'

'No idea,' I said with a shrug. 'But I'd say he's important, whoever he is.'

'Maybe Cara will tell you later tonight.'

'She kicked me out so I *wouldn't* find out who they were talking about. I doubt she's gonna just open up over a movie and popcorn.'

'Maybe, maybe not. Worth a try, though.'

I nodded. Maybe I'd approach the subject with Cara that night. I'd gauge her mood first. She was never in the best place mentally after Mum showed up with demands—rightfully so— and I didn't want to add to that if I could help it.

'Did you hear about Grayson and Arianna?' Layla asked me, changing the subject.

I also may have forgotten to mention to Layla that Grayson had asked me to be his girlfriend. Recently, I wasn't acting the way a best friend did, but the timing just hadn't been right.

Plus, Dean hated Grayson, and I didn't want to get into a fight with him about it. Not when it was still fresh and making me happy.

'No? What about them?'

'Just don't shoot the messenger,' she said, her face imploring me to understand whatever it was she was about to tell me. 'And that's all I am.'

'Okay,' I said with a nod, wondering what could be so serious.

'What were you doing last night?'

'I had a movie night with Cara,' I told her. 'Same I do any Saturday night you blow me out for your new hot footballer boyfriend.'

Layla's cheeks warmed and I could see the pride on her face mixing with her embarrassment at blowing off one of our longest traditions for her new relationship. At first it stung, and I had to adjust, but after so many months of it, it didn't bother me half as much anymore. If Layla was happy—truly happy—then that was all that mattered to me.

'I thought you spent Saturday night with Grayson now,' she said, digging for something, but without knowing what, I was a little stumped. Most weeks I was with Gray if we didn't already have plans.

'Sometimes,' I said, brushing some crumbs from the million-aire's shortbread I ate when I arrived off my lap. 'But he was busy last night. Something came up with the Rebels.'

'Huh,' she said. 'Is that what he told you?'

'Yeah…' I trailed off, her suspicious tone causing suspicion to rise within me. 'Why? What do you know?'

'Nothing serious. Just thought I'd pass it along.'

'Pass *what* along?' I spat, getting tired of the reluctance to tell me. 'Just spit it out, Layla.'

'Last night, Grayson was at a house party over in the Hills.'

'Okay?' It was news to me, but it wasn't exactly something shameful or something to be worried about. Grayson was always at some party or another, with or without me, and I wasn't going to be one of those girlfriends who got pissed at that. It was irrational. We were both teenagers with our own friends and our own lives. He could do what he wanted. Plus, if the party was over in the Hills, then it was with the rich kids in town who lived on the other side of the 'divide' and I probably didn't know half of them.

Because Gray grew up hanging around with Arianna in the Hawthorn Hills gated community, he knew other kids there, too.

Half of them attended Hollowdale, and the others were boarding students up at the school on the hill the estate was named after. Hawthorn Academy. They came home for the holidays, though, some of them, or the weekends. They had the money to do what they wanted.

Gray told me they threw the best parties because the alcohol was never the cheap stuff and although he hadn't explicitly said it, he implied the drugs were better, too.

It was why Arianna and Rock had thrown his birthday party at their place. It had the space, the location, and ultimately, they had the money to really go all-out in a way Gray didn't.

'He went with Arianna,' Layla continued. I stared at her with a blank expression, waiting for the punchline. The part of the story that would make me sad or angry or whatever emotion she thought it would elicit from me. 'They were really close.'

'They are really close,' I said, shrugging, not in the slightest bit worried. 'They're best friends. It'd be like me and you getting close at a party.'

'I don't mean just close as in sitting next to each other all night.' Layla winced.

'What do you mean, then? Because you're not exactly getting to the point, are you?'

Hurt flashed on her face and a stab of remorse shot through me, but only for a second. I didn't mean to lash out at her, but c'mon, she was trying to twist my mind against Gray without good reason.

'I have pictures,' she whispered, getting her phone from her pocket and getting up whatever conversation or pictures she needed to help her prove whatever the point was. 'Maybe they'll do a better job of explaining what I'm trying to say.'

She reached out her hand to me, and I took her phone from her, bringing it close to have a nose through the pictures she was showing me.

The first picture was innocent enough. Grayson and Arianna

sat next to one another on a sofa, Arianna whispering something in his ear while he smiled.

The next one they were a little closer. Arianna had moved from sitting *next* to Grayson on the sofa to being half-sat on his lap. Both of them were wrapped up in conversation, and even though the picture made it look bad, I knew it wasn't.

Gray had told me they were close and that something was happening in Arianna's life that made her need him a little more than usual. I hadn't asked what it was because it wasn't my place—Gray would tell me if it ever became an issue.

The last swipe of my finger was a video.

I pressed play, my thumb shaking even though the pictures themselves hadn't made me nervous.

For some reason, a video seemed a little more nefarious.

'Who sent you these?' I asked her, watching the party unfold in front of me from the video on her phone.

Arianna and Gray were in the same place on the sofa, but had moved, so she was fully seated on his lap, her arms wrapped around the back of his neck. He was whispering in her ear, or maybe even kissing her neck. The grainy image was hard to read. Either way, it didn't paint a *great* picture, but I wasn't worried.

Whether people knew it or not, he was my boyfriend, and that meant something.

The only thing that ticked me off was that he'd never mentioned the party. If I'd known he went, then I wouldn't have been so blindsided.

'Dean,' Layla said. 'He got them from Peter or Alex. Not sure which one, but they were there and thought you'd want to see it.'

'Thanks, I guess.'

'You know I'd never keep things like that from you. That's what best friends are for, right?'

'Right,' I agreed, handing her phone back to her. I'd have to talk to Gray about it, add it to the long list of things I needed to talk to him about but was putting off.

It made me hate myself, just a little, that I was being so secretive with everybody, but it was as if I couldn't help it. Any time I opened my mouth, the words wouldn't come. Like a ten-ton weight was sitting on my stomach and heart, refusing to budge.

'Do you think it was serious? Or one of those one-night flings he's so well known for?'

'Huh?' My mind was elsewhere. 'Oh. No. That was nothing.'

'But the video—'

'Means shit,' I snapped. 'Gray wouldn't do that to me.'

'How do you even know that?' she asked, her tone rising. 'You barely know him. Dean said he's been this way for years, always a new girl every weekend, never once going back for more. Arianna's been his only constant.'

'When was the last weekend anybody saw him with a new girl?' I asked, wanting her to think it over before coming back at me with more bullshit. Ever since we first connected that night on the field in the tent, he'd spent every weekend with me. 'Really think about it.'

'Well, I guess he hasn't,' she admitted. 'But doesn't mean he's not sleeping around still.'

'Are you trying to piss me off?' I swung my narrowed gaze her way. 'Because you're doing a good job of it.'

'I'm just being realistic! I don't want to see you hurt by some playboy. Especially not one who sleeps with you, doesn't talk about it after the fact, and was careless enough that you ended up in a pregnancy scare!'

God, she really wanted to paint a bad image of him, didn't she?

'We've cleared all that up,' I lied, not wanting her to know we hadn't spoken about his birthday at all. 'And for your information, I know him better than you think.'

'A few study dates and parties don't mean you know him, Beth.' Her exasperated tone was pissing me off. My hormones were already all over the place, and I didn't need my *best friend* doubting me and my judgement. 'It just means he's wooed you the same way he has dozens of other foolish girls and that you're one in a long line.'

The moment she finished, she slapped her hand over her mouth, her eyes filling with shame and sorrow in seconds.

'Shit, I didn't mean it like that.' She shook her head. 'I just meant that he's a charmer.'

'He also happens to be my boyfriend,' I said, my tone clear. 'So I'd like to think that maybe I'm not just another *foolish girl he's wooed.*'

'You're his girlfriend?' she asked, her eyebrow raised, confusion painted on her features. 'Since when?'

'Since he took me for cheesecake after he failed his mock test.'

'And you didn't think to tell me?' she whispered, hurt lacing every word. 'You're my best friend, Beth. We've always told each other everything.'

'I know,' I replied, trying not to let the tears in her eyes affect me. *Fuck.* If she was near to tears about me not telling her I had a boyfriend, I didn't want to see how she'd react when I finally told her I was pregnant. 'But we've just been in our own bubble. I didn't want to burst it.'

'I can understand that. And I know maybe you didn't want to tell me because I'd tell Dean and he'd be a judgemental prick about it all even if he's talking to them a bit more now, but know that it would just take a word from you and I wouldn't tell him shit.'

'Thanks,' I muttered, not believing her for a second but appreciating the gesture. 'I'll talk to him about the pictures.'

'Are you happy?' she asked, tilting her head, assessing me.

'I am. He's really not the guy he's painted to be, you know? We have chemistry and banter, and we enjoy spending time together.'

'Well, then I'm happy for you. And maybe I'll work on twisting Dean's arm so he's happy for you, too.'

'Thanks. I appreciate you. You know that, right?'

'I appreciate you, too. You're my best friend, Beth. You've always been there for me no matter what and it hurts my heart that you didn't tell me because you worried about how I'd react. That's crappy and I'm gonna do my best to make sure it doesn't happen again.'

My heart panged with guilt. Her words were beautiful, and yet they made me feel like the shittiest human alive because I was hiding a hell of a lot more from her—from everybody.

'I love you, Layla. No matter what.'

'I love you, too.'

Sixteen

Beth

ME AND MY sister were sitting on the sofa, both wrapped up in our fleece blankets, a bowl of popcorn in our hands watching a movie, when a sharp stab to the gut had me bolting up from my spot and dashing to the bathroom.

Shit.

I rushed to the toilet, throwing open the lip, and quickly dropped my head down before the vomit could leave my lips.

Once the entire contents of my stomach had left my body, I sat back on my haunches and wiped my mouth with the back of my hand, feeling sorry for myself.

Since the start of my pregnancy, I had been extremely lucky with sickness and nausea. And although my stomach turned at a lot of smells these days, it was rare that I was physically sick.

When the wave passed, I stood up and made my way to the sink to wash my hands.

My eyes were focused on my hands. On the lather of the soap and the suds as they washed down the drain.

I didn't notice the looming presence behind me until I stood up and looked at myself in the mirror.

And locked eyes with a pair startlingly like my own.

'Is there something you want to tell me?' my sister bit out, her eyes narrowed on me as I dried my hands on the towel to the side of the sink. 'Because I'd say there is.'

'What makes you say that?' I asked, brushing past her in the doorway to go back to my comfy spot on the sofa.

The blanket was warm and cosy and one of my favourites. I'd owned it ever since I was a kid, and it was one of my comfort items. One of the things that made me feel safe and loved.

I held my bowl aloft and asked, 'Want my popcorn?'

Cara's eyes were still narrowed in suspicion, but she came and sat beside me again, taking my bowl and putting the left-over popcorn and chocolate into her bowl.

'Beth,' she said, shaking her short black hair from her face. 'Please tell me this isn't what I think it is.'

'It depends…' I said, an edge to my tone.

'On?'

'On what you think it is.'

'Don't play with me. Don't turn this into a joke. Tell me the truth. Are you pregnant?'

My heart dropped to the floor.

Hearing the question out loud for the first time felt ickier than I thought it would. If I stayed pregnant, I would have to get used to listening to that question. Get used to answering with the truth.

'Define pregnant.'

'Beth!' she cried out, exasperated with my delaying tactics.

'Fine!' I conceded, shuffling in my spot to face her. It didn't feel right to tell her such life-changing shit facing away. 'Will you kill me if I am?'

'I—' She took a deep breath, her shoulders rising and falling with the effort, and I braced myself for her answer.

My sister was my best friend—alongside Layla—and her opinion meant everything to me. If she was ashamed of me or disappointed, I wasn't sure how well I'd take it.

It would gut me.

She still hadn't spoken and I may have thought that my body had nothing left to vomit up, but the wait was making me realise that wasn't quite true.

'Say something,' I whispered, wanting her to just spit it out.

'I'm trying to think of something I can say without sounding like a bitch,' she admitted, rubbing her hand on her forehead. 'Because a real big part of me just wants to lose my shit.'

'I didn't do any of it on purpose,' I said. 'Wasn't like I went out of my way to have unprotected sex and get pregnant, was it?'

'Doesn't matter,' she replied. 'No matter what you intended, it's happened now. Nothing you can do to take it back. Fuck, Beth. You're only seventeen. You've got so much of your life ahead of you and you're so smart. You were gonna be the whizz-kid of the family. The one who went off and truly made something of themselves. Now look at you.'

'What's *that* supposed to mean?' I snapped, not liking her tone at all. It had started so well. She was proud of me. She wanted what was best for me.

Then she said that last line.

Now look at you.

'Well, how the fuck are you going to go to university with a baby?'

'I haven't thought about it yet.'

'Haven't thought about it? Clearly, you haven't thought about a lot.' She scoffed, and it was the first time since I was a kid that I wanted to punch the smirk off my sister's face.

Was getting pregnant at seventeen my plan? Fuck no.

But it had happened and I couldn't go back in time and stop myself from going upstairs with Gray at his party, could I?

Every time I thought about telling Gray, the butterflies in my stomach became bats and everything turned dark. But I had to. I couldn't put it off much longer, or I'd be showing before he knew—and that wouldn't be great, would it?

'I get it,' I said. 'You're disappointed in me. You wish I'd made different choices and I fully get why. But we're here and it is what it is.'

'Please tell me you know who the father is.'

A slap would've hurt less.

The accusation, the venom in her eyes, all of it, were a lot worse than my imagination told me it could be.

Even when I debated telling her, she never looked at me with such disgust.

No. In my dreams, she held my hand and cried with me. Cried for all that I would lose, but also all that I could gain if I kept the baby.

'Of course I do!' I shouted, indignant. 'Funny enough, I'm dating him!'

'Grayson?' The shock covering her features was insulting. 'Really?'

'Yep.'

'But you've barely been dating for a couple weeks.'

'You can have sex with somebody you're not dating.'

'Don't get smart with me,' she huffed, and I knew I needed to get out of there. If I stayed, the conversation would only sink further and grow nasty. 'Does he know?'

'Nope. But I think I'm going to go tell him right now.'

'Right now? But we haven't finished talking. Or watching the movie.'

'Oh, we're definitely done here,' I said, standing up and brushing myself off. 'I don't wanna be around you right now.'

'I could say the same to you.'

'So glad we agree on something.'

My coat was on the rack by the door and I snatched it and threw it on as quickly as I could before I lost my nerve.

It was imperative that I saw Grayson as fast as possible.

No ifs, ands, or buts.

'WHAT ARE YOU DOING HERE?' Grayson bit out when he opened the door, his eyes narrowing on my face. Guess he must've seen something that made him pause because he opened the door wider and let me step inside. 'What's up?'

'Can we talk in your room?' I asked, looking around the room for any sign of his dad but not seeing anything. 'There's something I need to tell you.'

'And it couldn't wait?'

'No,' I said with a sigh, 'it couldn't.'

He took my hand in his and walked me through the living room to the stairs in the left corner of the room. It was the first time he'd let me inside his house, but he didn't let me linger long enough to take in the surroundings fully.

Once upstairs, he pushed me into the first room on the left, closing the door behind us.

'You can't be here long,' he said, walking over to his bed and sitting on the edge. 'My dad will be home soon and he can't find you here.'

I nodded and swallowed. Every time Gray spoke about his dad, a chill ran down my spine. I was yet to meet the man, but I got the vibe that not meeting him was a blessing. Gray may have fobbed off his black eye the other week to me as something he got during a bout with Tyler, but I knew otherwise.

'I need to tell you something important.' I took a deep breath, my lungs fit to burst, and I felt as if the weight of everything was coming down on me. Crushing me whole.

'Okay…' Gray grabbed my hand and pulled me down to sit beside him. The warmth of his calloused fingertips settled my stomach—only slightly—as he drew circles on the back of my hand. 'Clearly, it's important enough that you came here.'

Just do it, Beth. Just open your big fat mouth and tell him.

One more deep breath entered my lungs, and I spoke the two words I was terrified of putting into the universe. Because once I told him, it was real. All of it became real.

'I'm pregnant.'

Grayson's face changed in the blink of an eye. His once cheery disposition replaced with one filled with anger and frustration. Confusion.

'You're what?' he bit out, his voice made up of small—yet sharp and deadly—razor blades.

'I'm pregnant,' I repeated, my tone as small as I felt. I'd known the moment that second line appeared that shit was going to hit the fan. That Gray wouldn't take it well.

But the way he was staring at me—staring at me with disgust—made me want to run away and never look back.

'And why the fuck are you telling me?' he spat. 'Have you cheated on me, Jacobs? Fucked someone else when you're meant to be *my* girl?'

I stared back blankly. The air knocked from my lungs when it registered in my mind what his words meant.

I thought he didn't mention our night together because he was embarrassed. Or maybe because he was worried I'd become a stage ten cling-on or something.

But no.

He hadn't spoken about it because he didn't *remember* it. The pissed off look on his face told me he had no recollection of our night together. That he really believed I'd cheated on him.

I sucked in a deep lungful of air and set my shoulders in a firm line, hoping to find the resolve needed to tell him.

'I've not cheated on you. I'm telling you because we had sex.' It was simple. To the point. No added flourishes. No bullshitting.

Just cold, hard facts.

'No,' he replied, a sneer settling in place of his usual smile. 'We didn't.'

'I'm lying then?' I said, my voice rising with every word. 'Why would I lie about something like that?'

My eyes roved over his features, trying to get a read on him. To see beneath the stony exterior to the true feelings that lay under it, but it was like staring at a brick wall. Cold and unmoving.

'I don't know, Jacobs,' he said, standing to look down at me. 'Maybe you fucked somebody else and you don't want me to know.'

'I didn't *fuck* anybody but you,' I said, standing too so that I wasn't being looked down upon—in more ways than one. '*You* are the only person I've had sex with, Grayson, so if I'm telling you there's a baby in my stomach, then you better believe it's yours!'

Seventeen

Grayson

'I'M PREGNANT.'

Those two words reverberated through my mind, entering every nook and cranny of my brain and settling down. Getting too comfortable for my liking.

How the fuck could Beth be pregnant? Okay. I understood the how. But still.

Arianna told me she'd seen me slink upstairs with Beth, and that she'd seen her when she snuck out. Had accused me of sleeping with her, and I'd shot it down, adamant it hadn't happened.

The two of us were standing in my room, my eyes staring down at her as I processed her words. Her last sentence was filled with venom and anger. And I knew I was a cock for even hinting that she'd slept with somebody else. In the short time I'd known her, I knew Beth wasn't the type to sleep around—especially after we started dating. Every word out of her mouth when we watched films together told me she was a romantic at heart and she wouldn't mess me around.

The fight went out of her in front of my eyes. Her shoulders slumped and her face lost its colour.

'Say something,' Beth whispered, her large hazelnut-coloured eyes blinking, tears threatening to spill over. 'Don't just stare blankly at me like that.'

'Shit, Beth. What is there I can say?'

She winced when I used her name. It was rare that I did. She was always Jacobs. Never Beth.

My eyes strayed away from her face to the clock on the wall, and my blood froze when I saw the time. *Fuck*. It was even later than I thought it was. When Beth arrived, I was so shell-shocked to see her standing on my doorstep that I invited her in without fully thinking it through. I should've invited her to go to the field with me—or for a walk on the path.

I rarely invited people in. Even the other Rebels only came inside once in a blue moon.

She needed to leave—and fast.

'Say anything!' she said, her voice getting louder. 'Say that you're by my side. That you'll be there for me through this shit. Say anything, Grayson!'

I looked back at her and decided what to do next. What to say. And I knew she wouldn't like it one bit, but I needed her gone from this house before my old man got home. I didn't want him to know about her. Not her face. Her name. Anything. So I did what anyone in my position would do.

'The only thought running through my mind right now is that this is all your fault.'

She froze as my words settled around her. Saw the moment they sank into her skin and made roots there. Seeping into her pores like the filth they were.

'My fault?' Her eyes blazed. 'My. Fault?'

Each word was clipped, and I could tell she was holding back her full fire. She was pissed and I couldn't blame her. Yet she still wasn't leaving.

'I was wasted. I have no memory of what happened. You took advantage of me.'

'I—' She paused and took a step back from me, rubbing her hands together in agitation. 'I didn't.'

She didn't sound certain, though. And I pounced.

'You're telling me you didn't notice how drunk I was? That

you were just so thrilled to be with me alone that you didn't see the warning signs?' I scoffed, shaking my head. 'Bet you didn't even check we used a condom either, right?'

Before me, Beth floundered, her mouth opening and closing, with only air coming out. She had nothing to say. I'd achieved what I set out to do—even if I didn't truly believe the shit I'd spouted. Deep down, I knew Beth didn't take advantage of me, whether I could remember it or not.

'I've got to go,' Beth mumbled, the motion of her hand rubbing her stomach catching my eye. 'Text me when you've got something nice to say.'

She left my room without a backward glance, and within a moment, I heard the front door slam behind her.

And all I felt was a massive wave of relief. Relief that she was gone before my old man returned home. Relief that I could think about the bomb she dropped alone.

Pregnant?

I couldn't wrap my head around it. Somebody up there must be laughing, looking down at me, because surely nobody in their right mind would think I would be a good dad. Fuck. I didn't exactly have a good role model.

Jacobs deserved more than I just gave her. She deserved somebody who would listen to her talk it through. Her fears. Her doubts.

Yet all I'd done was make her feel crappy about it. It must have been hard to come here and tell me. I wondered how long she'd known. How long it had taken her to build up her courage and tell me.

I'd failed her already.

And what if she didn't even *want* to have the baby? Even just assuming she wanted it was dickish behaviour. As if all women wanted children just because they had wombs.

At least she had Layla to talk to. Maybe even her sister.

Who did I have?

Not like I could talk to my dad about any of it. And the guys would never understand. Maybe even turn it into a joke. The only real friend who may listen was Arianna, but I didn't want to do that to Beth. Not yet, anyway.

She should be able to talk about it on her own time. Tell people on her terms.

The door slamming brought me from my thoughts.

'Grayson!' my dad shouted, calling for me. 'Where the fuck are you, boy?'

'Coming!' I called down to him, brushing my hands on my thighs. He didn't sound drunk, but hell, what did I know? The man drank vodka like it was water and had built up such a tolerance that it was hard to know anymore just how close to the edge he was.

I made my way to the living room and the fumes coming off him hit me within seconds. Clearly, he'd had a lot to drink. More than usual.

'What's up?' I asked, moving into his eyeline.

'It reeks in here.'

I rolled my eyes, but not before turning my head so he wouldn't see my blatant disrespect. Of course it reeked. *He* reeked.

'Does it?' I asked, my tone flat.

'It reeks in here of girls' perfume,' he continued as if I'd never spoken before turning to me, his face already one of rage. 'Who have you had here? One of your whores?'

'Nobody's been here.' Sometimes, speaking to my dad was like talking to a younger child. You needed to speak plainly. Simple words for a simple man. 'And I don't have any whores, Dad.'

'Then who was that girl I saw crying at the corner?' He raised an eyebrow, and my palms began to sweat. Between Beth leaving and him arriving home, there were maybe ten minutes max. Just because she left the house straight away didn't mean she'd left the street.

'Huh?' I asked, nonchalant, hoping my act was enough for

him not to be too suspicious. The man could barely see in front of his face most of the time, so the fact he'd noticed any of his surroundings on the way home was odd enough.

'There was a girl standing by the street sign on the corner. Long black hair, quite short, jeans and a blue hoodie on. Seemed pretty sad when I walked past her. Smelled an awful lot like the perfume in here, too.'

Maybe he was bullshitting.

Maybe he was trying to call my bluff. See if I gave anything away. Gave him something he could use as ammo towards me.

Either way, he was describing Beth—even down to what she'd been wearing.

'No clue who you're talking about.' I shrugged and went to sit on the sofa, not looking him in the eye.

'That's funny, seeing as she was on the phone to somebody, telling them she'd just left Grayson's house.'

My heart beat too fast in my chest. That fucker. He knew the entire conversation the girl he'd seen was here before. Bet he couldn't smell shit in the room except for his own filth. He was just baiting me. Seeing if I said something—told him the truth.

And I hadn't.

Shit fucking balls.

I braced myself for what I knew was coming. Braced myself for the fists that would fly in my direction because I *disappointed* him. For somebody who spent their entire life drinking, he could still land a mean punch.

His fist connected with my eye, and the pain seared through me. *Fuck. Fuck. Fuck.*

His fists kept coming. And I didn't dodge a single blow, because on the occasions I had, it got a lot worse. I wanted to walk out of it as unscathed as possible.

And I didn't want him looking closer at what Beth was doing here, either.

Eighteen

Beth

My feet pounded the pavement, my head focused on said feet as I made my way from the bus stop to the hospital on the other side of town. I was lazy and got to the town circular, knowing I couldn't walk the entire way in my current state. I also wasn't in a fit state to drive myself.

Sleep had eluded me.

All night I was up tossing and turning, apprehensive for the day to come, but also confident, too—to a degree.

Oh, let's be honest, I didn't know *what* or *how* I was really thinking.

Once I reached my destination, I stopped to take a deep breath; the sun shining through the clouds into my eyes, spring on the horizon.

Hovering outside of the clinic, my entire body was on edge. Every nerve buzzing, my heart pounding.

I was acting rash. Or was I? I wasn't sure anymore.

My mind was at odds with itself, running around in circles.

Really, I should've tried harder to talk to Grayson, tell him how I was feeling about everything, but the way he looked at me the last time we spoke was burned into my mind.

He looked at me as if I was pond scum, ruining his new trainers.

He hadn't even given me the chance to talk it all through

with him—to talk of our options. He just dismissed me. The way I expected from others, but never from him.

When I made the appointment at the clinic, I wasn't sure I'd show. It wasn't a definitive appointment, but more one where I could learn my options. Consider all the alternatives and pick the one that sounded best for me.

And although the statement *my body, my choice* came to mind whenever I thought about it, so did the fact that for me personally, it didn't feel fair to exclude Gray from the decision entirely. No matter how shit he treated me. Because either way, it would affect him going forward—affect his life one way or the other.

The time on the large clock face on the front of the hospital told me it was nearly time to head inside, yet my feet wouldn't move from their spot.

All I had to do was enter the white door behind me that read Family Planning clinic and tell the receptionist my name. That was the first step.

My eyes were fixated on the door.

A familiar face barrelled into my line of vision and my feet had to move, so I wasn't flattened by her. She exited the door with such force I thought she might have taken it off its hinges, but when I looked back, it was still there.

'What are you doing here?' Remi spat, her eyes red-rimmed and bloodshot. She'd been crying, but the tears had dried now, her makeup-free face looking wholesome and so very sad. 'Did you follow me?'

'Why would I follow you?' I scoffed. Remi and I weren't exactly what you'd call friends. Especially after she was the one responsible for everybody learning Layla's past—and twisting it into something it wasn't—all so she could win Dean back.

A tactic that, funnily enough, didn't pay off.

'I don't know,' she said, looking over her shoulder before her worried eyes locked with mine once more. 'If you're not here to follow me, then why the fuck are you here?'

'For the reason most people come to the hospital,' I said, my tone bored. Remi was known for her dramatics, but even for her, her paranoia was extreme. 'For an appointment.'

'But you're standing outside Family Planning…'

'So?'

'And you were staring at the door for ages. I could see you.'

'Sorry, but I fail to see your point?' I said, acting nonchalant, but inside my pulse was rising rapidly. The only thing stopping me from a full-blown freak-out was the fact that she exited that same door I was contemplating entering. She, too, had been in the Family Planning clinic, and from the way she approached me, I doubted she wanted anybody to know about it.

'What are you doing *here*?' she emphasised, and my eyes blinked at her, the sting of tears starting.

'I could ask the same of you.'

Because we both knew that the morning appointments at the clinic on a Wednesday weren't just your run-of-the-mill sexual health classes. No. The appointments on a Wednesday morning were specifically for those already pregnant or actively trying. The receptionist had told me when I called and booked in.

'Want to go somewhere more… private?' she asked, still darting looks over her shoulders, no doubt worried somebody would see us both there.

Because we weren't friends, it would be even more suspicious.

My appointment was in five minutes. Even though it was an excuse, I knew I should walk through that door and find out what I wanted to do. Because I already knew the options available to me. I was just buying time. But whatever Remi wanted to talk about might help.

I weighed up my choices and decided on the one that my heart told me to.

'Fine,' I said to her, pushing my Cambridge satchel bag further up my shoulder. It was a gift from Cara to thank me for moving to Beurre with her, and it was probably one of the most expensive bags I'd ever owned. 'Where to?'

'I've got just the place.'

'THE WOODS?' I asked. 'When you said you had just the place, I thought you meant somewhere warm, at least.'

'We won't be overheard in here,' she said, as if I was being simple for not realising that. 'Nobody ever comes here.'

'Yeah,' I said, looking around us, 'and I'm sensing there's a reason why.'

'Nothing major,' she replied with a shrug of her coat-clad shoulders. 'People avoid it because at the end of the woods there's a mansion owned by a super rich dude who killed his wives.'

'Killed his wives? Plural?'

'Oh, don't look so scared. It's mostly rumours. My cousin's aunt works for him. Says it's all poppycock.'

'Right…' I trailed off, a chill running down my spine. 'We could just go to my house? It's not far from here.'

I pointed to the houses in the opposite direction from the mansion she had just mentioned.

'Of course you live this side of the divide,' she said with a roll of her eyes. 'Makes sense.'

'What's that supposed to mean?'

'You have the look of the wealthy about you,' she said, her tone bitter. 'Let me guess, you live in Hawthorn Hills.'

'Nope,' I said, making the word last, relishing in the fact she was wrong. 'I'm not quite that rich.'

'Hm,' she huffed, shaking her head. 'Whatever.'

'What did you bring me here for?' I asked, unhappy I was having to put my nice new bag down on the dirty woodland ground, but I was no longer able to hold its weight without effort.

'I wanted us to speak plainly. Without fear of being over-heard. When I nearly bumped into you, you looked terrified.'

'Because you were hurtling towards me like a freight train!'

'That's not it and you know it.'

I sighed, moving my weight to one leg, popping my hip with attitude. A bravado that was half false and half not. To further the image that I was unaffected, I placed a cherry drop in my mouth and sucked on that for a minute or two before responding to her.

'What do you want me to say? We're not friends. You're a bit of a bitch, let's be honest.'

'Maybe so'—she shrugged, not overly fussed I'd pegged her as a bitch—'but I would also bet money on the fact I'm the only person who knows where you were today.'

'I—' I paused, shaking my head. Technically, she was right, but only because I wanted to talk it through with somebody who wasn't my sister and a nurse seemed the next best option. 'Okay, you're right. Big whoop. You've got me sussed. What else do you think you know about me?'

'I know you don't have a boyfriend.'

'As far as I'm aware, Remi, neither do you.'

'Look, you can act catty as much as you want, but I genuinely want to help you. I didn't bring you here to torment you.'

Her ocean-blue eyes were wide, still slightly bloodshot, and for the first time, I took them in fully. It became clear to me she was holding herself back. On the surface, she was trying to seem calm and collected, but when you looked deeper, you could see her turmoil. Her despair at whatever was plaguing her.

'Okay,' I said, a deep breath leaving my nostrils, accepting her help in whatever way she wanted to give it. I was so tired of pretending to Layla that everything was okay. 'I was at the clinic because I'm pregnant.'

'No shit!' Her eyes locked with mine. 'For some reason, that was *not* what I expected you to say.'

'What did you think I was gonna say? You were there too.

You know that Wednesday mornings are appointments for pregnant people.'

Her eyes went even wider, and she swallowed, pursing her lips.

'No,' she said, 'I didn't know that.'

'Oh,' I replied, caught off guard. 'So you weren't there to… talk about your options?'

I looked down at her stomach, wondering if I would see something there, but she wrapped her coat tighter around herself and laughed. But there was no malice in it.

'No.' She winced. 'I promise you, Beth, that I won't repeat anything you tell me. I know that my word doesn't exactly mean shit to you, but I'm telling the truth. I'm here to listen if you want to talk.'

Did I want to talk to her?

Part of me felt as if I was betraying Layla by talking to the girl who caused her so much grief only a few months previously, but a much larger part needed to talk it out with somebody who didn't know me. Somebody who wouldn't have a biased opinion either way—for either option.

'You promise it won't go any further?' I asked, but it didn't have much gusto. We both knew I'd already made the decision to talk shit through with her. 'Because if it does, believe me, I wouldn't wanna be you.'

She gulped and nodded her head, whispering, 'Who's the father?'

Shit. Why hadn't it occurred to me that would be one of her first questions? Of course she wanted to know who he was. Who the father was could play a large part in any decision made.

'Grayson Smith,' I said, averting my gaze, not wanting to see her reaction.

'Grayson Smith?' she asked thoughtfully, with a hint of incredulity thrown in. 'Are you shitting me?'

'Nope,' I said, popping the P, scuffing my foot on the debris on the ground. 'Is it that hard to believe?'

'That's not it.' She raised her hand and touched my arm, a tentative smile on her face when I looked up at her. 'I just didn't expect it, that's all.'

I nodded. It made sense.

Fuck, if I was standing listening to me, I probably wouldn't have believed it either. One of the most revered guys at school, and then there was me, the new boring science nerd.

'Well, it's the truth,' I told her.

'Does he know?'

'Yeah,' I mumbled, the look on Gray's face when I told him flashing in my mind again. An image I hadn't been able to shake ever since it happened. The disappointment in his gaze, the anger aimed at me, all of it hurt. 'He knows.'

'And?'

'And he kicked me out of his house.'

'Shit, I'm sorry.' She looked it too. It didn't just look like empty words, and that alone filled me with a bit of strength I didn't have before. 'That really fucking sucks. Why are guys such wankers?'

'No idea,' I replied, a small smile playing on my lips. 'But I don't blame him. Not really. He just turned eighteen and he—' I cut myself off before I divulged any more of Grayson's secrets. Remi attended the field parties, and I'd seen her hanging around with Spencer and Tyler before. That first party I went to she'd even been trying it on with Gray before I arrived.

'He what?'

'He's just got a lot on his plate,' I murmured, deflecting.

'Well, without sounding like the bitch you seem to think I am, you've not exactly got an empty plate now, have you? Especially as you're eating for two.' Her lips curved at the edges, her poor attempt at a joke falling somewhat flat.

'I'm really good at science,' I said the words that popped into my head. 'My plan was always to go to uni, study chemistry, then go into the world and get a decent job that paid really well so me and my sister would never be poor again.'

'Don't exactly look poor to me,' she said, nudging her head in the direction of the town—and my house. 'Not like you live on my side of the divide.'

'Honestly, I have no idea how my sister pulled that shit off. We moved here for her new job that pays a lot better than her last. That's all I know.'

'Look, Beth. I'm not gonna stand here and pretend I know what you're feeling or how the future will go, but one thing I will say is that you need to talk to him again. Does he even know you went to the clinic today?'

My head shook violently, my heart picking up speed at the thought of him knowing what I'd potentially planned to do without talking to him about it first.

I was acting shitty, even when I didn't mean to be.

But by not trying harder to talk with Grayson, I was doing him a disservice. Ultimately, the decision would be mine, but that didn't mean I couldn't get his opinion.

'Do you want to have this baby?' Remi asked, tilting her head to the side, pointing at my stomach. 'Don't think. Just answer.'

'I—'

'The truth, Beth. What is your heart saying? Not your head.'

'Of course my heart wants this baby, but I'm also not stupid enough to lead with my heart.'

'Not gonna lie, new girl, but from what I've heard about you, you are *exactly* the type to lead with your heart.'

'Huh.' I pondered her words. She wasn't wrong, either. Wearing my heart on my sleeve had always been a part of my identity. Something I relied on when times were tough. 'I've no idea exactly what you've heard about me, but you're not wrong in saying I let my heart make a lot of my decisions. Partially the reason I'm in this mess in the first place.'

Both of us laughed, the tension between us easing with every minute spent alone in the woods. From what Dean had said, and Layla had told me, Remi didn't have many *real* friends. Not in the way I had Layla, who in turn also had Amber.

Maybe all the girl needed was a friend, and she'd stop being such a heinous bitch to everybody who got in her way.

'Thank you,' I said, meaning every word. 'I really appreciate you bringing me out here and talking to me. I think I know what I need to do.'

'Sorry, but I've got to be nosey. What do you need to do?'

I took in a deep lungful of air through my mouth, then exhaled through my nose, grounding myself. Preparing myself to say the words out loud, I'd known in my head and heart all along.

'I'm having this baby.'

'Of course you are!'

I GOT HOME from the woods, slammed the front door behind me, called out for my sister.

'Cara! Are you home?'

'I'm in here!' she called from the kitchen. 'What are you doing home?'

It was nearly three, so I would've been home within the hour anyway as I didn't have science stuff on a Wednesday, but I *was* home early, so of course she'd ask.

I made my way into the kitchen and looked at her across the counter in the middle of the room. She was hovering over the hob, stirring something that looked suspiciously like cheese sauce, and I had the feeling she was trying to get into my good graces by cooking one of my favourite meals.

'I didn't go to school today.' The two of us were always honest with each other, and I wasn't going to break that trust, even if I was slightly mad at her still. 'I went to the clinic.'

'The clinic?' she asked, looking up from the pan. 'Last time we spoke about it, you were going to talk to Grayson before making a decision. When you got back from his the past week-end, you said it went a lot better than expected.'

'I lied.'

'Oh, Beth,' she said, taking the pan off the heat and coming over to where I was standing. 'I'm so sorry.'

It was as if she knew what had happened without me even having to voice it. We'd always been really close. Close enough to be so in sync to share thoughts.

The moment her arms came around my shoulders, I sniffed and began to let out the tears I'd held back since I left Grayson's. I didn't want to cry anymore.

'It's okay,' I said through my sobs. 'It was wishful thinking that he'd react the way I hoped. We're not even a couple. We're only teenagers with our lives ahead of us.'

'And what's that supposed to mean?' she asked, leaning back a little to take in my face, her hands brushing my hair from my eyes.

'That I can't blame him for ignoring me.'

'He's been *ignoring* you?' Her indignant tone made me smile a little through my sorrow. Trust my big sister to get protective of me. She always stuck up for me, no matter what. Over the years, I'd begun to lean on her more than I should, but I couldn't help myself. 'Why didn't you tell me?'

'Because it seemed silly to make a big deal out of it.' I shrugged. 'Gray's life is hard enough as it is without me adding to it.'

'Hard, how?'

'I think his dad beats him,' I told her, voicing my suspicion. He may have never said anything to indicate it, but we all saw the bruises he tried to hide. 'He never lets me over to his house if his dad's due home. He doesn't want him to learn about me.'

'Right...'

'But I think I fucked up,' I said, my bottom lip wobbling as I recalled the weekend. 'When he told me to leave I was so sad. So lost. I couldn't bring myself to come home and face you yet, so I stood at the street sign for a bit and called Layla so I could hear a familiar voice to ground me.'

'Right…'

'And a drunk man walked past me at the exact moment I mentioned Gray's name.'

'That doesn't mean anything, Beth.'

'I would agree with you if I didn't see Gray's face at school on Monday. His eye was black and bruised and I just knew in my gut that I was the cause of it.'

'There's no way for you to know that,' she said, her tone soothing, as she pulled away from me to go back to the sauce on the stove. 'And he will come around eventually. I know it. He'll talk to you and everything will get sorted. And if not sorted, you'll at least come to a mutual agreement, I'm sure.'

I nodded. My sister's words made sense to me. Her wisdom always hit me in the heart—the way most things did—and she made me see things differently.

'I just don't know what to do.'

'Did the clinic give you any insight?'

'Well… I never actually went inside,' I admitted, shuffling around the counter to look at the rest of the food she was preparing.

'You didn't?'

'Nope. When I got there, I stared at the door until a girl from school came flying out of it.' I picked up a carrot from the side and bit down on it hard, the crunch strangely satisfying. 'And then the two of us went somewhere to talk.'

'I'm glad you have somebody to speak to that isn't me.' She took a deep breath, and I knew what was coming next. Knew exactly what the next words out of her mouth would be. 'I really think you should speak to Layla about all this, Beth. She's gonna be so upset when she learns the truth.'

'I know,' I replied. 'But every time I'm in front of her, I open my mouth and no words leave it. It's like a block I can't push through yet. I will tell her, though. Sort of have to, seeing as they'll be here in less than six months' time.'

I waited for her to realise what I'd said. To understand the gravity of my statement.

Any moment now.

'You're keeping the baby?' she croaked out, whirling around to face me, her eyes wide and uncertain. 'You're sure?'

'Yep. I know it isn't what you want for me, but it's what *I* want.'

'Well, then,' she said, coming close enough to grip my hand in hers, 'I'll help in any what I can.'

'Thanks. And you can start by letting me have tomorrow off school. I know I need to speak to Gray, but I'm just not ready yet.'

'One day off is fine, but you will talk to him soon. And Layla. Promise me that.'

'I promise.'

Nineteen

Beth

I STAYED home from school again. I couldn't look anybody in the eye—not yet. I needed to fully accept my decision before going in all guns blazing.

'Hey,' my sister said, coming into the lounge and sitting down next to me on the sofa. 'What you up to?'

'Just been writing down some names,' I said with a small shrug. 'Thought if I did that I'd feel a bit more sure about keeping the baby.'

'I don't think that's how it works.'

'Me neither, but I thought it was worth a try.'

She nodded, and I closed my notebook, not wanting her to see inside just yet. It was private.

'Maybe I'll pull a Tara and call my kid Seth,' I said with a smile. 'I've always wondered why she didn't try and call me Zara. Or even Mara.'

My sister's face turned serious, and she stared at me intently.

'Beth…' she trailed off, looking up at the ceiling in the way she always did to gather strength. 'I need to tell you something.'

'Can it wait?' I asked, standing up. 'I was going to have a bath and then thought we could watch a movie or something.'

'Beth,' Cara said again, her tone grabbing my attention. 'I really need to tell you something.'

'What's to tell? I've forgiven you for being mad if that's what you're talking about.'

'Please,' she pleaded, grabbing my hand and pulling me back down to the sofa. 'There's something important to tell you, and I'm so scared you won't forgive me for it.'

'You're being silly now,' I chastised. 'There's not much I wouldn't forgive you for.'

'Just… hear me out until you make that kind of statement, yeah?'

'Okay…' I trailed off, looking at her face, the worry lines around her eyes deeper than I'd seen them in a long time. It always happened when my sister was super stressed, and with the move to a new town and a new job—and now a pregnant teen sister—I could understand her stress.

'Shit,' she whispered, biting her bottom lip. 'I have no idea where to start.'

'If not the beginning'—I reached for her hand and placed it in mine—'then how about you start by telling me what brought this on?'

'Your pregnancy,' she replied in an instant. The words bubbled out of her mouth, already having sat on the tip of her tongue. 'I was so mad at you when you told me. So mad.'

'I know—'

'Let me finish,' she said, effectively cutting me off. She started again as if I hadn't interrupted. 'I was so mad. But not at you. No. I was mad at myself for not preventing this. For not making sure you knew to be safe. For not doing what any parent should.'

Cara had always acted like a mix between a big sister and a parent. With a mum like ours, she felt like she needed to be everything for me that Tara wasn't. Make up for the lack of a motherly bond between me and Tara.

Over the years, I made it clear to Cara that it wasn't her place to make me feel better. That it wasn't her duty. She'd done everything for me and more.

Fuck. Even making sure the move to Hollowdale was good

for me before she took the new job was more than she needed to do. Not that I would've wanted to stay with Mum, but still. I would've if she needed me to.

'Cara,' I said, squeezing her hand, attempting to put all my love and appreciation for her into that action. 'It's not your fault we have a crappy mother. And it is *not* your fault that I'm pregnant. I was stupid, and I forgot to take my pill that weekend. That's on *me*. Not you.'

'I don't think you understand, Beth,' she said, her voice cracking when she uttered my name. 'I've failed you in so many ways.'

'No, you haven't.'

'But I have!' She sniffed, tears leaking from her eyes. 'Because I've not been honest with you. We didn't just move here because I got a new job.'

'Then why did we move here?'

'Because your father insisted on it,' she said, her bottom lip wobbling as her sobs became louder. 'He wants to meet you. Wanted you to go to his old school. Hoped you'd love it here the way he does.'

'My father?' I snatched my hand from hers and moved to face her fully. 'You mean *our* father?'

'No,' she whispered. 'I mean, *your* dad. Shit, Beth. There's so much I should've told you. And now here we are. History repeating itself.'

'What does that even mean?' I cried, standing up to look down at her. 'Why the fuck are you being so cryptic? Just tell me what's going on!'

'Please sit down. Sit down and I promise I'll tell you everything.'

I paced up and down a couple of strides, my mind and body at war. Half of me wanted to listen to her plea. Go and sit by her side. The other half knew that a shit bomb was about to hit, and I wasn't sure if I wanted to be in a position I couldn't easily flee from.

My love for my sister won out, though, and I took my seat beside her once more.

She grabbed both of my hands and held them in hers, looking me dead in the eyes with her wide hazelnut ones that matched mine.

'When I was sixteen, I fell pregnant.'

Her words sent a shock wave through me. I hadn't expected that at all. Not that I even knew what I was expecting, but still.

'I'd been with the same guy since I was thirteen, and for all that we could be at that age, we were deeply in love. He came from the wealthy side of town, on the other side of the divide, but that didn't matter to us. When I took the test and found out, he was the first person I told. And he vowed to stand by me. Shit, Beth, the two of us were thrilled. We knew we were young and that people would frown at us, but we didn't care. We were happy.

'Until we told our parents and shit hit the fan.' She took a deep breath, removing one of her hands from on top of mine to wipe away some of her tears that were still silently streaking down her face. 'They were the opposite of supportive and they told us we either had to give our baby up for adoption or terminate the pregnancy altogether.

'And I couldn't do either of those things. Not to my precious baby. So Ethan's parents came up with another solution. One they believed would benefit everybody.'

She shook her head, her anger growing alongside the sorrow.

'Even back then, Mum had a drinking problem and the entire town knew it. We had little money, and we were barely keeping up the payments on our flat on the estate. And they had the money we so desperately needed. So, they paid us off essentially.'

'How?' I whispered, drawn into her words, wondering where on earth the story ended.

'They would pay us one hundred thousand pounds if we moved out of Beurre, stayed away until I had the baby, and when we returned, Mum would pretend the baby was hers and nobody would be any the wiser.'

My breathing sputtered, and I believed I was about to choke on the very air around us. *What is she telling me?*

'Mum, of course, jumped on it. I was apprehensive, but that kind of money for us at that time was life-changing. It could completely change our lives—and the life of my unborn child. And if we didn't take the money, they were going to send Ethan off to boarding school and I wouldn't see him for years, and I couldn't do that to him. I loved him too much to fuck up his life even more.

'So we moved away within the week, and at first, I heard from Ethan daily. But as time went on, our contact lessened. His parents were overbearing, and they controlled everything in his life to the point that when my baby was born, they never let him come visit. He was engaged within the year and I didn't hear from him, except for every year on our daughter's birthday.' She looked at me, her eyes boring into mine. *'Your* birthday.'

It was only then that I realised I started crying a while ago, completely caught up in her story, knowing in my gut where it was going, but too fearful of that possibility to put faith in it.

'You're my *mum?*' I stuttered, stumbling over my words.

My heart sank.

The beats were coming too slow as my breathing shallowed.

My sister's—no, my *mum's*—words repeated in my mind.

'I am so, so sorry, Elizabeth. I never wanted to hurt you.' Her vice-like grip on my hands turned her knuckles white with the effort. 'Everything I've done in this life was for you to have a better one than I had, and I've royally fucked that up. Mum blew through the money from the Bakers within five years, and by then, I was too embarrassed to move back to Beurre. I couldn't face Ethan and his new fiancée, for starters. Plus, we'd signed a contract, so even though the money had run out, I still couldn't be upfront and tell people I was your mum.'

I couldn't look away from her. Couldn't bring my eyes away from her grief.

'But why keep up the charade, then?' I asked, confused and hurt.

My head swam with different thoughts—some hateful, others pitying. *I* was the one who had been cheated of a true mother. *I* was the one in the dark my entire life. Lied to. By those who were meant to love me.

How could they look me in the eyes all those years, knowing what they knew?

'If you didn't move back to Beurre, then there was no reason to lie and say Tara was my mum,' I said, holding back my tears.

'By the time the money ran out, you were about to turn six. You'd started school, made friends, and introduced me to everybody as your cooler older sister. I didn't want to confuse you and uproot your life more than I already had. Hindsight is twenty-twenty, and I would do everything differently if I had my time again. But I don't, so I have to live with my poor choices. I was a twenty-one-year-old with no job and no way to sustain myself— let alone my daughter, too. So I wrote to the Bakers without Ethan's knowledge and asked for more money. Threatened that if they didn't cough up, I would show up on their doorstep with you in tow.'

'And they gave you more money?'

She nodded.

'They did, and I put it in a savings account for you straight away, so Mum couldn't get her grubby hands on it. From then on, I vowed to myself to be the best mum I could be for you, by being your sister.'

'How could you let me think my own mother hated me?' My lip wobbled and a deep-rooted sob left my throat. 'For years I've thought I was unlovable because of how that woman has treated me.'

Betrayal filled my gut. Bile, thick and heavy. Acidic. Weighing me down.

'I'm sorry,' she said. 'At first, the two of you had a bond. You were a mummy's girl, and while we had the money, Mum treated you like a little princess. It was only once she contacted the Bakers asking for more money and found out I'd already done that and hidden it from her that she turned nasty towards you. By then, you were ten, and I didn't want to ruin your life by shattering all you knew.'

'But it's okay to do that now?' I shouted, my anger bubbling to the surface, overriding the sadness filling my heart.

'There's nothing more I can say except I hope one day you accept my apology and you understand my decisions. I was a year younger than you, in the same position as you, and I was scared. The Bakers are a formidable family, Beth.'

I ripped my hand from hers and rubbed my stomach, feeling the warmth of my slight bump through my T-shirt, gathering strength from the baby I knew was growing in there. *My baby.* One I would do anything for.

'If the Bakers are so formidable, then why did you bow to Ethan's demands to return to Hollowdale this year? Why now?'

'Because your grandparents died last year, and he's divorced his wife. He has so many regrets about how it all went down, the same as me.'

I let her words sink in, a pang stabbing my heart. I had grandparents I never even knew about—and they were dead. I could see the anguish on her face. The regret. The sorrow. But I couldn't focus on how she felt yet. Not when I hadn't worked through my own emotions.

'What happened to the messages he sent on my birthday?'

'I kept them all, and the gifts, too. They're in the attic. If you want to see them, I'll get them down for you. I knew one day you'd learn the truth, and I wanted to have everything for you when you were ready.'

Inside, I was numb, but I nodded anyway. Of course I wanted to read those notes. See those gifts. My whole life, I had wondered why my parents didn't love me. Why I wasn't worthy of the love I saw the kids around me getting.

As much as I loved Layla, the way her parents were made me bitter on a couple of occasions over the years. They truly loved and cared for her. They were devastated when everything came out about Coach Driscoll and did everything in their power to ensure Layla healed from the ordeal.

'Can I go now?' I asked, wanting to escape the room. I had no idea where I was going to go, but I knew I couldn't sit here with her for a moment longer. Not until I got a better handle on myself.

'Do you hate me?' she whispered, her eyes wide. A flash of fear ran through them.

'No,' I said, being honest. 'But I'm also not ready to just pretend you haven't lied to me my whole life. Let me believe my mum was a drunken waste of space who didn't love me. I just… I need some time.'

She tilted her head and gave a slight nod of acceptance.

'I'll be here to talk whenever you're ready,' she replied. 'Just give me the word and I'll come running—even if I'm at work, okay?'

'Okay.' I stood up and moved away from the sofa.

To my bedroom? Or the front door?

My fingers grazed my stomach, and I knew where I needed to go.

I needed to go and see Grayson. Make things right between us. To tell him I'd made the drastic step of visiting the clinic, but that I knew in my heart I was keeping our baby—whether he liked it or not.

And mostly, I just needed to feel loved, even for a moment.

Twenty

Grayson

'I've got something to tell you.'

My words rang through the room, echoing off the walls and the ceiling, back to where Arianna and I were sitting on my bed. She was sitting cross-legged across from me and I was leaning up against my bed's headboard, my legs stretched out in front of me, lazily lounging.

I'd listened to her for the last half hour, and the fact she'd opened up to me only made me want to tell her more about the situation Beth and I found ourselves in.

It sat heavily on my gut that nobody knew about the pregnancy, but I'd respected that Jacobs didn't want anyone knowing just yet.

When Arianna arrived at mine, I was in the middle of getting ready to leave and go to see her. I'd fucked up. Let the fear of my own father shape the way I felt about becoming a father myself. But fuck, the fear of being a shit dad was overwhelming. Crashing through me and crushing me with every lungful of breath.

From one glance in Ree's eyes, though, I knew I couldn't leave her in that state. My plan was to sort out whatever shit Ree was going through and then head on over to the Jacobses' home. It was still the plan. It was just taking a little longer than expected.

And with Arianna in front of me, I wanted a girl's perspective, and she was the best thing I had.

'You finally gonna tell me why you've been acting strange the last couple of weeks?' she said, leaning forward. 'Or is it about that shiner you've been sporting since last weekend?'

'Bit of both, I guess.'

'Then hit me,' she said, getting comfortable. Her large brown eyes were a mixture of wariness and excitement. It killed her not to be in the know. And it was the first time I hadn't told her something the moment it took place. 'Least I can do, seeing as you've just listened to my crap.'

I nodded.

Inhale. Exhale.

'Okay, so remember my birthday party?'

'Yes...' she said, dragging out the S.

'You saw me go upstairs with Beth, right?'

She nodded, her eyes filled with questions, but her mouth stayed closed.

'We fucked that night.'

'*Fucking hell,*' she said, her eyes widening further. 'Have you *seriously* only just realised?'

'Sort of...' I trailed off. Guess it cleared up whether or not Arianna had known about it, but just kept it to herself. She'd accused me of it the morning after, but I didn't entertain the idea for even a moment. 'I still can't really remember much of that night.'

'You were plastered. I warned you not to get so drunk so fast.'

'Yes, Mum, I remember.' She stuck her tongue out at me and I continued. 'But either way, I don't remember it, and I feel fucking shit about it because she was a virgin.'

'Fucking hell, Grayson.' Her eyes locked with mine, the disappointment in me lingering there, hitting me in the heart. 'And you've just been dating the girl not even knowing you've already had sex with her?'

I winced. When she put it that way, it seemed even shittier.

'I suppose. But that's not even the worst of it.'

'I mean, can it get much worse?'

'Yeah, Ree. It can.' The seriousness in my tone made her pause in our back-and-forth. She raised a well-groomed eyebrow in my direction and waited for me to spit out the words sitting on my tongue. I sat forward, no longer able to lounge back when I was about to say something so serious. 'Beth's pregnant.'

'She's what now?' she shrieked.

'Beth's pregnant.'

'She told you that?'

'Yep. Last weekend.'

She nodded, mulling it over.

'Shit. She didn't give you the black eye, did she?'

'She's not like that, Ree,' I said with a deep sigh. 'But no, that's courtesy of the old man.'

'Oh.'

'Yeah. Oh.'

'What are you gonna do about it? Is she going to have an abortion?' she whispered.

Bile filled my stomach, and my vision blurred. *Why hasn't that crossed my mind?* Literally at no point during the last week when I thought about what we were going to do did I think she'd possibly want to get rid of the baby. Of *our* baby.

'I don't know,' I croaked out. 'It didn't even enter my mind.'

'That she may want that?'

'That it was even a thing she could do. All I've been thinking about the last week is a way we can make it work. A way the two of us can bring a life into the world. *This* world. And have it be a normal, healthy, and okay situation.'

'Any solutions?'

'Not one,' I admitted.

'Have you not spoken about it?' she asked, concern written on her face.

'I—' I stopped talking, sitting up even straighter. 'I haven't spoken to her at all.'

'*At all?*' The disappointment in her voice was a knife. The glare in her eyes a wound.

'No,' I said and swallowed. The shame in my gut manifested itself on my face as my cheeks warmed and all I wanted was for the bed to suck me in and spit me out in a fountain of blood like that dude in that horror film. 'I've avoided her.'

'Jesus, Gray! I didn't think you were that much of a dickhead. If I didn't want to hug you, I'd smother you.'

'I'll take the hug,' I told her. 'I'm sorry. I fucked up.'

'Don't be apologising to me. I only learned about it five minutes ago. The person you should be apologising to is your girl. You've really let her down. I can't even imagine the worries going through her mind right now. The fear. The absolute shame and terror of the kids at school learning about it.'

'You can't tell anybody.'

'Who do you think I am? Of course I'm not gonna tell anybody.' Arianna uncurled her legs from their crossed position and rose up on her knees to shuffle closer to me. I leaned in at the same time as she did, pulling her into my chest for a tight hug. My nose was buried in her hair, her scent comforting to me, and I inhaled.

'Dude. Are you smelling my head?' She chuckled, her body vibrating in my arms.

'Just let me have this,' I said, laughing a little for the first time in a week. The dark thoughts threatening to creep in—lurking at the edges.

The way I reacted when Beth told me, I wouldn't blame her if she wanted to have an abortion. If she'd lost all faith in me.

The courage it must've taken to show up at my home and tell me about it was vast, yet I'd shat on it from a high height.

'Gray,' Ari said from her spot buried in my chest. 'You have to talk to her. Listen to her. Let her cry. Comfort her. Whatever she needs, you have to do it. Fuck, man, you've got to grovel on your fucking knees and apologise until you're blue in the face.'

'I know,' I agreed. 'But it's hard. Not like I have a great father figure to use as a role model.'

'No, and I wouldn't exactly suggest you look at mine either for tips.' She sat back, a wince covering her face that she disguised in an instant. 'But the first thing on the agenda is talking to Beth. Properly. Without distraction and without you running off again!'

'You're right. I need to go see her.'

She pushed my shoulder in jest, a laugh trickling from her, as she shouted, 'Of course you do, you big idiot! What are you even still sitting here with me for?'

I stood up, the mattress bouncing Arianna with the loss of my weight, and I made my way out the door. Arianna's feet weren't far behind, and the two of us hotfooted it down the stairs, getting to the front door at the same time.

Ree reached out and unlocked the door, opening it wide for us both to leave through, but she paused and grabbed my hand to squeeze it.

Leaning up on tiptoes, she kissed my cheek and whispered, 'For the record, Gray, you're going to be the best dad.'

A small laugh left my mouth, and Arianna smiled back, a giggle bubbling out of her at the sheer insanity that was my life.

It was the gasp we heard as she did so that stopped our laughter.

'You two look like you're having fun,' Beth said, her face sour and unimpressed. 'I came over here to talk to you, but guess I'll just come back another time.'

'I was just on my way to yours,' I told her, trying to catch her eye, but she averted her gaze so I couldn't. 'Ree was just leaving.'

'The wrong thing to say, Gray,' Ree whispered from where she'd moved behind me.

'Oh, was she? Bored with her already and thought you'd crawl over to me?'

'No!' I said, my hand reaching forward to touch her, but she took a step away from me. The movement hurt more than her words. 'Arianna came over to talk. That's all.'

Arianna took a step to the left from where she was half-hidden behind me, coming into Beth's eyeline, and received the full force of her fury.

'Hey,' Ree said with a small wave. 'This is one hundred percent *not* what it looks like.'

'And what do you think it looks like?' Beth asked, and the cold air mixed with her tone gave me a chill. 'Like you were about to go out on a date, all laughing and joking around, while I was at home waiting for Gray to call?'

'I promise, Jacobs. That wasn't it at all. I was on my way to talk to you about…' I trailed off, not wanting her to know I'd told Arianna the situation we were in. '*Stuff.*'

'I'll leave you two to it,' Ree said, stepping out of the house and passing Beth quickly. 'I'll text you later.'

I nodded, waving her goodbye before turning my focus back on Beth.

'Want to come inside?'

'I don't want to go anywhere with you.'

'Don't be like that. It wasn't anything. Me and Ree are friends, Beth. Best friends. Of course I'm gonna talk to her without people around.'

'Even when the only person you should be wanting to talk to is me?'

'Beth, I—'

'Save it, Gray.' She shook her head, her disappointment towards me seeping out of every pore. 'Did you tell her?'

'I… I—'

'Did. You. Tell. Her?' she bit out each word, hugging her body with her arms. No, not her body. Her stomach.

I swallowed. The answer was not going to go down well.

'Yes,' I admitted with a wince. 'Just the same as I'm sure you've told Layla.'

'I haven't said a word to her.' Well, that was news to me. The two of them were best friends, so of course I'd assumed Layla would be the first person she told. 'I've only spoken to two people.'

'Two is more than my one!' I said, frustrated. 'Who have you been blabbing with?'

'Blabbing?' she spat. 'I've *talked* to my mum and Remi.'

'Remi Riley? What are you doing talking to her about us?' I sputtered. 'I didn't even know you were friends with her. That you knew her, even.'

'She saw me when I—' she stopped mid-sentence. 'It doesn't matter how it happened, but we're friends.'

'Do you want to come in and talk?'

'No,' she said. 'I think I'll head home.'

'Well, can I at least walk you there?'

'I drove,' replied, pointing at the car parked at the kerb.

'We could go somewhere neutral,' I pointed out. 'Please, just talk to me.'

'I can't. Not now. I need to get home.'

'Oh. Well, then I guess I'll leave you to it,' I said, not happy in the slightest that she was trying to avoid me. She'd come over for a reason and if Arianna's presence hadn't spooked her, I would've learned what she wanted to say. 'Message me when you get home. Please.'

'I'll talk to you soon,' she said, backing away. 'Bye, Gray.'

'Bye,' I said, watching her get in her car, a sinking feeling filling my gut. Why did that one sentence seem so much deeper than a mere goodbye?

Twenty-One

Beth

WHEN I GOT in my car at Gray's, I didn't want to go home. I wasn't ready to face Cara and tell her I still hadn't sorted things with him.

I was being stubborn.

I was being difficult, and I knew it, but I couldn't help myself. It was as if the hormonal monster that resided within had come to the surface and was taking over my limbs—my mouth.

Where could I go?

My usual place of refuge was Layla's, but I still hadn't told her about my pregnancy and with the way I was feeling, it wasn't the right time. She'd judge Gray too harshly, and I really didn't want to bash him at that moment. Even if he was acting like a prick.

Then I remembered my new friend, and although we weren't friends in public, she'd given me her number for when times got rough.

BETH: Hey. I went to Gray's tonight and things were crappy. Can I come over?

Remi: Sure thing. Turn right at the end of Gray's road, then left. My house is the one with a red telephone box outside. You can't miss it.

I PUT my phone down and within moments I parked my car in front of her house. Remi was waiting in the doorway for me, the light illuminating her from behind, causing a creepy shadow on the path that ran from the small gate to the front door.

'Thanks,' I said when I got to her. She said nothing, just turned around and walked inside, knowing I would follow.

The house was small but cosy. Once inside, there was a small square of space for shoes and coats, then on the right there was a staircase that overlooked the living room. Further ahead was the kitchen. The entire downstairs of her home could've fit in the dining room of my new house. No wonder she'd been salty about it when she found out where I lived.

'Welcome to my humble abode,' she said, gesturing around herself.

'Remi,' a voice called from the kitchen, hidden from our view. 'Remi, dear.'

Remi blinked and called back, 'Yes, Nan?'

'Did I hear the front door go?'

'My friend Beth's here,' Remi said, and it felt good to be called her friend. I'd thought of her as a friend since she helped me get my head on straight, but I wasn't sure if she thought the same. Remi kept to herself these days, even as the head cheerleader of our school's team. Layla had mentioned when I started that people turned on Remi when they discovered her lies about Layla, and that even those who'd been her friends through fear had ditched her.

A little older lady came out of the kitchen, a tea towel in her hands and a frilly apron tied around her waist. Her hair was white and her smile was kind. As somebody who hadn't grown up with grandparents, she filled my heart with joy.

'Hello, dear,' she said, coming forward and wrapping me into a tight hug. It caught me off-guard, but I welcomed it anyway. When was the last time an adult hugged me? Shit, even Cara hadn't hugged me since my pregnancy became a barrier between us. 'I'm Flo, Remi's nan. Remi told me about your situation. If you ever need anything, you can come to me and Ron.'

'Huh?' a man's voice called out, and Ron appeared from the kitchen, touching his ear. 'Did you say my name?'

'Yes, I did, you deaf bat.' Flo let me go and rolled her eyes at me as if we were in on a secret together. 'Sorry about him, dear. He turns his hearing aid down when it suits him.'

'Only when you don't stop talking,' he said gruffly. He looked at me and smiled, his white dentures a little too big for his face. 'Name's Ron.'

'Hello,' I said, beaming at them both. Remi sighed beside me and shifted her weight from her left to her right side. I didn't realise Remi lived with her grandparents. Why would I? 'Nice to meet you both.'

'Would you like some dinner? I'm in the middle of cooking macaroni and cheese.' My stomach growling answered for me, but I looked at Remi first for confirmation that she was cool with it. She tilted her head, and I took that as permission.

'Please. I love macaroni and cheese!'

'Just you wait!' Flo said, bustling with energy. 'I make the cheese sauce myself. Special recipe. You're going to love it.'

'I can't wait,' I said, salivating at the mere thought of it.

'We're gonna go upstairs while we wait, okay?' Remi asked, already taking one step towards the stairs. 'Are you making your homemade garlic bread, too?'

'Yes,' Flo said, nodding. 'Best get back to it. Don't want it to burn! Will call you down when it's ready.'

'Thank you,' I said, so happy I came over.

'No problem, dear. Got to feed you and that baby up!'

I smiled, holding the tears at bay as I followed Remi up the stairs. It was the first time since telling people I was pregnant that I didn't feel judged. Didn't feel like somebody was looking at my stomach more than my face.

Upstairs, there were four doors, two to the left and two to the right. Three bedrooms and a bathroom.

'This one's my room,' Remi said, opening the door on the left of the landing. The walls were white, except for the feature wall, which was pale pink. It was a nice enough room, but I could tell she was self-conscious about it. 'You can sit on my bed.'

I did as she said and got comfortable, my back up against the wall, facing out to the rest of her room. Remi came and sat beside me, also facing her room.

'What happened?'

'I went to Gray's to talk to him, but he was already there with Arianna. The front door was open when I walked up the path and they were hugging. He placed a kiss on her neck.'

'You don't think…?' Remi asked, and the moment she did, I knew my answer.

'No. I don't,' I said. My voice was firm. 'But it still hurt me to see. That he was seeking comfort in her and not me.'

'Does she know?'

'Yeah, he told her tonight, I think. And I can't even be mad about that because I've told you.'

'But you're mad about something?'

'I don't know,' I murmured. 'I don't know how I'm feeling other than really out of whack. Everything seems too much, you know? Like every emotion is heightened. Exaggerated. Making me doubt my mind and the way I feel about people. About Gray.'

'I get you.'

'I'm sorry I came here to trauma-dump on you. We've been friends for all of two minutes and I'm already here weighing you down with my shit.'

'Not like I had anything better to do tonight,' she replied. 'Like my nan said, you're always welcome here.'

'You spoke to them about me, ay?' I said, my tone teasing, as I gave her a slight pinch on the arm.

'Didn't exactly want you showing up one day with a stomach as big as a whale and them be none the wiser.'

'Valid.'

'You gonna talk to Gray?'

'Not yet. I'm just not ready for it. And I know he means well, and that I've overreacted, but I guess I need to come to terms with it all myself first. I'm having this baby, but I can still grieve the life I thought I was going to have. And I need to do that alone first.'

Remi raised her arm and put it around my shoulder. The touch was a surprise, but I welcomed it. Leaning in, I rested my head on her chest, thankful for her hug. Thankful for her friendship, no matter how young it was.

'Thank you,' I told her, not wanting to keep my gratitude to myself.

'No problem.' She laughed, but there was no mirth in it. 'Pretty sure at this point you're my only friend.'

'I doubt that.'

'Don't. It's the truth and yeah, it's all my fault, but it still stings, ya know?'

I nodded, lifting my head so I could see her face—or attempting to. Remi just pulled me closer, so I couldn't. Her voice rumbled through her chest.

'I understand we can't be friends at school just yet, but I am your friend and I'll be here when you need me.'

'Thanks. Same goes for you.'

'Thank you.' Her voice nearly broke me. She sounded so down and sad. I made a vow to myself that I would do what I could to help her with whatever was causing her grief.

'Girls!' Flo called up the stairs. 'Dinner's ready!'

'I hope you *really love* macaroni and cheese and weren't just bullshitting for the old lady,' Remi said, removing her arm from around me and standing up. 'She'll have made way too much.'

'It's my favourite dinner,' I told her. 'Don't you worry, I'll devour it all.'

She chuckled. 'Good!'

THE FIELD PARTY was warming up around me—as was the bonfire—and with every second, my distress grew.

Beth still wasn't talking to me.

After she'd left mine in her car, the night Arianna came over last weekend, she'd messaged me to say she was home safe but that she wasn't ready to talk to me.

A whole six days had passed, and all I was getting was radio silence.

No matter how many messages or pictures I sent her way.

I placed the bottle of vodka to my lips and took a large swig, already halfway through the bottle. Every car that arrived, every group that huddled closer to the fire, I looked for my girl.

Shit. Is she even still my girl?

Of course she was. She was carrying my baby. That tied us together, whether she wanted it to or not. It meant something.

I didn't even have the pleasure of Ree's company to stop me from getting too into my own head. She and Rock were having an important dinner with their parents, so neither of them was at the party.

Headlights lit up the area, and I looked over to where people parked their cars and saw Layla's old beat-up Ford. Hope rose in my chest. If Beth was gonna show, it would be with Layla and Dean.

I swaggered over, attempting to walk straight but failing. Maybe it was my second bottle of vodka?

I didn't even know anymore.

'Hello, hello, hello,' I said, reaching the car as they began to get out. Layla and Dean eyed me with suspicion, and Alex and Peter got out the back, but no Beth.

'Where is she?' I demanded, pissed that she wasn't there, but also not wanting them to see me lose my cool. They wouldn't tell me where she was if I did.

'Where do you think?' Dean asked, stepping in front of me, puffing out his chest. 'She's at home. Alone. Because of *you*.'

'Because of me?' I scoffed, taking another sip of my drink. 'You got proof of that, dickhead?'

I wondered if she'd told them about her pregnancy. She hadn't mentioned it to me, but she had mentioned nothing to me in a while. When I told her I'd told Arianna, she mentioned she was yet to tell Layla, but that was a week ago. Things may have changed during that time.

'As a matter of fact, I do. You've been having it off with Arianna behind Beth's back and she's had enough of it.'

Well, I wasn't expecting that.

'I have? That's news to me.'

'You were seen with her at a party a couple weeks ago, and then Beth found you at your place sharing an over-friendly kiss goodnight.'

Layla was staying silent, her body wrapped tightly to Dean's, his arm draped over her shoulders. The two of them were the perfect picture of a perfect teenage couple, and a shot of guilt went through me.

That should be me and Beth. A united front. Happy to spend time together and be public about it. I'd asked her to be my girlfriend and then from that moment on I'd been a massive prick, treating her like shit.

'You should go talk to her,' Layla said. 'She wanted to come tonight, but she's not feeling well.'

'Not feeling well?' I asked, my ears perking up, trying to decipher whether Layla was in on the secret or not. 'What's wrong with her?'

'Feeling sick, I think,' she said with a shrug. 'Maybe you could take her some cherry drops and energy drink? It's usually what she wants for comfort when she's not well.'

If she was feeling sick, it must be because of the baby, right? I wanted to go to her. Wanted to help where I could. Would she want to see me?

Fuck it. Even if she didn't, I needed to try. Everything was messed up between us, and I hated it. Jacobs made me laugh. She made me happy. And ever since she stopped talking to me, everything became a black pit, and I didn't want to dwell in it any longer.

'I'm gonna go see her.' My mind ran through the ways I could get to hers faster. At least I didn't have a license. Otherwise, I might do something stupid like getting behind a wheel drunk. My eyes scanned the field, resting on where Tyler and Remi were in a heated discussion, and I knew my next step.

'That's the right response, dickhead,' Dean said. 'But if I hear that you've made things worse, I *will* kick your arse.'

'Go for it!' I shouted at Dean over my shoulder as I stomped over to Tyler and Remi. When I got there, I blurted, 'I need a ride.'

'And why the fuck you asking us?' Tyler said, raising an eyebrow at me, a beer bottle in his hand.

'I wasn't asking you,' I said, turning my gaze to Remi's. Her eyes widened slightly, but she didn't look too surprised.

'Let me guess,' she said drily. 'You want a ride to Beth's? Want to make it up to her?'

'Please,' I said, ready to beg and plead if I had to. 'I need to talk to her.'

'You really do,' she agreed. 'Fine. Let me just finish here and I'll take you. Meet at my car in five.'

Tyler gave her a confused look, then turned his confusion to me, but all I did was shrug. Not like I was gonna explain Remi's tentative friendship with Beth to him. The two of them hated each other, so I didn't know why they were talking in the first place. Or arguing.

With a wave, I headed off in the direction of the cars once more.

'Thought you were going to see Beth?' Dean called out, and I gave him the middle finger, passing them to where Remi's car was parked.

I downed the vodka while I waited, trying to piece together what I would say to her. I owed her a thousand apologies and some.

'You ready to go?' Remi asked, her tone bored, holding up her car keys.

'Let's do this.'

'WHAT DO YOU KNOW?' I asked Remi the moment the two of us were seated in her car, heading away from the field.

'About what exactly?' she replied, not taking her eyes away from the road, but I could feel her peripheral gaze on me. 'About the fact that you're a knobhead who has disregarded his pregnant girlfriend's feelings? Or that said girlfriend has been stressing herself out because of your actions and potentially harming herself and your unborn child?'

'Wow, Remi. Didn't know you cared.'

'I don't care about you,' she spat. 'But I *do* care about Beth and the girl's mad about you. Not that I can see the appeal myself.'

'You were hanging off me at that first field party of the new year.'

'A momentary lapse in judgement,' she said, brushing it off. 'I've seen the error of my ways.'

'Maybe I've seen the error of mine.'

'You really think I believe that?' she scoffed. 'You're not even going into this conversation sober. I watched you at the field. You drank at least two bottles of cheap, shitty vodka, yet somehow you're still standing, which is a feat in itself.'

'Are you just gonna judge me the whole ride there?'

'Most likely.'

'Remind me again how you and Beth are even friends?'

She bristled at that, slowly blinking, and I didn't think she was going to answer me.

'What did she tell you?'

'She didn't. Just said that you're friends.'

'Accept that for what it is then,' she said, turning the car down Beth's street. 'Just know that I care about her, and if you so much as fuck this up even a little, you'll have me to answer to.'

'You and Dean Walters, it would seem.'

'The two of us can form a line. I'm sure there would be a few people wanting to punch you if they found out how you were treating her.'

'Thanks for the reality check,' I said with a laugh. 'Remind me to come to you when I need a confidence boost.'

Remi pulled up outside Beth's and parked, leaving the car idling.

'Don't go in there all guns blazing, Grayson,' Remi said. 'You need to talk to her properly.'

'I'm not a complete knobhead, Rem. I know what I need to do.'

'Do you?' she asked, swivelling in her chair to face me. 'Because if you did, you'd have done it already and not waited a week to get the balls to face her.'

'Look. I know you know what's happening between us.'

Remi nodded.

'And I know it looks like I've been a massive prick about it all.'

She nodded once more.

'But it's hard, you know?'

'I know,' she mumbled, her eyes glossing over. 'But the two of you need to sort this. Come to some sort of conclusion. Because you can't live like this.'

'Thanks for the ride,' I said, opening the door and stepping outside. 'I appreciate it.'

'Just go sort this shit out, Gray. I'll see you later.'

I shut the car door and turned to face Beth's house. Her sister's car wasn't in the driveway, and I hoped it meant she wasn't home. We needed to talk without fear of anybody over-hearing what we had to say.

My drunk feet carried me to the door, and I knocked on it, hard, using my fist. It irritated her when people ignored the door knocker, and I wanted to get her attention.

She opened the door, a sour look on her face, but her eyes lit up when she realised it was me.

'Oh. Hey, Gray.'

'Can I come in? We need to talk.'

Twenty-Three

Beth

Remi - Gray's asked for a lift. I'm bringing him over.

I stared at my phone for a minute before I responded.

Beth - Okay

It wasn't exactly a stellar message, but Remi would forgive me. The two of us were in contact daily, even if we had nothing to do with each other at school, and she was becoming a good friend to me. I hoped that maybe one day I could be her friend in public and sort out the rift between her and Layla, but I knew that was a thing to think about in the future.

My eyes caught my reflection in the hallway mirror, and I winced. I looked like shit. There was no other way to describe it.

My black hair was unbrushed and frizzy, a mess of curls atop my head, and the dark circles underneath my eyes were evidence of just how little sleep I was getting.

Every night I struggled to fall asleep, every thought swirling through my head, every decision I could make, every choice I could take, all jousting one another, fighting for precedence. That and the fact I felt like a failure as a parent before my baby even arrived.

I was still staring at myself in the mirror when a loud knock rang through the house. Of course Gray knocked on the door itself. The fucker. He knew how much it irritated me. That was probably why he did it. To annoy me.

He was standing on the other side of the door, looking two sheets to the wind already, and I knew he wasn't anywhere near sober. *Wonderful.*

'Oh. Hey, Gray,' I said, my tone bored, as if I didn't know it was going to be him.

'Can I come in?' he asked, his tone ominous. 'We need to talk.'

I nodded and opened the door wider for him to come in, then I gave a little wave to Remi, who had stayed in her car. She waved back before driving off, presumably back to the field.

'Smells good in here. You been baking?' he asked, sniffing his nose in the air, like a bloodhound on a scent.

'Just some cookies,' I said, walking us into the living room and taking a spot on the sofa. My sister, or should I say my mum, was out on a date—which, yes, was just as much a surprise to me as you—and had left me home alone.

Things still weren't back to normal between me and Cara. Ever since she dropped the parent bomb on me, I'd tried to act as if I wasn't bothered by it. As if the betrayal didn't sting me to my core and make me want to throw things and destroy everything in my path.

'Can I have one?' he asked, already reaching out his hand to the plate on the coffee table.

'Like you're not just gonna help yourself anyway,' I said, a faint smile gracing my lips for a second before it disappeared into the nether. 'Have as many as you like.'

'You sure?' he asked, already having stuffed one in his mouth. I nodded and turned to face him, waiting for him to finish eating and say whatever it was he came here to say.

Just looking at him hurt.

His light brown hair was all ruffled and I could tell he'd run his fingers through it all night. He also had dark circles under his eyes, but I wasn't sure if they were from lack of sleep or overindulging.

From the start, I could tell that Grayson drank a lot. That he enjoyed having drinks at parties and the likes. But the more time I spent with him, the more I worried that it was a bigger problem than I first realised. He was sitting next to me and I could smell the reek of cheap vodka that emanated from him.

I gave up waiting for him to speak first.

'How many drinks have you had?'

'A couple,' he replied, wiping his hands on his jeans, looking me in the eye. 'It's a Friday night, Jacobs. I was at the field. And you weren't.'

'Glad to know you're not too drunk to notice that.'

'Why weren't you there? I thought I'd invited you to all of them.'

I remembered the words. I was also surprised he remembered them, seeing as so much of the rest of our nights together seemed to have slipped his mind.

'A party in my current state doesn't seem like much fun,' I said, waving at my stomach. 'Can't exactly drink, can I?'

'I suppose not, although I thought you came to the field for other reasons. Clearly, I was mistaken.'

'Gray, don't be like that.'

'Like what?'

'In a mood at me. Fucking hell, it should be me mad at you! You're the one cosying up to your best friend and confiding in her instead of talking to me about our problems.'

'I was on my way to see you, yet you wouldn't hear me out. What was I supposed to do? All week I've sent you messages and you've ignored every single one.'

'I had a lot going on.'

'And I don't?' he asked, exasperated with me. 'I'm trying to pass science, keep my head afloat, not piss off my old man, *and* keep you happy and figure out a plan of action for us to move forward.'

'I've got something to tell you.'

'Go on.'

'You know me and Remi are friends?'

'Well, yeah. That's how I knew she'd bring me here.'

'Right...' I said, taking a deep breath. 'I never told you *how* we became friends.'

'No, you didn't. Assume you're gonna tell me now?'

I nodded. 'We bumped into one another the other week when I took the day off from school. Not sure if you remember, but anyway. It was the week after you showed up at school with a black eye, and I'd told you I was pregnant.'

'I remember,' he said, his gruff voice even rougher than usual.

'Well, that day I was booked in at the clinic.'

'The clinic?' he said, furrowing his brow. 'What clinic?'

'The one they run on Wednesdays at the hospital,' I told him. 'I went there to discuss my options.'

'*Your* options?'

'Yeah. I went to ask for an abortion.'

His eyes narrowed, and he fidgeted, agitation rife in his body. My hand reached out to grab his, but he snatched it away and moved an inch back so there was even more space between us.

'You were going to do that without telling me first?' he asked, his voice low. 'You were going to do that without *discussing* it with me first?'

'I—'

'You what?' he bit out through gritted teeth, his anger climbing. 'There's no explanation that makes this okay, Beth.'

'Isn't there?' I spat, my temper rising alongside his. My voice was shrill, but I couldn't help it. All of my frustration climbed to the surface, needing to be released. 'Because you kicked me out of your house when I told you I was pregnant. Told me it was my fault! That I *took advantage* of you! Then showed up at school with a black eye and ignored me! What else was I supposed to do? I had nobody else to turn to!'

'You had me!' he shouted. 'Okay, I kicked you out, but that was only because I didn't want my dad meeting you. I was going to talk to you afterwards, but then I got caught up in feeling shit about myself. My dad is awful, and worry smothered me I'd be the same way to our kid. But I snapped out of it, and the moment I did, I came to see you, to talk to you.'

'You were with Arianna.'

'We're going around in fucking circles,' he said, his eyes still flashing with a glint of anger aimed towards me. 'You've hurt me.'

The low admission gutted me. Grayson seemed so calm and above it all most of the time, and even though I knew he was soft-hearted underneath it all, even I had forgotten at the most crucial of times. By not talking to him and going to the clinic, I'd dismissed his feelings as if they didn't matter.

As if *he* didn't matter.

Which was exactly how his mum and dad had treated him his whole life. I wasn't any better than them, and that made me sick.

'I'm sorry, Gray. I didn't mean to make you feel like shit, even if you made me feel like shit first.'

'I know,' he said. 'But you managed it, anyway.'

I HAD to get out of there.

Had to leave and go back to the field. Drink myself into oblivion.

Literally do anything other than sit across from her and feel so much hatred towards her. It was irrational, and I knew my anger wasn't for Beth, but I couldn't stop myself. Like a sink about to overflow, the poison seeping into every crack, I would explode and the result wouldn't be pretty.

'I'm leaving,' I announced, standing abruptly and making my way to the front door. I couldn't look at her wide, rich-brown eyes any longer without cracking. 'Don't follow me.'

A sob came from behind me, but I didn't turn around to look. Beth crying would tip me over the precarious ledge I was balancing on.

'Where are you going?' she cried, yet I still didn't answer her.

I couldn't.

The door slammed behind me as I moved on angry feet away from her fucking large palace of a house and her rich, wealthy life. It never bothered me when I was at Arianna's mansion, but with Jacobs, it made me realise just how inferior I was to her. Who the fuck was I, really? A boy from the wrong side of the tracks who lived on the estate, who got one of the girls on the right side of the 'divide' pregnant.

It made me sick. *I* made me sick.

And I couldn't even remember it. Couldn't even remember the night she got pregnant in the first place because I was so fucking wankered I barely knew my name the morning afterwards. Barely knew where I was. Assumed our time together was a fucking dream I'd had.

When Arianna had told me that maybe Beth would be considering not having the baby, it cut me, but I didn't think it was an actual thing to worry about. The way Beth stormed into my bedroom, telling me she was pregnant, wanting to figure out a way we could make it work as parents, made me never consider the alternative.

Did she want an abortion because of me? Because of the way I treated her?

Thoughts filled with self-hatred and loathing consumed me.

I wasn't fit to be a father, and I for sure wasn't fit to be Elizabeth Jacobs' boyfriend.

The only thing I was good at was getting drunk on a Friday night. And sometimes on a Saturday night. And occasionally on a weekday.

Was my drinking becoming a problem? Fuck if I knew. I just knew it made the days more bearable. The looks from others in town easier to swallow.

Everybody knew my old man. Knew that he was likely to be pissed at one of the seedier spots, like Pleasure Island, the local strip bar. It was what he'd done for as long as I could remember. Ever since Mum left, if I was putting a date on it.

Lights burned my eyes, and I blinked, staring around, trying to place myself. My anger had taken me back towards the field, back to the alcohol, but I still had at least fifteen minutes until I got back there.

Would Remi come get me? I doubted it. She wanted me to sort things out with her *friend*. Remi never did something if it didn't benefit her, and I knew Beth believed her, but I wasn't so sure.

Of course, her giving me a lift was nice and all that. But one generous action didn't mean a person was changed.

The fountain in the middle of the town centre loomed up ahead, ominous and spooky-looking. The perfect place to pause and take stock of my situation. But then the lights of the local supermarket caught my eye, and seeing as I was out of vodka, it only made sense to go buy another bottle.

One more bottle wouldn't hurt, would it?

Next thing I knew, I was back at the field, the bonfire raging next to me and some girl sat on my lap.

'Want me to stay?' she whispered in my ear, her words slurred. 'I'm more than happy to sleep in your tent.'

I shook my head, knowing that whatever was happening wasn't right, but my limbs were too heavy to throw her off. My tongue too tired to say anything.

'Oh, for fuck's sake,' Arianna growled, ripping the girl off my lap. 'What the fuck do you think you're doing?'

'Are you talking to me?' the girl squealed from where she'd fallen on the floor.

'No,' Ree spat. 'I'm talking to this prick.'

'Ouch,' I said, rubbing my head. 'Not so loud.'

'Get over yourself.'

'What are you even doing here? You had a family dinner.'

'Which was a disaster. Thanks for asking.' The venom in her tone wasn't completely aimed at me, it would seem. 'I got a text from Spencer and came straight here.'

'He should keep his nose in his own business.'

'He cares about you and can tell you're drowning!' She grabbed my arm and hauled me up. 'We're not talking about this here.'

'About what?' I called out. 'The fact that Jacobs—'

'DO. NOT,' Ree warned. 'You *will* regret it.'

I nodded, ashamed that my first instinct was to call her out in front of so many people. To divulge Beth's secret to people she didn't know or like.

She dragged me to a spot behind her car, shoving me to the floor and then sitting down beside me.

'Where's Rock?' I asked.

'Sorting out something with Tyler,' she said, her tone telling me that I wasn't in a position to be the one asking questions. 'Stop trying to change the subject.'

'My head is fucked right now. Can't we talk about this later?'

'Grayson,' she said, forcing my face to look at her with her finger. 'You need to hear this shit. Get it through your thick skull.'

'Get *what* through my skull?' I asked, gripping her chin to keep her in place, too. 'I've already accepted that I'm gonna be a shit dad!'

'You're not gonna be a shit dad, Gray. Keep your fucking voice down.'

'There's no way of knowing that.'

'If you continue to drink yourself into stupidity every day and let random girls sit on your lap when you have a girlfriend, then sure. You'll be the worst fucking dad there is.' She ran her hand through her hair, her tired eyes still locked on mine, her finger underneath my chin. 'But if you sort yourself out. Stop drinking. Actually act like a guy with a great girl who wants to be with them. Then maybe you won't go the same way as your old man.'

'How dare you compare me with that lowlife,' I growled.

'What?' she said with a bitter laugh. 'The same way you've been comparing yourself ever since Beth dropped the baby bomb on you?'

I didn't give her the satisfaction of letting her know she'd hit a nerve.

'Gray,' she said, her tone softening. 'You're my best friend. I love you like a brother.'

'I don't want you to love me like *that*,' I joked, and she shoved my shoulder, disconnecting our touch. 'I'm messing with you. You know I love you like a sister.'

'Then hear me when I say that you're worth so much better than this shit. Look, I don't know the girl that well, but from what I've seen, Beth's one of the good ones. She cares about you and whether you like it or not, the two of you are tied together now.'

'Is that what you think?' I mumbled, her words swimming in my mind.

'Huh?'

'Do you think I don't like the fact we're tied together?'

'Can't say you've exactly shown otherwise,' she said with a shrug, her dark hair falling in front of her shoulder. 'I know you like her. But liking her and having a life together as parents are two totally different things.'

'She's more than just the girl I like,' I said, my fuzzy thoughts trying—and failing—to grasp what it was I was trying to say. The feelings I had towards her. The emotions she brought out in me. Only one sentence came to me that made sense. That showed the true extent of it all. 'She's mine.'

'Maybe in your head,' Arianna replied, and I winced at the callousness of it.

'I fucked up.'

'Pretty sure I've heard you say that before.'

'Well, I've fucked up *again*. Help me fix it?'

'Gray, I hate to be that person.' She took a deep breath. 'But the only one who can help fix it—no, fix *you*, is you.'

'I know,' I whispered, my voice barely audible. 'I just don't know where to start.'

Twenty-Five

Beth

GRAYSON'S DRINKING worried me more than I wanted to admit to even myself.

At first, it was a harmless thing he did at parties—like everyone our age who attended them. But as time went on, I began to notice just how often he drank and just how much he had.

His birthday should've been a big indicator to me of the truth.

He didn't remember our time together. Something that meant a lot to me meant absolutely fuck all to him and although I'd come to terms with it, it still hurt.

'I'm sorry,' Layla said, and I nodded. She and Amber had come over to see if I was okay after what happened Friday night. The two of them didn't know the whole of it but had been at the field when Gray left with Remi. They were also there when he returned in a worse state than he left mine and let some girl in the year below drape herself over him like a foul smell.

It only stopped because Arianna pulled him away.

Never knew she cared so much about me.

'It's not your fault,' I said, shrugging my shoulders, resigned to it all. Grayson was acting like a grade-A wanker, and even though half of me was sympathetic, the other half just wanted to rage at him and knock some sense into his—albeit beautiful —head.

'You're taking it better than I would,' Amber said from her spot on my beanbag in the corner of my room. It was one of those large ones that ate you; one you sank so far into, you struggled for an age to get up again. Not that I'd mentioned that to Amber when she sat on it. The amusement at watching her get up was too good to pass up.

It wasn't like I could sit in it for much longer.

'It's complicated,' I mumbled, burying myself further into my duvet. In my head, my stomach was the size of a watermelon and the most obvious thing when you looked at me. Cara told me I was just imagining it. *"At most, Beth, it looks like you ate a massive roast dinner or something. A food bloat."*

I was sure she was right, and it wasn't noticeable at all, but the girls had blindsided me with their arrival and I was wearing a tight tank top I wanted to keep hidden.

'What's going on with you and Gray?' Layla asked from her spot in my desk chair, helping herself to my stash of sweets from the bag on the floor under my desk that I kept for when I had cravings.

'Yeah, I wanna know that too!' Amber said, taking a strawberry cable from Layla's outstretched hand. 'You've been so secretive lately, which ain't like you.'

My head turned to them both in turn, and I took in their open and smiling faces, feeling like a total bitch. It was time to tell them, even if my climbing heart rate told me to do anything else.

'Girls,' I said, and just that one word made them pause and look at me with serious expressions, their smiles fading. 'I've actually got to tell you something important.'

'Okay…' Amber said, sitting up a bit in the beanbag. Layla stopped slowly twirling the desk chair around and placed her feet on the floor to anchor herself, her expression one of concern.

'Don't hate me,' I pleaded, tears creeping into my eyes. 'There's so much I haven't told you guys.'

'You can tell us. We could never hate you,' Layla promised. It was easy to promise something before you even knew what you were promising, but I hoped she meant it no matter what. My white knuckles gripped the duvet closer, the soft material between my hands a comfort to me.

'So, what bomb would you like me to drop first?' I asked. 'The one about my mum and dad, or the one about me and Gray?'

'Whatever one you feel makes sense to tell first,' Layla said, and Amber nodded in agreement. I guessed it made sense to tell them my story first and then explain how it tied into my parents'.

'Okay…' I steeled myself for their reactions. 'I'm pregnant.'

You could drop a pin in the room, and you'd hear it. The two of them were so shocked at my statement, no words left their mouths. Amber opened and closed hers a couple of times like a fish, and Layla blinked twice. But other than that, there was little reaction from either of them.

'Please say something,' I said, experiencing déjà vu from the time I told my sister and I had to say the same thing to her. Fingers crossed that their next words were better than hers.

'You're pregnant?' Layla finally said, leaning forward in her chair a little, looking like she'd pass out at any second. 'Since when? You took a test at mine and you said it was negative!'

'I know.'

'Did you and Grayson sleep together again, then?' Layla asked, doing the maths in her head.

I shook my head. It was eight weeks ago that I took that test in her room. I knew that, because I had my twelve-week scan coming up the next day.

'That test wasn't negative?' she asked, and the tears I'd held back sprang into my eyes, with one breaking free and streaming down my face.

'No.' My voice was a hushed whisper. An admission of

shame, guilt, and betrayal. Every bone in my body ached at the thought of letting my longest friend down. 'I lied.'

'Why?' Amber asked, raising her eyebrow at me, sensing the tension between me and Layla. 'Why lie?'

'I'm so sorry, Layla. I saw that second line on the test and freaked. Then I wanted to tell Gray before I told anyone else, but that went to shit.'

'Why's that?'

'Once I came to terms with it all, I just couldn't bring myself to tell him. He asked me to be his girlfriend, and I just knew that if he knew the truth, he wouldn't want to be with me anymore. Plus, he never mentioned our time together on his birthday and I didn't want to make shit awkward by bringing it up.'

'We would've been there for you if you only told us.'

'I never doubted you'd be there for me,' I said, wanting to make it clear that I hadn't thought that about them. 'I just needed to accept it myself first.'

'And have you now?' Layla asked. 'Accepted it, I mean?'

'I have,' I said. 'It took some time and some conversations, but I'm ready for what's coming.'

'Has Grayson?'

'He's…' I trailed off, wondering what frame of mind Gray would be in the next time I spoke to him. 'He's terrified.'

'Makes sense,' Amber said. 'From what I know of his home life, his dad's a wanker.'

'An abusive wanker.' I looked over at Layla, waiting for her to talk, but she didn't, so I continued talking. 'Gray's worried he's going to turn out like his dad. It's causing us some… setbacks.'

'Setbacks like his behaviour Friday night?' Layla asked, and I nodded, thankful she'd said something. 'Why did he ask Remi to bring him over here, Beth? It was me and Dean who told him you'd stayed home, but instead of asking me for a ride, he turned around and went over to *her*,' she spat, 'to ask.'

I knew the Remi issue was going to come up at some point,

but I didn't think it'd be so soon, and I also didn't want to tell them how we became friends. That wasn't my story to tell.

I could lie. Of course I could. But if I was being honest with myself, I'd already told enough lies and they hadn't got me anywhere good.

'Remi knows,' I told her, the truth tumbling from my lips. Then a half-truth followed, wanting to soften the blow. 'She guessed.'

'So let me get this straight,' Layla seethed, her eyes narrowed into slits my way. 'You told *Remi Riley* before you told me?'

'It wasn't like that.'

'What was it like then?'

'I told you, she guessed. I bumped into her one day in town on my way to the hospital and I was crying. She was at Gray's birthday party and put two and two together and came up with the right answer.'

It wasn't the right time to tell her we'd become friends. I'd cross that bridge when things died down a little.

'What made you decide to finally tell us?'

'Honestly? I didn't want to tell you before I made my decision. If I wasn't going to keep the baby, I didn't want to tell you guys and have you judge me for it.' I held up my hands to stop them from cutting in. 'I know you wouldn't have judged me, but my mind was in a funny place and all I could think about was the fact that somebody would have an opinion on it that wasn't the same as mine.'

'So you're keeping it?' Layla asked, at the same time Amber spoke.

'What makes you think we won't judge you for keeping it?'

I swallowed. That thought hadn't crossed my mind. Abortion was one of those things that was deemed as shameful—something society didn't talk about—and I just assumed people would judge me if I had one, not the other way around.

'And do you?' I asked, looking over at Amber. 'Judge me?'

'For wanting to keep the kid?' She shook her head, grabbing

another cable from the bag Layla had dropped to the floor in her shock. 'Narh, not at all. If anything, I think it's brave.'

'Thanks,' I whispered, finally letting go of my death grip on the duvet to rub my stomach. Even though I couldn't feel anything yet other than a slight hardness, I still imagined I could feel my baby moving. Whenever I thought of Grayson, a flutter travelled through me and I imagined it was the small, defenceless baby growing in my stomach.

'Are you ready for that?' Layla asked. 'Are you truly ready to be a mum?'

I laughed, the first genuine smile in days covering my face, not feeling entirely sane.

'Oh, I am definitely not ready for that shit. But I know it's what I want. And I know Gray wants it, too. Or at least I think he does. He's a hard nut to crack.'

'Neither of you has great parental role models,' Amber pointed out. 'So it makes sense that you'll navigate this together in the best way you can. Not like you'd want to repeat their mistakes.'

'Well...'

'Didn't you say there was something to tell us about your mum and dad?'

I nodded, ready to tell the crazy tale. At least it had nothing to do with my poor decisions.

'When I found out I was pregnant, I wanted to tell Gray first, but one night Cara and I were watching a film together and the mix of popcorn and sweets made me vomit. She followed me to the bathroom, and the jig was up. She knew straight away and I couldn't lie to her face.'

'Nice to know there's somebody you can't lie to,' Layla said drily, and I threw one of my cushions at her.

'Shut up,' I said with a laugh. 'Anyway, she knew straight away, and it was talking to her about it that gave me the courage to go round to Gray's and tell him.

'He didn't take it well, but that's another conversation for another day. Anyway, once I returned from my disastrous talk with Gray, I booked the appointment at the clinic.'

'And talked to Remi.'

'Layla, I get it and I promise you, you can be sour about it forever if you want, but let me finish my story.'

'Fine,' she huffed, crossing her arms across her chest, but her smile told me she was joking with me—for the most part.

'When I got home, I told Cara where I'd been. She apologised for her harsh words from the night she found out, and she told me why she'd been so sad and disappointed in me.'

'Come on,' Amber said, hurrying me along. 'I'm on the edge of my bloody beanbag.'

'I don't know if I've ever mentioned it to you,' I said, looking at Amber, 'but my mum's a mess and I've never known my dad.'

Amber nodded, and I continued, 'Turns out, my sister got pregnant at sixteen and had a baby girl.'

'No shit?' Layla said as Amber sat there open-mouthed.

'Yep. History repeating and all that.' Then I dropped the real kicker. 'And it turns out, I'm that baby. Tara's not my biological mum. It was Cara all along.'

'Are you fucking shitting me?' Amber swore.

'Swear on my unborn child,' I said, and the two of them knew then how serious I was. 'My dad's a rich dude who lives in Beurre, and it was him who gave Cara the new job and helped pay for this house.' I gestured to my room with my hand and laughed. 'Apparently, his parents weren't very nice people and wanted him to marry someone of their choosing, so they paid off Cara and Tara to move and have me raised as Tara's child so nobody would question shit.'

'That's heavy, Beth.'

'Tell me about it.'

'How long have you known?'

'Six weeks or so now, I guess?' I said, thinking back to that night. 'I'm still a little in shock, I think, and because I've been dealing with my own baby stuff and Grayson, we've not really discussed it much. But get this.'

'What?' Layla asked, once more reaching into the sweet bag, no longer too shocked to stuff her face with some toffees.

'Cara wants me to meet my dad. Or should I say, he wants to meet me and Cara thinks it's a good idea. She's even dating him again!'

'Cara's dating?' Layla began to choke on the fudge, and I threw a bottle of water to her that she caught with expert fingers.

'Yep,' I said, not quite believing it myself. 'The two of them are trying to work out their shit before dragging me into it, I suppose? I've been given a reprieve because of my own baby daddy drama, but I'm sure they'll arrange a dinner or something soon.'

'Shit, Beth. There was me thinking I had it rough because the girl I like is still not out.' Amber shook her head, a small smile on her lips. 'You win this round, dude.'

'Thanks,' I said with a laugh, reaching forward for the fudge, a weight having lifted now that I'd told them the truth.

Twenty Six

Beth

THE DAY of my first scan arrived, and I was so nervous, I didn't even want to eat breakfast.

'Remember, you need a full bladder,' Cara told me and I nodded, not giving her my full attention.

'Thanks for the reminder,' I said with a wince, putting down my glass of water. There was nothing worse in my eyes than having to hold your bladder. It was cruel and unnatural. But whenever I said as much to anybody, they laughed at me and brushed it away as if I was saying it merely to make them laugh.

I wasn't.

'What time's the appointment?' she asked, popping up some toast and covering it with a sparse amount of butter. I rolled my eyes at her dry toast. There was no pleasure in that piece of bread. None at all.

'Ten,' I replied, grabbing the piece of paper on the counter with the details of the appointment. 'I'm a bit nervous.'

'That's normal,' she assured me. 'I remember my first scan with you. I was shitting it. And of course Tara didn't care enough to come with me.'

Her eyes glazed over as she lost herself in the past, and I wasn't sure how to react. Was I thankful she was coming with me? Of course I was! But we still hadn't spoken about the implications of what her being *my mum* meant.

'Did Ethan come with you?' I asked, his name tasting like tar. As much as I wanted to meet Ethan, there was something holding me back. Whether he gave me up because he wanted to or not didn't really matter in my eyes. No matter the circumstances, I grew up without a father. That wasn't going to change overnight.

'He did. The two of us cried so much, just seeing you on that screen. Or what would become you.' She laughed. 'Babies don't exactly look much like babies at this stage. What are they the size of now?'

I got up my pregnancy app on my phone and looked at what fruit or vegetable they were comparing my baby to that week.

'A passion fruit, apparently.'

'Yum,' Cara said, and I smiled. 'You going to school afterwards?'

'Yeah,' I said, knowing I needed to show my face there. 'I need to talk to Grayson.'

'Have you told him about today?'

'Nope.'

'Do you plan to tell him about today?'

'Nope,' I repeated.

'Elizabeth,' she said, reprimanding me with my full name. The full name always came out when she was unimpressed with me. 'You're not being fair to that boy.'

'I'm the one not being fair?' My voice rose to shrill levels, and I turned it down a notch when I said, 'If anyone is being unfair, it definitely isn't me.'

'You should give him the chance to show, though. He might surprise you.'

'Look, I don't want this ruined. I want to see my baby and feel all the good shit that comes with that and smile about it whenever I tell the story in the future.'

'What if you frown when you tell it because you know you're acting like a bitch to prove a point?'

'Nice to know that even as a mother, you still talk to me like your sister.'

'The dynamic isn't going to change between us because you know I'm your mum, Beth.'

I rolled my eyes and went to put my coat and shoes on, letting her follow behind me at her own pace.

It was good to know that our dynamic wasn't going to change, but then again, maybe it should?

Fuck if I knew what was best.

Not like I knew anybody else whose sister turned out to be their mum to talk to about it.

Cara came into the hall and put her shoes and coat on, while I shuffled from foot to foot, anxious to leave even though we still had forty-five minutes until the appointment.

The shuffling also came from the fact that I was bursting for the toilet and still had a long time to wait until I could go.

Nobody ever mentioned that, did they? They made the scans out to be all fun and games, but I could tell you it wasn't no picnic.

'If Grayson talks to me later and is a good human about it, then I'll invite him to the next one. How about that?'

'Guess that's better than nothing,' she said, still sour-faced. 'You ready to go?'

'Ready as I'll ever be.'

'Let's do this shit.'

THE MOMENT my baby came up on the ultrasound monitor, my heart stopped in my mouth. Every emotion flooded through me: love, sadness, caring, and even more love.

But one emotion overrode them all.

Anger.

An acute anger that stabbed my gut. One I couldn't ignore.

Looking at the monitor, I couldn't imagine handing that little bundle of, well, whatever they were at that point, over to somebody else. No matter how much money was at stake. No matter if it would result in me being shunned or kicked out. I wouldn't do it. I *couldn't* do it.

And when my eyes locked on Cara sitting on the stool beside me, I saw red.

'Oh, Beth,' she gushed, wiping a tear away from the bottom of her eye. 'How precious.'

My pulse thrummed in my ears.

'Get out,' I whispered, my voice barely audible over the many sounds in the room and the clinic on the other side of the thin walls.

'What?' Her eyes squinted, her smile slowly leaking away from her face.

'Get. Out,' I repeated, biting each word out.

My anger only grew as Cara stumbled from the room, holding her hand over her mouth to cover the sob that leaked from her lips.

'I'm sorry,' I whispered to the sonographer who was standing next to the monitor, looking a little confused about whatever had just happened. Bet she could tell plenty of stories about the shit she saw and heard during scans.

'No need to apologise to me, love,' she said with a small shake of her head. 'You're emotional and this is a big moment for you.'

I nodded, grateful for her kind words and understanding.

'I should've told the father I was coming,' I said, wishing I'd listened to Cara earlier that morning. She was right. I would feel regret when I told the story in the future.

No matter how I was feeling towards Grayson, happy or sad, anger or love, our child should never suffer because of it.

There was nothing worse than parents who used their kids as a bargaining tool. A pawn in their war.

I vowed then and there to never be that person. To never treat our child that way, even if all I wanted to do was wring Grayson's neck.

'There will be other scans, dear,' she said, patting my hand. 'This baby is strong. Look at that heartbeat fluttering away.'

My eyes went back to the monitor, and I focused in on that flutter.

A heartbeat.

After another five minutes, the scan was finished, and I got myself together and left the clinic.

On exiting the building, I expected to see Cara standing there waiting for me.

And there *was* somebody there waiting for me.

It just wasn't Cara.

TWENTY-SEVEN
GRAYSON

BETH WASN'T AT SCHOOL.

I couldn't see her anywhere, and the messages I sent her were all opened but unanswered. The two of us still hadn't spoken after I left hers in a rage on Friday night.

It was already Wednesday, and nothing.

Not one word, or glance, or *anything*.

'Yo, Grayson,' a voice called across the study hall and I followed the voice to see Dean ushering me over to his spot in the corner.

I made my way over, dragging my feet until I was standing in front of him.

'Take a seat,' he said, gesturing to the spot next to him on the sofa. I did as he asked, wondering what the fuck was happening, when he leaned in to whisper, 'Beth's at her scan.'

'Scan?' I breathed back, racking my brain for any texts or conversations about a scan coming up. 'She didn't mention no scan to me.'

'I know,' he said. 'That's why I'm telling you, arsehole.'

'Why hasn't Beth told me?'

He gave me a look that said, *why the fuck would she tell you after the way you've treated her?* and I couldn't say I disagreed with him. I'd acted like a prick, treating her like shit. No wonder she hadn't told me anything.

'Message received,' I said, and he gave a chuckle.

'Why are you telling me this? How do you even know?'

'Beth finally told Layla what was going on, who of course told me.' He shrugged as if it were a given that Layla passed it on to him. If the roles were reversed, Beth probably would've told me too. 'And I'm telling you because I think you deserve to know. Don't make me regret this.'

'Where and when is it?'

'The hospital clinic. At ten.'

I looked at the large clock on the far wall. It was already ten to ten. Even if I tried to catch the town circular bus, I wouldn't be there in time.

'Couldn't have told me a little earlier?'

'Couldn't see you,' he said. 'You're lucky I'm telling you at all given the way you've acted the last few weeks.'

'Thanks, man. I owe you one.'

'You do,' he agreed with a nod. 'Want a lift?'

'Serious?'

'No, I'm just getting your hopes up to be a knob about it afterwards. Yes, of course I'm serious. Get your shit and let's go.'

'Thank you,' I said again, meaning it. Dean and I may not be friendly anymore, but he was a good friend to Beth, and that mattered to me. 'I appreciate it.'

'Just make this worth my time. Apologise to her and sort it out. You're going to be parents and you need to grow up.'

'I will,' I vowed.

I WASN'T sure how long I paced outside the clinic before she came hurtling through the door, her eyes red-rimmed, pulling her coat tighter around herself.

When she spotted me waiting for her, her eyes widened further.

'What are you doing here?'

'Dean brought me.'

'Dean?' she asked, furrowing her brows. 'Why would Dean bring you here?'

'Because he, like me, believes that you should've told me.'

Her face crinkled. The cute wrinkle between her eyes that happened when she concentrated came out and I smiled. There were times when her cuteness overwhelmed me and made me see nothing but her.

'Want to go somewhere private?' I asked. 'I really wanna talk to you, Jacobs. We need to sort shit out between us. I'm only letting this'—I pointed at the door she exited from—'slide because I understand why you didn't wanna tell me.'

'If it helps, I felt like a big load of dog shit the entire time.'

'No, baby, that doesn't help,' I said, her eyes softening when I called her baby. It was the first time, and it slipped from my mouth with natural ease, as if I'd called her that many times before. Maybe I had in my head, or in my dreams. 'I don't want you to feel shitty for that.'

'I should've invited you.'

'Yeah,' I agreed with an easiness I didn't fully feel within. 'But it's happened and all we can do is move on from it. Let's go get some cake and you can show me the pictures.'

She nodded, sniffling, holding her tears at bay. All I wanted to do was demand she tell me what was going on, and why she was crying, but I held off.

'I don't have my car,' she told me, her eyes filling with tears again. 'I came here with Cara.'

'Where is she? Not like your sister to leave without you.'

Her bottom lip wobbled, and she whispered, 'We had a fight. I kicked her out of the room.'

Of all the things I expected her to say, that wasn't it.

'Well, you can tell me all about it over coffee and cake.'

'As long as the coffee's decaf,' she said, taking the last step to close the distance between us and reach out for my arm, looping hers through it. 'Shall we walk? It's a nice day, and it gives us time to talk.'

'Things too juicy to talk about at the café?' I asked, raising my brows at her.

'Something like that,' she said with a laugh. The two of us started walking in the direction of the town centre and I smiled at the warmth of her arm in mine. 'Where do I even start?'

There were so many places the conversation could start; so many things I wanted her to tell me. But I settled on the one I thought would be the easiest to talk about.

'Why did you kick your sister out of the scan?'

A sob came from her, and a sharp pain shot through my gut. *Huh.* Maybe I hadn't started with the easiest, after all.

'I'm gonna say something right now,' she started, 'and it's gonna sound wild. And it is wild. But Cara isn't my sister.'

'Cara isn't...?' Images flashed in my mind of the times I'd spent with them both. Of course they were related. They both had the same hazelnut brown eyes, the same button nose, the same expression covering their faces when they were happy...

'She's my mum,' Beth said, her voice cracking on the last word. 'She's my mum, Gray.'

For the first time around her, I was speechless. No words zapped into my mind or rolled off my tongue. We kept walking, our paces in step with one another, and I looked down at her face, but she was resolute in looking ahead.

'She told me after...' She shook her head, then turned her head so our eyes locked. 'After I went to the clinic that day'—she stressed the word, letting me know the dark day she was referring to—'she sat me down and told me she'd had a baby girl at seventeen. That *I* was that baby girl.'

'What? How?'

I listened as she told me the story of her parents, and how Tara had taken the money to pretend she was Beth's mum. Both of us had bonded over our shitty parents, and even though that was before we learned the truth, I still believed we'd both suffered at the hands of those who were meant to love and care about us more than anything.

'And now she's dating the guy!' she said, exasperated. 'My *dad*. He wants to meet me and Cara's all for it, as if I'm meant to just jump at the chance of meeting a dude who gave me some DNA and fucked off because his rich-as-sin parents told him to.'

'If you ever do want to meet him, I'll come with you,' I told her, stopping us on the pavement and pulling her over to the side so we weren't in anyone's way if they passed. My fingers trailed down her cheek, wiping away the tears that were still falling. 'Look, I know I've not exactly been great'—she chuckled at that, and I cracked a smile in return—'but I really do care about you. I want to make all this work for us. And if that means meeting your dad with you and helping you come to terms with the fact your sister is actually your mum, then I'll do that, no questions asked.'

A short burst of wind came at us, and we stepped closer together to huddle and keep warm. Having her pressed up against me, having her smiling at me, and happy to be in my presence, was better than any swig of vodka. Beth Jacobs was a shining light in my darkness. A beacon of hope and a future I never thought I'd have but was now well within my grasp. She was pregnant with our future and that just made me love her more.

Shit.

I was in love with her.

How had I not realised that earlier? How had I not seen the truth before that moment, standing on a pavement, the wind blowing around us?

I was in love with Elizabeth Jacobs. And I needed to sort the shit out between us.

Twenty Eight
Beth

'HERE'S OUR BABY,' I said, removing the printout from the scan from my bag and placing it on the table in front of us in between the plates of cakes and cookies.

Gray's eyes went to the printout, and he picked it up with tentative fingers, lifting it to take a closer look.

Then he looked at me with wide eyes.

'You may need to show me just what part of this is our baby.'

I laughed and leaned forward, pointing over the top of the image to where the tiny blip of our baby was.

'Right there. That's our baby.'

'Shit,' he whispered, his face going pale. 'It's real.'

'Bit of a cruel joke if I lied about it,' I said, my tone teasing. I knew he wasn't actually implying I'd lied. He was just in shock. I'd known from that very first test that I was pregnant. From the very first time I was sick that I had a baby growing inside me. But for him, it was only words until he saw the scan. And I couldn't blame him for that.

'I—' he said, his eyes lifting to mine, worry shining in them that he'd offended me somehow.

'I know.' I placed my hand on his and squeezed before I removed it to pick up my fork and continue taking small bites of the many sweet treats Gray had treated me to. 'I promise you I'll tell you about the next one.'

'When will that be?'

'In a month or so. We find out the sex then.'

'That's cool,' he said, putting the scan down and looking at me with an expression I would say was love if it was coming from Layla or Cara, but from Gray I wasn't sure. 'I'm sorry, Beth.'

'What are you apologising for this time?' I said, my tongue poking the side of my cheek as I kept myself from laughing in his face.

'I'm serious,' he said, a small smile playing on his lips. 'I'm sorry for all of it. I'm a prick. And yeah, I could blame my parents, but they weren't the ones who treated you the way I did.'

I nodded, letting him get it all out.

'I've always blamed my shitty actions on my mum leaving or my dad's drinking, so I wouldn't have to look at myself harder.' He gulped, and I knew how hard it was for him to open himself up to me. 'But I don't want that for our kid. I want them to have two loving parents who love them and care for them and would do anything for them.'

'I want that too.'

'And I want us to do it together. Be a real team. 'He took a deep breath. 'I want us to try again. Start fresh and wipe the slate clean. You're still my girlfriend in my eyes, Jacobs.'

'I never doubted we were still a couple, Gray,' I said, warmth filling me when his eyes lit up with hope. 'I just needed space from your bullshit. It's not just about me anymore and I needed to protect that.'

'I get it. And I will never stop saying sorry.'

'How about you just not do shit to say sorry for and we can do our best to move past it?'

'Yeah?'

I nodded.

'You're the best, Jacobs. I mean that.'

'You're not so bad yourself,' I replied. 'Did you mean what you said? About coming to meet my dad with me?'

'Yeah, of course. What you thinking?'

'We could go to his place for dinner with Cara on Friday night instead of hitting the field. It doesn't exactly appeal to me to spend the night with drunk teenagers when I can't drink and my stomach's gonna be noticeable enough soon for people to have an opinion.'

'Okay,' he agreed. 'Sounds like a plan.'

CARA WAS beside herself when I agreed to attend a dinner at my dad's house with her on Friday night. I made it clear from the start, though, that I would only show if Gray was able to come, too.

She agreed in a heartbeat.

Cara knew when to pick a fight, and Gray coming definitely wasn't one of them. She was still pissed at him for his actions, but I was still pissed at her for hers, so it was all a moot point.

After I got home from the café, I found her crying in the living room, a video playing on the TV from when I was younger, dressed as a princess, dancing around the room with a wand gripped in my hand.

I didn't apologise for kicking her out of the scan.

I didn't tell her I understood her actions, or that I forgave them.

But I handed her a bone in offering to attend the dinner and that would have to be enough for her for the time being.

'Do you think the food will be super fancy?' Gray asked, straightening his jacket as we stood at the front door of what could only be called a mansion. Yeah, Cara had said my dad was wealthy, and it wasn't as if I didn't believe her, but seeing his home in the flesh made it even more real.

'I hope not,' I said, rubbing my stomach. 'I can't stomach fancy food on a good day.'

'Unless it's a fancy dessert. Then you'd be game.'

'Well, of course. Who wouldn't be?'

The door opened and a man in a suit was on the other side, ready to greet us.

'Hello, Miss Jacobs, Mr Smith. I'm Jefferson, the butler.'

Butler? Oh, for fuck's sake. Course the prick who sired me had a butler.

'Hello,' Grayson said, finding his manners a lot faster than I found mine. My mouth was agape as I took in the hallway behind the man. It was a vast space with minimal furniture.

'Do come in.'

The two of us stepped over the threshold and I had to stop myself from letting out a little gasp.

I grew up in a small flat without heating most winters and then there was this man living in a palace. Anger I didn't even know I possessed bubbled up inside me, threatening to explode and shatter the expensive vases on the side tables dotted around the hall.

'Your parents are waiting in the dining hall.'

My parents. Fuck, that was going to take some getting used to.

'Are you ready for this?' Gray whispered in my ear and I nodded, rubbing my hand on my stomach. It had become a comforting habit. I couldn't wait until I could feel my baby move. It was that one step that would make everything even more real than it already was.

'No,' I said, even though I just nodded. 'If I need rescuing, you promise you'll be the one to save me?'

'Always.'

With a deep breath, I stepped into the dining room with Grayson close on my heels.

'Let's do this shit,' I mumbled under my breath, so only Gray could hear me.

The sight that greeted us made my heart stutter, and I could've sworn it was going to pack up and stop working altogether.

Because seeing my parents together for the first time was fucking unreal, and I wasn't sure that my heart—or my head—could take it.

They looked so at ease around each other. So happy to be looking at *me*, their daughter, finally.

'You're beautiful,' Ethan said in a hushed whisper. My cheeks flushed with his words, and I swallowed, taking my seat opposite Cara as Gray took his next to me opposite Ethan.

I still couldn't bring myself to call Cara anything other than her name. At times I even still slipped up in my head, calling her my sister, and I had to scold myself that she wasn't, and never would be, my sister.

'Elizabeth,' Cara said, and I squinted, wondering why she was full-naming me when I wasn't in trouble. 'This is your dad, Ethan. Ethan, this is Elizabeth.'

'Pretty sure we all knew that,' I mumbled.

'Ethan, this is Grayson, Beth's boyfriend.'

Grayson, sensing that I was about to have a full-blown meltdown at the table, said, 'Nice to meet you, sir. I've heard such great things about you.'

Which was utter bullshit because we barely knew crap about him, but I thanked Gray with a squeeze on his knee under the table, grateful he was taking the spotlight off of me.

'Please,' he said, 'call me Ethan.'

Gray nodded and continued, 'Well, *Ethan*, thank you for inviting us both to dinner. Beth and I are happy to be here.'

A sharp kick under the table from Cara had me locking eyes with hers, a look that could only be described as pleading on her face.

She wanted me to play nice.

She wanted me to act as if we were one big fucking happy family, even though we were the complete opposite.

'Yes,' I spat out, my voice sounding as if I'd swallowed gravel on the way here. 'Thank you for having us.'

'You're welcome,' Ethan said, his eyes dancing with amusement. Were the thoughts in my head plain for everybody to see? 'I understand this has all been an enormous shock for you and I can only apologise for that.'

'It wasn't your fault, Ethan,' Cara said, placing her hand on top of his, and I squirmed, a war breaking out inside of me. For so long I'd wanted to see Cara happy and in a relationship, yet now that she was, the circumstances of it all meant I couldn't be happy for her in the way I always wanted. And that sucked.

So much of my thoughts and emotions since it all went down have been from grief.

I've grieved the fact I never had a typical upbringing, knowing who my true parents were.

I've grieved for Cara and the way her love was stolen from her, and then her child was stolen from her too, in a sense.

Sometimes, the world fucking sucked and there was no other way to say or express that.

It was just how things were.

'I hear from your mother that you excel in science.'

A shiver ran down my spine. It was the first time anybody had referred to Cara as my mother, and it made me burn with rage whilst also simultaneously shine from pride that she'd been talking about me. Telling him things about me, no doubt with pride in her voice.

Cara had always been proud of me. She was the one who showed up to every Science Fair, every competition and maths-related thing I'd taken part in. The one who drove me around when I needed to be at various school events, and the one who put on my favourite movie to cheer me up whenever I lost or got something wrong.

Why was all of it so hard?

Beneath the table, Grayson's hand planted itself firmly on mine, and he gave me a reassuring squeeze. The support I needed to croak out something—anything.

'I love science,' I said, looking down at the multiple plates in front of me. Why on earth were there so many plates? Why were there so many forks? *Ignore it, Beth.* 'I've always loved things with a set answer, you know? Something that can't be left up to interpretation.'

A member of staff came and filled the glasses in front of us with water, and we thanked them, everybody taking the brief reprieve to bolster themselves for the rest of the meal.

'That's great,' Ethan said, his eyes blaring with pride. 'I know I can't claim any of it, but I'm proud of your achievements, Beth.'

I swallowed, a warm feeling travelling down to the tips of my toes at his words. At the praise. I loved being told I'd made somebody proud. Probably stemmed from how Tara treated me when I was young and I thought my mum didn't give a shit about my accomplishments.

I sought out praise from everybody after that.

'Look,' I said, locking eyes with Cara, then moving to gaze at Ethan. 'Can we cut the crap?'

They both stared back, waiting for whatever I'd say next. The two of them were so in sync, I wondered if they were eerily similar in general or if the two of them had discussed how to react in the weeks they'd reconnected.

When I didn't continue, Ethan said, 'Go on,' with an amused tilt to his lips.

'This is bloody weird for all of us.' I let out the breath I was holding and assessed the situation. 'And I know that you both want it to go well. I'm not saying I don't. But I am saying that I'm not sure where I'm at mentally regarding all this.' I waved my hand around, somehow encompassing the entire room, the whole mansion, into my point. 'I've only just found out you exist'—I pointed at Ethan—'and it feels weird to even be sitting across from somebody who has the same dimples in their cheeks that I do.'

Grayson was still silent, letting me air out whatever it was I needed to say. The point I was hoping to get across but was probably getting lost in translation because I found talking about what was going on in my mind hard at times.

Not that I couldn't talk about my feelings when pushed or provoked. It just wasn't something that came as naturally to me as it did to others.

'So,' I continued, 'I guess what I'm asking is if we can just pretend this is a normal meal. That my sis—' I faltered, shaking my head. 'That *Cara* has a new boyfriend and you've asked us here so we can all meet. As if we're four normal people who don't have a fuck-ton of baggage weighing us down.'

Ethan was the first to speak, a warm smile on his face, those dimples I saw in the mirror glaring back at me.

'If that's what you want, then that's what we'll do. We want this all to be in your time, Beth. I acted like a fool when I was a teenager and I've regretted it every day since. If you need time, then I can give that to you. After all, what's another six months in the grand scheme of life?'

My eyes thanked him, my words stuck in my throat.

Twenty-Nine
Grayson

MY HANDS SHOOK with nerves as I waited for Mr Taylor to grade the mock science test I'd just handed across.

Every study session with Jacobs, every moment we spent together in the science labs, had led to that test.

All I needed was for him to tell me I'd passed, and I knew I'd go into the actual test positive and, yeah, probably a little cocky.

I'd worked harder ever since I found out about Beth's pregnancy. I couldn't fail her. She deserved a heck of a lot more than me, but I would do everything in my power to make sure I did all I could for her. For our child.

'Mr Smith,' the teacher finally said, and I bristled at him using my surname. *Shit.* It was bad news, wasn't it?

'Yes, sir,' I called back from the stool I was perched on in the science labs, a sink to my right.

He beckoned me forward with his hand, and on slow feet, I went to the front of the room until I was standing before his desk, awaiting my result.

'Grayson,' he said, and a little of the tension seeped from my bones. 'You've passed.'

'I passed?'

'You more than passed,' he said, taking his glasses off and wiping them with his cleaner before putting them back on and smiling at me. 'There are only two students who got a better grade than you on this test, and I bet you know who one of them is.'

Of course Beth had done better. She'd probably done the best knowing her. It was something she excelled in, thrived on, even when her life was crumbling around her. Or should I say, her life crumbled around her. Because it wasn't crumbling anymore. It was slowly, brick by brick, being built up again.

By me. By Ethan. By Cara.

Layla, Dean, Amber, and Remi, too.

With everything out in the open, Beth had a bigger support unit than she'd expected. And once the other kids at school found out she was pregnant—and that I was the dad—nobody said shit about it. Not to our faces, at least.

Not that there weren't whispers behind our backs.

But we could overcome them. Just the same as I'd overcome my hatred of science, which wasn't in the same ballpark at all, but still.

'Congratulations, Grayson. I have a good feeling that you're going to ace the exam.'

'Thanks, sir. I do too.'

'And if you or Beth ever need anything,' he said, tilting his head downwards, his eyes conveying what his words didn't, 'just let me know.'

'Thank you,' I said, meaning it. 'We appreciate it.'

Our teachers knew what was happening. Gossip that spread like wildfire through the student body reached the teachers in a matter of moments.

'Now go tell her the good news. I'm sure she's dying to hear how you did.'

I laughed, knowing that Beth was most likely waiting outside the door, wanting to know how I did.

The door opened before I could reach it, and there she was, tapping her toe on the floor in agitation.

'Sorry to burst in,' she said, looking the least bit sorry. 'But it's been enough time now and I know you know how he did. I could hear the two of you mumbling and I couldn't wait any longer.'

'Hello to you too, Beth,' Mr Taylor said with a deep chuckle. 'I was just telling Grayson here that he passed with flying colours. Only a few marks beneath you, if I'm being honest.'

'Seriously?' she squealed, ready to catapult herself at me but trying to show restraint.

'Yes, seriously. Now go celebrate, you two.'

'We will!' Beth said enthused, bouncing on her tiptoes with excitement. 'C'mon, Gray. I've got just the place to celebrate.'

We both gave Mr Taylor a wave before we made our way out of the science block, turning right to head towards the parking lot.

'I'm so proud of you, Gray,' Beth said, lacing her fingers with mine, dragging me along at her fast clip. 'I knew you could do it. I've always known.'

'Thanks for always keeping faith in me. You're the only one who ever has.'

'That's not true,' she pointed out. 'Mr Taylor had faith in you too. Otherwise, he wouldn't have given you me as a tutor.'

'Valid point, Jacobs.'

She kept pulling me forward, not daring to stop for a moment.

'Where are you dragging me off to?'

'My lair,' she said with a laugh. 'Just kidding… Kind of.'

'Just tell me where we're rushing off to.'

'To mine,' she said, a wicked glint in her eye. 'Cara's away for the weekend with Ethan.'

'So you mean…'

'Yep.' She chuckled at me when my feet began moving as fast as hers. 'How about we pretend to be a married couple for the weekend? Play house and all that good shit.'

'Sounds perfect. And it'll be good practise for when the baby arrives.'

She paused, her hand going to her stomach the way it always did these days.

'I hadn't even thought about that.'

'Huh?' I asked, turning to face her, trying to get her feet back into action. Now that I knew there was an empty house awaiting us, I wanted to get back there and show her just how much I appreciated her tutoring me. How much I loved her.

'Gray,' she whispered, biting her bottom lip. 'What *are* we going to do when the baby comes?'

'We'll figure it out, okay? We've got more than enough time to come up with something.'

She nodded, her fingers still lightly trailing across her stomach. Her belly was showing, just a little, and every time I looked down and saw it, I got giddy.

Our baby was in there. Growing. One day soon, it would be in our arms and as much as that thought scared me shitless, it was also one I welcomed.

'Now let's go,' I said, my tone urgent, grabbing her hand to pull her along. 'We've got a whole weekend to see what our future looks like.'

She smiled, but it didn't reach her eyes.

'You're right. We'll figure it out. We always do.'

THE ENTIRE WEEKEND WAS PERFECT.

Beth and I spent the whole time acting as if we were living in our own place, and it made me realise it was exactly what I wanted for my future.

For *our* future.

A nice, warm home, filled with love. A place our son or daughter could grow up and know they were special. That everything we'd done was for them.

We would be the parents we hadn't had.

It was going back home on Sunday evening that put dread in my stomach, rocks weighing me down.

I needed to tell my dad the truth about Beth's pregnancy. Needed to open up about just what was going on in my life these days and deal with the consequences of my actions, whatever they would be.

I would be a dad myself in a matter of months, and it only made sense that my dad knew about that.

The front door loomed in front of me, and I stood there, staring at it for a lot longer than intended. That door—what lay behind it—was my own personal nemesis. Something, or should I say *someone*, I needed to overcome before I could move on with my life. Before I could walk into the sunset of my future, I needed to accept my failings and his.

Steeling myself, I took a deep breath, filling my lungs with the warm air until they were close to bursting.

It was now or never.

'Grayson, is that you?' my dad called from the kitchen when the door shut behind me, the sound alerting him to my presence.

'Who else would let themselves in the door as if they lived here?' I asked, unable to bite down my retort. The man got under my skin. Even just hearing his voice, his inane questions he knew the answers to, pissed me off. Made me hate him a little more than before.

'Don't get smart with me,' he growled, his large red face appearing around the doorframe. He was shorter than me, rounder than me, yet still struck fear into my heart when I least expected it. Pretty sure a therapist would have a field day going over why, at eighteen, I was still scared shitless of my old man. It was easy to say, 'Just fight back.'

But in reality, it wasn't as simple to do.

Because I could fight back.

I'd been physically strong enough to fight him off for a few years. Mentally, not so much.

'Where the fuck have you been?' he demanded, his beady eyes taking me in, probably sensing that wherever it was made me happier than being with him.

'Out.'

'Out where?'

'At my girlfriend's,' I said, fessing up. It was what I planned to do, and I needed to see it through. 'We're having a baby.'

He moved closer, his forehead furrowed, running a hand through his matted, unwashed hair.

'You're what?' he seethed, his anger escalating the closer he got.

'We're having a baby,' I repeated, shuffling back an inch. 'In November.'

'Not under my roof you're not!' he roared, rushing towards me. 'You're a disgrace! I should've forced your mother to take your sorry arse with her when she abandoned us!'

'It's a good thing Beth doesn't live under your roof, isn't it?' I snapped, feeling bold.

'Do her parents know about this?'

'Yes.'

'And they're okay with it?'

'Her mum had her at sixteen, so she's understanding of the situation, yes.' My words came out clipped. The man, no matter what words he said, no matter what actions he did, got under my skin. Made my blood boil and my eyes saw red.

'So she's gutter trash, and she was born from gutter trash.'

My fists clenched at my sides. How dare he call Beth and Cara gutter trash? Didn't the man ever look in the fucking mirror? Assess his own life before judging the lives of others?

'Actually,' I said, knowing my next sentence would drop a verbal bomb in the room. 'Her dad's Ethan Baker.'

'Ethan Baker of Baker Enterprises?' he asked, a small decibel of awe in his voice that he coughed to disguise.

'The very same,' I said, a cocksure attitude rising within me. He hadn't expected that. I wasn't even sure that Beth really understood who her father was, or the empire her dad owned. The empire she was now an heir to. 'I've met him. Nice bloke.'

Dad bristled, stopping his advance on me.

'Met him?' he asked, and even though it was to my advantage that he'd stopped coming closer, I wasn't sure why he seemed so vexed about it all.

'Had dinner at his mansion. Nice place.'

'So you've knocked up a rich girl on purpose?' He came back to his senses. To the matter at hand. 'You've sold yourself out, have you? Thought you'd have a cushy life if you had a baby with a Baker?'

Fucking hell. The man really thought the worst of me.

'No,' I bit out. 'I didn't know she was a Baker when she got pregnant. Fuck, she didn't even know she was a Baker.'

'Don't use that foul language in front of me, boy. You're not with your pathetic school friends now.'

'No shit,' I said, riling him up further. 'I'm looking at you.'

'You think you're so smart.' He sneered at me, hatred evident on his face. 'That cockiness of yours will be your downfall, Son. I can guarantee that.'

Laughter barked from me. The man was fucking deluded, and I was sick of having to deal with his shit.

In the eyes of the law, I was an adult. And it was high time I started acting like one.

'I *am* smart. And I'm sick of the way you treat me. For years I've let you punch me around. Treat me like shit. And I'm done. You're the scum. You're the person who has a miserable life and will never amount to anything.'

'You dare talk to your father like that, boy?' A step closer. Heavy breathing filling the room.

'I do.' I stood my ground. Staring him down.

'If you're going to be a disappointment to me, then I want you out of this house. You're not to live under my roof any longer. You want to play adults, get your girl knocked up, then you can act like an adult and get the hell off my property.'

'What?' I said, a laugh escaping me. I was expecting his anger. I was expecting his disappointment and derision. But I wasn't expecting him to kick me out.

He'd threatened to kick me out plenty of times over the years, but he'd never sounded as serious as he did at that moment.

'You. Will. Leave. This. House.' The anger, the steam he'd kept a lid on since I walked through the door and told him about Beth being pregnant, boiled over and came spilling out in every pore. His nostrils flared and his face turned a dark burgundy— an unnatural, unhealthy colour. I was so focused, so distracted by his face, that I didn't see his fist.

My jaw smarted the moment his fist connected with my face.

For a man shorter than me, he'd figured out the correct angle years ago to hit me where it hurt.

Fuck.

Like the gun had gone off at the start of a race, like the gates opening at the start of a horse race, all bets were off. His fists came thick and fast, pummelling me, pushing me backwards until my back was up against the wall and I couldn't escape. And because of my stupid fear, I froze.

My bones locked together, unmoving. And I just stood there and took what his fists were handing out. I winced. I held my breath. I opened and closed my fists, not even attempting to shield myself from the blows.

'You.' *Hit.* 'Are.' *Hit.* 'A.' *Hit.* 'Waste.' *Hit.* 'Of.' *Hit.* 'Space.'

His words were wrong. I wasn't a waste of space. And I wasn't a useless piece of shit.

Before Jacobs, I would've believed his bullshit. Would've let him say those words, let them seep into my bones and slither into my veins.

But she'd changed me for the better. Had helped me see my worth. My value.

I would pass my exams. I would get decent grades and for

the first time, I had the potential to get into a university and get away from the life I was born into if I chose.

Standing still and letting him abuse me was no longer an option. No father should treat their child that way, and for the first time, I knew I could break free.

Of the chains. Of *him*.

'No,' I muttered, my voice a small croak. Then I repeated it, louder. 'No!'

The word stopped his fists for a brief moment, and that was when my bones unlocked. The padlock on my mind, my fists, finally breaking free. A key, hidden before, now available to me.

And it was that brief reprieve of his fists that gave me the opportunity my younger self had craved for but never had the courage to execute.

My fist connected with his face. The force of it knocked him to the side. The crash of him hitting the cabinet settled over me, and what I'd done became very, very real.

Shit. I needed to leave. *Now.*

Without waiting for him to get up. Without another look in his direction. I fled.

My feet carried me without really knowing where they would end up. But I ran. Ran. Ran.

Until I was standing in front of the supermarket in town and I knew exactly what I would do to ease the dread seeping into every nook and cranny of my being.

Thirty
Beth

I HADN'T HEARD from Gray since he left mine earlier in the evening.

I thought he'd text me when he got home or something, but it'd been radio silence for at least two hours.

Should I be worried?

Maybe. His dad was an arsehole, and I knew he abused Gray more than Gray would ever admit to me. It was his secret shame. The thing I'd never got him to speak about.

The door opened, and in came Cara, a big smile on her face.

'Beth!' she said, pulling me into a deep hug. 'I've missed you.'

'You were only gone for three days,' I said, hugging her back with a laugh. Her responding laugh rattled through me and I took a step back, taking her in.

Ever since she reconnected with Ethan, there was an aura of light around her at all times. A happiness I'd never seen from her. A true happiness that came from within.

'I know, but with everything that's happened recently, I still felt bad about leaving you.'

'I wasn't alone,' I told her, and she gave me a cheeky grin, her eyebrows raised at my admission. 'Gray stayed for the weekend.'

I hadn't told her before she left in case she'd tell me it wasn't allowed, but now that she'd returned I didn't want to lie to her. I mean, what was the worst that could happen? I was already pregnant.

'Did you have a good time?' she said with a bright smile, the fresh evening air travelling in from the open front door. 'Guess it's a good idea for the future if you plan to live together one day.'

'It was the best,' I told her, meaning every word. 'The two of us got along and even when we disagreed over what dinner to have, it felt natural, you know? Like it was meant to be. Like *we* are meant to be.'

She laughed but nodded, understanding what I meant. We may be young. We may have been stupid. But there was something in my gut that just knew Gray and I were going to be happy together.

'I'm happy for you both, truly.' She had tears in her eyes, her bottom lip threatening to break as it wobbled. 'Me and your dad spoke about it this weekend, and we're going to help you both the best way we can.'

'He pays for this house, right?'

'Yeah,' she said, looking around the entrance hall. 'But we spoke about that too.'

'Sounds like the weekend was filled with a lot of talking.'

'Amongst other things,' she said, a sly smile on her face that had me close to gagging. I may have only just learned the truth, but now that I knew, no kid wanted to hear their parents hint at *that*.

'And?'

'And we're going to sell this house.' She tilted my chin up, so we were looking into each other's eyes. Like looking in a mirror. 'Your dad wants us to move in with him. He has the space and the staff. His home is perfect for when the baby arrives.'

It made sense to move to his house. The man was paying for two homes, and now that he and Cara were slowly making their relationship work, of course he wanted her living with him.

They'd lost how many years because of the actions of others? I got it.

Even if I wasn't overly thrilled about it.

'I know the two of you still don't know each other that well, but I hope that by living together, you'll get to bond. He really is a great guy, Beth. I promise.'

'I know. And I know you want us to get along and for everything to be the way it should have always been, but you've gotta work with me here,' I said, holding her forearms and looking right at her. 'You've always known about him and about me. I haven't. I'm trying, though.'

'That's all we hoped for.'

A crashing noise came from the open front door, and the two of us swirled around in terror, wondering what the fuck the noise was. We lived in a nice neighbourhood. There was barely any crime that we knew of at least, and since we moved here, we hadn't worried about the front door being unlocked during the day. But that crashing noise made me doubt our trust.

Until I spotted Grayson, face down in the bushes, the crashing noise having come from the gravel he'd tripped over on his way to the front door.

'What the...' Cara said, turning her gaze to me, but I had no explanation for her. I hadn't heard from him in over two hours and as far as I knew, he was going home to tell his dad we were having a baby.

Oh...

Shit.

When he told me that was his plan, it didn't even register in my mind. What an idiot. I should've gone with him. Should have been there to support him.

'Gray?' I called out, leaving the house to go crouch down beside him. 'Are you okay?'

'I fucking love you,' he said, his words mumbled by the rose bush he was currently face down in. 'You are the light of my life.'

'And you are very drunk.'

I could hear it in his voice. We'd attended enough parties together for me to know how the boy sounded when he was wasted and his voice when he told me I was the light of his life was no different to those times.

He'd never told me he loved me.

Then there he was, saying it when he wasn't sober.

The fucking cheek of it made me mad, but also, I knew he was acting that way because of whatever happened when he went home.

Cara came over to where I was crouched on Gray's left and crouched down on his right, mirroring me.

'Want help turning him?' she asked, and I nodded. The two of us turned him around, so he was lying on his back, looking up at the sky, a soft and dazed look on his face.

It was a good thing I liked him enough to overlook his stupidity.

But then I spotted the darkening of his skin. The bruises that were slowly appearing on various spots of his body, and my stomach fell away.

'Shit, Gray. Are you okay?'

'Can you help me up?' he whispered, reminding me of a small kid who fell down in the dirt of the park, wanting to seem brave but struggling.

With Cara's help, I got Gray into a sitting position and eventually upright. Small, hobbled steps got us to the front door, and even more hobbled steps got us to the sofa in the living room.

The moment the sofa was beneath him, Gray flopped down onto it, exhausted, energy leaving his body the moment he hit the cushions.

'I'll get some water,' Cara announced, leaving us alone to give us some privacy.

'You look so beautiful when you smile,' Gray told me through half-mast eyes. 'It lights up your whole face.'

'Well, don't you wax lyrical when plastered?' I said, a smile on my face, disguising the heartbreak within. He looked like a boy, a scared boy who had suffered for too long but didn't know how to break free. 'You look pretty handsome yourself.'

'Why don't you come and lie on me?' he asked, waggling his eyebrows at me, and all I could do was laugh at him. 'Hey! What are you laughing about? Don't you wanna cover my body with yours?'

'Knock it off, dickhead,' I said, shoving him in the shoulder. 'Tell me what happened.'

'Dad. He got mad.'

'How mad is mad?'

'Very mad,' he said, his voice barely audible. 'Hurt me.'

'I know, baby,' I whispered, wanting to soothe him. I sat down on the empty spot on the sofa and within a moment Gray's head was resting in my lap, looking up at me. His enormous eyes and long eyelashes were blinking up at me in slow movements, taking me in.

My fingers found their way into his hair and, using a light touch, I drew patterns in it. A soft moan came from his lips, and he closed his eyes in pleasure.

'Why does he hate me?'

'I don't know. I don't know how anybody could hate you.'

'Because I'm bad.'

'You're not bad, Gray.'

'I am.' His bottom lip wobbled. 'I always have been.'

'I've never thought so,' I told him, my heart breaking for him. For the boy who felt unloved. Who'd never been heard. 'To me, you could never be bad.'

'I don't even remember that night.'

'I know.'

'You should hate me.'

'I don't hate you, Gray. And talking about not remembering things, I'm not even sure you will remember this conversation.'

'I'm sorry.'

'It's okay. What happened?'

'My dad didn't take the news well. Hates me. Hates you. Hurt me. Kicked me out.'

'What?'

'Kicked me out,' he said, his breathing slowing. A soft snore left him and I didn't have the heart to wake him up.

'His dad kicked him out, huh?' Cara asked, leaning against the doorframe, a glass of water in her hand.

I nodded, still running my fingers through Gray's dark brown hair, not wanting him to wake.

'That sucks.'

'Yeah… His dad hits him. He can't go back there.'

'We'll make sure he doesn't have to.'

'You promise?'

'I promise.'

Thirty-One
Beth

GRAYSON SLEPT off his alcohol stupor on the sofa, and I swear I must've got up at least five times in the night to make sure he was still breathing and hadn't choked on his own vomit or anything ridiculous like that.

The fear of losing him was real, and I couldn't place why.

All I knew was that I couldn't lose Gray. Not even a small fraction.

I went downstairs, ready to face him and find out exactly what had gone down between him and his dad. Last night he was too drunk, too vulnerable to get a sensible answer out of.

The living room was silent except for an old movie that was playing on the large television.

'Are you watching *Casablanca*?' I asked, shocked at his choice of TV viewing. 'Without me?'

'Is there a right answer here? Or is it a trick question?' He turned his head to the door and a tentative smile graced his lips, filling me with warmth. 'Because I'll answer with whatever you want me to.'

'Budge over,' I said, moving through the room to sit next to him. He grabbed my ankles and draped them over his lap, covering my legs with the blanket he'd slept under.

'Morning, Jacobs.'

'Morning, Gray,' I said with a laugh. 'Bit different to how we've woken up the last two mornings, huh?'

'Just a bit,' he said with a playful expression. 'This is nowhere near as fun.'

'And whose fault is that?'

'Definitely Cara's,' he joked, rubbing my leg with the back of his hand. Goosebumps rose on my legs from his touch and joy overtook me. It all felt so natural. So *normal.* I loved it. 'I'm sorry about last night.'

'What do you remember?'

'Lying face down in the rosebush.' He laughed, tilting his head back, and my eyes became transfixed on his neck. On the way his Adam's apple bobbed in his throat, his strong jawline making my mouth water. The bastard knew it, too, because he stayed in the position a fraction longer than necessary. 'It all gets a little fuzzy after that.'

'That's a shame,' I said. 'Because you told me, and I quote, that you "fucking love me".'

'Nice to know I'm a charmer under the influence.'

'You always have been. We wouldn't be in this position without that being the case.' I gestured at my stomach and laughed, but instead of joining in, his eyes went downcast, his mood sombre.

'I will never forgive myself for not remembering that time with you, B.'

How on earth could a single letter make my heart flutter so much? He'd never called me *B* before. Never really called me a nickname at all. I was usually Jacobs to him and nothing more. But I could feel his pain in that one letter. The vulnerable side he was showing me.

'It's okay.' His eyes remained down, zoned in on my legs, and I didn't know what to say to make things better. And they needed to be better. I couldn't have him regretting it his whole life. Not when we were about to spend forever being in one another's lives in some capacity. We were just yet to define what that would look like. 'I don't regret a moment of it.'

'Even though we're teenagers with a baby on the way?'

'I came from two teenagers and I've turned out okay.'

He snapped his head up to stare at me.

'Okay, so I've turned out okay, not *knowing* I came from two teenagers, but whatever. Not the point here.'

'I will spend my whole life making it up to you.'

'There's really no need for that,' I said, waving him off. 'All I want is for you to talk to me and for us to combat the future together.'

'And how do we do that?'

'We start by you telling me what happened last night.'

'Do I have to?' he grumbled, and my eyes shot daggers at him.

'Yes, you do. Otherwise, you'll wake up on the sofa for a very long time.'

He didn't know yet that Cara had said he could move in with us—under certain conditions. We'd hashed it all out together the night before, and I couldn't wait to tell Gray about it all. I just needed him to start the conversation first. To tell me sober that his dad kicked him out.

'Fine…' He looked at the film still playing on the screen, the words muted at the touch of a button, and started talking. 'I went home and told Dad we were having a baby. He started in the usual way. Told me I was a waste of space. Would never amount to anything. That kind of thing. Kicked me out of the house. Told me I wasn't welcome there anymore. Then he hit me. And he just wouldn't stop. So I hit him back. Knocked him down.'

'What happened after that?'

'I bolted. Got out of there as quickly as I could.' He shook his head, his haunted eyes lost in the past. 'Didn't even know where I was heading until I found myself outside the supermarket. I went in and got myself a bottle of vodka, then made my way here.'

'I'm sorry that your dad's such a dick, Gray.'

'Not your fault,' he murmured. 'Thanks for letting me stay last night. Not like I could've gone home.'

'We weren't gonna kick you out when you could barely stand upright, were we?' I laughed, wondering if he actually thought we'd do that to him or if he was just trying to work through shit in his own way. 'Where would you have gone?'

'To Tyler's, I guess. He lives in a flat in town on his own.' Then he shook his head as if remembering something. 'Nope. Wouldn't have gone there. He's got *guests* at the moment.'

Hm. Would file that away as something to find out later.

'So… your dad meant it? You can't live there anymore?'

'Oh, he meant it. He's threatened it over the years, but this time was different. I could tell, you know? Something in my gut just knew it was real.'

'Cara wants us to move in with Ethan,' I said, telling him the major news she'd dropped on me before he found himself with a face full of roses. 'Sell this place.'

'Seriously? How do you feel about that?'

'I don't know.' I shrugged. 'I guess I feel like a lot of my life is being decided for me and I've got no idea what I really want.'

'I feel you.'

'But,' I added, locking my gaze to his. 'Cara has said you can live with us there, too. You never have to go back to your dad.'

'I—' He gulped, looking small. 'I don't know what to say.'

'Hear me out first before you say anything 'cause there's a catch.'

'What is it?'

'You have to go to get some help,' I whispered, hoping he didn't shoot the messenger.

'Help?'

'My dad's willing to pay for a top-notch counsellor that deals with alcohol-related issues in teens with a shitty upbringing. They can help you.'

'Is that the only condition?'

'And we have to have separate bedrooms.' We smiled at that one. Trust my parents to act like parents the moment they had the chance to. As if I wasn't already pregnant enough for it to make a difference. 'But they can be next door to each other so that when the baby comes, you can hear the screams and come help me. Minor victories and all that.'

'We still have time,' he replied. 'Maybe we could find a place of our own before then?'

'Maybe,' I whispered, warmth spreading across my cheeks at the hope in his voice. In his eyes. 'I'd like that.'

'Me too.'

'I know I said it last night, and I'm sorry that was the first time I said it, but I really do love you, Beth. I'm *in* love with you. And I know we're young, and we've got a fuck ton of obstacles in our path, but I'll jump every one if it means I get to see that smile on your face.'

The smile that was plastered on my face at that exact moment. *Probably looks a little manic, thinking about it.* The sincerity in his eyes gutted me. He meant every word. My heart gave a kick—and so did my stomach.

What?

There it was again!

'Are you okay?' Gray asked, a worried look on his face. 'What's happening?'

I didn't answer with words.

Instead, I grabbed his hand and pulled him to the side, placing it on my stomach, waiting for the next movement to come. *Kick.* There it was again.

Gray's eyes met mine, blinking in awe, as he whispered, 'Is that...?'

I nodded with enthusiasm, beyond grateful that we were together to experience the moment. After I hadn't invited him to my first scan, I didn't want him to miss any other firsts on our journey as parents.

'Our baby loves you, too,' I said, unable to take the smile off my face.

'But do you?' he asked.

'Do I what?' I knew what he wanted to know, and it may be a tad mean, but I wanted him to sweat a little. Wanted him to work for it, just a bit.

'Are you gonna make me say it, Jacobs?'

'Uh-huh.'

'Do you see a future for us?' He amended. 'Aside from the whole, we're having a child together situation.'

'Gray,' I said, finally letting him off the hook. 'I love you, too. I'm *in* love with you, too. And of course I want to have a future with you. Who else is gonna put up with your shit?'

'You make a fair point.'

'I've been known to do that once or twice.'

He laughed and looked up at me from underneath his eyelashes.

'I'm so glad I get to do this life with you, Jacobs.'

'Ditto.'

And when he leaned in for a kiss, I closed my eyes and kissed him with all the love in my heart. His tongue grazed mine, and I moaned, wishing we weren't in an awkward position on the sofa in my living room.

'If you two have finished,' Cara said, her tone cutting through the sexual tension growing between us, 'there's breakfast waiting in the kitchen. Ethan will be here in five.'

Gray laughed, and I went red, a small chuckle leaving me.

'We'll continue this later, Jacobs,' he said, placing one last kiss on my lips before moving my legs from his.

'Is that a threat?' My toes curled at the possession in his eyes.

'It's a promise.'

Thirty-Two

Beth

THE MOOD around the kitchen table was a little stilted.

'Could you please pass the jam?' Cara asked me, and I raised an eyebrow at her but passed her the jam, anyway. The whole scenario was bloody bizarre. Breakfast was something we grabbed before rushing out the door, not something we sat down and took our time with.

And Cara had gone all out.

The table was laden with so many pastries, jams, and other items that it looked like a hotel's continental breakfast had spat up on it. Somebody was trying their best to impress.

'Grayson,' Ethan said, placing his coffee mug down on the table, a serious expression on his face. 'Has Beth spoken to you about our conditions?'

In my peripheral, Grayson sat up a little straighter, putting his toast down on his plate rather than continue eating now that my dad had asked him a question.

'She has, sir.'

'And?'

'And they're no problem, sir. I want to work on myself. I'm extremely thankful for all the help you and Cara have given me.'

'It's no problem. Grayson,' Cara said, cracking a smile for the first time since we all sat down at the table. 'We know things are hard for you and we don't want things to be as hard for you two as they were for us.'

Ethan moved his hand to take hers, the gesture one of love and care. I had to admit that it warmed my heart to see them like that. Not that I'd tell them that.

'Right,' Ethan agreed. 'We want to help you two and we've got a little sweetener.'

'What's that?' I asked, mumbling through the toast slathered in butter and chocolate spread I'd just shoved in my mouth.

'If Grayson completes three months of counselling and stays sober during that time, then we will help the two of you find your own place.'

'Seriously?' I asked, rife with scepticism, even if they'd never given me reason to be suspicious. 'You'd help us do that?'

'Why not?' He shrugged. 'Unless you've got a reason why we shouldn't?'

'Nope,' I said, popping the P. 'Not that I can think of.'

'Then it's a deal.'

'Thanks, I guess…' Was he trying to buy my love? Or did he really want to help me? I hated the thoughts fighting in my mind. Hated that I couldn't just see his help as help with no strings attached.

'No need to sound so suspicious, Beth.' Cara stared at me, or more like gave me the evil eye. Things were still hard between the two of us, and every time I tried to make things better, I stopped myself. Or something happened with Gray and I forgot about it. 'Your dad's just trying to help where he can.'

'I know that,' I said, taking a sip of my apple juice. 'And I'm doing the best I can.'

Everybody fell silent and went back to eating. Grayson's hand on my knee was a source of comfort, and once again, I was so thankful that he was in my life. That he wanted to do life by my side.

Once most of the food was consumed, Ethan shuffled in his seat, a slight look of discomfort on his face.

'Beth,' he said, and I looked at him, wondering what was coming next. 'How would you like to come to the Science Museum with me this weekend?'

'Just us two?'

'Mhm.' He nodded, not taking his eyes off my face. 'I thought it'd be nice to get to know one another better in a setting you like.'

'Er...' My gaze wandered around the room, taking in everything, not sure how to respond. I knew he was trying his hardest to bond and connect with me, and I couldn't judge him for that. And I didn't need to make it harder for him than it already was, right? I took a deep breath, returning my eyes to his. 'Sure. I'd like that.'

'Great,' he said, the flash of relief in his eyes shining at me. 'I look forward to it.'

'Me too.'

It surprised me to find that I meant it.

WHEN CARA TOLD me the truth, she'd mentioned that my dad had sent gifts and letters for my birthday every year.

She'd said I could go through them whenever I wanted, had even put them in my bedroom for when I was ready, but I'd put them in the walk-in wardrobe and ignored them ever since.

I wasn't ready to face them then. Especially when things between me and Gray were so up in the air. My pregnancy hormones were all over the place and I knew that reading those letters and cards would either make me mourn what I had never had or make me livid that I grew up believing such lies.

'Come upstairs with me,' I whispered in Gray's ear once breakfast was finally over, and he gave a slight nod.

I went upstairs into my bedroom, collected the pile of things from my wardrobe, placed them on my bed, and waited for him.

'What's up, B?' he asked the moment he entered, coming to sit beside me on the bed. He leafed through the items on the bed with his fingers, his brows furrowed. 'What are these?'

'Letters and birthday things from my dad.'

'You wanna read them?'

I dipped my head, staring down at my name on the seventeen envelopes in front of me. Why did it feel so daunting?

'I'm scared,' I admitted in a low murmur.

'Of what?'

'I don't even know. I guess I'm still a little angry at them both and I'm worried these letters will make me forget that anger.'

'You're allowed to be angry, babe,' he said, putting his arm around my shoulder and tucking me into his side. 'They did something pretty shitty. There's no beating around the bush about it.'

'No, you'd rather just fall into the bush.'

'Oh, ha-ha,' he said, but I could feel the vibration of his body as he gave a small laugh at my poor joke. 'Just read one. Just one. And see how you feel after that.'

I hummed my agreement and found the letter addressed to me from my most recent birthday. Cara had helpfully put my age in the top left corner of each envelope.

My fingers shook as I opened the letter and took it out.

Gray grabbed the side of it to keep it still for me.

'Thanks.'

'I've got you, no matter what.' His eyes flared, an emotion there and then gone before I could figure out what was happening. 'I love you. You know that, right?'

'Yeah, I do.' We both smiled, and I loved that he was trying to distract me from how nervous I was. 'I love you, too.'

'And together we can jump any hurdle. Get through anything the world throws at us.'

'Okay,' I said, my tone breathy. 'I'm going in.'

My eyes scanned the paper. A slight procrastination. But once my eyes caught on the opening sentence, I began to read.

My darling daughter, Beth,

I don't know when you will get to read this letter, but I still feel compelled to write every year without fail.

Every birthday that comes and goes causes my heart to hurt in a way I've never experienced before. Knowing that you are growing up unaware of my existence is a pain I wish on nobody.

Turning seventeen is a big year. When I turned seventeen, you entered the world and I couldn't have been happier. Although I only got to see one photo of you before you were cruelly taken out of my life, I've often wondered what you look like now. Do you have your mother's wide eyes and optimism? Do we share any features at all? I won't mind if we don't. After all, your mother is the most beautiful woman I've ever seen, and if you look like her, then we're both extremely lucky.

Please don't judge us for the decisions we made at your age. We never thought it would go on for this long. Go this far.

I hope to one day meet you. Talk to you. Laugh with you. Get to be the father I've dreamed of being since the day I learned of you.

I hope one day the mistakes your mother and I made will make sense to you, or at least that you will understand and listen to us, regardless of whether you forgive us.

All I want is for us to be a family. A true family.

Who knows? Maybe one day we will be.

I love you and I love your mum more than anything in the world.

I am so, so sorry. I wish everything were different.

Happy birthday, my love. Maybe the next one we will spend it together.

Your dad, Ethan x

Tears were pouring down my face and I wasn't sure I could stop them.

I was right. Reading the letter made my anger ebb away, like the ocean, going out with the tide. As if it were never there, or almost never there, the odd debris giving it away.

My sobs came thick and fast, everything crashing down around me. Heavy footsteps came up the stairs and stopped outside the room, stopping Gray from whatever he was about to say.

'Beth!' Cara called through the door. 'Beth, are you okay? I can hear you crying.'

'I'm okay,' I said, my voice a low wobble.

'Can we come in?' she asked, worry laced in her tone, and from the '*we*' I knew they were both standing out there, probably worried they'd said something wrong at breakfast or upset me in some way.

I didn't answer, my sobs overwhelming me.

'If you don't reply, we're coming in,' she said, and I still didn't answer. Did I want them to see me or not? Did I want Dad to know I'd read his letter? That I was ready to call him Dad to his face?

The door opened and the two of them stood on the other side. Cara looked frantic and Ethan worried.

How many years had I wished for parents who cared?

And there they were. Two of them. Caring very much. And I knew I couldn't push them away any longer. Couldn't hold a grudge for a crappy decision they made as teens.

It was Cara who spotted the letters first.

'Oh, Beth,' she said, coming into the room and kneeling down on the floor beside my legs. 'I hope this stupid lughead didn't say anything too damning.'

'Oi,' Dad said, going to sit beside her on the floor. 'I would never.'

Wordlessly, I passed the letter to Cara for her to read. There was no way I could repeat the words out loud.

I watched as she read it. Watched as her eyes filled with tears, too.

She stopped reading, her bottom lip wobbling. My heart broke for her. For all of us. For the actions of so many who had led to everything we'd *all* lost.

And that was when it clicked in my mind that all three of us had lost something. That I wasn't the only one who had suffered.

'I'm so sorry.' I sobbed. 'I've been such a bitch.'

'Beth, baby,' Cara said, grabbing my knee and looking at me, her tears streaming down her face. 'If that was you being a bitch, then we're pretty lucky parents.'

'We're lucky parents, period,' Dad said, his hand coming on my other knee. 'We love you, Beth. We'd never judge you for any emotion you feel. You've gone through a rough few months and we're a big part of that.'

'I forgive you both,' I said, meaning every word. 'And I'm sorry for judging you both for your decisions.'

'We'll be the first to admit they were shitty, Beth.' Dad looked at Cara and his eyes softened. 'And that we were wrong. No excuse is good enough.'

'Can you forgive me?' I asked, my voice cracking.

'There's nothing to forgive you for,' Dad said. 'You've done nothing wrong.'

'Your dad's right. It's all on us, Beth. Not you. Never you.'

I moved to the floor, sweeping the letters out of the way and falling in between my parents. Their arms came around me and the three of us shared a tight hug, the tears free-flowing. I wasn't sure, but I think even my dad shed a tear.

My eyes locked with Gray's, and he smiled at me, happy that I'd forgiven them. Even though he'd never told me I should, I knew he wanted me to fix the things between us. Or at least start to.

I was beyond lucky to have him.

He was my everything and I would be forever grateful that he demanded I tutor him in science at the start of the year.

It was something I would never regret. Could never regret.

BETH and her parents had gone out for dinner, just the three of them, and I'd stayed home alone.

I didn't mind.

Giving them time to connect was important, and I knew my girl appreciated me staying home and letting them have their space.

Before she'd read the letter from her dad, I said something to her and it was as if a lightbulb went off in my mind. It had taken me off guard.

One innocent sentence, and the 'dream' I had the night of my birthday came flooding into my brain. The memory was hazy and blurred, but whole and there.

When I said, 'I've got you,' it all rushed back.

'I WANT TO. I've wanted to for a while.' Her whisper caught me off guard. The admission filled me with a euphoria that travelled from my head down to my toes.

'Yeah?'

'Fuck yeah,' she whispered, and I smiled widely at her enthusiasm. I leaned down and swept my lips across hers, loving the visible reaction as her skin flushed with goosebumps.

'I'll be gentle,' I whispered. 'You can trust me on that, Jacobs. I've got you.'

'I do trust you. If I didn't, I wouldn't be here.' Her words were like a balm to my soul. Nobody had ever trusted me like that before. Her face was open and honest, and she meant every word.

I trailed kisses up and down her neck, then I moved to her ear, placing a tender kiss on her sweet spot. A shiver ran through her and I smiled at her reaction to my touch.

'Lie down, Jacobs,' I said, my lips grazing her ear.

She obeyed my command.

'I've got you,' I whispered, my fingers trailing a scorching path up and down her ribcage. 'Breathe, Jacobs.'

NEITHER OF US had spoken about that night afterwards, and I assumed it was because we'd done the same things we did in the tent at the field or whatever.

Jacobs must've been so confused. Why I didn't talk to her about it, or even acknowledge it after the fact.

I just acted normal around her—the way we'd acted around each other from the start—and thought nothing of it.

Since everything blew up in our faces, we'd taken things slowly. Continued to get to know one another better and start a genuine relationship with no lies or half-truths between us.

The weekend we played house things got a little hot under the collar, but we both stopped anything from progressing further.

When we had sex again, I wanted to remember every second. Every touch of her hand, every breathy moan, every sound, and everything else in between.

It wasn't like we needed to rush. We weren't on a timeline.

The two of us were having a baby, about to take our exams, and we would decide the future from there. No talk of university had come up, but I knew that one day soon I'd talk to her about it. Not for me, but for her. Beth was smart as fuck, and I wanted the world to know about it the same way I did.

She'd worked so hard all these years and, in current times, having a baby didn't mean you couldn't achieve great things in your career too.

It wasn't an either/or situation.

No matter what she decided, I would support her. She was my one, and nothing would change that.

MY HAND SHOOK as I reached out for the door handle, the cold metal under my touch chilling me to the bone. Or maybe my nerves were doing that for me.

It was the day I would finally see my baby. Hear their heartbeat.

The day it would become even more real to me. Feeling our baby kick was the first time it hit me that all of it was real. That the two of us really were about to become parents in the not-so-distant future. The scan would just solidify that.

'There's no need to be nervous, Gray,' B said, taking my hand in hers. 'We're gonna see our baby and find out the sex, and it's all gonna be gravy.'

'Promise?'

'Why wouldn't it be?' she said, checking us in at the reception desk before taking us over to the waiting area. We were having one of those fancy 3D scans, and no matter how much Jacobs told me they were all the rage, I still thought they looked a little freaky. 'Everything's good.'

'If you say so.'

'I do say so. And you'll say so too once we've seen our angel and we know they're healthy and well.'

'Okay, okay,' I said in a placating manner. 'After today, we can start discussing names.'

'Oh, I've already started compiling a short list,' she said with a nod, her black fringe falling into her face. 'It's got a name from every letter of the alphabet and some.'

'Have you just basically recreated the list in that book you were reading?'

I'd spotted her reading some *1000 top names for babies* book the other day, and knowing her, she had at least half of that number on her 'short' list.

'I wouldn't say I've recreated it.' She bristled, a light pink flushing her cheeks, giving her away. 'I've narrowed it down.'

'By how much?'

'Enough,' she bit out at the same time a nurse called out her name.

'Saved by the nurse,' I teased and she just stood up, my hand still in hers.

'Come on, dickhead.'

I chuckled but followed her like an obedient puppy. I'd follow her anywhere, after all. No matter when or where.

The room was clean and bright white. That typical sterile kind of room you found in clinics, but it didn't feel uncomfortable either.

I looked at the posters on the walls, the various pieces of equipment in the room, not paying attention to whatever it was the nurse was saying to Jacobs.

'Are you ready to see your baby?' the nurse asked us both, and I coughed, my heart rate escalating.

'Yeah,' I said, my voice rough and broken. 'I'm ready.'

'This might be a little cold,' the nurse said to Beth, who nodded, her eyes fixed on the screen in the same way mine were. She gripped my hand in hers, anchoring each other to the moment.

Slowly, an image formed on the screen, and my heart stopped beating.

It was our baby. There, on the screen, in front of our eyes. I swallowed the emotion sitting in my throat as tears formed in my eyes.

The nurse talked us through what we could see on the screen and we hummed and nodded in response, both of us lost in a trance.

'Would the two of you like to know the sex of your baby?'

The two of us had discussed it, and even though it didn't matter to either of us what sex our baby was, we'd decided we were gonna find out. Easier to pick a name that way and personalise all the baby's things—or at least that was what Jacobs had tried to convince me was the better thing to do.

'Yes, please,' B said, her eyes locking with mine, a smile covering her face. The shine from her eyes told me how happy she was. She was light and air. Beautiful.

The nurse technician moved the wand around on her stomach, seeking the right angle, and after a moment, she'd located what she needed to know.

'Your baby is a girl,' the nurse said, also beaming. 'A healthy baby girl.'

The tears in my eyes that had threatened to spill ever since our baby appeared on the screen finally leaked from my eyes and travelled down my face. My sobs were silent, but the emotion overtook me in a way that surprised me.

I leaned into Beth's face and whispered, 'I love you. So much.'

'I love you too, Gray.'

For the next few minutes, the tech took pictures of our baby for us and we stayed silent, watching with awe and wonder at the little spark of life we'd created together.

Everything in my life was only going to get better from there on out.

Epilogue
Beth

Living in a home with Gray was 1000 percent better than I'd hoped it would be.

The two of us were happy, healthy, and oh so fucking ready for our daughter to enter the world.

My stomach was enormous, and it had got to the point where I couldn't remember what my feet looked like. The moment I asked Gray to help me shave my legs was a low point, but he did it without batting an eyelid—I think he even had a smile on his face that he could help out in some way.

'Babe!' he called from the kitchen. 'Did you want some food? A drink?'

'Narh, I'm good, thanks!' I called back, not hungry at all. 'My stomach's feeling a little tight.'

My Braxton Hicks started the day before, and if they were a judge of anything, I was decidedly *not* looking forward to having a baby.

That was a lie.

I just wished I could skip the giving birth part and be firmly in the holding my baby part. Smelling her skin, touching her, and holding her tight.

I shuffled on the sofa, trying—and failing—to change my position without causing myself too much pain. The TV remote was on the coffee table and if I could move just an inch closer, I'd be able to grab it and turn on the subtitles.

'Shit!' I called out, a whooshing feeling rushing through my body. Then I felt the gushing of fluid and looked down at my lap, knowing exactly what I would see there, but afraid of it. 'Gray!'

The panic in my voice must've sounded even worse to him than it did to me because he ran through the door from the kitchen within seconds, his eyes wide with worry.

'What's going on?' he said. His gaze assessed me, starting at my face before travelling down my body, until he spotted the large patch of liquid seeping into the teal sofa cushion. 'Shit! Is that what I think it is?'

'Yeah!' I squealed, not knowing what to do next. Should I pack? Wait, I'd already packed and unpacked, then packed again multiple times. Should I prepare to leave? Or did we still have hours before we could go to the hospital? 'Call Cara.'

'Already on it,' he said, his phone in his hand. 'Hey, Cara!'

Grayson started talking, telling her what was going on, when a contraction shot through me. My fingers went white from my tight grip on the arm of the sofa as the pain subsided—leaving almost as fast as it arrived.

'Cara's on her way,' Gray said. He'd hung up the phone and came over to crouch down in front of me. 'Then she's gonna get us over to the hospital.'

I nodded, staring into his azure blue eyes that were swimming with love and pride.

'Okay.' I breathed out slowly, not wanting to lose my cool, but being oh so close to it happening. 'Okay. I'm gonna be fine, right?'

'Right!' A trail of tingles jolted through me when his fingers grazed my cheek, brushing my hair away from my face and behind my ear. 'You've got this.'

My heart calmed at his certain words. The reassuring whispers.

Within hours, I could be holding my baby in my arms, and that was what mattered the most.

Pushing a baby out of my vagina was a lot harder than I expected it to be.

Not that I thought it would be easy or anything—I'd watched enough episodes of *One Born Every Minute* and *Teen Mom* to know that wasn't the case—but maybe I'd gone in a little *too* overconfident about my abilities. And my pain threshold.

But it was all worth it.

The moment they placed my baby on my chest, I couldn't contain the emotions swirling through my body. Overwhelming every sense. I could barely see her through the tears filling my eyes.

My daughter.

Her beautiful face and full head of dark brown hair that was a mix of mine and Gray's, warmed my heart to the point I thought it was going to burst inside my chest.

'She's beautiful,' Gray whispered in my ear, his voice cracking. Seeing him break down and cry when she entered the world made me love him even more than I thought possible. We may only be eighteen, but we'd experienced something together that would bond us forever.

Our daughter would bond us forever.

'She's precious,' Cara said from where she was standing beside the door. When I found out I could have two people in the room with me when I gave birth, I knew straight away that I wanted her in there with me as much as I wanted Gray.

'I'm so scared, Mum,' I said in a hushed tone, looking over at her. It was the first time I'd called her Mum. Ever since I found out the truth, it hadn't felt right to call her anything but Cara.

But looking down at my innocent baby, knowing I would do absolutely *anything* for her, I could understand a little more what she went through eighteen years ago.

Even in eighteen years, times had changed enough that it wasn't as frowned upon to have a baby at eighteen.

'You just called me Mum,' she replied, her voice filled with emotion, as she came to stand closer to the three of us. Tears sprang to her eyes that were so like mine and she swallowed. 'I don't know what to say.'

'Just tell me I have nothing to be scared about. Tell me I've got this.'

'Of course you have.' She touched my hand that was under my baby's body and gave a small reassuring squeeze. 'You two are going to ace this, and you're gonna do a lot better than I did.'

We all gave a small chuckle.

I would be lying if I said that a sharp stab of anger aimed at my mum hadn't run through my body when I saw my daughter for the first time. Yes, I knew I would do anything for her. But I also knew that no part of me would be able to hand her over as if she wasn't mine. Let my mum raise her as her own—and poorly at that.

But I knew I had to let my anger go.

Had to move on. Be happier and healthier.

Layla had given me the number for her therapist, and when things were settled, I would make a call and schedule myself some appointments. And then, when I was ready, I would invite my mum to come, too.

Things weren't going to get better unless we all made an active effort to make them so. If my boyfriend could go to counselling and face his demons, then I could face my insecurities and sorrow.

'What's her name?' Mum asked, running her finger up and down my hand, gazing blissfully at her granddaughter. She looked too young to be a grandparent. 'I've been dying to know, seeing as you've kept it a secret!'

'We didn't want anyone to give a negative opinion and ruin the way we felt about it,' Gray said, sticking up for me. Everybody had wanted to know the name early, but I kept it super close to my chest.

I'd seen too many horror stories on online forums about baby names and how family members or friends had ruined a name for a couple before they used it—and then they regretted it ever after.

'Maybe we should wait until my dad gets here,' I said, not meaning a word of it but wanting to torment her a little longer. 'Tell you both together.'

'Your dad's working away,' Mum whined, snapping her eyes to lock with mine. 'You know he won't be here for a day, minimum.'

I *did* know that. But even just watching her panic for a minute was good enough for me.

'I'm joking,' I admitted, smiling widely at her. 'Dad already knows.'

'Are you serious?' she shrieked, then realised her mistake and covered her mouth with her hand. In my arms, my little bundle of joy squirmed before settling once more. The room let out a collective sigh of relief that she hadn't begun to scream. 'He didn't tell me!'

'Relax, I'm kidding again.' I laughed, shaking my head at how gullible she could be sometimes. 'Her name is Penelope Rose Smith.'

Her eyes welled up once more, and she swallowed before asking in a hushed whisper, 'You gave her my middle name?'

'Of course we did. You've always been the most important person in my life. Well, before these two came along and my circle of important people got a bit bigger.'

'I love it! Where did the name Penelope come from?'

My mind went back to one of Gray's and my *many* conversations about baby names.

• • •

'WE NEED to at least narrow it down!' I said, brandishing my list in front of his face, waving the piece of paper around with enough force his fringe blew up in the breeze. I rubbed my stomach with my other hand —something I did more and more the further along I got. 'Gray, I need to think of her as a person with a name. Baby and daughter aren't cutting it for me anymore.'

We had lived in our home for a month, and the two of us were finding our rhythm now that we were no longer living with my parents. Our new routine. Cara and my dad had helped us find a one-bedroom starter family home near their house in Hawthorn Hills. It was picturesque and everything a young family needed, and I couldn't wait to raise our child there. Thanks to my dad's generosity—in both the form of my savings fund and his bank balance—we never needed to worry about paying off the mortgage either, as the house was paid for up-front.

'We've already narrowed it down to twenty from your original list of ONE HUNDRED,' he said, blowing out a breath in exasperation. 'Who knew you'd like literally every name on the planet?'

'I don't like every name on the planet. Just this top one hundred I spent hours making.' I sniffed, trying to keep the tears threatening to escape at bay. My hormones were all over the place and I'd already cried once that day because Gray made me macaroni and cheese—the cheese sauce from scratch—and it overwhelmed me. My love for him grew every single day, and when he made an effort to show me just how much he loved me in return, I couldn't help but get a little emo about it all.

He grabbed my wrist and pulled me over to the sofa, sitting down first and then half pulling me onto his lap. His lips were warm as he placed a tender kiss on my neck, breathing in my scent. He told me I always smelled like cherries. At first I worried my love of cherry drops would disappear due to some pregnancy crap, but luckily for me—and my rather large stash—my love for them was as strong as ever.

Maybe even more so.

'I've got a name suggestion,' he murmured against my neck,

placing more kisses down my neck, leaving a trail of tingles until he reached my shoulder. 'And it isn't one on your list.'

'Oh? What is it?'

'Don't laugh at it,' he said, his self-conscious tone causing me to sit up a little straighter. My finger on his chin moved him to face me, and I raised a questioning brow.

'Why would I laugh at it?'

'Good point. You had the name Vivien on yours.'

'I'll have you know that name means lively.'

'Either way, we ain't calling our daughter that.' He laughed, rubbing my arm with a circling motion, grounding us both.

'Just tell me. I'm on the edge of my seat.'

'No, you're on the edge of my lap, and if you keep wriggling like that, then you're gonna land arse first on the floor.'

'Graysonnn,' I whined, batting my eyelashes at him and jutting out my bottom lip into a pout. 'I promise I won't laugh.'

'Well, I've been thinking about Vanellope.'

'Vanellope?' I asked. When he told me he had a name in mind, at no point would I ever have jumped to the name Vanellope as his sugges-tion. 'Like the cartoon race car driver?'

'Yeah.'

'Right…' I trailed off, unsure what to say. 'Why?'

'Because she reminds me of you,' he said, his tone shy. A shrug of his shoulders told me he was a little embarrassed by his admission.

'She does? How so?'

'Well, like you, she loves sweets. She lives in a candyland after all.' I nodded, understanding his reasoning. He continued before I opened my mouth. 'She has black hair, she's petite and cute, and has freckles on her nose the same way you do.'

'Who knew you could be such a sweet romantic?' I teased, keeping it light, but really my entire body was battling a storm on the inside. It was one of the cutest things the boy had ever said to me, and I knew his suggestion came from the heart.

'I love it, I truly do,' I replied, meaning every word. 'But…'

'But?'

'I don't want our daughter bullied because of something we can prevent.'

'Surely you don't want our daughter bullied for any reason?'

'Of course not. But kids are cruel and there are some things we won't ever be able to control. But her name is one of those things and I want to be careful.'

He nodded, agreeing with me. My logic was sound and he couldn't argue with it.

'But I do have a name on this list that's pretty similar to Vanellope.'

'Oh yeah? What's that then?'

'Penelope.'

'Penelope,' he repeated, mulling it over. Tasting it on his tongue. 'I love it.'

'Yeah?'

'Yeah!'

'Then we agree...' I said, not wanting to get my hopes up straight away, but also getting a little excited to know that soon I wouldn't have to refer to my baby as baby or peanut in my mind or when I spoke aloud to my stomach. 'Our daughter's name is Penelope?'

'Penelope Smith.'

'Penelope Rose Smith,' I said. Rose was Cara's middle name, and from the moment I found out I was expecting a girl, I knew I would use it for her middle name. 'For my mum.'

'I love it!' he enthused, wrapping his arms around me and pulling me tighter into his chest. 'And I love you!'

'I love you right back.'

'Good. You're stuck with me now.'

'I wouldn't want it any other way.'

'THAT'S SUCH A BEAUTIFUL STORY,' my mum said, and I blinked, wondering what I'd missed during my trip down memory lane. She looked down at Penelope and cooed, 'Hello, baby Penelope. I'm your nanny.'

A smile split my face. By far, it was the happiest moment of my entire life. And no matter what speed bumps and hurdles we had to face to get there, I wouldn't change any of them. Because at that moment, in the hospital bed surrounded by the ones I loved most, I knew everything had happened for a reason.

And that the heart I wore on my sleeve had once again never steered me wrong.

Epilogue
Grayson

Seeing my daughter for the first time was unlike anything I'd expected it to be.

I felt a lot more than I thought I would, that was for damn sure. The moment Penelope's first cry entered the universe, I knew I would do anything for her. Would do anything to keep her safe, sane, healthy, and whole.

Would do anything for her and her mum.

Beth transformed in front of my eyes into a warrior. Somebody who would do everything in their power to protect our precious baby girl—rain or shine.

'She's precious,' Arianna said, looking down at Penelope bundled in her arms. 'I think she's got your nose, Gray.'

My smile widened at the comparison. To me, she looked like a mini version of Beth. The black hair, the button nose, the bow-shaped lips, all of it. It wouldn't bother me if she had none of my features at all—not when she looked like the most beautiful person alive.

'Doesn't she!' Beth said from where she was lying in the hospital bed still. 'It curves at the bottom in the same way as his.'

If there was one good thing to come out of everything—well, aside from my daughter and my love for Beth—it was that Arianna and Beth were friendly enough to be in the same room. They weren't best friends, and I doubted they ever would be, but they both realised they only had my best interests at heart and that was what mattered the most.

'I see it,' Rock agreed, coming over to stand beside Arianna, his hand resting on the small of her back. 'You two have made a very beautiful human. Congrats!'

'Cheers, man. I appreciate it.'

'Have any of you heard from Remi?' Beth asked, and it was as if the entire mood in the room shifted. 'I thought she'd come with you. I texted her to tell her Penelope has arrived.'

'Er…' Rock trailed off, looking around the room for a distraction. 'Tyler mentioned they'd swing by in the next couple of days, maybe.'

Beth nodded, a tense smile on her face. She put on a brave face for everybody else, but I knew her well enough to know the sadness lying underneath. She and Remi became close ever since that talk in the woods on the day Beth decided she was keeping our baby, and even though Remi wasn't everybody's favourite person, Beth didn't care about that. She'd even gone up against Layla and Dean to stick up for some of Remi's recent actions, and yet Remi hadn't shown up here to congratulate her.

I kept my thoughts to myself, not wanting to voice them aloud and ruin shit for Beth, but I'd be messaging Remi later that evening, that was for sure.

'I'm sure she's just busy with her grandparents,' Beth said, once again making excuses for her friend. 'Layla and Dean are on their way up anyway, so maybe it's best she's not here.'

After that, the conversation went back to lighter topics. Like how much hair Penelope had, and bets on whether she'd grow up to resemble me or her mother more and break some hearts along the way.

Layla and Dean arrived, so Ari and Rock left, and once again we went through the motions of telling them her name, why we chose it, who we thought she looked like, etc.

Things between me and Dean were good. Any grudges we were holding onto disappeared once I got my shit together and moved in with Beth. Ever since then, the four of us had spent more time together. Sometimes with Amber and her new girl-friend, Jaime—the pink-haired girl she was with so long ago—tagging along, too.

The day passed that way, with visitors all day long, until the two of us were ready to drop on the spot and sleep for eternity.

Then our daughter wailed, and we realised that maybe sleeping for eternity was off the table—at least for the foresee-able future.

'Are you happy?' Beth mumbled, her lips on Penelope's head, her eyes tired but happy.

'The happiest I've ever been,' I said without skipping a beat. No hint of a lie because I meant it. It was the happiest I'd ever been by a long shot.

'Have you heard from your dad?' she asked, and I shook my head. All day I had been getting my phone out of my pocket, bringing up his number and typing out a message to let him know he was a grandparent but then deleting it all before I pressed send.

Something was holding me back, but I didn't know for sure what that *something* was.

He may not even reply. Or care. One day, maybe I could forgive him, but there was a lot that needed to happen first.

'I haven't told him,' I whispered, the beeps of the hospital nearly drowning my words out.

'Text him,' Beth said, her large brown eyes locking on mine. 'He may surprise you.'

'Have you told Tara?' The relationship between Tara and Beth was a complicated one, and even though she realised there was a lot more to it than she knew at the time, it still hurt her to know that Tara pretended to be her mum for so many years because of a payout. And although Beth had forgiven both Tara and Cara for their part in the deception, she would never forget it.

I may have gone and sought help for my drinking demons,

but neither my dad nor Tara had, even when given the chance on a silver platter.

'I did,' she said, kissing Penelope's hair, closing her eyes as she did so. She was beautiful. They were beautiful. My heart swelled with pride and love once more, looking at them both. All that mattered in the world was them.

Nobody else mattered.

'What did she say?'

'That she's happy for us. She's gonna come visit sometime next week to meet her. I can't be arsed to live in the past anymore. Holding our daughter today has made me see that. So I'm just gonna take it for what it is. The woman has her flaws, and she needs help, but you can't give help to those who don't want it.'

I nodded, her words settling in. As usual, she was right. You couldn't help those who didn't want to be helped. But you could lend them a hand just in case they ever wanted or needed it.

My phone was in my hand in moments, and I tapped out a quick message to my dad.

GRAYSON - HEY DAD. Your granddaughter Penelope was born today at 2.05pm. She's beautiful and I hope one day you'll get to meet her.

I ATTACHED an image and pressed send, flinging my phone away from me on the side of Beth's bed the moment the two ticks arrived to say it had been delivered.

'You're so dramatic,' Beth said with a chuckle. 'You remind me of the way I reacted once I messaged you that first night.'

'Oh, yeah? I don't think you've ever told me about that.'

'Yeah, so you messaged me, remember, arranging when we'd study or whatever? And after every single message I sent back, I would throw my phone face down on the bed, not wanting to see whether you'd read it or not. Because if you read it and then didn't reply, I would've been devastated.'

'It's a good thing I replied then, isn't it? Wouldn't have wanted you to not show up to school the next week.'

'I'd love to say that you're full of shit, but I one hundred percent wouldn't have come to school on Monday had you ignored me.'

My phone vibrated on the bed, and I jumped, my nerves reaching their peak.

'You gonna look at it?'

'Give me a moment.' I laughed, both at her and at myself for being too pussy to pick up my phone and see what he said. The message may not have even come from him.

'Just do it. You'll feel better after you've looked.'

My hand reached for my phone, shaking as it did so, and I turned it around to see the notification on the other side.

DAD - PROUD OF YOU, son. Be the dad I'm not.

I SWALLOWED, my emotions threatening to take over.

'What did he say?' Beth asked, and I moved my phone so she could see. 'That's nice, Gray. Maybe one day we can talk with him.'

'Yeah, maybe.'

'The way things went with him wasn't your fault. You know that, right?' I nodded and mumbled in agreement. 'I love you.'

Her hair was in a messy bun on top of her head, the dark circles under her eyes like bruises that were only going to get worse as the next few days passed, but to me, she'd never looked better.

'I love you. So much,' I whispered, taking a step closer to place a deep kiss on her forehead. 'Thank you for never giving up on me.'

'I did nothing,' she replied, brushing me off. 'It was you who never gave up on yourself. And you saved us both in the process.'

'Elizabeth Louise Jacobs, you get this through your skull, yeah?' I placed a finger on her chin and lifted her head so our eyes were locked together. 'You saved me. I owe my life to you. You've made me a better person. You've made me a father. There is nothing I wouldn't do for you.'

'Nothing?'

'Nothing.'

'Well, then…' she said, an evil glint appearing in her gaze, 'you can do all the nappies for the next two weeks while I do all the nighttime feeds.'

'Deal,' I agreed, smiling at her. 'Whatever this life throws at us, we can get through it, as long as we have each other.'

'Sounds like a solid plan to me.'

acknowledgements

I wrote this book during a particularly hard time in my life, and I am beyond chuffed with how it turned out. As always, there are people to thank, without whom I would've struggled.

To Meg, thank you for everything that you do. Everything that you are.

To Bills, as always, you are the macaroni to my cheese and I am so thankful that the two of us are taking this journey together. Great things are coming for us both, and I cannot wait for the beach.

To Els, thank you for all that you do! There are days where we don't talk, and those days always feel a little bit wrong. I'm glad you loved Gray and Beth's story, even if it is a pregnancy one.

To Jess and Jess, thank you for always being there. I am beyond glad that the four of us found each other when we did, and that no matter the question, or problem, or decision, we can turn to one another.

To Fi, one day we will have that life we want. I just know it.

To Tay, soulmates come in many forms, and you are one of mine.

To my BETAs, Eszter, Chloe, Robin, and Louise, thank you so much for your input and advice. You helped me realise that my story wasn't total trash. I'm so glad you're on my team!

To my readers, thank you once more for picking up one of my books. I truly appreciate every single one of you and I hope you'll continue reading the Hollowdale series.

about the author

Katie Lowrie is a twenty something year old Brit who loves to write the stories trapped in her mind.

A list in no particular order of her greatest loves:
- Henry VIII and the Tudor era
- Her baby cat, Cress
- Musicals
- Disney
- Cheese

She loves to stalk people online (in a good way) and understands if you do too.

instagram.com/katielowrieauthor
goodreads.com/katielowrieauthor
facebook.com/katielowrieauthor
bookbub.com/authors/katie-lowrie

also by katie lowrie

Rebels of Hollowdale High:

Haven at Hollowdale High

Hero of Hollowdale High

Heirs of Hollowdale High

Hated at Hollowdale High

Heartless at Hollowdale High

Hitched at Hollowdale High

Re-Imagined Series:

Key of Cunning (**Dark** Billionaire Romance)

The Sleep Eternal (**Dark** Mafia Romance)

Hawthorn Academy Series:

Disorder

Disease

Disturbed

Under the pen name K. Lowrie:

Model (mis)Behaviour

Acting Out